DESTINED

Book One of the Blood Games Trilogy

JORDAN PINCKNEY and WILL LENZEN JR

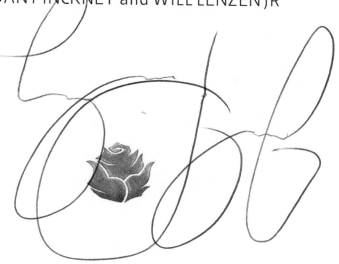

Destined
A Novel By Jordan Pinckney and Will Lenzen Jr.

April 2016

Published by
Destined Productions

*To all those who have ever encouraged us
to dream big and reach for the stars.*

PROLOGUE

Worried eyes looked out the window tonight. Otis lifted the lower sash, allowing the fresh night's breeze in. He braced his arms against the windowsill and stared out into Core City's neighborhood of Bertram with a different perspective, one where he truly hated himself. He held his breath, trying to keep his composure, at first paying no attention to how the air smelled. Eventually, in the long silence of his attempt to mentally escape, he couldn't help but notice the familiar scent of his surroundings. He breathed in the clean laundry smell of his home combined with the freshly cut grass he mowed just earlier that evening.

Usually it would bring a smile to his rough, chiseled face, but tonight it filled him with even more misery.

The stress continued to build up inside as he pressed his hands down on the windowsill, feeling slivers of wood pierce his palms. Otis looked down at his tanned hands, flipping them over to see his pale palms with two fresh slivers sticking into his callused hands. He stared blankly for a moment before looking back out the window.

The crescent moon splintered the sky, softly illuminating the homes below. Tree branches shook and leaves ruffled in the breeze. Otis filled his lungs with the open air again, soaking in this cool moment. This life was a dream come true, he thought, as he held onto his love of being a husband and a father. But his stomach twisted in a terrible knot as reality settled further in. Tonight everything changed, and he hated it. He never imagined it would come to this.

He put that thought deep in the back of his mind for now. Time to focus on something more important. He sniffed and ran his hand over his forehead through his hair, removing the sweat. He wiped the dried blood away on his red unbuttoned flannel shirt.

1

"Better?" His voice was gentle.

"Mhmm," agreed a little voice behind him.

He turned around with a half-smile. "Yeah?"

Behind him stood his three-year-old, Leana, holding her stuffed wolf as she swayed side to side, humming a song he'd never heard.

These kinds of moments, intimate ones with his family, were what he treasured most. His heart constantly melted at the sound of his daughter's gentle voice. He never thought he deserved the blessing of such a perfect life. He doubted the good things that ever came to him; he didn't think he deserved them.

"What that?" she timidly asked, pointing her tiny finger out the window.

"That, little rose petal," he explained, walking over to her and lifting her into his arms, "is the wind."

She slung her right arm around his neck, and gripped her stuffed animal with the other. She laid her head into his shoulder, holding her body tight to his. The warmth of her made him feel weak, but strong at the same time.

"No, that." She raised her finger weakly towards the window again, fighting off the exhaustion of a young child.

"Those, rose petal, are crickets." He bent down, holding her with one strong arm, and throwing open the bed spread with the other. He lowered his treasured girl into bed, and knelt down next to her. "And you know what?" he whispered. "They're playing music just for you."

She curled up closer to him.

Above her headboard on the wall were individual letters, each childishly painted, reading "L-E-A-N-A." At the end of her bed was a chest filled with toys. Her art desk sat in the corner of the room next to her bedroom window. The only light that filled the room came from the lamp on her side table, displaying a picture of Otis, his wife, and Leana as a baby, wearing red overalls. Her dresser stood along the opposite wall from the bed, each drawer open with clothes hanging out as if refusing to be tidy and kept.

She yawned, her eyes slightly watering from feeling so tired.

"You sleepy, baby girl?" he asked, crossing his arms on the bed and leaning closer.

"Hmm mm," she grumbled. "Stowy?"

He smiled at her words.

"No story."

"Pwease?" She blinked her big, chestnut brown eyes.

"Just one. Okay?"

She nodded.

Otis pushed off the bed. "How about this one?" said a soothing voice. Otis turned to the bedroom door. His wife, Danielle, stood there, leaning against the door frame, holding a book out.

He looked over to his wife and took note of her flawless, brown skin.

Standing to the height of Otis' chest with one of her hands resting on her hips, Danielle stared up. Her curly, black hair was tied back, and hanging loosely above her shoulders. Her full lips smiled and her hazel eyes gazed back at him adoringly, but with a flicker of sadness. Otis could tell she was trying to be strong. She wore the green bathrobe he'd gotten her last Christmas. He didn't blink, momentarily lost in the vision of the only woman who gave him a chance to live a meaningful life. The thought lingered, turning his smile into painful awareness once again. Tonight was unbearably difficult.

"Here," Danielle said, holding out the book.

Otis stepped forward to take it, but she didn't let go. Instead, Danielle pulled him to her. She felt his muscular figure under his flannel shirt. She hugged him tightly. He kissed her head before letting go and stepping back towards his daughter.

"Hi, Mommy." Leana smiled.

"Hi, baby girl."

He tucked the blanket tight around her body, just the way she liked it. "There you go."

Leana rested her head on her pillow, cuddling with her wolf. Otis ran his hand through her hair, and then wiggled her nose with his fingers. She laughed.

"Ready?"

She nodded.

Having his back to Danielle made it easier for him to avoid seeing her sadness and disappointment. *I can't look at her right now.* He didn't know what to do, or how to make things safe for them. The only thing he could do right now was read this story to his daughter.

He scanned his eyes across the words of each page, telling the story the best he could, hoping she'd remember it when she grew up. Each time he took his eyes off the page he saw her eyelids become heavier and heavier.

"I love you, Leana. More than you could possibly imagine," he said as he closed the book.

She was already fast asleep, unable to stay awake through the entire story. Her little lips puckered as she slept. Her dark curly hair framed her face.

Otis leaned in and whispered in her ear. "I am so sorry. I will love you forever to the stars and beyond." He kissed her tiny forehead. "I hope someday you will forgive me."

After saying a quick prayer, Otis left the bedroom.

He closed the bedroom door and turned to his wife. "I don't want to do this."

The consequences of his choice filled him with sadness, and then anger. He clenched his fists and jaw as he stood before his wife, staring at the floor, overwhelmed.

"Hey," Danielle said, cupping his face. "You are doing this to keep her safe, to protect her. That's all you've ever done for her. For us."

Otis sighed. His head was heavy and his stomach was in knots.

"Otis, honey, listen to me. She's only a child. She won't understand why you did this now, but she will when she's older. Everything is going to be okay. I'll be here with her." She kissed him. "I promise."

"Yeah." He cleared his throat, sighing deeply in an attempt to keep his emotions at bay, and then added, "You know what to do when she--"

"*If* that happens," she interjected. "I'll know what to do. This is going to work. She *will* live a normal life."

"She'll grow to hate me."

"She will only grow to hate you if I hate you, and that will never happen."

Otis pulled her into his arms.

I can't let go.

"I think it's time I leave," he said, slowly pulling away from her.

She wrapped her arms a little tighter, stopping him. "No… not yet."

"But I--"

"Otis, I love you with my whole heart, but I can't watch you leave."

"Danielle…"

She interrupted. "Please, just stay with me until I'm asleep."

Otis thumbed away the tears streaming down her cheeks. He knew his wife was a strong woman, but he knew tonight would hurt, so he silently led her to bed.

"Just give me a minute, okay?"

"Yeah," she said softly.

Danielle shuffled to her side of the bed as Otis made his way into the bathroom. Quietly shutting the door, he turned and braced himself on the sink, staring at himself in the mirror. He felt the gut-wrenching anxiety in his chest. His face was warm and his eyes were weighed down by the black bags underneath. The shame he felt from his past made him feel like a monster, and being away from Leana was the best way to keep her from that, and potential repercussions. He'd rather her be angry he left, than be terrified of who he was if he stayed.

He took one last glance at his reflection, at the face he could hardly bear to look at any longer. He bent down slightly to center his face in the mirror, studying the tawny skin and blue eyes. Forcing himself to stare into the eyes of a coward made him sick to his stomach, but he buried those feelings, flicking the light off quickly to hide his face. He headed back into the bedroom and joined Danielle.

Otis lay in bed, holding his wife like he wasn't ever going to let her go. He noticed the recently opened bottle of sleeping pills on her side table. He wondered and worried how many more she was going to need in the future. He kept silent since there wasn't anything he could say to make the situation better for her. The ceiling fan spun directly overhead as he gently rubbed his wife's ear. The thought of the struggles and obstacles ahead filled his mind. For a brief moment, he even considered staying, but he knew that would cause even more hardship. He had to go, for Leana's sake. He couldn't let her know who he truly was.

From the sound of Danielle's steady breathing, Otis knew it was time for him to leave. He grabbed his bag and tiptoed to the door. He looked back at his wife one last time. "I love you," he said, fearing he would never see them again.

CHAPTER 1

I was in my dreams again; lost in a world I knew nothing about. Was this real? Was I really here? I could feel the cold touch of the armor strapped to my body. It was bulky, but not heavy. The ornate patterns on the metal gleamed in the moonlight. I could smell the strange musk of the soldiers in front and behind me. I could barely see through the helmet on my face.

I knew one thing: I was marching. To where, I didn't know, but we were all armed. The thought of killing others filled my mind, but these weren't my thoughts. They were another's. Feelings of anger and murder filled me without permission. Who was I? I wasn't me. I was her. A soldier.

The armor I wore was crimson and gold with pale silver bordering the edges. The soldiers leading the march were wearing capes, marking them as high ranking officers. I didn't know how I knew this. They looked human, but I knew they weren't. The red and gray moons illuminated us with an eerie glow from a dark sky filled with infinite stars; constellations I didn't recognize.

The weapons were made of blue steel, and like veins in a body, pink crystal lines flowed through the metal. I didn't recognize the emblems and symbols on their armor. Our march was in perfect unison and formation. I couldn't hear anything above the cadence of footsteps and clanking metal.

I felt the breeze blow through the gaps of my armor as we marched between two high walls into a dark alley. The structures were incredible, reaching up to the sky. The walls looked as if they were forged of metal, but were textured like concrete. The marching feet echoed through the alleyway, growing in intensity. I could barely see the end. Where were we going?

Abruptly, the sounds of marching turned to sounds of a screaming, angry crowd. The end of the alley led to an enormous, round open-air arena. There were people violently throwing their fists in the air. They were enraged. I could see it in their eyes. I could feel the fear within this body I was in.

The crowd looked human, but I know they weren't. Their hands and eyes glowed pink.

I made my way to the left, circling around the angry mob. The soldiers ahead of me charged forward, straight into the seething crowd along the far wall. Cornered there, floating inches off the ground, were seven figures, facing the oncomers. Their hands were up in surrender, their bright white cloaks tarnished with dark, purplish blood. They were ancient looking men with long, white beards and grizzly hair. They would all look quite frail, if it weren't for their glowing hands and eyes. A pink haze vented off their bodies like smoke from a fire. All seven were similar in appearance. One stood slightly shorter than the others. He lowered his heavy brow, clenching his jaw and glaring at the crowd.

I charged uncontrollably at them with my spear pointing directly at the ancient one on the farthest left. What was I doing?! I was terrified and angry as the one closest to me stared into the crowd. His eyes were defeated, scanning the crowd as if searching for someone. He looked like he had accepted his doom. His head panned to the side, looking directly at me, and I could see something change in his eyes. My heart raced. He recognized me.

All the noise muted. I heard nothing. My eyes were locked on his.

He opened his mouth slightly.

"Leana."

Leana's muscles flexed and tightened as she shot up from her bed, choking on a bloodcurdling scream, still feeling like she was in the dream. Her pajamas and bed sheets were soaked in sweat, sticking to her skin. As her lungs emptied she looked wildly around the room.

The dim glow from the moon gleamed in through the two bedroom windows, reassuring Leana that she was still in her room. Relieved but breathing heavily, she slumped back down on her pillows.

Leana stared up at the ceiling, trying to control the images flashing through her mind. Her joints ached as her heart pounded heavy inside her chest. She rolled over and grabbed her pocket watch from the side table. As she held it tightly in her hand, she stared at a picture frame face down next to the lamp. Dust had collected on the back of the frame. Turning back, Leana gazed at the mirror over her dresser at the moon's reflection through her window.

Still breathing raggedly, Leana rubbed her face, soaking her fingers in sweat. Scrubbing her hands dry on the bed sheets and taking as many deep breaths as she could, Leana struggled to calm down.

They've gotten worse, she thought to herself. Her lungs were on fire and her throat felt sore. She could feel the oncoming headache that always followed these dreams. Her hand hurt too, possibly from punching the wall in her sleep.

The dreams that haunted her weren't subsiding despite her mother's reassurances. Instead, they were becoming more and more real, plaguing her reality. The dreams progressively trapped her in moments of confusion where she awoke screaming, unable to tell what was real from what wasn't.

The fear that she was going crazy was constant. These dreams, and nightmares, weren't normal. She felt like a freak.

Leana hugged her knees, hoping for one of her friends to distract her with a message. She picked up her phone, but was disappointed to find no blinking message notifications. She placed it back on the table, staring at it, trying to avoid sleep. She grasped the sides of her head, seeing the images flash and fade in her mind. She took the pocket watch in her hand and pressed it against her ear, listening to the ticking. With her other hand, she slid open the small drawer from her side table and pulled out a jungle green notebook. Slapping it open to the middle, she clicked her pen and jotted down her dream as quickly as possible. Her wrist strained to keep up with her thoughts as the pen raced across the page. With each tick of the watch, the detailed images started to leave her mind's eye.

"Why did you say my name?" she said between inhalations, speaking into the darkness.

She stopped scribbling and stared at her now tranquil hand holding the pen above the paper. She couldn't remember any more of the dream. In fact, she couldn't recall any of it at all now, which frustrated her, but she was also relieved the images were gone. She was still trying to get ahold of her breathing, struggling with the adrenaline coursing through her body. *And they wonder why I'm scared to close my eyes.*

The anxious current racing through her body made her want to puke and cry at the same time. She didn't want to move from her bed, but she didn't want to lie back down, fearing her dreams would consume her once again.

It was a very unsettling feeling to fear something she couldn't recall at all.

A click from the hallway pulled Leana's attention away from her thoughts, and drew her to the light glowing from underneath her bedroom door. Following quickly were footsteps moving down the hallway, growing louder as they approached. Leana jumped out of bed and sprinted to the door. Shouldering into it, Leana fiddled with the knob, finally getting it locked. She pressed her back against the door, barricading herself inside.

The knob rattled, and then someone began knocking.

"Ana, baby." Danielle's voice was tense. "Honey, let me in. Are you okay?" she said urgently through the door. "Was it a dream?"

Leana's frustration grew the more she struggled to catch her breath and calm down. Her adrenaline wouldn't seem to let up. Her shaking kept getting worse as adrenaline spiked again. She needed the pocket watch, but she had left it on her bed.

"Ana, they're dreams, not real life. You're going to be okay."

"I'm not okay!" Leana shouted. "I can't do this anymore!"

Leana had struggled with these nightmares almost every night for the past five years. She knew as well as her mother did that the dreams were getting worse. The trauma was starting to leave its mark on her.

"It'll pass," Danielle said comfortingly. "You hear me?" Leana heard her mother press her body against the door.

Leaning against the other side, Leana slid to the floor and hugged her knees. "They won't stop!" she said, exasperated. "I don't want this!"

"I know, I know. They're still just dreams." Danielle hesitated. "Really bad dreams." Leana knew her mother wanted to be with her, but the two inches of thick oak wood and a lock separated them. Locking her out of the room spared Leana from seeing the hurt on her mother's face; she'd seen it too many times. When her mother worried it only made Leana feel worse.

"Why won't they stop, Mom?" Leana said weakly, finally beginning to catch her breath. She knew before asking that her mother didn't have the answers. She knew her mother wasn't going to be able to comfort her. She felt how each nightmare tore a little bit more sanity away like they were slowly killing her.

Leana heard her mother sigh deeply. "You gotta be strong, baby girl."

Leana was silent, staring at the floor with her eyes wide open. She was fighting to stay awake.

"Ana?"

Leana wanted to believe her. There was no one else she could turn to with this… problem. She even hid her secret from her friends. They were great people, but she still wondered if this was so crazy even they'd turn away from her. She nodded. "Yeah—yeah, Mom." Leana took a deep breath, wiping the tears from her face. "I'm okay. I'm good." Leana slowly stood, still leaning against the door.

"If you would let me in, we could talk—"

"No, I'm fine," Leana interrupted. "I'm okay." Her chest still burned.

"Baby, please, let me in."

Leana raised her voice. "Mom, no! I'm going to bed."

"Ana…"

"Goodnight, Mom."

The dreams were so real, and so frightening. After dealing with these nightmares for such a long time Leana stopped wanting to talk about it. That's all her mom did was talk, and it got them nowhere. Leana knew her mother was the only person who'd understand, but that wasn't going to fix the problem. Even though she couldn't remember the images of her dreams outside of what was in her notebook, the intense anxiety and fear lingered, clinging to each nerve and pore in her body.

Leana could hear Danielle step back from the door. "Alright, then. I love you."

Leana sighed. "I love you too."

Danielle turned back to her room. Leana listened to the slow steps fade farther down the hallway. Her own memories of when she was a little girl ran through her mind. She pictured her mother at the end of the hall on her knees, her arms wide open. Leana remembered how she would run to her and throw herself into those comforting, safe arms, especially when she was too scared to sleep, or too scared to be alone. Leana knew what she had put her through all these years, and it made it that much harder listening to her mother's footsteps trail back to her room, where she would most likely take her pills, and then fall asleep alone.

Leana felt isolated once again the moment the hallway light switched off and her mom's bedroom door latched shut. She shuffled back to the foot of her bed and sat down. She was angry with herself, hating herself for pushing her mother away; for not being a normal teenager. Instead, she felt more like a freak that had to be contained deep inside a seemingly normal girl. The moonlight was like a blanket, wrapping around her as she hugged her knees and cried alone. Tears streamed down her cheeks as she stared forward. Her mind went back to that one single thought that had haunted her since the nightmares started:

"What's wrong with me?"

CHAPTER 2

Sunlight finally filled Leana's room, lighting the walls with a warm spring glow. Leana couldn't have been happier that the night was over. She'd sat awake at the end of her bed for hours during the night staring at her journal in fear of falling asleep again. After each episode, she would hear her psychiatrist's advice play through her mind to look over her journal each morning to process the feelings, thoughts and trauma that filled her. Leana didn't like going over what she'd written, but she trusted Dr. Amber Bennett with her secrets and did what she suggested. Leana had read and reread what she'd written, attempting to remember her nightmare, but no matter how many times she recited her dream-log she could never recall her dream specifically. It felt detached from her, which was strange since she was reading her own handwriting.

She squinted as she gazed out the window. Hearing the birds chirping in the trees brought to mind her friends she would soon see at school. With the night over, relief finally settled in. The rest of the day would be filled with sunlight and school. She closed her eyes for a moment to collect the warmth of the rising sun and breathed deep, sighing as she exhaled.

Leana got up, ready to start her day. She showered, and tied her shoulder long, ash brown hair back. Her hair had a natural wavy curl to it that didn't need much attention to look good.

Taking a last look in the mirror, she wrapped herself in a towel then headed back to her room. She shivered at the cool air hitting her damp skin.

Her crimson and gold soccer uniform lay neatly on her bed. The team wore their jerseys on game day, and today was the biggest game of the year. On the floor next to her bed sat three bags: her jungle green backpack, her soccer bag, and her overnight bag. She stared at the last one, thinking about how ridiculous it was to even have this bag today. Leana had to go to her father's house this weekend and she was not okay with that. It was pointless. *Why am I even going?*

She hadn't seen or heard from him in over a decade, and now she suddenly had to spend the weekend with him because her mom 'said so'. He was supposed to have been there for her all these years, but he hadn't and it made her furious. Each thought she had of her father filled her with an overflowing sense of resentment.

Danielle had said he was going to help Leana figure out what had been going on with her dreams, but she knew he wasn't a doctor or a psychiatrist; he was a stranger. Leana hated him.

She turned her head and stared at her reflection in the mirror, trying to make sense of his abandonment. Her mother's words ran through her head over and over again: *"Do not hate him. Hate is ugly."*

The thought of seeing her father for the first time since she was three made her stomach churn. Leana didn't want to meet him. Since she could remember Leana has asked her mother about him and never got a good answer, so Leana formed her own opinions. She had imagined what kind of terrible man he was for years, but each miserable scenario she believed he lived was quickly torn down by her mother's words. Danielle had been consistent in reminding Leana that she was very wrong about her father, that he loved her very much, but whenever Leana pushed for answers about why he left, Danielle would fall silent.

Leana picked up the old, silver pocket watch off her side table, opening the cover to see the crimson hands pointing at the time. Her mother had told her it was her father's, that he had made it with his own hands. She'd said it was a gift he had left for Leana. Year after year, staring at that watch, Leana had sometimes caught herself wishing her father had died instead of just leaving. She was usually filled with shame and guilt for those thoughts, despite her anger. She was angry, but not cruel. Other times, she thought of what it'd be like if he came home, appearing in the front door. Leana instantly erased those thoughts the moment they appeared. There was never a reason to be hopeful. She could have easily thrown the watch away too, crushed it into tiny pieces, or thrown it into the river. But, for some unknown reason, she never did.

Instead, Leana took it everywhere she went. She had it with her at school, when she was with friends, and sometimes even when she slept. It was never far from her side.

She rubbed her thumb over the watch, feeling the engraved lining on the cover. In the center was a metallic rose. Leana, as she grew older, learned the rose symbolized her father's nickname for her, 'rose petal.' There was a quotation that circled the rose that she read hundreds of times, never understanding what it meant: *"Chur um'i bala"*. Leana researched this quote for years, but had never found the answer.

Leana's head twisted towards her door at the sound of laughter downstairs. If her mother was already up and in the kitchen, then it meant that Leana needed to hustle to get to school on time. She wasn't even dressed yet. She quickly pulled on her #20 soccer uniform, grabbed all three bags, and hurried downstairs. Dropping her bags off at the front door, she rounded the stairs and headed down the hallway, into the kitchen.

Danielle's coordinating white cabinets and gray-blue walls looked like they came out of a home magazine. The window above the kitchen sink made for the best view of the morning sunrise. Her mother was on the phone and surprisingly had the HoloVision on. Her mother never had the HV on.

It was on the wall, across from the table, displaying the news. The holographic center screen was transparent enough to show the kitchen wall behind it, while still clearly displaying the morning report. A man's voice was saying, "—d morning, everyone. This is Keith Williams with the Channel 8 news, reporting to you live on a beautiful Friday morning." The anchorman was fully dressed in a blue suit with overly tanned skin, bleached white teeth and a hardened comb-over hairdo covering his balding head.

Danielle's energetic voice rose above the sound of the HV as she fidgeted with the bracelets on her wrists, which were lit with various notifications from her phone. She had on her sky blue scrubs as she leaned against the center island talking animatedly. At first it appeared her mother was speaking to herself, but Leana could see that one of her hazel eyes glowed bright blue, a clear sign that she was on the phone with someone special. Usually, Leana's mother used her bracelets' projected holographic screen, but today she'd connected to the contact lens' interface. Obviously her mother was keeping something from her.

"Morning," announced Leana to her oblivious mother.

"Yeah. She's...excited," Danielle responded into the phone.

Never mind, Leana thought, rolling her eyes. She wanted to pretend it was someone else Danielle was talking to, but she knew it wasn't. It was her father.

Danielle gave Leana a big smile. "Good morning, honey," she mouthed back.

Leana raised her eyebrows in question. "Is that him?"

Danielle made a shushing motion.

She already knew. "It's him, isn't it?

She turned around, avoiding Leana's irritated gaze.

"Mom?!" Leana exclaimed.

Danielle turned back and nodded, then spoke into the phone again. "Yeah, that was her. She's right here." Danielle waved Leana away.

Leana felt the knot in her gut as she watched her mother smile, not for Leana but for him.

Leana growled under her breath, shook her head, and walked over to the Brew Spout at the counter behind her mother. The metal frame had a scrolling display reading *"Ready to Brew for You"* above a row of buttons listing the different drinks it could make. Leana pushed two buttons and placed two cups under the spouts. The machine dispensed white foam into a green cup, and plain black coffee into a white one which she topped off with a squirt of creamer.

Leana handed Danielle the steaming white cup which slowly revealed a picture of a younger Leana holding up a trophy with her mother on the outside. She mouthed "Thank you," but Leana didn't care and turned to sit at the kitchen table. Attempting to cover the sound of her mother's conversation, Leana pressed a button on the end of the table, turning up the volume on the newscast.

"And now for Core City's top news," the anchorman smirked and paused for effect, overly dramatic as always. Leana groaned at the anchorman's annoyingly perky smile. *"It's almost that day, ladies and gentleman. Twenty years to the day when the crash occurred in our great city. Core City will be throwing the 20th Annual Welcome Fish Fry tomorrow night at Landings Park where the crash occurred two decades ago. More details can be found..."* Leana couldn't take the anchorman's voice any longer; she shut off the HV and leaned back in her chair with a sigh.

"Alright, we'll see you tonight. Okay. Bye..." Danielle tapped a button on her left bracelet, ending the call with a smile. Leana could see the blue contact lens become clear. She shook her head jealously.

"Gross," grunted Leana.

"Oh, honey." Danielle chuckled. With her coffee, she sat down next to Leana. "He's excited to see you."

"Him?! Excited?" Leana was getting more irritated.

Having one of the biggest games of the year tonight, and then going straight to her father's through the weekend was not something she wanted to deal with. She wanted to spend her three-day weekend with her friends like she always did. Eight hours of school, four days a week, wasn't enough time to have with her friends, especially when she was so involved with sports. Now, this weekend was going to be taken away from her.

"Leana—" Danielle started saying.

"Mom!" Leana interrupted. "I don't think I'm ready yet."

"Ready for what?"

"For him to come back into our lives, my life especially. He didn't want anything to do with me when I was a kid, and now, thirteen years later, he thinks all is forgiven? No way, Mom."

Her mother sat, pursing her lips as if she had something to say, but was holding herself back. "Ana, there's a reason your father and I are talking more now. I had to tell him..." she hesitated.

14

"What? What'd you tell him?" snapped Leana. She crossed her arms and leaned back.

"I told him about your nightmares," Danielle finished in a rush.

Leana's hand shot up to her face. "You what?! Oh my god, Mom, seriously?!" she exclaimed. "Why would you do that? He's basically a stranger who I know nothing about, which is exactly how I want things between him and me. I really don't want him knowing anything about me, especially not that!"

She sighed in frustration. Now another person knew her secrets and was probably going to try and fix her just like all the other adults in her life. Leana glared at her mother. "I can't believe you told him. He's going to think I'm crazy."

"Honey, you're not crazy," whispered Danielle as she leaned in to take hold of Leana's hand. Leana took a deep breath and interlocked fingers with her mother. She was tired of being disappointed by the doctors and their *help*; nothing worked. "How do you know?"

"He can help. Trust me on this one. Okay?" Danielle smiled.

"I don't know, Mom. How could he?"

Danielle looked away for a second to check the time, then stood quickly and finished the rest of her coffee. "Mmm, not now. We're late. Grab your things."

"Mom?" Leana sighed exasperatedly. "Mom?!" Danielle hurried from the kitchen.

Leana chugged the rest of her overly sweetened coffee and sucked at the leftover white foam, then pushed back from the table and grabbed her bags, following her mother to the garage.

She glanced at her mother. Her eyes told Leana she wasn't angry, or sad, or frustrated. The only thought running through Leana's mind was how she should probably just give up arguing because change wasn't going to come even if she wanted it to.

CHAPTER 3

Sunlight flickered between the branches of the tree limbs that reached over the road while Leana drove, her hands tightly gripped the steering wheel. The drive to school was actually quite pretty. The sky was filled with fluffy white clouds innocently floating up above. Focused on everything going by the car, she was completely oblivious to whatever her mother was attempting to say to her. The clean, white interior of the car matched the floating clouds. She could smell the freshly cut grass as it wafted in through the cracked window.

Leana had fought to keep ahold of herself while lines from her journal about last night's dream repeated over and over in her head.

Her psychiatrist, Dr. Bennett, had once tried helping Leana process her dreams and cope emotionally. She told Leana, who was only eleven at the time, that if she didn't deal with this trauma, it would slowly fog up her thoughts, progressively getting worse and harder to deal with, to the point of living an arduous life. *Easier said than done.*

To try to help her cope, Dr. Bennett had encouraged Leana to surround herself with other friends and family, to be outside, and to be active. Leana tried to do what her doctor suggested, but no one really had a clue what was wrong with her, not even the doctor. Outwardly, she was a perfectly healthy teenager, but there were no answers to 'why' and 'how' these dreams kept happening. Tests were done, and her diet was changed more times than she could count. Medication was utilized and failed.

Different sleep cycles were tried, but that only made the dreams more vivid. Leana had struggled more and more. She couldn't focus, couldn't think, couldn't listen. This past week had been no exception. In fact, it had been worse.

These dreams were becoming her obsession. Each one was more

intense than the last. She could see more, hear more, even feel more. They were almost like memories. The thing she benefited from most was getting her thoughts out and into her journal. After each episode, Leana would journal, writing the feelings that she experienced: the intense fear and, at times, wonder. Her diary was the only thing that truly knew what was going on inside of her. She kept as much away from her mother as possible, and especially her friends, fearing they would think she was crazy and no longer wanted anything to do with her. She collected her filled diaries, stacking them in a box hidden away in her closet.

"…need to slow down, Leana," exclaimed Danielle, but Leana didn't hear her. "Leana?!" Danielle touched Leana's forearm.

"Huh? What?" Leana readjusted her body in the driver's seat trying to pretend she hadn't been a million miles away, and eased her foot off the gas pedal slightly.

"Are you okay?" Danielle barely took her eyes off the road while Leana drove.

"I'm fine, Mom," she blurted.

"—Okay."

For a moment, neither of them talked. Leana wanted to bring up, again, how badly she didn't want to be going to her father's house, but didn't want to hear the same rebuttal her mother had already given her a hundred times. They were both tired of fighting back and forth on the same topic. Besides, Leana knew her mom had a long week of work ahead of her and had gotten very little sleep the night before, so her patience would already be thin.

Nonetheless, Leana couldn't hold it in any longer. "I really don't want to go!"

Danielle sighed. "I know, and I'm sorry honey, but it's not up to you."

Leana turned to her mother quickly and opened her mouth, but for a moment, no words came out. She gripped the steering wheel even tighter.

"Why do I have to go? Why don't I have a say in this?"

Danielle stared straight ahead. "Almost every night you scream yourself *and* me awake. That's why. And you don't have a say in this because you are still a child and I am still your parent. You're going to see your father and let him help figure this out."

"Well…I feel like you're just trying to get rid of me." Leana responded weakly.

Danielle chuckled, "I wish it was that easy."

"Hey, that's not funny." Leana paused for a moment. "It's weird, Mom. I don't even know him."

"Well I do and that's why you need to trust me. You're going."

"This is so stupid!" she said, slapping the steering wheel. The more frustrated she felt the more she unconsciously accelerated.

The car raced down the road towards a red light, with no sign of slowing down. Danielle grabbed for the steering wheel. "Leana! Stop!" she screamed, instinctually pressing her foot down on her non-existent brake pedal.

Leana gasped and slammed on the brakes, screeching to a halt just as a semi-truck barreled through the intersection.

"What is the matter with you?! Pay attention to the road!" Danielle breathed heavily and gripped her head, collecting herself quickly. "I'm sorry. I didn't mean to yell."

Leana sunk down into her seat, feeling like a little child getting in trouble. "No, I'm sorry. I'm sorry," she replied. Her heart was racing.

Danielle caught her breath and ran her hands over her hair, attempting to regain composure. Turning her body toward Leana, she spoke calmly, "Ana, I know you don't like my decision, but this is something you need to do. Your father is going to help you."

Leana sat, staring at the wheel. "I still can't believe you told him that, Mom. You shouldn't have said anything to him."

"He has a better understanding of what you're dealing with than I do."

"How do you know, Mom?"

"Look at me, Ana. I'm someone who believes in doctors and medicine, but even I have to admit that they have only made it worse for you. Your father is truly the only person we can talk to who will understand."

Leana looked at her mom. "How can he help me?"

"Because he says he can."

A driver behind them honked impatiently. Leana sat up startled, checked both ways then drove through the green light. Her head was full of questions and thoughts about her father's sudden interest in her.

"So...what exactly does he do?" asked Leana, trying to change the tone of the conversation.

"He's a farmer."

"What? You're joking, a farmer? Like cows and stuff? That's kind of lame... and gross."

"Why's that?"

"Because of all the stuff that comes out of farms like... *you* know."

"Poop?"

Leana gasped and rolled her eyes. "Yes and it reeks."

Danielle laughed. "Oh, Leana."

"What, Mom? It's gross."

"I see your point, but listen."

"Plus, machines run the farms, farmers get paid to babysit the machines and sit on their porch while they do nothing as androids do everything. That's not farming."

"He's not that type of farmer. He does all the work himself like they used to over half a century ago. He runs the machines, he does the planting, harvesting, everything."

"No way. How does he manage that?" Leana was genuinely surprised.

"It's how farming used to be done when my parents were really young. It's possible, but it's really hard work... just like he wants it."

"So how did he come into *old*-school farming?"

"It was actually kind of an accident," Danielle replied. "One day he was driving along and saw an old farmer struggling with his stalled tractor in the middle of the road. Your father stopped and helped the man. The farmer told him he could use an extra set of hands at his farm. Since your dad was looking for work at the time, he accepted the offer. He eventually took it over after about five years when the farmer passed away. He left the house, acreage, everything to your father."

"Huh... Well that's pretty cool. I've never been to a farm. Do you think he has horses?"

"Last time I asked he did."

Leana started to smile, but put it away stubbornly. "So is that all he does? Just farm?"

"Two or three times a month he attends veteran support groups near Prescott, traveling around the counties looking to help veterans get back on their feet."

"You mean like a sponsor?"

"Yes, exactly. Is he still sounding lame?"

"Wait... Was he in the military?" Leana asked, sitting upright. She was intrigued despite herself.

Danielle clarified. "Yes, he was, but he never talked about it. Now, he sponsors vets who've returned from wartime and who need to get back on their feet."

"Oh, wow... That's... kind of cool."

"Yes, but don't tell him that. He hates war."

"Then why did he join?"

"He didn't have a choice. Sometimes things happen that can't be changed. He's worked for a long, long time to escape his past."

"Yeah, right." Leana's anger resurfaced.

"You're going to like him, Ana. You're actually a lot alike. There's a lot you don't know about him, so you'll finally have a chance to ask."

Leana shrugged, defensively. "I still don't want to go."

Danielle sighed. "Leana."

"Mom..."

Danielle shook her head and looked at her daughter. "Leana... I love you with all my heart, but..." Danielle hesitated.

"But what?" Leana hated it when her mother used the word 'but.'

Danielle turned on and peered into the center camera. She spoke firmly, "Car! Passenger-side override. Danielle Rayne." The camera angled at the passenger.

"Mom?" Leana bounced her eyes back and forth between the road and Danielle.

"Override accepted, Mrs. Rayne. Command?"

"Mom?!"

Danielle glanced at her daughter then out the side window. "Initiate Auto-Drive," she commanded, feeling satisfied with her next decision.

Leana's hands struggled to control the now useless steering wheel, finally giving up and letting go of it entirely, allowing the car to drive itself. "Mom, what are you doing?"

"Find nearest parking zone and park."

"Nearest location is 150 meters."

"That will do fine, thank you."

"Mom?!"

"Yes?" Danielle responded.

Leana met her mother's innocent stare. "What are you doing?"

"I'm going to work. *You* are getting out."

The car made a perfect parallel park along the side of the road. "Destination acquired."

"What'd I do?"

"That."

"What?"

"Arguing. Constantly."

"So what, Mom? I'm allowed to argue."

"No, you are allowed to tell me your feelings and then accept my decisions. The walk will give you time to think."

"I'm not walking. It's too far of a walk."

Danielle looked back into the central nav-camera and spoke, "How far from Chandler M.A.S.?"

"Chandler High School of Merit and Advanced Studies is approximately zero-point-nine-two-three miles, Mrs. Rayne."

Danielle looked calmly at Leana, raising her eyebrows and smiled from the side of her mouth. "So... Hop out please."

"No." Leana crossed her arms and slouched in her seat.

"Car. Ignition off."

The engine shut down as it sat in the parking space.

"You have two choices. Sit here and pout until it's time to go to your father's. Or..." paused Danielle as she leaned closer. "You can get out of the car, make it to school on time, and be allowed to start in your soccer game tonight. Your choice."

Leana glared holes through her mother, but knew she was right; soccer was one thing she was not willing to give up. Leana hated when her mother was right, which was most of the time.

"Whatever," she exclaimed, throwing up her arm in defeat. "I'll walk."

Danielle nodded her head. "Thank you," she said calmly. She rubbed her legs and smiled. "Unlock please," she added.

The car doors unlocked. Danielle pushed a button on the center console and both doors lifted like wings. "Come on, honey."

Leana sighed deeply and exited the car. She shouldered her soccer bag and backpack and walked around the rear of the vehicle, leaving the travel bag behind for her father's.

"I love you, honey," teased Danielle, standing as she opened her arms for a hug. Leana let her mother hold her briefly, pretending like she didn't want it, but deep down she knew a hug was what she really needed. And her mom seemed to know, too.

"Love you too," mumbled Leana as she pulled away and headed towards the sidewalk. "Bye... and sorry."

She walked away quickly, trying to avoid further conversation.

"Hey?!" yelled Danielle. Leana turned. "Good luck at your game, baby girl. I don't know if I'll make it in time, but I'll try, okay?"

"Yeah, okay, Mom," Leana said disappointedly. She waved. "Bye."

Danielle waved and got back in the car, closing both doors. Leana felt her mother's eyes watching her as she trudged down the sidewalk for a moment, but soon heard the car get onto the road and drive away.

"This totally sucks," grumbled Leana to herself.

She walked briskly down the sidewalk, anxious to get to school and to her friends.

She wasn't enjoying the solitude. Not after last night and this morning. The last thing Leana wanted right now was to be left alone to her thoughts.

CHAPTER 4

Leana's mother was right, stretching her legs and taking a walk helped make Leana's morning feel a little more stress-free. It was still early morning and the breeze was a bit chilly, but she soaked up the warmth from the sun as it darted in and out of the clouds floating above. Walking along the sidewalk, she ignored all the traffic driving by, as people rushed to work and school and wherever else they went these days. Being in the open, outside with the world, was what she needed to regain perspective and balance within herself and her rollercoaster of emotions.

As she looked around, she found that all the lights, advertisements and people made her hometown seem so crowded. Everything was so distracting, so overwhelming. One of the billboards announced the brand-new "Put It Together Yourself" Android Systems that had released just last weekend. Below the advertisement, Leana could see bumper-to-bumper morning traffic. This walk wasn't going to be as relaxing and peaceful as she'd hoped.

Leana made good time on her walk to school; she was a naturally a fast walker. She was already halfway there and she knew she would have around twenty minutes before the first bell. She never liked how her mother always stressed out about being on time. Personally, Leana couldn't have cared less. The big soccer game tonight was the only thing that made it important for her to be on time.

Making her way around First Avenue, Leana came upon a historical park that was built well before her time. The landscaping around the park was very well maintained. The property extended out into some old woods, but the actual antique playground could be seen from the main road. In front of the park was a large monument framed perfectly by several elegantly sculpted trees – it read: "Thomas Park – established in 1917 and later renamed Landings Park in 2054. '*A park where young and old come to play and grow.*'"

A chipper, male voice suddenly spoke out from the sign.

"*Landings Park, which was once known as Thomas Park, was established back in 1917. It has become the main park of Core City, which originated from a time when all the towns came together nearly twenty years ago to become one single city. Cedar Rapids, Marion, Fairfax, Hiawatha, Robins and Bertram united to create our glorious Core City. Would you like to learn more?*"

"No thank you," Leana replied irritably as she walked away.

The structure of the playground was still in one piece, held together by old wood with metal framing. The ground underneath was covered in moist woodchips; some areas had empty splotches of dirt where people played, but obviously weren't supposed to, as a nearby sign read: "PLEASE KEEP OFF". The swings were still attached to a tall overhead bar with their antique chain links, and still had their original hard plastic seats. Flanking the swings were two long, metal slides, both worn-down with countless scratch marks, most likely from all the buttons, zippers, and toys that had slid down these once magnificent rides.

In the distance where the grassy acreage stretched out to the horizon of the woods was the "up-to-date" Landings Park playground. Leana could see a parent sitting alone as three kids screamed and ran around the enormous plastic, colorful playground. It was more advanced, with electric rides that moved around, music playing within the playground, and safety harnesses on the swings. The slides even had padding at the bottom. Leana wasn't impressed, she preferred the old stuff.

After setting down her backpack, Leana approached the old playground, ignoring the "PLEASE KEEP OFF" sign. She reached for a long, metal handle and pulled herself up to the first few steps. The shaky handle had rusted over the century. She walked cautiously across a hanging bridge held up with rattling chain links. Her feet sank into the old wooden boards. Some of the planks lifted from the framing where rot had replaced the nails and bolts that once held these boards safely intact.

"Oh, this isn't safe at all." She smiled and bit down on her lips, carefully moving along the structure.

She finally reached the peak of the playground that overlooked the rest of the park. It was built like a large bird cage, barred all the way around. Leana could feel the fresh, cool breeze sweep over her face and through her hair. She shut her eyes, taking in a deep breath while gripping a metal bar with both hands. She peered around the large area, scanning the cars in the distance, old pavilions, people and their families, and the little wildlife scattered about the area. She smiled at the sight and sound of the children's laughter, screams, and cries as they adventured through the newer, bigger playground.

A high-pitched and scratchy sound distracted Leana, drawing her attention below. Off to the side was an extremely rusted and dirty roundabout swaying slightly in the breeze. The handles lining the center of the ride had been rotted and chewed away by rust over time.

Descending carelessly, she hopped off the play-structure and approached the old ride, which hid in the shade under a large tree next to a picnic table. The base was about two feet off the ground. Vaguely resembling a moat without water, the ground had deep, rough drag marks all the way around it from years of quick-footed laps and hard stops. Leana gripped the handle with her left hand, and then pushed it softly. Rusty metal screeched in protest as the ride moved in a circular motion for a few feet, then stopped. She gripped another handle, but this time she walked around in a circle, watching the ride slowly spin, loosening the gears underneath the metal framing.

Very carefully, avoiding any cuts from the ragged edges, Leana sat down between two handles, holding herself in place with each hand on a handle. Looking down at her feet, she pushed off the ground, forcing the ride to spin in a circle. The more she kicked her feet the more it would spin, and the louder the squeaking became. After a few cycles, the sounds became quieter. Again, Leana pushed hard with her feet, spinning herself faster and faster around.

The fresh breeze cooled her face, relaxing her as she lay back on the dirty metal. She peered up into the blue morning sky as birds flew overhead, darting between the clouds. The sun was hidden behind the thick clouds now. The chirping mixed well with the children's laughter, soothing Leana and putting her in a good place.

Just for a moment, she forgot about her troubles - she forgot about her father and this weekend, the terrible nightmares, and feeling like a freak at school. Her deep breath and a sense of peace filled her body and thoughts. As the sun came out of hiding, Leana gladly welcomed the heat as the bright rays blinded her, soaking it all in.

She could still see the flashing light of the sun through her eyelids after closing her eyes. It was relaxing at first, but the bright flashes began blinking faster and faster. She tried pinching her eyes tighter, but it didn't help.

She couldn't tell if the Round-About was spinning faster, or if the trees were being blown around more, but the lights kept getting worse. Everything felt like it was spinning, and the gaps between the flashes were getting darker. She wanted to open her eyes, but couldn't. It felt like she was trapped in a vortex, blinded and helpless. She shot up her hand to block the bright light and without warning a car spun out of control right in front of her. The squealing of the tires was ear-shrieking.

. . .

...

Where am I? I was looking around and finally saw something. I wasn't in the park, but was instead standing in a dark alleyway looking out towards a road. I was getting soaked from the heavy, freezing rain that was drenching everything it touched. With such a dark night and heavy rain I could only see the lights of the spinning car and the two buildings I stood between. I lost sight of the car as it disappeared around the corner. I jumped back and gasped as I heard it violently crash.

I sprinted to the end of the alley, breathing heavily. I looked around the corner, praying the driver wasn't hurt. The car sat still as smoke spewed from the hood. The headlights were the only source of light, creating two beacons from the wreck. There was a gigantic opening in the front window like something had shot out from the vehicle, and the front end was caved in on the driver's side. I could tell someone had been thrown from the driver's seat when it crashed, but I didn't see anyone lying on the pavement. I could see a nearby light pole that had been smashed to the ground. Sparks flew in all directions on the other side of the car.

Out of my peripheral view, I could see a man in a black hoodie standing in the middle of the road, opposite of the accident. The hooded stranger breathed deep as his chest rose and fell. I couldn't see his face, but his eyes… I could see his eyes. They glowed with a pink haze, misting underneath his hood. I watched him strain as he clenched his hands into fists. The glow illuminated his hands with the same colored haze.

He watched the car as a woman started to crawl out from the vehicle.

"Oh my—" I stopped myself by covering my mouth, trying to stay hidden from the stranger.

From of the passenger side door the woman continued to struggle out, grasping her round belly. She was hurt, but her body language only showed concern for the child inside her. I couldn't make out the woman's face because it was so dark. The woman's breath fogged in the cold air and she shook uncontrollably from the icy rain. Her long, white blouse clung to her skin as she leaned her hand against the wrecked car, slipping and falling to the pavement. Her shoulders quivered, and she started to sob.

I screamed out, trying to get the woman's attention. "Get out of here!" but my voice was strangely muted. I cupped my mouth with my hands, trying again and again. I screamed with all my might over and over. Nothing.

I looked back to the hooded man; he was still standing there. I felt panic overcome me the moment he took his first step towards the wounded woman. His steps became faster and faster until he was sprinting towards her. I tried to call out again; still nothing.

As I watched the hooded man approach, suddenly the sound of a loud horn pierced the night. I twisted my head around to see the enormous beams from the headlights of a semi-truck heading right for the woman. I heard the truck's tires squeal as it tried to brake, but the trailer on the back swung around and wasn't stopping. I knew the truck driver couldn't see the woman on the other side of the car. She and the hooded man were both about to die. I felt my eyes strain as they grew wide and my mouth opened. I tried once more to scream.

Leana's eyes shot open. "No!" Her voice rang out loudly in the air as she breathed heavily.

She realized she was still looking up at the sky. Leana sat up and looked around the park, realizing she was still on the Round-About which had come to a stop.

She was terrified. Nothing like this had ever occurred during the day. Unlike her dreams, these images weren't fading. This was something different. Her chest and heart throbbed from the intensity of what she had just experienced. An alarm on her wrist phone suddenly buzzed, causing her to jump. She looked down.

"That can't be right," Leana muttered confused. She turned off the alarm that reminded her she had ten minutes until school.

According to the time, Leana had been on the Round-About for less than two minutes. *But that seemed like so much longer*, she thought.

She rested her feet on the dirt ground. Her attention was drawn to an old married couple holding hands. They stood on the sidewalk, staring at Leana with shock written all over their faces. As Leana made eye contact, the old woman began pulling the old man along away.

"Hm. Kids doing drugs again, Dorene," grumbled the old man.

"I know. I know," she replied with a raspy voice. They continued shuffling down the sidewalk with their hands still interlocked, wagging their heads.

Leana's hands were still shaking as she watched the disapproving couple walk away. She struggled to focus her eyes; everything seemed so blurry. Without warning, a ringing noise pierced her ears. She whipped her head around, looking for the source. The high-pitched ringing grew louder. It felt like screams erupting in her mind. She gripped her head and leaned forward in pain.

"Stop, stop... Stop!" she screamed, rocking back and forth.

She winced in pain, her head throbbing and feeling like it was about to explode.

"It's too much. It's too much," she whispered desperately.

As quickly as it came, the ringing faded away, and the pain along with it. She looked at her hands as her vision suddenly became clear like a 'reality reset.'

"What is wrong with me?"

She started sobbing. Her anger and confusion was too overwhelming. She wanted it all to stop, but it never would. It never had. She wanted to be normal, but she knew that would never be. She wanted to be like her friends, but she was too alone, even amongst them.

She sniffed, trying to regain control. "I'm a freak," she said to herself. "Oh great, now I'm talking to myself." She snarled and stood up. "I *am* a freak."

Leana grabbed her backpack and left the park as quickly as possible, not wanting to ever come back again. Bolting down the sidewalk, she turned briefly around and glanced back at the Round-About. It was out of sight.

"'Keep Off', the sign said. 'Break the rules', I said." She swallowed hard, trying to keep herself from crying. She didn't want her friends to notice she'd been crying most of the morning.

"Today sucks," she whispered, choking on her words as she held back more tears.

CHAPTER 5

Leana could finally see the many buildings of Chandler High School. Built and completed nearly fifteen years earlier, this prestigious school was named after the first president of the United Countries of the World, William Chandler, who was from the same area of Iowa as Core City. Chandler High attracted the most exceptional teenagers. Leana loved walking up to the front of the enormous, white brick building. The lawn and trees were well trimmed and mowed; the gravel that led to the entrance stairwell was off-white and always maintained. The main part of the building, where most of the classes took place, was three stories of nearly all glass walls, creating an open atmosphere for the nearly one-thousand students.

The school was built from a portion of the many contributions and donations the town received after the crash occurred. There were extra funds for rebuilding, so the people voted to construct a new school in hopes of attracting the best and brightest. It had worked. The town had quickly filled with people from all over the world. Students gifted in fields of arts, sciences, mathematics, technology, and more applied, hoping to learn from the best. It didn't take long for the school to garner a reputation for excellent college preparation, since most graduates received scholarships to their college of choice.

Making her way through the smooth automatic doors, she passed by a floating, holographic image of a man standing upright and broad-chested. The name 'President William Chandler' floated below his feet. Leana was greeted mechanically by the robotic, but soothing, voice of a woman.

"Welcome, Miss Leana Rayne. Good luck with your soccer match tonight. Bring the Rayne."

Many of the students packing the hallways were on their phones, some with their displays activated. Leana thought they looked stupid talking to the heads-up display that appeared in the single eyepiece they wore. A lot of students thought the eyepieces were "nitro", but Leana thought they were ridiculous. There were always a handful of students with their displays popped up in front of them while they hung out with friends by their lockers. Leana often watched kids run into each other, not paying attention to where they were walking. They looked like zombies who were completely absorbed in their digital world.

Some of the less preoccupied students greeted her and wished her luck, most of whom were wildly decked out in school colors. Team devotees always went above and beyond on game day. While students were encouraged to wear school colors on a daily basis with appropriate uniforms, athletes were required to wear their jerseys to represent their team if they were playing that night.

Naturally, there was also an elite group of kids who felt they were above the school recommendations. They made up their own rules, were referred to as "trophs" by the rest of the student body, and were usually avoided. Hanging with trophs usually led to trouble, and since getting in trouble at this school meant instant suspension, most students gave them a wide berth.

Leana was proud to wear her uniform at school, representing the team she captained. While she didn't particularly like the added attention, after last year's successful season of being captain, she was used to it.

The teachers at Chandler were all old-school looking with their suits, messy hair, glasses, and timeworn touchscreen phones. Their classrooms were very advanced with the latest software and technology – the school was used as a test school for the latest educational technology – and the teachers were each a genius in their individual fields. They cared greatly about their students' education. They used technology masterfully out of necessity, but anyone could tell it was the craft and joy of teaching that truly inspired them to be the very best – which is why most of them were at Chandler; it cultivated the best in all areas.

Making it to class just as the bell rang, Leana walked around the white desks to the far side of the room, next to the windows. The windows were always good to her whenever she suffered long, dark nights lost in her dreams. Now, while in class, she was able to look out, gathering in the beautiful view of the school's property.

The grass was cut perfectly on all areas of the grounds, accented beautifully with tree lines bordering the school, and tasteful landscaping articulating the various patios available. She enjoyed watching students having class outside with their teachers, or the occasional drama breakout between random girlfriends and boyfriends in places she was sure they thought were more private. Leana truly appreciated and enjoyed her school.

Not just because of her education and the amenities Chandler provided, but also because of her friends, teachers, and, of course, playing soccer on a nationally ranked team.

At the front of the classroom, placed directly in the middle of the rows of desks, was a blue and white, mushroom-shaped unit that stood a few feet from the ground, topped with a display hub. Engraved around its trunk was "Educational Hologram Interface." The top-half of the unit, a near replica of the bottom, hung from the ceiling directly over it. Around the rim of the bottom half were lights displayed in various hues. Some had labels underneath the indicator lights showing which features were on or off. When activated through finger and eye identification, teachers could access 3D holograms of information, chapters, tests and quizzes for their daily topics and classes.

The teachers at this school never used desks. They always taught on their feet, fully involved in the students' education. In the back of each classroom was a long display case lit with blue lights within the glass shelves. Each case was unique and filled with historical antiques, books, and clothes all relevant to the subject taught in that particular classroom. This was one of the things Chandler School for the Gifted insisted on to keep students grounded in their history. The school's original headmaster, Headmaster Privet, always said "The future is an amazing place you will help create, but remember the dots in time from which you came."

The students' desks were made of white wood with white metal framing, and were very thin, matching the white floors. Each classroom looked nearly alike, pristine and perfectly set up.

"Hey, Leana," greeted Justin, exposing his white teeth in a charming smile.

She sat down in front of him. "Hey, Justin." As usual, the butterflies she tried so hard to fight when he smiled were wrestling in her stomach.

Justin Edwards was the captain of the cheerleading team and a Junior Olympic gold medalist in gymnastics, and the poster-child of the world renowned elite Midwest training facility: The Anvil Gym. Even though they had been friends since they were six years old, Leana always thought him to be a troph; cocky and flirtatious. It still surprised her when she was a bit annoyed, and even impressed at the number of girls drooling over him whenever he walked by. Leana stayed friends with him because, despite the female attention, he was a gentleman to the girls. He acted like a lady-killer, but never made bad choices when it came to girls, and that's what Leana respected. Besides, she knew he'd had the biggest crush on her since high school started, always wanting to be more than friends, but never acting on it. Leana smiled every time she thought about him. She wanted the kind of attention he wanted to give, but she had a hard time opening up to him like that. She didn't want to get too close to Justin. She knew if she did, something would go wrong and he'd leave her just like her father. Keeping distant emotionally made this friendship work. *Trust your intuition.*

"You ready for tonight?" he asked enthusiastically. Leana liked his support.

"More than I'll ever be," she responded. School was a good distraction for Leana, helping her think about other things like hanging around people she loved. She was still mentally struggling with what happened at the park, but was trying not to. The feelings she had experienced and felt during the car crash still lingered like a stone in her stomach.

He smirked and pumped her shoulder. "You're not scared are you?"

"You're such a troph, Justin," said a short, curvy girl as she walked past to her desk.

"Now that's not very nice, Emily," he said with a grin, putting his pen in his mouth and leaning back in his chair.

He crossed his bulky arms as two more girls walked by, smiling at him. He ignored them, turning his smile back to Leana.

Emily slid smoothly into the seat next to Leana. "Well, I think you're going to totally *ice* them!" She zigzagged her fingers through her long, brunette hair.

"Thanks," responded Leana.

Emily Hayden was Drama Queen of the junior class, but not the type of drama most people would think with that title. Being ranked "Drama Queen" as a junior in this school was a huge achievement in the Arts & Drama clubs. She hated the actual high school drama that went on at school amongst her peers and avoided it at all costs. With her parents' rocky relationship and their unrelenting pressure on her to perform above average at school, she had enough drama of her own to deal with at home.

Emily's mother ran the theatre courses, but Emily had still earned the peer appointed title fair and square. She loved her mother, but they often butted heads even at school. She purposely hung out with a small, unique group of friends who understood and accepted her without argument.

At the age of eight, Emily had earned her first supporting role in a children's movie. Her dream had always been to be a famous actress once she graduated from Julliard. This was a goal she was well on her way to accomplishing, since she had been able to land small, extra parts in independent films once or twice a year ever since.

"Hey, guys. What's snappin'?" exclaimed an athletically built girl with dreadlocks, plopping down at the desk in front of Leana. She wore an earth-toned sleeveless blouse, exposing her muscular arms and dark brown skin.

Annette Willows, or Annette "Causes Pain" Willows as her competitors liked calling her, was Leana's best friend. Her father ran the Jayne Boyd Community House, which his grandfather had bought out before it closed down for good. Since then it had been passed down through the family. She had learned to fight as a young child, coached under her own father since she was three-years-old. Leana loved playing with Annette's dreadlocks, especially when she got bored during class, occasionally braiding them when the teacher wasn't looking.

Leana knew she could trust Annette like a sister, as they knew everything about each other... or *almost* everything. Practically growing up together since second grade, they'd been through a lot over the years, but no matter what happened, no major conflicts ever came between them. No one knew Leana better than Annette. It was a relationship that Leana hoped would last forever. Leana knew that under Annette's perfect skin and well-defined muscles were the most tender, caring heart and personality ever.

Leana had met Justin through Annette who was also a Junior Olympic gold medalist; for boxing. Leana was all too accustomed to hearing Annette passionately refuse to accept boxing as a dying sport. In her championship match, Annette had knocked her opponent out in the first forty-five seconds. She still joked about how long her opponent had lasted in the ring that match. She may have been competitive and cocky, but she was largely fair and honorable, especially in school.

"Hey, Annette. How'd training go last night with your dad?" asked Justin.

"Same old. Coach isn't letting up on me. He's getting me ready for my *bigger* competitions once I turn eighteen this summer. I'm so ready," she said, shadow boxing in his direction. She had explained to Leana once that she always called her father 'Coach' out of respect for his title and how the community recognized him.

"Really, guys?!" groaned Emily. "Can we not talk about fighting and muscles and sweating for like two minutes?" She switched back to her overwhelming happy attitude. "So... Who's ready for prom?" She clapped her hands quickly.

"Ughh!" exclaimed Annette and Justin together, rolling their eyes.

"What?" Emily looked at them both.

"Not again, Emily," pleaded Justin. "Prom isn't for another month."

"That's only four weeks! Look, I know you muscle bound meatheads don't like talking about this, but it's important. I mean... I've already been asked—"

"Yeah, yeah," Justin interrupted, "we know you've already been asked. He's probably regretting it by now," he teased.

"Oh shut up... And no he isn't," Emily said defiantly as Justin chuckled.

Slouching in her seat, Leana was unintentionally ignoring the back-and-forth and was instead staring out the window. She was lost in her mind, again still thinking about the plaguing dream and vision she'd had today.

Annette placed her hand on her friend's arm. "Leana?"

32

Startled, Leana choked back the slight tears she suddenly realized had formed, sucking in air through her noise. "What?"

"You okay?" Annette leaned her head to the side, attempting to get Leana's eye contact as she gazed out the window.

"Yeah," she whispered. She rubbed her cheek and shifted her body uncomfortably. "Yeah, I'm fine."

"Huh." Annette slowly turned to face forward, appearing unconvinced as the starting bell blared in the halls and classrooms. All phones deactivated, as well as the wrist- and eyepiece displays, shutting down all forms of communication. As always, the students groaned the moment the old-fashioned "No Cell After the Bell" school policy was automatically enforced.

Justin leaned forward; his voice low. "Psst, Emily."

Emily cocked her head slightly to the side, being sure it *looked* like she was still paying attention in class. "What?"

"You hear the 'Teacher Rumor of the Week' yet?"

"Duh, of course I did, but I don't believe it."

Sarah, a cute girl with red, curly hair and freckles, sitting directly behind Emily, piped in softly. "I didn't. What was it?"

"Well, *supposedly*, Dr. Vincent was once a renowned professor for Core City University." Dr. Vincent was their United Countries of the World History teacher and had not yet entered the room.

Emily leaned her head back toward Sarah and encouraged softly, "Don't believe this story."

Sarah looked at Emily confused, and then back at Justin. "And?"

"Apparently he had some kind of mental breakdown twenty years ago and got kicked out of the university."

"Nuh-uh. Where'd you hear that?" whispered Sarah.

"It's true. A guy from Phys-Ed told me."

"What'd he teach there?"

"Something space related. Don't know really." Justin shrugged. "I guess the guy heard it from some student whose grandfather worked with Dr. Vincent back then."

Emily looked back at them with her finger to mouth. "Shh."

The door opened and an eccentrically dressed man in his sixties waltzed into class. Dr. Charles Vincent always got chuckles from his students due to his turn of the twentieth century fashion.

"Quiet, class! We have much to discuss today…" he pronounced slowly, adjusting his dark-rimmed glasses. Dr. Vincent turned his body to the side and covered his mouth partially with his hand. He spoke fast and quiet. The students leaned forward, trying to listen in on what he was saying to himself. After mumbling unintelligibly for a moment, he raked his hands through his hair and straightened the waist of his bright red fitted pants.

He turned quickly to face the class, his eyes wide open. Some of the students jumped back in their chairs. His eyes glared at each pair of eyes staring back at him. "And not much time to do it!" He smiled excitedly as he adjusted his glasses. A few students giggled.

Leana continued to stare out the window, struggling to take her mind off her cursed vision and dream from today. The teacher's voice was but a mere muffle in the background of her thoughts. The images running through her mind overrode what her eyes wanted to see out the window. *I'm sure it's a lovely day.* Her heart was beating fast and she was struggling to control it.

"What's this weekend? Anyone?" Dr. Vincent raised his hands inviting the class to respond.

"Saturday?!" announced a kid from the back row. The class laughed.

"Boy…" The teacher paced back and forth, shaking his finger. "We have a bright one in the class today, don't we? Thank you, Warren. No." He cleared his throat.

The teacher was visibly frustrated and began picking at a spot on his face. He grunted and stared at the ground for a second, then jerking his leg, he kicked the Educational Hologram Interface. His breath was heavy enough that the kids in the back row knew he was upset. Two girls in the far end of the room gasped.

Dr. Vincent shot up his hands and chuckled. "I'm sorry… Sorry. Okay? Okay."

He looked around at all the wide eyes staring at him. His unpredictable behaviors never failed to alternately entertain and terrify. This was why most students enjoyed his class.

"Light!" The ceiling lights turned off. He pressed a button on the E.H.I. hub and the interface display appeared. The open space between the hanging portion and the mounted half on the ground lit up. The room was now blue and green from the hologram, weaving into images and letters. There was a soft buzzing sound. An image of Earth spun below letters that read: "Twenty Years After Knowing Others Were Out There!"

Dr. Vincent removed his glasses and cleaned them with the hem of his fitted plaid button down shirt that he yanked from his beltline. "Twenty years ago is when everything changed. Why?"

"The crash?" offered Annette, twirling her fingers through her dreadlocks.

He walked towards Annette, pointing. "Yes. Yes." He turned back to the class. "The crash! Twenty years ago was the beginning of an era when human beings finally *knew* we weren't alone in the galaxy." The doctor continued excitedly, "We all know the story by now. Twenty years ago, an alien spacecraft crash landed in the city originally called Cedar Rapids. There were thousands of people who witnessed the ship fly overhead. The government, of course, initially tried covering it up through the media, but there was too much video and pictorial evidence; not to mention satellite feeds showing there was *indeed* a ship. What did the government do next?"

The students sat quietly, knowing he would answer his own question. Leana's mind tried to focus on the discussion since it was a subject that interested her, but her mind kept sneaking back to the vision. She was fixated on what she had seen. The image of the man with pink, glowing eyes burned in her head.

"Anyone?" asked the teacher again. His eyes bouncing from one child to another.

Each time the teacher spoke there was a ringing in her ears. She ignored the sounds while thinking back to the moment in the alley way. She remembered the cold rain and sound of squealing tires… and the pregnant woman. Leana didn't know why, but she knew it somehow related to her dreams.

"The government," he paused, "funded the city with an unlimited amount of resources which allowed Cedar Rapids to", using air quotes, "*negotiate with* the surrounding towns. It became one great, big city… Core City… and started this school which focuses on finding the most exceptional children."

"Why would they do that? It seems kind of pointless," said a boy in the back of the classroom.

"Isn't it obvious? They made a deal with the city. Money for…?" He waited for a response, but didn't wait long for an answer. "For the ship. They wanted the ship. In order to acquire it, they compensated the city so generously that the city was able to fund pretty much everything around you. This school, for example, or the fleet of city maintenance and educational androids, and new construction of the new stadium et cetera, et cetera. This gave the government free reign to search for whatever else came down with the ship."

"Like a pay-off?" blurted out a girl from the back.

"Possibly," responded the professor. "That's one opinion."

"We don't even know if the crash happened for sure," exclaimed Emily with her hand in the air. The scratching of chairs sounded together as students shifted to look at Emily. "They never found a pilot to go with the spacecraft, which means there are still some people who believe it wasn't a ship, but a meteor. A lot of people still believe it was a hoax."

"Oh, there was a ship and enough video evidence that the world believed in it."

"The footage could have been faked, professor," she replied quickly.

"Possible, but not probable that that many people faked the same footage or evidence. *And* you're right. To our knowledge, they never did find a pilot, *or* a meteor, but think about it," he said, holding up his pointer finger. "Have you ever heard of the government giving money without getting something in return? Quid pro quo, if you will. There was a ship."

"How do you know that, professor?" asked a boy next to Emily.

"I've seen it. I've touched it. You haven't seen it because they confiscated it and continue research to this day."

"No way. You're lying," said a girl in the front row.

"Cross my heart, Eva," he said, making the cross sign over his chest. "I was on the team that retrieved it."

Some of the students gasped in surprise. Emily sighed exasperatedly, clearly still unconvinced.

Annette spoke without raising her hand. "What do you think happened to the pilot, Professor Vincent?"

"Interesting question, Miss Willows. Now," he stepped towards the student with his hands up and palms facing them, saying in a lowered voice, "if you want to know my opinion, here it is. This isn't something you'll find in your textbooks. Being a part of the research team twenty years ago gave me time to form my own hypothesis." He paused with his index finger and thumb on his chin.

"Which is?" Annette asked intrigued.

"I don't believe the ship we found was the actual ship."

A couple of the kids' heads jerked back startled.

The professor's posture straightened. "I think what we found was a smaller, detached piece of a much larger craft. An escape pod, perhaps," he said.

Justin chimed in, "How'd you come up with that idea?!"

"Listen, Mr. Edwards," he said. He scanned the rest of the room. "When we were able to open the hatch, there was no evidence anyone had been inside. It was clean and appeared unused. Our *earth* technology was unable to detect fingerprints or DNA residue of any sort. There was no steering mechanisms or navigation equipment of any sort. I truly don't believe this small craft could have traveled through space on its own. Of course, I could be wrong." He turned around and whispered to himself, "It wouldn't be the first time."

The kids in the front row laughed.

"This is all very dramatic professor – a great story – but it doesn't make any sense and goes against everything we've been told. But *if* you're right, which I don't think you are," several students nodded in agreement, "what do you think all that means?" asked Emily not hiding her attitude.

"I think it means whatever flew the original craft dropped that smaller pod for us to find which gave him or her time to hide the ship and blend in with us."

The professor paused as several students spoke up at the same time. He held up his hands to silence the class. "Which means what?" He pointed to

36

a girl in the front row.

"Intelligent life?" suggested a girl.

"Yes! Intelligence," repeated the doctor. "What else?"

A kid in the back raised his hand, speaking up hesitantly, "Maybe the pilot or... alien is still, uh, here?"

"Yes! Correct. Good hypothesis," said the professor with a wide grin. "Which means what for us?"

The room sat quietly as the doctor's eyes peered over the students. They silently exchanged looks with one another.

"Fear. Our government was afraid."

"Nah," spoke up Justin. "We are the United Countries of the World now. The crash made us stronger, and more unified as a people. Not scared."

"Your pride for our planet is duly noted Mr. Edwards, but arrogance and ignorance can crush any world if not cautious. It did bring fear. Why else do you think the government had to change? Why did they adapt?" Again, the students sat quietly and stared. "This time I want an answer. Someone, anyone."

Sarah raised her hand and answered. "The government used this event to grow and became stronger. By grouping up with other governments around the world, the wars stopped, and the genocides and massacres going on in the communist countries stopped. Those rulers realized they weren't the most powerful anymore. They realized how small they were. They joined with the other countries around the world to form one government."

"Very good, Sarah. Look at how our world reacted to this moment in history. N.A.S.A. was brought out of retirement to revive any sort of intergalactic communication satellites. We've advanced our planetary space modules and spacecrafts, and we've exchanged and obtained incredible resources from other countries to advance our military defenses in case of an invasion. Awesome, awesome stuff, and quite scary when you think of—"

"But how is that scary?" interrupted Justin. "Shouldn't we strive to be unified and armed against threats to our lives? What has happened is obviously working. So it's great the crash happened because we're in a better place, and whatever crashed has left us alone."

Their teacher smiled. "I agree that there is a lot of good happening right now, Mr. Edwards, but I'd encourage you to think of the long-term ramifications if we don't strive to be peaceful *galactic* citizens too. Someone knows we're here now. He... she... they could be walking among us still."

"What do you think we should expect, Dr. Vincent?" a student to Vincent's left asked meekly through the tension.

The doctor removed his glasses. "When a planet's resources die and those indigenous species have nowhere to survive, it's only logical that they may leave their world looking for somewhere to flourish. Honestly, I don't know, but anything is possible. We can only hope for the best… and prepare for the worst."

Leana groaned suddenly, drawing attention from the teacher. She gripped her head.

The ringing… It's getting worse. Her vision blurred and her body started getting hotter. She could feel dampness breakout on her forehead.

"Leana… Are you okay?" asked Dr. Vincent.

Annette twisted around, grabbing at Leana's hand. "Hey? You okay?"

Leana pulled her hand away. She wobbled as she rose from her chair, stumbling against the wall, delirious from the ringing in her head.

"I—I'm sorry." She quickly regained her balance as best she could, and realized that she was now standing in the middle of the room with everyone present staring at her. Some gaping, some sniggering – all staring. Overwhelmed, Leana bolted for the hallway, flinging the door violently open against the wall.

"Leana?!" yelled Annette and Dr. Vincent in unison.

"You two, go!" Dr. Vincent barked to Annette and Emily. "Follow her and make sure she's alright."

Justin started to get out of his chair, but Dr. Vincent raised his palm. "Mr. Edwards, you can stay here."

"But—" He was interrupted by the simple gesture to sit.

Annette and Emily sprinted out of class, their rapid footfalls slowly dissipating as they shot down the hallway.

Leana was down the hall ahead of them as she careened into a few unwary students, unintentionally knocking some of them to the ground or into each other as she raced by.

The ringing was getting louder and louder. *Go away!* Her muscles tightened, her heart raced, and she couldn't think straight. Nothing was working right. Sprinting around the corner, she slammed into the bathroom door, nearly smacking it into a girl who plastered herself against the wall to avoid the collision. The girl hurriedly left the bathroom, mumbling angry words that Leana paid no attention to.

Taking her hands from her ears, she shoved her hands under the sink, activating the faucet. She felt the cool water overload her senses as she splashed her face, and rubbed it on her neck. A small chill ran down her spine as the cold liquid trickled down her neck and into her soccer jersey. Despite this very brief moment of relief, the ringing kept getting louder. She struggled to breathe and had to brace herself up with both arms on the edge of the sink.

A stall door opened and a girl emerged with a concerned look on her face. "Are you—"

Leana waved her out. "Get out!" was all she could say without pain tearing through her head. The girl quickly washed her hands and left.

Leana's mind began playing tricks as the ringing sound turned into bloodcurdling screams, piercing inside her head. The walls of the bathroom were coming in and out of focus as flashes of her dreams and vision suddenly began taking over. An explosion seemed to BURST out of the stall next to her accompanied by the screams of people around her, running for their lives. She couldn't tell what was reality and what wasn't. The pulsing sounds drowned her mind beyond comprehension.

"Stop," she screamed, "please stop!"

A single sound suddenly broke through the pandemonium. A small, and yet, utterly familiar, ticking sound. *The watch.*

She desperately reached into her pocket, pulling out the watch wrapped in a bandana. She threw the rag to the ground and pressed the pocket watch against her ear, focusing on the ticking... only the ticking. The beat of Leana's heart began to slow as her mind was instantly wiped of all the terror she had been experiencing just seconds before. Soon her breathing calmed and the bathroom came into sharp focus. She could see herself in the mirror at the sink she was bracing herself on, the water still running and her wet hair dripping all over the floor around her. The watch was in her hand; she was clutching it so hard her knuckles were pale. Despite being physically and mentally exhausted, she noticed something about the watch. Something she'd never seen before. A pink light coming from the edges of the closed watch.

She stared at the light transfixed, but the experiences of the last few minutes had taken their toll. The last thing Leana heard before collapsing was the door banging open and her friends' voices calling out her name.

. . .

. . .

Annette and Emily skidded on the wet floor to Leana's unconscious body.

Emily cupped her hand to her mouth in horror. "Oh my god."

CHAPTER 6

Annette checked a text message on her phone. "They're on their way," she said to Leana comfortingly.

Leana was slouched on the white and crimson bleachers. She stared out at the vast practice stadium. Besides the school's athletes using it for practice, it was often used for class sessions and extracurricular activities for the students. The sheer size of it helped Leana feel free from the previous event. Annette watched Leana who hadn't said a word for about ten minutes; she had just sat there, looking at the empty green turf.

"You doing okay?" Annette asked gently.

There was a moment of silence. The sound of students participating in their P.E. class carried across the track.

"I've been having these… dreams."

"What dreams?" Annette said still concerned.

"I, uh… I've had them for years, you know… but the last few weeks they've been the worst… and they scare me." Leana choked on her words as a tear ran down her cheek. "I, uh, can't sleep."

Annette reached up and gently wiped the tear away, her hand lingering on Leana's cheek.

Leana cleared her throat and pulled away, feeling awkward.

"Last night was the worst one. And now I'm starting to… *see* things during the day." She checked Annette's reaction, but saw nothing but concern.

"My mom is making me stay with my dad over the weekend to…. '*help* me.'" She hesitated a moment. "I don't know what's wrong with me, but these dreams… these nightmares… they are so vivid, so real."

"What do you mean?" Annette rubbed Leana's back. Leana could tell Annette's calm demeanor was fake; she was nervous.

I shouldn't have said anything, she thought to herself. Leana sighed, wiping her face dry. "Nothing. Never mind. I'm being an emotional sixteen-year-old, you know...." Leana forced a weak chuckle, attempting to shift focus.

"Hey, hey. You don't have to push me away, Leana."

"I know. I'm sorry, but I'd actually rather *not* talk about it. I'm sorry I brought it up."

Annette stared patiently at Leana, waiting.

"The more I talk about it the more afraid I am that it'll become real, and these things in my head are already too real."

"You *need* to talk about it. What's going to happen if this starts getting worse?"

"Honestly... I don't know. I just have to make it through the game tonight."

"You're actually going to play tonight?" Annette paused. "You collapsed in the bathroom. Remember?"

"I have to, okay?" snapped Leana.

"Okay, okay. I'm only trying to help," Annette said, raising her hands in surrender.

Leana knew how much Annette cared for her, but she also knew no one on this planet could possibly understand the rollercoaster of emotions she had been experiencing.

"I'm... sorry. I didn't mean to snap." The weight of regret filled Leana's eyes.

"It's okay," Annette said calmly.

Annette shifted herself closer to Leana. "Look, maybe going to your dad's place will, I don't know, be better. I know how great it is to have a father. Now's your chance. Who knows... Maybe you'll like each other."

Leana chuckled dryly. "Yeah, um, I don't even know him. He's a total stranger to me."

She pulled out the pocket watch. "This is the only thing I have from him. I don't even know why I keep it."

"What is it?"

Leana showed her the shiny pocket watch.

"Wow. This is sizzlin', Leana," exclaimed Annette. "It's beautiful."

For a moment, Leana was tempted to just give it to Annette, but something stopped her.

"Where'd he get this?"

"He made it."

Annette jerked her head up. "*Way*?!"

"Way."

Annette started laughing. "It's incredible. I want it."

"...okay."

"Seriously?"

"No!" They laughed, bumping shoulders, forgetting for a moment how fresh Leana's pain was from the dreams. Annette paused, staring deep into Leana's eyes, a strange expression crossing her face. Leana blinked and quickly broke eye contact, ending the moment.

"What's so funny?" Justin vaulted up the steps of the stadium.

Show-off, Leana thought as she shared a look with Annette that told her she was thinking the same thing.

Emily followed him, taking her time up the stairs. Justin slid himself across the bleachers and stopped next to Leana.

"Emily, you are oh-so slow!" he proclaimed.

"Shut up. You're such a troph, Justin." Emily sat down in front of the girls.

"No can do," he replied.

Leana flinched at Emily's cold hand on her knee. "Are you doing okay?" she asked Leana.

"Yeah, I think I am. Thanks, Em." A breeze of cool air blew through the stadium.

"What's that?" Justin grabbed at the pocket watch.

"Careful!" blurted Annette as she snatched it out of reach.

"I will... Dang. You girls get so emotional," he said mockingly.

Annette handed him the pocket watch gently. The girls watched him look at it with curiosity.

"You have no idea what that is, do you?" Annette grinned.

"It's a watch, I think... It's a watch, right?"

The girls laughed.

"It's pretty nitro. Where'd you get it, Annette?" He handed it back, but Leana intercepted it.

"*My* dad." She said, stuffing it back into her pocket. "He made it. My mom said he was good with mechanical stuff, and this was something he made for me when I was a baby I guess."

"Well, it's pretty nitro, Lee."

"Why don't you ever say her whole name?" Emily piped in.

It was obvious to everyone that Justin had a crush on Leana, and making him uncomfortable always made for a good time. His eyes bounced between the girls, each of them waiting for an answer as he squirmed.

"I, uh... because I don't know. I just... don't. Why are you asking me questions? We're focused on *LEEAANNAA*." He drug out the name purposefully. "Right, Annette?"

Emily laughed. "Yeah okay. *Anyway*, since Leana's doing better, then let's... talk ... prom. Who's wearing what?" she asked, clapping her hands again at her favorite subject.

Leana could always count on Emily to make the group laugh. Even though she wasn't a physical athlete like the other three, she was quick with her mind and mouth.

Annette spoke first. "I looked through all the magazines and links you gave me, and I think I know what I want." She stood up and gestured as she described her dress. "It's a bit out of my style, but I think it'll fit perfect. It's a red mermaid dress, strapless, probably with red heels... not sure yet."

"Oh, that sounds *sparklin'*," Emily squeeled. "You're going to look so beautiful, Annette."

"Thanks. It shows off my back muscles." She flexed like a figure competitor.

"And that's what really matters," laughed Justin.

"Thank you, sir." Annette bowed.

"You're welcome, m'lady."

"Okay, weirdos." Emily got up from her seat and slowly spun. "I'm going with a replica of *the* famous pink dress worn by the great legend herself, Marilyn Monroe, from 1953 when she performed *Diamonds are a Girl's Best Friend*," She squealed again. "Ah! I'm so excited. Leana, what about you?"

"Well I can tell you this much... No pink. I see enough of that hanging out with you. But I was thinking... maybe jungle green? Sweetheart neckline. Empire waist. Floor-length."

"Oh, yeah. I can totally see you in that. You'll look sparklin' too, Leana. What do you think, Justin?"

"I think you girls can have fun talking dresses, and I've got places to be and photos to take. See ya." He looked directly at Leana and winked. "Bye."

Justin took off and hurdled the stadium railing, heading for the exit. Emily rolled her eyes. "He's such a show-off."

Annette leaned in. "Yeah, but he's showing off for her," she nodded in Leana's direction.

That's okay with me.

"Okay," Leana stretched her elbows out. "Ready to head out?"

"Yep," they replied.

"By the way, girls?" said Leana. They looked at her. "Thank you. I couldn't be okay without you."

The three girls hugged and stood up.

It always seemed like no matter how hard things were for Leana, she never had to face anything alone because she had these three friends. She couldn't imagine life without them.

CHAPTER 7

The last bell rang, releasing the students from their weekly grind. Thursdays were the best day of the week, starting off their three-day weekend, which meant sporting events, family time, and parties.

Most of the student body was heading home for dinner before the big soccer game at the Kingman's Stadium that night. Leana and her teammates exited the school doors towards the bus as swarms of students ran around them.

Waiting alongside the travel bus was Coach Shepard. His wide shoulders and chiseled legs were an obvious testament to his athleticism. He always wore an old silver whistle his father had given him when he was very young. Rumor had it that Coach Shepard's great grandfather was one of the greatest soccer coaches of all time in the Midwest back in the mid-80's. The whistle was a symbolic part of his token look, since nowadays professional coaches and referees had whistle implants they used directly out of their own vocal chords.

The girls always respected Coach Shepard's expert guidance, and experience, and they never questioned him. It didn't hurt that he was also extremely handsome.

"Hey, Coach," greeted Myanna, the first player on the bus.

He forced a slight smile and a head nod, but avoided eye contact, looking instead at the team roster as he marked off her name.

It was well known that Myanna had recently been caught writing Coach Shepard notes and leaving them on his truck's windshield. A security camera had recorded her doing it and an astute guard had reported it to the principal. At first, no one saw the harm, but when Coach Shepard took his letters to the principal people found out quick what she had done. These weren't just love notes; they were borderline inappropriate. Normally such behavior would have merited suspension or even removal from school, but her father was a major contributor on the school board, so she was given a second chance. Coach Shepard was careful not to encourage any misbehavior. The team needed her.

The rest of the girls followed close behind Myanna, greeting their coach as they got on the bus.

He checked off their names as they got on. "Wiltkens. Hart. Mussman. Rayne... Oh wait, Rayne hold up."

"Yeah, Coach?"

"I never got your confirmation about your parents..." Coach Shepard paused awkwardly, "Sorry. I mean, your mom. Is she attending the game tonight?" It was Parent's Night. All the players would be walking with their parents on the field, being recognized for their accomplishments during the final home game. "This ringing a bell?"

"Oh... yeah. Um, I don't know. Probably." She walked by with her head down.

He watched Leana make her way up the steps before stopping her again. "Hey. You okay?"

"Ugh! Why do people keep asking me that? I just want to get through this game." She continued into the bus before Coach Shepard could respond. She was sick of talking.

Once all the girls were accounted for, Coach Shepard and his assistant coaches got on the bus. The doors shut behind them. Half the girls immediately pulled out their phones to listen to whatever music they needed to get pumped up for the game, while the other half chatted amongst themselves. Leana didn't enjoy traveling on the bus with her team; she usually preferred being around her friends or her family, but at this particular moment, she would have rather been completely alone. She knew half the bus wasn't even focused on the game, their minds were on the parties that were planned for the weekend.

Partying wasn't really Leana's style. She lived for soccer. She was fueled by competition, and especially by a victory at the end of a game. It was very obvious, with this group however, she was in the minority. She wished her teammates shared her passion.

Frustration from being around her unfocused teammates gave Leana a bitter feeling. Her day's emotions soaked into her mind, affecting the way she thought about them. She wanted to scream at them to shut up and focus on the game ahead. She wanted to slap some of them awake, but she sat there quietly, staring out the window and trying to ignore the annoying noise of gossip, chatter, and babbling.

Leana tried thinking about something positive. She thought of her friends and the conversations they'd had earlier. Then her thoughts drifted to her mother. The moment her mother came into her mind, Leana remembered the last conversation they'd had. All the questions she wanted answered. Why did she have to see her father? What was happening to her? Why was she such a freak? Her emotions churned in her gut, filling her mind with depressing thoughts. She did not want to be here. She wanted to be in her room, alone. Her mind continued to wander to dark places. Places she didn't want to go and that scared her even more.

The dreams and visions were beginning to tear her world apart.

She refocused herself as Myanna shook her shoulder.

"Leana! You okay?"

"Wh—yeah. Of course I am. Why wouldn't I be?"

"Because we're at the stadium and you're still on the bus. Let's go." Myanna shuffled towards the door, hefting her game bag over the seats.

"We're here already?" she whispered to herself, looking out the windows. She hadn't even gotten around to thinking about the game yet.

Now I'm losing track of time?!

Leana grabbed her bag under the seat and scuttled off the bus. She glanced up at the outside wall of the Kingsman Stadium. She felt so small compared to the enormous structure.

As a cool breeze blew by, a cold chill caught Leana's focus. She was surprised to discover that she'd been sweating badly in her uniform.

"Great," she said annoyed.

Leana watched her teammates run out onto the field to begin their warm-up routines. She wanted to get to a sink to cool down and compose herself before joining her team. The moment she stepped into the locker room, the humid and pungent scent of sweat, dirt, and sour moisture hit her. The locker room's structure was very old, obviously made well before Coach Shepard's time.

At the center of the concrete room were the bathroom stalls. Leana headed for the sinks in front of them. The running water was a relaxing sound. She cupped her hands, splashing cold water on her face and drenching her hair. She could feel the chill move into her pores. Her skin welcomed the cold as her muscles relaxed, her breathing slowed, and her mind calmed. She grabbed some paper towels to dry off with, but they had the same rank odor as the locker room, so she threw them unused into the trash.

The flickering lights highlighted locker areas along the walls where the girls could put their things. One corner, with a burnt out light, stood out to Leana in the back area of the locker room. She felt an instant desire to be alone in that dim place.

She put her bag in the rusty locker and slumped down on a wooden bench. She was finally alone... in the half dark, thinking about her insanity, confusion, and frustration.

Finally.

Just when she was getting relaxed – as relaxed as she could possibly muster, at least – her wrist lit up blue. Her mother had sent a text message. She pressed a small button on her black bracelet, popping up a display above her wrist. Words scrolled across: "NOT GOING TO MAKE IT. WORK. SORRY. SEE YOU AFTER. GOOD LUCK. LOVE YOU. MOM."

"Awesome. And your messaging sucks, Mom." Leana thought, wondering why her mom still typed in all-caps.

She scanned the locker room, hoping no one heard her. She already felt crazy enough without others realizing their team captain talked to herself.

Leana yanked the bracelets from her wrist and shoved them into her bag, slamming the door shut before punching it. She grunted, rubbing her face with her hands.

I don't know how much more I can take, she thought. Her hand throbbed and her frustration grew.

CHAPTER 8

The door swung open to a quickly silenced locker room. The coaches marched in confidently, standing around the Chandler players. Shepard took his position at the center, staring at all the athletes he'd trained throughout the season. Some looked intimidated, and others just plain scared, their legs jiggling nervously. Leana was the only one without expression; her gaze seemingly far away.

The team waited for his strong words of encouragement. Cleats slapped the concrete floor and heavy breathing filled the air.

"Alright, Owls... Get them going," he yelled, beginning to clap his hands together.

Rhythmically and with near perfect cadence, the girls began to pound the ground with their cleats like a beat of a battle drum.

Coach Shepard raised his voice, pep talking his team. "I know you're nervous and afraid, but I also know your hearts and your abilities. You've given your blood, sweat and tears for this team over the last year, working harder than ever before." He moved around the center, staring at each player. "This is one of the biggest games of the year. Of the decade, even! I know you are scared, but I'm not. Believe me when I say that if you work together, you are the better team. If you play as a team, you will win as a team. Have faith in the girl next to you and you will come out of this victoriously. I promise."

Leana, along with her team, looked up, listening as the stadium above them began vibrating and shaking, cheers erupting through the concrete structure. Leana knew she needed to get her head right, she needed her distractions turned to focus. It was time. Her fear and confusion turned to awareness. She was going to win this game. She had to.

"Do you hear that?" Coach Shepard pointed up. "That's for all of you.

They believe in you. They know that this is *your* game. Now it's time for you to believe in yourselves." He paused momentarily as the girls escalated the pounding of their cleats, and then yelled, "It's our game!"

His words ignited the locker room. The team shot to their feet screaming and embracing each other like they had already won. The roar of the crowd rumbled louder outside the locker room door, filling the players' bones with confidence. Leana alone remained calm. She stood, staring intently at the doors to the stadium, waiting for them to open.

"Tonight's the night, girls," yelled one of the assistant coaches. "This is the game you've all been waiting for. And everyone here's for you. No backing down. One minute at a time."

Leana pushed her way to the front of her team, squeezing between them and the door. She turned and looked at the girls. All eyes were on her. "We're going up against a tough team and all we have is each other out there. If you want this… I mean really want this… Then take it." The girls hooted with fists in the air. "Years from now you'll remember this game and how great it felt to win. You'll remember each other and how we fought, bled, and won as a team. Come on, Owls! Let's go!" She slapped the hands in the air then turned, roaring along with her team.

They burst through the door and ran down the dark, damp walkway, directly under the stadium seats. At the end were large swinging doors, sealed and ready to open any second.

Just inches from the door, Leana could feel her heart beat through her chest.

Here we go.

As the doors swung open the crowd's screams were almost deafening. Sirens, horns, and fans belted out encouragement for Core City's team. Leana felt the wave of confidence sweeping over her. *We're not losing tonight.*

The girls ran out to the center of the stadium, warming up and soaking in their fans' cheers. A moment passed when a blaring horn went off at the other end of the field, and as if a wind carried away the cheers, a hush swept over the stadium. Suddenly, cheers erupted at the opposite end of the stadium.

Leana watched the far doors swing open as the rival team charged the field. The booming cheers ushered in the Reavers' arrival. This team was known for their unorthodox antics to disrupt the traditional pre-game of a match. Not a hint of fear was in Leana; she stood watching, calm and focused. She blocked out the crowd and continued warming up.

At the front of the Reavers' team was Thea Williams, their captain and the most ruthless player in the Midwest. Her father was a highly decorated Marine, Elite Class, who served three tours in the Final War twenty years ago. She wore his strength in every game. A great leader, a phenomenal player, and merciless throughout her four years of varsity soccer, this girl had gotten kicked out of nearly ten games for "careless, reckless, and excessive force." All Leana knew was Thea was going to play her best tonight, which was exactly what Leana wanted.

"Game on!" Leana slapped her legs, giving them a jolt of energy and getting the blood flowing.

The crowd stood for the "World Allegiance Anthem," sung by students of both schools. It was created after the Final War. Leana and Thea stared at each other across the field, paying no attention to the song or the United World Allegiance flag as it snapped in the night sky.

The crowd cheered at the end of the song, and a man in white and black waved Leana over, emptying his lungs into his vocal whistle. "Team Captains!"

All eyes were on Leana and Thea as they met at the center of the field. Thea shook out her long legs. Hover-cams circled the two captains and the referee, filming and projecting the game live on HV nationwide, as well as in the rabble room filled with the reporters around the Midwest. Each was giving their take on the top two teams in the nation competing for their final regular season game before playoffs. These relentless reporters would verbally claw at each other, tooth and nail, in order to get their take on one of the most important games of the year.

The reporters watched through their Holo-Visions as the game started.

"I'm Roger Feegal. I'll be the center referee tonight. Names, please." The ref's voice echoed through the stadium speakers as he pulled out his game card and removed a little pencil from behind his ear. The fans loved the new coin-flip ceremony.

"Thea Williams."

"Leana Rayne."

"Okay, thank you. Thea, you're away, so call it in the air." The ref reached into his pocket. *"Ready?"* he asked, holding up both sides of the coin. *"This is heads, this is tails. Call it."* The coins flipped in the air.

"Heads."

"It's tails. Home's call. Leana, do you want to start with the ball or have it the second half?"

"We'll start with the ball. Thanks."

"Okay. Reavers, you'll be defending here. Owls kick off first." He jotted down his notes in his game card. *"Shake hands."*

Thea's handshake was tight. Leana felt the sweat collect between their hands.

"Head back to your sidelines and good luck."

Leana tried turning away, but Thea didn't let go.

"Good luck." Thea smiled sarcastically.

Leana squeezed back tightly. She smiled as well and squeezed a bit harder until Thea let go.

"See you out there."

Thea turned confidently and ran back to her team.

Leana, her coach, and the rest of the Owls collected at their sideline.

"Okay… It's time. Bring it in!" Coach Shepard hollered. "On three. 1…2…3…"

The crowd near the team sideline and players screamed together, "GAME NIGHT! HOO!" The team cheered as the starters ran out to centerfield. Leana bumped fists with Myanna who squared off next to the Reavers' team captain. Thea's stare practically burned a hole through Myanna.

"Hey, Myanna," Leana said out of the side of her mouth, her eyes never leaving Thea's. "Let's ice these guys." Myanna nodded.

Leana waited for the whistle with her foot on the ball. The instant the whistle blew, Leana passed the ball to Myanna. Leana moved up the field with incredible speed, sprinting past the forwards and mid-fielders. Myanna booted the ball high into the air.

Leana looked up and watched the ball descending perfectly. Right before colliding with the defender, Leana turned and jumped, popping the ball off her head and behind the defender. She spun and sprinted at the ball… Just her and the goalie. Leana dribbled left then cocked back her leg, kicking hard to the right corner.

"GOAL!" screamed the announcer. The crowd went crazy, chanting Leana's name, "LET IT RAYNE, LET IT RAYNE, LET IT RAYNE!" The Owls' student section broke down in their ritualistic 'Rayne Dance.'

"Let's go," she screamed, clapping her hands. "We're just getting started."

The girls crowded around her. "1…2…3…"

"HOO!"

"This stops now, ladies," Thea yelled, encouraging her team to turn it up.

The rest of the first half stayed exciting, both goalies being more aggressive, stopping everything until the buzzer. Yellow cards got held up and the crowd stayed on their feet screaming.

"*Score 1-0 at the half,*" proclaimed the announcer, as both teams jogged to their locker rooms.

The rabble room of reporters quickly emptied as they pushed towards the field, hoping to get a quick interview with one of the coaches. Leana almost made it off the field before getting stopped by someone with a camera. He asked Leana if she wanted to talk, but she declined and instead threw a wet towel over her head. She made her way through the doors.

Both tired and hyped, Leana sat quietly in the locker room while the rest of the girls kept up their excitement. The vibrations from the cheering still shook above them.

"Great job! Great job!" Coach Shepard clapped entering the locker room. "That's how you play. This is your game… Your game. Take a breather. Honor students, you've got five minutes before they need you on the field with your parents. Everyone else, stay focused." Before exiting out the door, he turned to his players. "HEY! I'm proud of you girls, but it's not over."

He smiled and opened the door, instantly bombarded by reporters and cameras.

This is our game, Leana thought.

After a few minutes, the locker room emptied of the honor students, as well as the rest of the team to cheer them on. Leana was the only one still in the locker room. She was lost in thought. With all the quiet, her mind quickly switched back to earlier. The soccer game was a much needed mental break, but once she was alone the images and thoughts were able to swarm her mind once again. She couldn't ignore how it made her feel. Her teammates saw her as a captain, but she saw herself as a freak and a psycho. All of a sudden, she was back to not wanting to be there. She wanted to be at home in her bed. She didn't want to see her father, or think about prom or, strangely, even the game.

Before long, her chattering teammates burst back into the locker room. She forced herself to snap back to playing the part of a leader and captain, hiding her weakness from the other girls. She hated herself for allowing those images and thoughts to come over her again, and now she was scared she wouldn't regain her focus. She needed to keep her game face; not for her, but for her teammates. She knew she couldn't allow her mental state to get the best of her right now. She needed to stay strong for her team.

Some of the girls were exchanging smiles and looks about Leana. She could tell they were pity smiles, feeling bad Leana's parents hadn't come to the game. She let them think her missing mother was the reason for her discomfort. It was a good cover for the truth. She felt like a spotlight was directly on her and all of her stress was showing. They didn't need to know why.

The buzzer blared. *Game on.* Both starting teams went centerfield, and the Reavers started the second half with the ball.

Coach Shepard screamed out to his girls. "45 more minutes. This is your game."

The entire crowd roared. The hover-cams continued to circle centerfield as the referee blew his whistle.

"*The Reavers are out for blood this half, looking more vicious and aggressive with the ball. They want this game bad, but the Owls aren't giving up their victory without a fight,*" broadcasted the announcer from the overhead speakers.

For ten minutes, both teams kept pushing the envelope, competing aggressively both on offense and defense. "*An incredible game of head-to-head, back-and-forth as both teams are playing well, driving the ball down the field, only to have both goalies defend each shot brilliantly. Amazing!"* called the announcer, causing the crowd to erupt.

Thea Williams played smart against Myanna, who seemed to be reveling in the competition. Leana watched Myanna battle back and ignore all of Thea's cheap shots, insults, and patronizing comments. The Reavers' best wasn't breaking the Owl's player. Leana was actually a bit grateful Thea was there with her bad attitude, it was distracting her from her own internal battle and focusing her frustration and energy on showing Thea who the better team was. Leana's team was staying strong, but Leana knew she had to keep her eyes on Thea, watching for any foul play beyond what Thea was already dishing out. Leana knew Thea's track record.

As the game went into the final 20 minutes, Leana could tell Thea was getting desperate. Her team was losing, and she was starting to make simple mistakes. Leana watched Thea switch positions with the other Reavers' midfielder. Right away, Leana knew Thea was up to something. Thea's eyes were focused on Myanna with deadly intent. She didn't know how or why she realized it, but Leana knew something bad was about to happen. Leana glanced at the coach, but there wasn't time to get a switch out. She wanted to scream at Myanna to keep an eye out, but it was too late. The ball got kicked out of bounds, capturing the ref and players' focus, and then it happened. Too far away to intervene, Leana watched helplessly as Thea sidestepped Myanna's ankle, dropping her hard to the turf.

Myanna's piercing scream confirmed the snap of her ankle, immediately drawing the attention of the coaches and players. The side ref ran up to Thea, holding up the red card, kicking her out of the game, but Leana knew Thea's tirade wasn't over.

Leana sprinted across the field, ignoring the other players, and slid in next to Myanna who was grasping her ankle and grimacing in pain.

"Coach! Coach!" Leana yelled, seeing he was already running towards them with the trainers behind him.

The whistle blew for an injury time-out. Myanna lay back, rolling on the ground in agony. Leana felt Thea's gaze as she turned and screamed in Thea's face. "You're a pathetic troph! What's the matter with you?!" She turned back to her teammate. "It's going to be okay, Myanna."

"Who you calling troph?" Thea cleated Leana in the back, sending her to her knees as other players tried to pull Thea back, but she broke away.

In that moment, everything slowed down. The screams of angry fans became muffled. Leana could feel her heavy, beating heart and raspy breath. She could hear a muted whistle as the ref ordered Thea's disqualification. Every fiber of her being was filled with adrenaline, shooting like lightening through her body. Her emotions turned to rage, but somehow she still felt in control.

Leana felt Thea's hand grab at her shoulder. Before Leana could think about it, her elbow made contact with Thea's stomach, digging deep. Leana sprang up and turned with the world in slow motion. The moment she hit Thea in the gut she realized she was out of control. Her rage fumed through her. After making quick eye contact with Thea, her hand swung out, hard. Leana felt the throbbing on her palm as it connected with Thea's face. She breathed hard. Abruptly, a whistle broke through the haze and the world around her became clear again.

Thea Williams lay on the turf below her, unconscious.

The noise, voices, screams became clear again, overpoweringly loud. *What'd I just do?* Leana touched her mouth with her stinging hands. "I... I'm sorry." She backed away.

The referee pulled out the red card. "Get off my field! You're out of the game too!" he yelled. He pulled Leana away from the two girls on the turf, gripping Leana's arm tightly. "Coach! Get her out of here."

Leana struggled to breath. Her brain pounded with angry thoughts. She struggled to block them out. As suddenly as she found herself striking Thea, the images began flashing through her mind again, making it hard for her to maintain focus on reality. *Not now!*

A hand turned her around and her eyes widened, her body filled with terror. A hulking figure with gray, dry skin dressed entirely in black stood facing her, looking down on her. It reached out its claws. She gasped.

"Leana! What's wrong with you?!" Coach Shepard stood inches from her, his hands on her shoulders.

"What?! What?" Leana stammered out feebly.

"You need to get off the field. Now!" He looked to one of the assistant coaches. "Get her to the locker room, quickly. She can't be out here any longer."

The hover-cams zoomed between Leana with her coach and the two girls lying on the field. Other cams scanned over the roiling crowd of screaming people.

Owls players stared stunned as Leana ran by them. Thea was still unconscious with her coach and trainers kneeling next to her, trying to wake her up. Myanna was being carried off on a stretcher by paramedics, writhing in pain. An ambulance waited on the sideline.

Leana didn't know what had happened or what she had been thinking. Seeing Thea on the ground and Myanna heading towards the ambulance sent waves of sadness, embarrassment, and shame over her. Heading into the stadium walkway, fans around the entrance yelled and screamed at her. "What was that?!" "You call yourself a Captain?!" One individual fan yelled out in encouragement, "Thunder AND Rayne! Hoo!" Some just stared as if shocked the team's leader would display such poor control. The locker room door slammed behind her.

After quickly changing, Leana paced back and forth in her street clothes, listening to the game continue. From the moans of her school's fans it didn't sound like the game was going well for the Owls. Before the final buzzer, Leana packed up all her things and got out of the locker room, too embarrassed to face her teammates. She headed for the parking lot, still hearing the game from outside the stadium.

A few minutes later, the game was over. The crowd erupted at the buzzer. The Owls had lost.

I did this, it's my fault. We lost because of me! Blaming herself, Leana climbed on top of an old Light Tank M3 that decorated the lawn outside the stadium, and waited for her mother to pick her up. She knew she had to either face the shaming eyes of her team, or her mother who didn't know anything yet. Being around her team wasn't an option. Knowing she was the reason they lost put a knot in her stomach and sour taste in her mouth. She wanted to vomit, but hot tears was all she could muster.

"Way to go, Leana. You failed everyone. Everyone everywhere got to see how much you suck," she whispered, choking on each word. "I hate my life so much."

Shoving her hand in her bag, she pulled out the pocket watch. She clicked open the cover and pressed it against her ear, listening to the ticking, hoping to find stability. She felt the cold metal of the tank on her back as she gazed upward.

The dark lead sky revealed the glimmering beauty of the stars. No planes, no clouds… just stars. She envied the solitude.

"That's where I want to be. That's where I belong, away from all this." She wiped the tears away as they fell down her cheeks. *I'm sick of crying.*

A peace came over her, listening to the ticking and looking into the quiet expanse. For a brief moment, she forgot about her self-diagnosed insanity. She completely escaped into the black abyss, leaving this world behind.

Her attention was drawn to the trickling of the crowd exiting the stadium.

Just then, Danielle pulled up. Leana hopped off the tank quickly, shoved her bags into the back seat and slammed the door shut.

"Let's go."

"What's the rush, honey? You okay?"

"Mom, can you please drive?"

Danielle sighed, pulling out of the stadium parking lot as jubilant and disappointed fans walked back to their cars. Leana looked out the back window where the locker room was, and then hunched down in her seat so no one would see the team captain leave the parking lot in dishonor. She finally stopped trying to wipe her tears away, and let the streaks on her cheeks shine in the flickering lights as her mother drove them away from her humiliation.

Baring her shame to her mother, she spoke, "Mom… I failed."

CHAPTER 9

An awkward silence settled in as soon as the words left her mouth. She ignored the inevitable questions from her mother. She just wanted to sit quietly, fuming in her thoughts of shame and regret as they drove to her father's house. The feelings from the game replayed in her mind, while the images of her visions also began to flicker in and out. It was becoming too much to bear.

The woman on the radio sounded overly chipper, like she had to force her positive attitude to please listeners.

"The weather for most of this weekend looks warm and sunny. High chance of rain Sunday night, so get out those umbrellas. Back to you, Frank."

While Leana struggled to regain her composure, she continued to stare out her window, avoiding eye contact and conversation with her mother. Her thoughts were on the game, the mistake she made and the vision she had. It was all so confusing. *How could I have done that to Thea and not know what I was doing? What happened to me?*

Her mother's voice finally broke through her thoughts. "Do you mind telling me what's going on, Leana?"

"I don't know, Mom. A lot."

"You don't have to tell me anything, but it would be much better if you did."

"What do you want me to tell you?"

"Let's start with school. Anything interesting happen today?"

Leana chuckled in surprise at the question because it was so absurd in comparison to her day. She wanted to tell her mother everything, from collapsing in the bathroom to her mental breakdown at the game, but she felt if she talked about it she'd have to relive it all over again.

"It was just another day, I guess."

"Okay... How about the game?"

"We lost."

"Honey?" Danielle hinted.

"Yeah?" she mumbled.

"What happened?"

The window collected condensation from Leana's long, drawn out sigh. She turned to her mother. "I had another one, Mom."

"A dream? At school?"

"Sort of. I walked to Landings Park this morning and had another one there, but I wasn't asleep, and then I..." Her words failed her.

"You what, sweetheart?"

"I collapsed in the bathroom. It was weird, my head felt like it was exploding, and I was hearing and seeing things that weren't there. Images just pounded and pounded in my head. I didn't think my body could take it."

"Oh, no! Sweetheart, why didn't you call me? Why didn't the school call me?"

"Because I didn't want you to be mad... or freak out."

"Honey. Why would I be mad?"

"I don't know... Because I am, I guess?"

"Leana—"

"Mom, listen. Something is going on with me. I feel like I'm in Hell, right now, because I don't know what it is... No one does. It's scaring the crap out of me, Mom. I don't know what to do."

She looked back out the window. It had started sprinkling and water drops had collected outside of the glass. The lights from passing cars refracted in the droplets.

"The game went even worse."

"I know, Leana."

"What?"

"Your coach called me right before I picked you up, and told me what happened."

"Oh," she said shamefully, struggling to get the next question out around a lump in her throat. "Are you mad?"

"Oh honey, don't cry. It's going to be okay," Danielle comforted, grabbing Leana's hand.

"Did you hear I hit a gi—"

"Yes, Leana, I heard. He told me you seemed *off* from the moment you stepped on the bus after school."

"I saw something on the field... right after I slapped her. That's three visions in one day, and that's after my nightmare. That's never happened. I think it was a creature from my dreams. It felt familiar. It was so real, Mom. I—" The knot in her throat loosened as tears began flowing freely from her eyes. "Am I crazy?"

"No. You're not crazy, Leana."

"Easy for you to say. Your brain isn't filled with..." She gestured with her hands to try to find the words. "Whatever this is."

"No, it's not. But don't, for a second, think you're the only one going through this. I'm right here with you, watching this happen. Being unable to stop it tears me up inside."

"I'm sorry, Mom. I don't know what to do. It's not just dreams and nightmares anymore. It's visions and voices. I just... What's wrong with me, Mom?" She swiped her arm across her face, drying her cheeks for a moment before more tears continued to stream down.

"Leana, it's not your fault. I know you don't want to hear this, but your father..." Leana looked up. "He *will* take care of this. I promise."

"How do you know that?"

"I just do. You can trust him."

"Trust him? Why would I?"

"Because I know him, and I love him. I hate that he had to leave us, but I don't hate him. He's a good man, and he will do everything in his power to help you."

Silence set in for a few moments, moving Leana to turn on the radio.

"—*almost here ladies and gentlemen. The twentieth anniversary of...drum roll please...the alien crash landing in the center of Core City, once known as the small city of Cedar Rapids.*" Canned applause echoed through the car speakers.

"Mom, I can remember something from one of them."

For a moment, Danielle hesitated. She looked over at her daughter with wide eyes, but then flashed Leana her comforting smile. "Tell me."

"I was in this dark alleyway by a street. It was raining really hard and I could feel how cold it was, Mom. I was freezing, but it wasn't even real... I don't know."

"Okay. Keep going, baby girl."

Then, out of nowhere, this car spins out of control right in front of me and crashed into a pole. There was a pregnant woman crawling out and a semi-truck."

Her mother twisting her head towards Leana at the mention of the pregnant woman.

"And there was this guy in a hoodie, I think?!"

"In a hoodie?" asked Danielle, sounding stunned.

Leana nodded, her brow raised. "Right?! It was super detailed."

"Leana?" her mother hesitated. "That sounds more like a memory."

"What? How could it be?"

"Remember the day we sat down and read through your journal?"

"Um, yeah?"

"Those were dreams you didn't remember, and they took place on an alien planet and couldn't have ever occurred in real life."

"I know. So what?"

"Well, it sounds like your visions are about Earth. So maybe, they're just your mind converting your memories somehow."

Leana looked down, realizing her mother might be onto something she'd never thought about. She couldn't understand how she remembered the visions, but she did, and maybe her mother was right. She usually was. "Okay, so what memory was it, Mom?"

"I honestly don't know. I could be the man in the hoodie or the pregnant woman. I mean, maybe I'm the person in the alleyway."

"No, no, Mom. You see, I was the person in the alleyway. I wasn't in some body of someone else. It was me, watching this happen."

She sighed. "Then I don't know, Ana. I'm sorry. Your father might be better at understanding this." Danielle gently set her hand on Leana's.

"But—"

"Leana, I don't have all the answers. This is something I encourage you to ask him."

"Mom, I don't *want* to ask him."

The anchorman on the radio continued. *"—hat's right. Everything from the old smartphones to security cameras to first-hand witnesses caught on site the real life extraterr—"*

Leana flipped the radio off and sat back. "Why is everyone so obsessed with the crash landing thing?" She was anxious for a subject change.

"I remember that day," Danielle said, turning her head to her daughter and smiling, "like it was yesterday."

"Why? What's the big deal? It's just some stupid day where we celebrate a potential hoax. Yay! All the small towns came together to become the *great* Core City and the government search for a spaceship they never found." She rolled her eyes sarcastically.

"That was the day I met your father."

Leana's head twisted around. "Wait. Really?!"

Danielle laughed. "Yeah, just a little while after the crash."

"Why didn't you ever tell me?"

"You don't like talking about your father. Remember?"

"Well, you can tell me now. Might as well." Leana needed the distraction. She turned her body towards her mother.

Danielle began. "I think it was a little over a week after the crash happened. Doesn't matter. Anyway, I was waitressing at an old dive-bar, called The Rut. It was just a hole-in-the-wall joint with a handful of regulars normally. That night though, the whole place was packed, everyone's eyes peeled on the news, completely silent. People had been talking non-stop about this for the entire week. Some of them were terrified, others excited, but there was this one guy who walked in, paying no attention to the news.

He just sat there staring at the empty seat across from him."

"Dad?"

Danielle nodded. "He seemed exhausted like any of the other regulars, so I asked him if he was hungry."

"What'd he say?"

"He stuttered a bit, sounding like he'd lost his voice. He apologized and said he didn't have any money. He got up to leave, but there was something about him that intrigued me. I grabbed his arm, and the strangest thing happened... He flinched. It was kind of pitiful. I don't know why, but I bought him a burger and a beer."

"Weird. Then what?"

"He stayed 'til the end of my shift. The food seemed to relax him, and since most people were glued to the HV I didn't have anything better to do, so we talked. Well, I did most of the talking, and eventually asked him if he wanted to go out sometime."

"Wait, wait, wait. You asked *him* out?"

"I did." She felt Leana's gaze. "What?! He was cute. Did I mention that? And there was something about him that I just... liked. Anyway, that's when everything started."

"Wow, Mom. Look at you, making the moves. Ow! Ow!"

"Couldn't resist."

"So, you asked out a hot farmer?"

"Well, at this point he was still a soldier."

"Oh, really?!"

"Yes, but he really didn't talk about it. Later, when we dated, I tried asking him more, but the only thing he'd say was how he served his time in a war not many people knew about. He never talked about it in detail, but he did say he couldn't believe he made it out in one piece."

"Oh... That's kind of awesome. And now he farms, huh?"

"Yep."

"That's pretty crazy."

Yeah. It was a huge switch, I'm sure, but he's good at it. Always loved to grow and make things."

"Why?"

"I don't know. Just because, I guess."

"Mom, why didn't you tell me this before?"

"I told you. You hated talking about him."

"You should have made me listen anyway."

"I probably should have, but to tell you the truth, baby girl, it hurts a lot to talk about him sometimes. Even though he and I talk occasionally, I was still afraid talking to you about him would hurt because he hasn't been part of *our* life, and I didn't want you to see me hurting for him. You resent him so much already."

I never thought about how Mom *felt.* She felt selfish for even bringing him up now.

"I'm sorry, Mom."

"It's okay. You didn't know."

The car passed a green sign with white letters: "Prescott 10 miles."

Danielle pointed to it. "We're almost there."

Leana leaned against the door with her chin in her hand. "Can't wait," she said, sighing. Deep down a tiny part of her meant it.

CHAPTER 10

The crunching of the tires driving down the long gravel road distracted Leana from the feeling of dread she couldn't avoid. The headlights illuminated the road ahead of the car. Leana's eyes watched out the window, staring in surprise at her father's property, impressed despite herself. The rain had stopped about half an hour before and the damp trees now reflected the moonlight, glistening in the night.

White fencing lined each side of the driveway and trees lined the driver's side fence, separating the large acreage from the car. On Leana's side was a small pond with prairie grass just starting to grow for the season, and a willow tree that looked like it had survived centuries. Above it all was the clearest night sky she'd ever seen. There were no street or city lights for miles to pollute the view.

Pulling up to the house, Leana felt her mother's energy transform and become more energetic, like she had completely forgotten anything they had discussed on the drive up. Leana felt slightly betrayed and frustrated that Danielle's emotions were so easily charged with happiness. It was a happiness that sickened Leana because she wanted it too, but that giddiness wasn't going to come to her any time soon, especially now that they had arrived at her father's.

They parked in front of the porch of a large gray house with white trim. Leana hesitated to move as she watched Danielle open the door and step out.

On the porch in the dark, sat two figures in shadow; presumably, her father in his chair and some kind of large dog. Leana felt like both pairs of eyes were staring at her.

Together, the figures stood up. The dog stayed at the top of the stairs, still in the shadows, while the man made his way down the steps into the moonlight. Leana observed him walking towards her and her mother. Despite wearing a loose flannel shirt, she could tell he was tall and well built. As he got closer she could see how tanned his face was from working outside, and could make out dark hair that curled out from under his cap.

"Danielle." He had a strong, yet gentle, voice. The closer he got to her mother the faster his pace became.

"Otis." She wrapped her raised arms around his neck as he bent down and embraced her. "I've missed you," she whispered.

"I've missed you too. It's been too long this time."

Leana couldn't make out what they were saying, and she didn't care to. She wanted to stay in the car. Part of her still hoped if she was defiant and distant enough, he wouldn't want her there and she could go back home.

Otis approached the car and looked in the windshield, one arm still around Danielle and the other shoved into his pocket. He jerked his head at Leana, gesturing for her to come out.

Leana took a deep breath before opening the door. Stepping out, she felt fresh air fill her lungs, clean and pure. Even the air was better outside the city. Her breath suddenly turned into a gasp as she found herself staring into the eyes of a large, gray wolf that stood in front of her, exposing its teeth. She pressed her back against the car.

"Uh… uh…" were the only words she could force from her mouth, terror filling every cell in her body. She couldn't move, couldn't breathe, couldn't think. She turned her head and shut her eyes tightly, hoping it was only another vision.

"El! Down, girl," Otis commanded, shaking his head when the wolf looked over at him. "She's family."

Leana turned her head back just enough to peak at the wolf with one eye. It backed away and sat on its haunches like nothing had happened.

"I'm sorry, Leana. El's very protective around new people, but she's not dangerous. Are you, girl?" Otis stroked the wolf's head.

Awesome. Glad I peed my pants for nothing! She glared at her mother.

Leana tried to play it off like she was fine, but her heart was beating through her chest. This was not what she needed right now. "Not cool."

"Honey, come over here."

Leana yanked her bag from the car and slammed the door. She marched over to her mother.

Awkwardly, Danielle tried to introduce them, "Leana, this is your Father… This is Otis."

Nice, Mom, I had no idea, Leana thought sarcastically to herself.

Leana stuck out her still-sweaty hand, hoping it would disgust him. Whatever kept him from hugging her.

He accepted and shook firmly. "I'm happy you're here, Leana."

"Thanks. Me too." Her fake smile said otherwise. *Not!*

Otis turned to Danielle, smiling as he spoke hopefully. "Do you want to stay for dinner?"

She replied, regret in her voice, "I can't. I'm sorry, Otis. I have to work the overnight shift."

"It's okay. It was good to see you though." Otis smiled lovingly, but Leana saw the disappointment in his eyes.

"You too."

Danielle leaned in and encircled her daughter in her arms. "Make the most of it, baby girl," she whispered.

Leana wanted to run away and hide in the car again, but instead she hugged her mother tightly as if they'd never see each other again. It felt like the end for Leana, like she would be alone forever. For a second, she hoped if she gave her mom a *really* good hug maybe she wouldn't leave her here. No such luck.

Danielle released her then smiled once more at Otis and headed back to the car.

"Danny?" Otis called, following behind her.

She twisted around. "Yeah?"

Without words, Otis grabbed her tightly once again. Leana saw her mom hold on to the back of her father's shirt. She'd never seen her mother be treated so tenderly before.

"Forever love," he whispered.

Danielle tilted her head slightly upward toward Otis' ear "Forever love."

Leana watched, somewhat confused as they struggled to say goodbye, then Otis opened the car door for his wife, who got in without taking her eyes off him. Leana pursed her lips in disgust.

Leana watched her mom mouth the words to start the car and tell it where to take her, and then saw the tears start to roll down her cheeks just as the car began to pull away. Otis stood silently with his back to Leana.

She didn't know what to think of all this. Watching the deep love between her parents, and then the real struggle to let each other go completely contradicted what she thought of their relationship. That moment her parents had made it seem like they had been in love for all these years, but that didn't make sense to her. Her father had left them. He had exiled himself from her and her mother, but in the past five minutes they made it seem as if those thirteen years was only a mere flicker in time. Leana had spent so much time hating her father, and here he was clearly still in love with her mother, and her mother clearly loved him back.

Turning around, Otis approached Leana, and asked with an energetic tone that didn't match what just happened, "So, you hungry?" He rubbed his hands together.

"Sure."

Leana begrudgingly turned to walk into the house, but stopped suddenly. El was standing in her way, gazing at her as if she was still trying to figure out if Leana was a threat or not. At first, she thought it was shadows playing with the thick fur, but when El changed her posture the shadow didn't. Leana noticed black streaks ran down El's spine. *Strange,* Leana thought. *I've never seen markings like that before in any pictures of wolves.*

Her father cleared his throat and put his hand on the wolf's head again.

"Don't mind her. First impressions aren't always great, but she'll get used to you. I promise." He ran his hand along the wolf's back. "Come on, El. Food."

El slowly turned and followed Otis up the porch with Leana close behind. He opened the door to the house.

"Come on in," Otis said happily.

The first thing Leana noticed was the smell of fresh roses in a pot sitting at the bottom of the stairwell, directly inside the front door. She paused at the doorstep, taking in the beautiful house. He didn't have much, but the house was clean and organized. A Holo-Vision sat in the living room, which was good because she was probably going to get bored.

"You clean this place yourself?"

Otis' smile said '*no*'.

"Actually, I have—".

The banging of pots and pans snagged Leana's attention. Someone was in the kitchen. *Another woman?!* she thought to herself.

A high-pitched voice rang around the corner through the living room. It sounded almost robotic. "She's here!"

Springing into the living room and zooming toward the entrance was a man in a white shirt and jeans. His expression was static with no distinguishable features, until he got closer. Leana could see circuit boards, pistons, and skeletal parts underneath an almost transparent layer of skin. He was an android.

He hugged her tightly and without permission.

"Umm… Hi," said Leana. She looked at Otis, noticing he was covering a smile with his hand.

"It's okay," he said, reaching out and patting his fingers on her shoulder. "This is Esu."

"Esu? What kind of name is that?"

"I am E.S.U. Your father's android. I'm an Emotional Stabilizing Unit made for the company of others." He happily remained entangled in the awkward hug with Leana.

"You can let go anytime, Esu," she grunted uncomfortably, trying to back away.

Esu released her, but laid his hands on her shoulders, examining her from head to toe. "Beautiful. Well, I can honestly say I'm extremely happy you're here."

66

"Thanks?" *This day is getting weirder and weirder*, she thought.

There was an extremely awkward silence as Esu continued to stare. Otis broke in. "Esu, how is supper coming along?"

"Ah, supper. Please, head into the kitchen. Food will be ready in three minutes and twenty-eight seconds."

"Would you take her bags up to her room, please?"

"Of course! May I?" he asked, holding out his hand to Leana. She handed them over and he scurried up the stairs. "Such a good night!" he exclaimed to himself.

"Wow. Was he just talking to himself?"

"That he was. He can be a little much, but he's part of my home."

"So, what, like a butler?"

"No actually. I made him. He's interesting company to have around." He saw the questioning look on Leana's face. Her confusion made him smile.

"Like *made him…* made him?" she asked. Otis nodded. "That's pretty nitro. What else can he do?"

"Well, he has a wide variety of skills I programmed him with. He's not just a cook or housekeeper." He held out his hand towards the dining room. "Come on. Let's eat. I'll tell you how I made him if you want."

Making her way through the living room, Leana caught the incredible scent of a hot, freshly cooked meal. Stepping into the dining room, she saw on the table an assortment of steaming foods that filled the bowls and platters on the dining table. Two glasses for drinks, as well as multiple pieces of silverware were at each play-setting. Candles burned in the center of the table. *Uh, my father obviously doesn't know me*, she thought.

"Where do I sit?" she asked.

Esu whisked into the room from the kitchen. "How about," Esu pulled out the chair at one end of the table, which was directly across from where Otis would sit, "here?"

"Thanks. There's, uh, a lot of food here. I don't think I can eat all this."

"I'd be impressed if you did." Otis laughed. "He always makes too much." He sat down across from her.

"So what will you do with what's leftover?"

"I'll take it to a veteran's care center in the morning. I go once a week, sometimes twice. We don't waste it if that's what you were wondering."

"That's… cool." Leana was suddenly aware of how hungry she was. She slopped a heaping pile of mashed potatoes onto her plate, "So, the android."

"The android," he repeated, adding a bit of everything to his plate, but focusing mostly on the steak and corn.

"How'd you learn to make him?"

"I've just always been good with my hands. Making thing, fixing things.

When I look at something mechanical, I understand it."

"Mom mentioned that once." She hurried to add, "Mom doesn't talk about you very much." She didn't want him thinking he was a popular topic of conversation back home.

The food was incredible. Her mouth salivated with every bite, distracting her from the emotional rollercoaster she'd ridden all day. She hadn't had a meal like this in a very long time. Both the food and company weren't nearly as horrible as she'd expected.

"I see. So your mom does talk about me?" He filled his mouth with a piece of well-done, juicy steak.

"She tries," she replied, slathering gravy and corn on her potatoes.

Esu interrupted their conversation as he yelled from the living room. "How's the food?!"

"Oh my god, it's incredible. Thank you." Leana managed through a mouthful.

He walked around the dining table, looking for dirty dishes to take away. "Well, good." His voice was bubbly. "There's dessert afterwards, so save room."

He bustled back into the kitchen, banging around and doing god-knows what.

Leana flinched and looked down at a wet cold nose bumping her arm. "Agh!" She was surprised to find El seeking her attention.

She slowly and cautiously moved her hand as El leaned in closer, giving Leana permission to pet her. She could more clearly see the black markings along El's spine. The dark color stood out from the rest of the gray fur. It was angular and sweeping down to the tip of her tail. Leana's hand shook slightly as she brushed lightly over the rough coat, then set it back down in her lap to hide her nerves.

"What breed is she?" Leana asked.

"Well…" Otis placed his napkin over his plate and stood up, walking around the table. He knelt down by El. He placed his hand under El's chin then encouraged Leana to do the same. She hesitantly complied.

"She's a Canis Lupus." He acknowledged Leana's confused look and smiled. "She's a Gray Wolf." Leana knew Otis could tell she was nervous. Her hands were sweating badly. "You don't have to be scared, Leana. She will never hurt you."

"Yeah, okay," she whispered. She looked at her father. "Her fur is so soft."

"Only under her chin."

"Well, why am I rubbing under her chin?"

"This is a submissive touch. You are being compliant, nonviolent. Obedient," he said, educating his daughter. He slowly took her hand and turned it palm down, guiding it across the top of El's head. "And this is a

68

dominant touch."

"What's that mean?"

"It means you are managing her. It means you're the leader and in control."

"That's intense," she said, cautiously rubbing the fur. "It's so much rougher."

"Crazy, huh?" The look in his eyes made Leana want to trust him. This man was a complete stranger, yet they shared the same blood. She felt herself drawn to him already and she didn't like it. The feeling betrayed everything she had been convinced of for so long.

She slipped her hand out of his, brushing off some fur from her palm. "Sorry," she apologized to avoid further awkwardness. "I thought wolves were supposed to be extinct."

"Well they're not supposed to be, but they are. Except one; this one. She is the last gray wolf now."

"That sounds so... lonely."

"It is..." Otis trailed off distantly. Leana thought she saw a flicker of unexplainable sadness in him.

Otis held out his hand again, "It's okay." He guided her palm along El's back. Her fingers coursed through the black markings.

El closed her eyes, grunting quietly at Leana's gentle touch. "See? No sweat."

Otis patted El's side and sat in the chair next to Leana.

"How did you get her?" Leana asked.

Esu entered again from the kitchen, quickly and carefully clearing Otis' plate and napkins.

"Do you two need anything else?"

Before either Otis or Leana could respond he dashed back into the kitchen.

"Okay... Anyway, a few years ago I, uh, wasn't doing too good." He cleared his throat. "And one night, I found myself in the back woods." He gestured over his shoulder. "I followed a whimpering sound, which I could barely hear through the heavy wind. I found her lying in a patch of red snow. She growled and dragged herself away from me into a small hole under a tree. I was patient and waited, trying to show her she could trust me."

Leana's hand unconsciously raked across El's fur. She felt a deep, pitiful sadness for the wolf. She understood being lost and alone.

"She was scared and hurt bad. I don't know what happened. After a while of just looking at each other, we kind of came to an agreement to get out of the storm. That's when she stumbled out of the hole and collapsed in my arms, so I picked her up and brought her home.

"Esu and I patched her up and fed her. After a few days of healing, she was healthy enough to go off on her own again."

El surprised Leana by licking her hand affectionately.

Otis continued, "When the time came for her to go back to the woods, she didn't. She's stayed here with me and Esu ever since."

Leana continued rubbing El after Otis finished his story. "That's a good story."

El's ears twitched as Leana's phone beeped on her wrist. "I'm sorry." She tapped a button and the beeping stopped.

"It's okay. Did you need to take that?"

"No, it's okay. Probably just one my friends wondering how I'm doing."

"You are welcome to take that."

"No, I'll call them back later."

"Okay. So, what do you think so far?" He leaned in to pet El.

Leana was caught off guard. "What do you mean?"

"About being here with me."

"Oh, well," she began cautiously as she slid her plate away from the edge of the table. "I was expecting something completely different."

"I'm hoping that's a good thing."

Leana smirked and shrugged.

"DESSERT IS FINISHED!!" Esu blared, busting through the kitchen door.

Leana jumped and twisted her finger in her ear, hoping she wouldn't go deaf. "Do you ever get used to that?"

Otis laughed. "No. Not really."

"Great," she moaned. "What's dessert?"

"Pumpkin pie, apple pie, or cherry pie," Esu stated with much pride.

"Cherry please."

Esu placed a giant slice of pie in front of Leana and one in front of Otis. He held up a bowl with a big spoon. "Whipped cream? It's homemade."

Her eyes lit up. "Please."

He scooped a glob of the white topping on the still steaming piece of pie. "Enjoy," he encouraged.

Leana groaned in pleasure at her first delicious bite, prompting a self-satisfied smile from the android.

"Good, isn't it?" stated Esu.

"Nitro-good, thank you so much!" Leana responded blissfully.

Esu glared at Otis, still waiting for an answer.

"Oh, yes, it is *that* good."

Silently, they finished their desserts without saying another word. Finished with the dinner serves, Esu cleared the rest of the plates.

Leana wiped her face. "Mmm, that was good."

"I'm happy you enjoyed that," Esu purred.

When Esu made his exit, Leana exclaimed, "I like him."

"He has that effect."

Leana felt herself overtaken by a huge yawn, stretching her arms out wide. Looking down, she saw El's fangs and tongue exposed as she yawned just as hard.

"You tired, Leana?"

"Yeah, it's been a long day."

"I'll show you your room so you can get some rest."

Suddenly, Leana remembered everything that had happened from the time she'd awoke that morning. She was scared to be alone tonight. She didn't want to sleep. What if there were monsters in her dreams?

CHAPTER 11

The flight of stairs that started at the front door curved up to the second floor. At the top of the stairs were two doors flanking a short hallway, a third door at the end, and a trap door in the ceiling that led to the attic. On the left was a hall closet. On the right was Leana's bedroom, and at the very end was the master bedroom.

"Here you are." Otis pushed open the bedroom door, revealing a queen-size bed with a brown comforter and white pillows. A window at the far wall framed a dresser which held a vase with a rose in it. A small door to the left of the dresser led to her own private bathroom and closet. Leana instantly liked this room, and wished for a similar set-up back home.

As she stepped in, El whined from the hallway.

"What's wrong with El?"

"I don't let her into the bedrooms."

"Oh, okay." She scanned her room again. "Um, thank you for tonight."

"You bet." He smiled. "If you need anything my door is at the end of the hall. El usually sleeps in the hallway, so if you do leave your room in the middle of the night, just be careful where you walk."

"'Kay."

Leana knelt down to scratch El's chin, but hurriedly jumped back up to wipe slobber from her now soaked face. "Oh, gross. Thanks, El."

Leana threw her bags on the bed and took a deep breath, noticing the scent of the fresh rose. She flopped backward onto the bed, arms spread wide. Being in this room filled her with a calm and peace she didn't expect, and she really liked the lighting and colors. She felt more welcome here than she had expected.

"Everything okay?" asked Otis from the doorway.

She lifted her head. "Yes. It's great, thank you." She lay flat back down on the bed, taking another deep breath. "I like the rose."

"I thought you might." His arms crossed as he leaned against the doorframe. "You probably don't remember, but ever since you were born, I'd put a rose on your side table or dresser every night as you slept, so when you woke up your room smelled like roses."

"Oh... Yeah, I don't remember that." She sat up and stared at her father awkwardly. The silence made her feel a bit uneasy.

"Well, goodnight, Leana. I'll see you in the morning," Otis said.

Leana rubbed her thighs. "Okay. Night." She couldn't quite bring herself to call him 'Dad' yet.

Otis pulled the door shut behind him as Leana sat watching her father's shadow underneath the door. She knew that tonight would be rougher without her mother. *I don't want to be alone tonight.* Leana waited, surprised to find herself wanting more time with him, more time with anyone. She had hoped El could stay in her room. She stared at the unmoving shadow.

Why is he just standing there? The shadow left a gap beneath the door as her father walked away down the hallway.

Her stomach ached with a raw disappointment. For a split second she felt completely alone until she heard El's clicking toenails as the wolf settled in outside her bedroom door.

"Thanks, El," she whispered.

Leana got to her feet and placed her bag on the dresser next to the flower, which she leaned in to smell one more time. She pulled out pajamas and her tooth brush and headed for the bathroom to get ready for bed.

Fresh and cozy, Leana hopped into the bed. Pulling the blankets over her, she slid up the bracelets of her wrist-phone. Holo-Lights beamed images from the phone, revealing a missed message from Annette. She opened the message and a screen displayed the faces of Annette, Justin and Emily. Annette's voice was crystal clear as if she was in the room with Leana. "*Hey girly. How has it been going so far? We miss you. Message us back as quickly as humanly possible. We're dying to know the details. Hope you're okay from after the game. We're here if you need us.*"

Leana slid her finger across the blue-light display, erasing the voice message. Another display screen took its place, revealing Leana's reflected face.

"Record." A red light blinked on the top-left corner.

"Hey guys, just got to my room. The night didn't go so bad. You won't believe the stuff that he has here. And, uh... he's kind of okay, actually. I don't know. Anyway, it's been good so far. Miss you and love you guys. Goodnight." She puckered her lips followed by kissing sounds, and finished the voice message with a small wave.

The screen zoomed out with a notification saying her message was sent. Leana slid her bracelets down to her wrist and unbuckled them. She got up to open the window, allowing fresh, cool air to fill the room then hit the lights and listened to the outdoors.

"Please... just tonight. No nightmares," she said to the dark room. Her palms began to sweat as she fought to keep her eyes open.

Her eyes slowly shut.

CHAPTER 12

I was climbing the face of a cliff, and I could feel the jagged rocks against my palms. My hands were old and wrinkled. They ached as I climbed, but the adrenaline coursing through my body told me that to let go meant certain death, so I clutched desperately with each grip and didn't look down. The wind had a bitter scent I'd never smelled before, unlike the smell of the sweat soaking my white cloak — this was a smell caused by fear.

The wind caught my cloak and made it even harder to hold on. If I lost my grip I would plummet to the ground. Terror surged through my body. I didn't know why, maybe desperation, but I looked down. Below were hundreds of thousands of people fighting. I was too high to make out the details, but the booming currents of light and sound burst up to me, and so did the screams.

I stared too long and felt my arms begin to shake violently; thankfully as I looked up I could see the edge of the cliff. I was only two hand-holds away. I stretched out my arm for the closest hold, then mustered the energy for the next, and last, reaching for the ledge. With the very last ounce of energy I could collect, I pulled myself up. I only had to get my waist above the edge and fall forward, the rest would be easier.

I got my knee up and rolled myself away from the edge of the cliff. I made it, but I didn't know where I was yet. I turned my head and felt instant defeat. As if they had been waiting, standing over me were a dozen enormous, gray-skinned beings guarding a large, round silver door. I recognized them. I had seen them before... somewhere. A couple of them were female, the rest were male, but they were all hulking. Slowly, my hands rose, extended directly at the beings who were looking at me. Was I surrendering? There was a tense moment where I saw two of them grab for their weapons, and another one yelled something I couldn't understand. The female on the right charged at me, and a male on the left tried to flank me. Suddenly, I was blinded by an explosion and a flash of light that illuminated the entire area, reflecting off the great, silver door.

The overpowering light disappeared and I could tell some unknown amount of time had passed, as I was unexplainably heaving the last guard over the cliff. He snarled and screamed as he fell to his death. When I turned around there were three who had fallen from the blast alone. They were all dead. I, on the other hand, had not a single scratch.

I trudged past the bodies, feeling the pain in my weak body as I approached the gigantic, metallic door. I didn't sense any hint of remorse, anger, or sadness within myself. I just felt like I had to get behind the door. I pulled up my sleeves as I walked and I could feel a heat within my body start to build deep within my bones. I shot out my hands, and felt an intense focus on the door emanate from inside my very core. I paid no attention to the ground as it began to shake.

That's when I felt a buzzing in my right hand and the sensation as if my hand was connected to the door. I'm the key to this door. *The door spiraled open from the center, revealing a deep, dark cave.*

Without warning, I felt the body I was in somehow separate from my mind. The bond I had been sharing with this person had severed, and now an old man was walking into the cave, leaving me behind. He had taken only two steps when his long cloak began scraping the ground behind him, and he stopped. He looked backward and stared directly into my eyes as though he could see me.

He opened his bearded mouth. "Leana. Find me."

As he spoke, glowing clouds formed around me, growing so thick I could no longer see him or anything else around me. I tried to speak before the door spiraled shut with him inside. I called out, but couldn't make a sound. The clouds engulfed me, making me feel like I was going to suffocate.

Leana's eyes opened suddenly, and for once she wasn't waking up from her dream in a panic. Instead, she was totally bewildered. She stared at the ceiling.

Instead of her own scream waking her she could only sigh. "Who are you?"

Out of the corner of her eye, she thought she saw a pink haze at her bedside, but when she turned her head she only saw her bracelets blinking red. She thought she had placed her pocket watch next to her phone when she went to bed, but it wasn't there now. Still lost in the bewildered state of her dream, she didn't try to find it.

She sat up confused and disoriented in the unfamiliar room. It was relieving not to wake up screaming in terror for once, but still this dream was so focused, so real, so physical that she could still feel it. This one was so different. It had to mean something.

"Oh, no," she whimpered quietly. "I forgot my journal." She groaned, and then lay there as the nighttime bugs filled the silence. She couldn't stop thinking about the old man in white.

Who was that guy and how did he know my name?

She wiped sweat from her face and pulled away her now damp sheets, swinging her legs to the side of the bed. Without her journal she knew she was going to lose the details of this dream. That's what always happened when she didn't write them down. For the first time in a long time, she tried to relax and simply allowed the images and feelings of the dream to fade slowly from her memory, forgetting bits and pieces second-by-second.

It was still dark out which meant, if she couldn't fall back asleep, it was going to be another long day. At least this one wasn't going to start with the feeling of fear. There was just enough moonlight coming through the window to help her clearly see the room and confirm that she was actually awake, and not still in the dream. The quiet sound of El whimpering in her sleep outside the door also helped. Leana was definitely awake. Looking for reality-grounding facts whenever she had a dream always helped stabilize her mind.

She stared at the blinking light on her bracelet, still tired. *Well, I'm not going back to sleep now*, she thought to herself.

She yawned as she slipped her wrist bands on and attempted to focus her eyes, fighting against her heavy eyelids.

El growled quietly in the hallway. From the muffled scratching noises, Leana assumed El was probably chasing a rabbit in her dreams. She smiled to herself.

A collection of blue and teal hues filled her bedroom as her phone's display activated. There was a missed message from her mother. When she opened the message, Danielle's face popped up. The recording showed how tired and worn out she was from a late night at the hospital.

"Hey honey. I'm just getting home. God knows what time it is. I'm going to bed. I love you, miss you, and want to kiss you, baby girl. I hope tonight went okay. Goodnight."

Leana was too tired to care or call back. Besides, she wasn't going to wake up her mother for no reason. She closed the message and stared at the display screen. Being bored and not wanting to go back to sleep, she began to flip through her old pictures, running her fingers through her photo gallery. Leana stopped at an image of her and Annette hanging out at Landings Park when they were freshmen. Old memories with her best friend filled Leana with loneliness.

"Call Annette."

Tired of sitting upright, she slid out a clear lens from the side of her bracelet, and then gently placed it over her right iris. The holographic display disappeared back into the bracelets, relinquishing the room back to the moonlight. As Leana lay back on her pillow, her right eye lit up in the same bluish tint of the miniaturized display.

Annette didn't pick up.

"Hey, it's me. Can't sleep. Thinking of you guys. Miss you."

She slid off the bracelets and tossed them on the side table disappointed. When they bounced to the floor Leana groaned, rolled over, and slung her arm off the side of the bed.

Instead of the bracelets, her hand brushed a round, metallic object. "How'd you get down there?"

Rolling over more, she saw the pocket watch lying on the floor next to her bracelets. She picked it up and rolled back over, staring at the watch and running her thumb over the cover, lost in thought. Her body slowly relaxed, as she held the watch tight against her chest and felt the engravings and etchings of the cold metal beneath her thumb.

Chirping birds outside the window woke Leana. It was morning, early morning, and she had fallen back asleep. She felt the warmth of the sun coming into her room, and it had never felt better. She felt uncharacteristically energetic and happy. So far, being at her father's had been a good choice. For a brief moment, Leana thought about apologizing to her mother for the constant battles about coming here. *But it's still early, plenty of time for something to go wrong*, she thought.

Leana put on her phone and opened the display. Annette still hadn't returned Leana's call from early morning. She opened her voice messages and sent a recording to Annette, encouraging her to come out if she and the others were free that morning.

She threw on her red and black flannel hoodie and jeans, and made her way into the hallway. El was sitting in front of the door, waiting for her.

"Good morning, El." Leana scratched under El's chin. "Come on."

They descended the stairs, to be greeted by Esu.

"Good morning, Leana." He gazed down at the wolf. "El," he acknowledged coolly.

"Hey, Esu. What's for breakfast?"

"Everything! Hungry?"

"I'm starving."

"Good heavens, we can't have that. The food is not quite ready. How about a beverage for now? Coffee? Tea? Milk? Juice?" He hurried through a list of options.

"Whoa, whoa. Too much talking too early, Esu. I'll just wait until whatever you have is ready. Okay?"

"Certainly. Food will be ready in about 10 minutes."

"Thanks. Um, where's..." Leana trailed off.

He stared blankly.

"You know? My..."

Esu stared confused.

"My dad. Where is my dad?" she choked a little on the words.

"He is dropping off last night's leftovers at the veteran's care center. He'll be back any minute."

"Oh, okay. Well, where should I go?"

"You can take the Canis Lupus outside if you'd like."

El replied with a growl.

"You know you can just say her name, right?" Leana bent down and patted the wolf.

"Of course." Esu stared blankly at El.

El leaned against Leana's leg.

"Do you ever?"

"Not if I don't have to."

"Why?"

"Because I don't want to give her the satisfaction." El growled again. Esu pointed his finger. "I'm never going to forget what you did."

"What'd she do?"

Esu whispered, "She urinated on my circuit board while I was in sleep mode."

Leana covered her mouth, trying not to laugh. "El!"

El spun excitedly as if she knew what was being said about her.

"I'm glad to see she's happy about it. Remove that gray beast from my sight. I have cooking to do." Esu stomped off back to the kitchen.

Leana continued laughing even after Esu walked away. After a moment she went to the front door and pulled it open slowly. She hadn't experienced the farm in daylight yet, and as the door opened a cool spring breeze filled her lungs with the smell of fresh dew and damp fields. So refreshing.

El sprang out the door and off the porch, nearly taking Leana's feet out from under her. She dashed from sight around the corner then reappeared, circling the house over and over again.

"Wow. You're... so fast."

As El zoomed around the house and across the yard, Leana followed her down the steps and picked up a well-chewed softball. She idly tossed it in the air with one hand as she admired the wolf's speed. On the last lap El stopped suddenly at the stairs noticing what Leana was doing. When Leana had first met El, the wolf had seemed like a ferocious animal, but now Leana saw her playful side as El's head followed the ball in Leana's hand up and down.

"Oh... You want this?"

She threw the ball across the front yard. The wolf took off, leaving paw prints in the glistening morning grass and snatched the ball with her jaw after one bounce. She sprinted back to Leana.

She wasn't slowing down.

Leana shot out her hands. "Ah! El. Stop!"

She covered her face, bracing for impact. At the last moment, El dug her paws into the damp ground, and slid to a stop, just inches from Leana. Through the blast of kicked up dirt and water from her wet fur, the wolf dropped the drooled-on ball at Leana's feet.

Leana stuttered with her eyes wide open. "I have no words for you, pup."

Hesitantly, Leana picked up the ball. El crouched down, ready to dash away for another round. She stared at the wolf, still marveling at how this magnificent beast came to be here. *They're supposed to be extinct*, she thought. El looked back one last time right before Leana threw the ball with all her might, spraying her with more water and dirt as the wolf took off.

This game went on for several more minutes. Leana was bemused by where she was finding herself at this moment, playing a game of catch, with a wolf, at the farm of her father she never knew. There was something about El that felt so comforting. Leana hoped she could spend more time with her. *Guess that depends on how this weekend goes.*

After a short while, Otis pulled up in his white truck with several empty crates in the back. El pranced through the mud towards the truck, her paws darkened by the wet dirt. She hopped up on the door of the truck, coating the white paint with mud streaks and prints.

"Great," he growled good-naturedly. "Alright, El. Move back."

He stepped out of the truck, calling out to Leana. "Morning. How'd you sleep?"

"Best sleep I've gotten in a long time."

"That's good—"

Leana interrupted. "I never knew wolves were so fast."

Otis held out his hand for the ball and Leana tossed it to him. "She's actually much faster than most." He threw the ball down the driveway.

El came skidding back in, ball in mouth. With some effort, Otis pried the ball away.

"Okay, I'm gonna go hose off El around back, then I'll be inside. Want to wash up before we eat?"

"Yeah, that's fine. Want any help?"

"Sure, okay, yeah. Come on."

Water squirted from the green hose Leana was holding as she sprayed it over El's thick gray fur and paws, removing the chunks of mud. Leana laughed as El shook her fur, spraying both Leana and Otis. Otis threw a dry towel at Leana, making it clear that drying El was going to be Leana's task.

Once the towel was soaking and El was mostly clean they went back inside, hungry and ready for food.

The house was filled with the aroma of hot, fresh breakfast. Hot syrup steamed in the center of the table, circled by bowls of scrambled eggs, hash browns, bacon, and sausage. El ran around the table, jumping to get a closer smell and knocking over a chair in her excitement.

Otis picked up the chair, set it next to Leana's seat, and sat down beside her. Leana's eyes connected with her father's, and she felt as if he was asking permission to sit next to her. She responded with a hesitant smile. A calm flowed over her. With him sitting next to her, she felt peaceful. Surprisingly, this day was starting out great.

"Does he always cook like this?" Leana asked.

"Always. He never disappoints, but he's also trying to impress our guest."

"Me?" Leana laughed. "Oh, I'm definitely impressed."

Otis rubbed his hands together and absorbed the smell of the food in front of his face. El yelped and whined.

"Easy, girl. You'll get some."

She continued yelping, circling in place and pacing back and forth.

"I think she's going to jump up," warned Leana.

Otis leaned forward to fork some pancakes onto his plate, "I don't think she will. She knows better—"

El suddenly stood on her hind legs with her front paws slapping a heaping spoonful of scrambled eggs out of a bowl. It shot in Otis' direction, covering his face with egg. Surprised, Otis sprang up with his pancake-holding hand high in the air. The pancakes left the fork and flew across to the other side of the table. With perfect speed and agility, El caught them in her mouth.

"El!" he exclaimed.

Leana felt her eyes opening wide, unsure whether to laugh or stay quiet. The giggles started building up in her throat. "Told you," she joked, her face turning red as she tried not to laugh.

Otis sat down as chunks of egg slid down his face and dropped in his lap. "I don't want to say it, but yeah... You did." He threw the fork on the table and shook the rest of the eggs free from his arms.

A loud thump resounded as El resumed her hind-legged stance at the table and looked at Otis expectantly, smiling.

"El, down!" Otis reprimanded sharply.

His flailing arms and loud tone startled El. She flinched away, splashing hash browns onto Leana's plate and lap.

"Oh no. El!"

Leana sprang up covered in potatoes.

El scooted back and darted under the table into the living room, knocking over another chair before sliding uncontrollably into the sofa. She yelped and lay on the ground next to the sofa, panting loudly.

Leana couldn't contain herself any longer. She looked at her father as she let out an uncontainable laugh. She struggled to catch her breath and braced herself up against her chair, but couldn't stop laughing. Tears rolled down her cheeks, blurring the sight of Otis laughing just as hard.

Their laughter was so loud that they almost missed the slamming kitchen door. Esu's surprised expression only made them laugh harder.

"What happened?" he exclaimed. "Why is this so funny? This isn't funny!" Esu pointed at the egg and potatoes coating the floor and their clothes.

"Oh, my circuits… El!"

"It's okay Esu. It was an accident—"

"It wasn't an accident. She did this intentionally, and stop laughing!"

Otis threw a pancake. "Here… have a flap jack." It slapped Esu in the face and stuck.

Leana belted out again, forcing out words between breaths. "What's. A. Flap jack?"

Otis inhaled heavily catching his breath. "Are you serious? You don't know what a flapjack is? It's another name for pancake."

Leana was wiping her eyes and trying to catch her breath too. "I'm sorry. It must be an *old man* term."

"Hey hey. Easy with the 'old man', kiddo. You could hurt my feelings speaking like that."

Leana giggled. She didn't realize how great it would feel to hear him call her "kiddo." She started helping Esu clean up the mess, sore but exhilarated from the laughter. They sat back down. The rest of breakfast proceeded smoothly.

"So," Otis asked, "how's city life?"

"It's loud, busy, and packed," was all she could think of to say. "What about you? You like farm life?"

"I do. I get a chance to grow and create. I feel like I'm doing a good thing here. I feel purpose here. So, yeah, I do like it."

Otis started telling her about how he got into farming. It was the same story her mother had already told her, but she let him talk. The more she learned about how Otis fell into farming and why he enjoyed doing so much for veterans the more she realized how different his life was from hers. Still, they did have a lot in common when it came to people. They both wanted to help. As he talked about the people he'd met and things he'd done she found herself more tempted to like him. There was still a part of her, though, that didn't want to.

As the meal ended, Esu started clearing the bowls and plates quickly and quietly. Leana picked up on the android's frustration, and she wondered if his emotions were real or just programmed.

Leana watched Esu enter the kitchen. "Is he really upset?" she whispered.

"What do you mean?"

"I mean is he creating the emotion or is he just programmed to express emotions when appropriate?"

"It's kind of both. He was programmed with emotions, but the longer he's alive and exposed to human interaction the more they evolve into his own versions of expression. Kind of like a human baby. It's our environment that truly shapes our emotions."

Otis took a rolled ball cap from his back pocket and shoved it on his head.

"Listen, I have a few chores to finish up, and then we'll hang out the rest of the afternoon. Sound good?" Esu exited the kitchen one more time for the final stacks of plates. "Esu, could you give Leana the tour of the place while I'm working?"

"Of course. It would be my pleasure." Esu zoomed back into the kitchen, his shoulders a bit higher.

"Well, he's back to happy again." Leana said smiling.

"Good. Have fun, and if you need me I'll be outside."

Otis headed out the front door as Leana crouched down next to El, petting her softly. Leana pulled out two biscuits and a piece of bacon, setting it in front of her nose. The food practically disappeared in an instant. El licked every crumb off the floor, then turned quickly and started licking Leana's face.

"Okay, okay. Gross." She rubbed the slobber off her face again. "You happy now?" she asked, leaning her forehead against El's.

Her phone began to vibrate on her wrist. She opened up the display in the contact lens she'd left in earlier. The screen popped up, revealing a message from Annette.

"Hey girl, Justin and I are heading out there right now. We'll be there in about an hour. Hope you get this in time to respond. Loves, girl!"

That's when she realized she had completely forgotten to ask permission for her friends to come. She wanted to ask him over breakfast, but with all the commotion she hadn't. She didn't know how he'd react, but she decided to wait to ask him until after the tour. She returned a message.

"I'm excited. See you soon."

After sending the message, she pressed a button on her bracelet to turn off the device and her contact lens. As if he'd been waiting, Esu sprang from behind the kitchen door.

"Okay, are you ready for the tour?"

He's definitely more excited about this than I am, she thought. Leana stood up. "Where we starting?"

Esu pointed behind him. "Dining room?"

"Seen the dining room, Esu."

"Living ro—"

"Esu... We're in the living room," she interrupted.

"Ah... kitchen."

"Uh... I guess." Leana rubbed her arm, already bored and followed Esu through the door he seemed to live behind during meals.

This kitchen seemed made for a five-star restaurant. Large and inviting, it had shiny food prep surfaces and numerous cabinets. The ceiling was lined with rows of pots and pans of different shapes and sizes. The huge oven along the sidewall had six burners. There was a door to a walk-in freezer next to an enormous refrigerator, and a pantry on the opposite wall. The floor had gray and white tile, perfectly clean and spotless.

Even though Leana was impressed she was ready for adventure which she doubted she'd find in the kitchen. "Esu, can you show me the basement or attic or something I haven't already seen? I want to go somewhere interesting."

"Right. The basement. This way."

Leana followed behind hopeful. They passed the stairwell and headed down the hallway. The first door on the left was a room she hadn't seen yet.

"What's this one?"

"This is Otis' office. His place to be alone. No one is allowed in without permission."

"Really? Can we look?"

"Of course not. Come now. The basement is up ahead."

Further down the hallway on the left, Esu opened a door that led to a dark, descending stairwell. "Lights," commanded Leana. The darkness remained.

"That's not how it works Leana. Here, pull this," he instructed, pointing at a string dangling from the ceiling.

"Oh, okay." Leana reached her hand up, pulling the string. Dust fell from the bulb above them.

"There. Much better." Esu clasped his hands behind him and proceeded down the stairs.

She cautiously followed, excited to discover a new space of the house. She was disappointed to discover nothing but boxes, dozens of boxes. Most of them were closed, but what was open was filled with junk she didn't recognize. The place was dusty and dirty and the walls were plain cement. It was a completely dull and normal basement.

"This is boring. Can we go now?"

"But this is where your father keeps all his parts."

"That's great. Let's move on."

"You don't want to see what all is down here?"

"No, not really. There's a lot of stuff, Esu. A lot of junk."

"Everything down here has a purpose. Maybe not today, or tomorrow. But sometime a certain part will be needed. And your father will know when and where to use it. He's never been a person to waste anything, and is always quick to fix what's broken." Esu paused then added, "Usually."

Leana was already halfway up the stairs by the time he was done talking. "Yeah, I've noticed. Now let's go," she yelled.

Esu scurried from the basement. "Okay. On to the rest of the house then," he pronounced.

The rough start to the tour only made Leana think about her friends getting to the house sooner. She was ready to be outside with other people she actually knew and could talk to without being misunderstood. She made a quick glance at El who lay on the floor by the door, waiting for someone to play with. Making their way upstairs, Leana happened to glance in her room in passing, seeing a fresh rose on the dresser that hadn't been there this morning.

She smiled to herself in surprise, catching a quick scent of the rose as she continued down the hallway. Apparently, Otis had made a trip to her bedroom when she wasn't paying attention. Halfway down the hall, Esu stopped and reached up, pulling down the attic door.

"Here we are."

"Great."

The stairs unfolded, leading up into the dark.

"How old is this house?" she asked, looking at the dust that collected on her fingers as she ascended up.

"Older than I am."

"Yeah, that doesn't help. I don't know how old you are, but, I assume you're not much older than me." Leana continued up on stairs.

"Okay. Not as old as your father."

She stopped just one step from the top and looked back, realizing she had no idea how old her father was either. "Still doesn't help."

Before Esu could answer, Otis called indistinctly from outside.

"A moment, please. Your father seems to need my assistance. Take a look around. I'll be back shortly."

"Umm… Okay."

She watched Esu turn back down the stairs.

"That was weird." She wondered why he didn't just answer the question. She knew her father couldn't be that old either, and the house obviously was. "Whatever."

Leana lifted herself into the attic as she heard footsteps padding below her. El had decided to keep her company but apparently couldn't make it up the attic stairs. "Sorry, El." Leana turned away from the stairs and looked around, promptly running face first into a light string. She pulled it, illuminating the enormous attic.

There was enough room for her to stand and walk around without bumping her head or running into anything. There were trunks full of clothes and blankets. There were old lamps and antique things that looked even older than the house.

At the far end of the attic was a small, round window right below the ceiling. Directly below it, on a dusty, old dresser was a long object partially covered with a tattered blanket. Just the tip of the object was uncovered and it reflected light from the attic bulb. She couldn't take her eyes off of it. It was as if it was calling to her. *Finally, something interesting.*

She pulled the blanket off and saw before her a sword resting on a stand still in its scabbard. The handle was ornate, with crimson and gold running through it in an intricate pattern, but the handle itself looked like ancient, petrified wood.

She checked behind her to make sure Esu hadn't returned yet and stepped closer, reaching out tentatively for the sword. She wanted to get a better look; she had to. She gripped the handle and removed it from its stand.

It was surprisingly light. Holding the handle of the sword firmly in her right hand, Leana slowly removed the scabbard with her left. It sang a high-pitched tone as the scabbard left the blade. It was about the length of her arm, and appeared sharp. Despite being surrounded by dusty relics, it looked brand new.

"This is so nitro."

After setting down the scabbard, she held out the sword with both hands as if she were ready for a fight. The heft of it in her hand felt oddly familiar, but she knew that wasn't possible. She was pretty sure she'd never touched anything like this, but now that she had she really liked it.

"No one mess with me or you *will* get diced," she spoke to the empty room.

Her hands gripped tighter around the handle. A tingling began to run over her palm. A sudden surge of energy vibrated violently through her hand, forcing her grip to tighten even more. Starting from the handle, a vein running down the center of the blade began to glow pink and the metal of the blade began to expand, growing in length. Shocked, she released her grip and dropped the weapon to the ground, scattering years of attic dust up in the air. The clang of the metal echoed through the wooden walls.

She looked at her hands and rubbed them hard against the front of her pants trying to remove the physical sensation from her body. "What was that?" The connection with the sword went deep into her arm, which now felt like pins and needles.

"Okay. Don't touch. Got it."

She picked up the old rag that was covering the sword originally and used it to lift the sword gently, carefully avoiding the handle and placing it back on its stand.

Backing away from the sword still shocked by what just happened, she now noticed a soft humming sound coming from behind her. She turned and took a few more steps looking for the source of the sound. It grew louder the closer she got. It was coming from a tall statue-like figure draped with a blanket. She hadn't noticed it before. The closer she got, the louder the noise grew.

Now about a foot away, the pulsing noise was loud enough to cover the sound of the creaks of the floor panels underneath her timid steps. Suddenly the sounds stopped.

Leana looked the blanketed object up and down. Her curiosity outweighed her nerves. She stretched up onto her tiptoes, reaching for the top of the blanket. Her hand grasped the dusty old cloth tightly and she started to pull it off.

B'VVVV. B'VVVV. B'VVVV

Leana gasped in surprise as her wrist vibrated violently at the alert of a new caller. She let go of the tarp covering whatever was underneath.

"Seriously?!" She laughed at herself, shaking off the shot of adrenaline. Leana accepted the call, illuminating the holographic display. "Hey, Annette! What's up?"

"We're here! Get your butt outside."

"What?! Already? I thought it'd be at least an hour."

"Yeah, well, Justin and I were already close. We wanted to surprise you. That cool?"

"Well, yeah. I mean, of course. I'll be right there." Leana turned off the screen. With the distractions found in the attic, she had completely forgotten her friends were coming. She sprinted out of the attic, looking back one more time at the mysterious object. The moment she shut the attic door she realized her mistake.

"Oh no, I forgot to remind Otis."

CHAPTER 13

Leana sprinted down the stairs, slamming against the front door. El followed close behind at her heels. Turning the knob, Leana paused as she considered how her friends might react to seeing a wolf. Based on her own first impression of El, she thought it might be best for her friends to meet the family pet later. It was going to be awkward enough introducing them to her father.

Leana stared at El for a moment, thinking, then got an idea. "Come on, girl. You hungry?"

El sprang up on her hind legs in excitement. Leana turned and led the bounding wolf through the dining room into the kitchen. Swinging open the door, she saw Esu holding two large boxes with one hand while stirring a bubbling pot on the stove with the other. He turned to see who had entered, peering around the big packages at Leana.

"Hello, what can I do for you?"

Leana spoke in a rush, "Hey Esu, my friends are here, can you take care of El for me? Great! Thanks." She turned and exited the kitchen before Esu could respond.

Leana had made it halfway into the living room before she heard a loud crash coming from the kitchen, followed by Esu yelling El's name. Leana couldn't help but giggle as she headed out the door.

By the time she reached the porch, Otis was already standing outside with her friends next to their car, his arms crossed, a rag in one hand.

"Leana, you have guests."

She quickly felt relief at his relaxed voice tone.

"Yeah, I'm sorry. I totally forgot to ask you at breakfast... And after."

"No, it's okay. We just introduced ourselves." He pointed at her friends. "Annette and... Justin."

"Yep. Got it, Mr. Rayne." Annette approached Leana and wrapped her arms around her. "Hey, girl."

Justin stepped forward. "Hey, Leana." He cleared his throat.

Leana turned and hugged Justin, but the fact that Otis was there watching made it feel awkward. She could tell Justin wanted the hug, but she didn't want her dad reading into it.

Leana's eyes caught her father's, and she thought she caught a flicker of something like discomfort, but she wasn't sure. She broke her hug with Justin and noticed the camera bag at his feet. "Plan on getting some shots while you're here?"

"Well, yeah," he said, looking at Otis. "That is… if you don't mind, Mr. Rayne. This place will make for some real nitro photos for my little shooter here."

"Well, a few places are off limits, but other than that I don't mind."

"Uh, yeah. Thank you, sir."

"No pictures of or in the house, please. I like my home private."

"Yes, sir."

"The greenhouse is fine, but stay out of the garage," he said, pointing to the different locations. Otis looked at Justin and clarified, "Tools and stuff. I don't want anyone getting hurt."

"Sure. Anything else?" Justin asked.

"I have two barns. Stay out of the red one closest to the house. The white one has horses. You are welcome in there. Any parts of the acreage outside of the fence is fine. If you can follow those guidelines, then all is well." After straightening the bill on his hat, Otis shoved his hands deep into his pockets. "Nice to meet you two. I've got more chores to get done, so you kids have fun." He looked at Justin one last time. "I'll be close."

Justin nodded and cleared his throat again.

Otis smiled at Leana one last time, and headed to the garage.

Annette chuckled and bit her lower lip. "Okay, so… yeah. Your dad is really cute."

"Gross. You're going to make me puke."

"What? He is." Annette gripped Leana's arm, acting like a fainting damsel with the back of her hand on her forehead.

"Okay, you can go home now," Leana joked as she shook her arm free, but her friend wrapped her arms tightly around her waist again.

"It's only been one day and I already missed you."

"Me too. So where's Emily?"

The answer to that question came from the ringing of Annette's phone. "Uh-oh."

"What?"

"That's her."

"So answer it, Annette."

The display activated for all three to see. "Hey, Emily. What's up?"

"*I'll tell you what's up, Annette...*"

Justin massaged his eyes uncomfortably as Annette marched around the other end of the car, apparently wanting to keep the conversation private. "Emily's kind of mad at us."

"Why?"

"We didn't wait for her. She wanted to come out and see you, but you know how she is in the morning. She takes two hours, *at least*, to get ready, and we didn't want to wait that long, you know?"

"Got ya. It would have been nice to have all of us together out here, though."

Justin knelt down to take out his camera. "Yeah, I know. We left at six in the morning to get here. There's no way she could have been ready."

"True, but you could have asked. She is one of us." She thought about Emily's exhaustive morning routines and chuckled. "But I understand what you mean."

"Yeah, so we let her sleep," he said, gritting his teeth. "And now we are facing her wrath."

Leana pulled Justin by the arm, "Come on."

Justin gripped his camera carefully as he was yanked away followed by the unintelligible sound of Emily's angry voice floating over the car. They walked out along the fence line where a beautiful pasture filled with green grass waved rhythmically with the soft wind. There were five well-groomed horses grazing and playing in the field, and on the horizon was a clear, blue sky. The birds overhead cued the feeling of springtime. The smell of damp grass drying in the warm sun was so refreshing. This place was truly stunning.

Justin peered through the eyepiece of his camera. "What do you see?" He panned his camera across the open pasture playing with the zoom and focus.

"What do you mean?" Leana latched her hands on the top rail of the fence, trying to stay out of the way of Justin's lens. The old wooden fence smelled of a recent coat of oil.

"Out there. What do you see?" Leana looked out beyond the pasture unaware that Justin was pointing his lens at her.

"I don't know. Horses? Birds?" Leana stepped up to the lower rail.

"Well yeah, but not just the obvious. What else?"

She heard the clicking behind her. "A clear sky, green pasture, fresh air, a cool breeze." She closed her eyes for a moment, feeling the breeze on her face.

Leana was always embarrassed talking about anything artsy with Justin. The way he saw the world around him amazed her because she couldn't see what he saw. It was a quality that drew her to him. Since the school year had started, she had found herself admiring him more and more, but she wasn't sure what those feelings meant or how to define them. She had begun noticing each time Justin was looking at her in class, in the hall, or at lunch. Sometimes she was even shy to look at him, worried he would catch her. At times, she even had butterflies in her stomach when she talked to him, which annoyed her. She knew he liked her, but she wasn't sure she wanted it to be mutual. Having him here right now felt complicated.

"I don't know, Justin. What do you want me to see?"

He stepped forward, gesturing. "It's just so picturesque out here. Look at the way the field slopes slightly upward, you can see the horses grazing in the background but you also have this amazing, old fence right here. It's framed so perfectly. And if I catch the timing just right I can get the changing waves of the grass in the shot. See what I'm talking about?"

"Yeah, I guess so." She looked back at the scene.

Justin took a few steps away from the fence. "This is pretty perfect."

Leana kept staring out in the open field as a foal and filly raced along the fence line. She very much wanted to see what Justin was seeing as he kept taking photos, but she knew her perspective would never quite match his.

"Here look," he said shyly as he walked up to Leana at the fence. "See? Beautiful."

Leana leaned back to look. In the camera's preview was a picture of herself looking out, wind blowing her hair into her face. She smiled, suddenly shy herself.

Nerves ran through her as he slowly leaned toward her. She felt frozen, suddenly realizing what was happening. She didn't know how to respond. The breeze continued to blow her hair back, exposing her features; she wondered if she was blushing.

Justin gently pressed his lips against hers. His breath blew softly on her skin. The touch of his stubble made the kiss very real, but strange. It didn't feel the way she had expected her first kiss to feel.

He pulled back only for a moment to stare into her silver-blue eyes before kissing her again. She could feel the rough skin of his fingers on her cheeks. She stepped back hesitantly, looking down at the ground.

Justin placed his hand on her shoulder, leaning his forehead against hers. "Are you okay?" he asked softly.

Leana wrapped her arm around his waist, and tucked herself tight into his body. *I have no idea.*

"Yes," she responded.

At the sound of footsteps approaching, they quickly broke apart. "There you are… Oh."

Leana, Justin and Annette all stared at each other uncomfortably. Annette cleared her throat. "Wow. Nice… view," she awkwardly gestured past the fence. She stretched her arms wide. "It's amazing out here."

Leana reached out an arm to pull Annette to her side. "I missed you guys."

For a moment, Annette paused, avoiding the embrace. Ignoring her hesitation, Leana stepped forward to close the distance between them. She squeezed her friend tight despite Annette's half-hearted response.

Leana had to get rid of the tension. "How'd she take it?" Leana asked.

"Emily? Oh, you know. Not… good. The last thing she said before hanging up was how *we*," Annette gestured with air quotes, "frustrate the crap out of her sometimes, but that she forgives us."

Leana sighed. "I love that girl. No matter how upset she is she always wants to fix things. No drama from the 'Queen of Drama'."

"Annette, a champion boxer, and Emily, a theater fanatic, best of friends to the end." Justin chuckled, "Talk about your odd couple."

"Justin," Leana said, tapping his back, "I can truly say you have the best girlfriends any guy on this planet could ever have."

"You're welcome," said both the girls in unison. They looked at each other and laughed.

"Okay…" he laughed awkwardly. "You mind if I go take some shots around the farm?" Justin fidgeted with his camera's settings then clicked a quick picture of the girls. "Beautiful," he said again, glancing at Leana with a smile.

"Aw, come on. You don't want to hang out with us anymore?" joked Annette. "We're gonna talk about menstrual cycles and boys." She smirked and wiggled her eyebrows.

Leana couldn't help but laugh.

"Okay. I'm gone." He winked at Leana and walked away, the girls' laughter following him.

Annette fidgeted with her dreads for a moment. She looked at Leana. "So… Did he kiss you?"

Leana thought she sensed a note of jealousy in Annette's voice. She looked away.

"He did, didn't he?!"

"No," Leana lied unconvincingly.

"Yes, he did."

"Stop, I don't want to talk about it."

"Just tell me, Leana."

Leana bit her lower lip, trying not to make eye contact.

"So, is he a good kisser?"

"You're ridiculous." Leana walked away, shaking her head.

Annette quickly caught up, gripping Leana's hand. "Hey, was that your first kiss?"

"You know it was. Don't play *troph* with me." They kept walking, heading towards Otis' barn. "Let's go see the horses."

"You know he's gonna ask you to the dance, right?" Annette asked her wistfully.

"I don't know. I think he would've asked me already," Leana responded. "Besides, I thought he already planned on going with someone else."

Annette laughed humorlessly. "Why else do you think he came all the way out here? To take photos? You're so naive when it comes to boys, Leana. You know that?"

"Well, I know he likes me... What if he does ask me? What if it screws up our friendship?"

"You worry *way* too much. We all knew this was coming. If you ask me, all relationships are risky." Annette looked down at the ground as they walked.

"I don't know, Annette. We'll see if he even asks."

"He will."

As they approached a red trimmed, white barn, they heard the sounds of horses whinnying. The warm smell of hay wafted through the opened top half of the door.

"I'm not sure I want to go in," said Annette nervously.

"What?" Leana said, looking at her sarcastically. "You're a boxer; you beat people up for a hobby. Are... Are you scared of horses?"

"They make me nervous."

"Come on." Leana laughed and punched Annette's arm.

Unlatching the bottom half of the door, Leana stepped in, pulling Annette behind her. The first thing Leana noticed was the back end which opened out to the pasture. A small gated fence kept free-roaming horses from entering the barn. On the girls' side of the gate six large stalls with windows lined a concrete aisle. Two stalls were occupied by horses, snorting a greeting to Annette and Leana. On the other side of the fence, a couple curious horses moved towards the barn.

Leana confidently approached the white and caramel horse in the nearest stall.

"Careful," Annette said softly.

Leana smiled. "Shut up." Leana reached out and rubbed the horse's smooth forehead. "They're sparklin', Annette." The horse snorted and tossed its head, making Leana laugh. "See?"

Annette continued to hang back.

"Come on."

Annette shook her head. "Nope."

Leana moved across the aisle to the all-black horse in the other stall. "Hello, handsome. What's your name?" The horse rolled his eyes and bucked his head, letting out a shrill, unfriendly sound.

"I don't think it likes you," warned Annette.

Leana stepped closer, reaching out her hand slowly. "Easy... Easy."

With her eyes locked with the horse's, Leana remained calm. "It's okay," she said softly. Leana noticed the horse's ears were back, but he had quieted and stopped tossing his head. Slowly, she placed her hand on the horse's forehead. He snorted, but didn't move. "There you go," she whispered. "See? I'm not so bad."

"Uhh... How did you know how to do that?" asked Annette.

"I don't know."

"That was freaky, and you're crazy. Speaking of crazy... Did you hear about, Thea?"

Leana was oblivious; her attention still on the animal.

"Leana!" Annette said louder.

"What?" She whipped her head around, causing the horse to startle again.

"Did you hear about Thea?"

"Oh. Uh... No. She okay?" She turned her head back to the horse. "Easy, easy."

"She has a hairline fracture in her jaw. She just left the hospital this morning."

"Wait, what?" Leana's hand stopped petting. She turned around, giving Annette her full attention.

"Yeah. Her parents are pretty angry. They're looking into going after the school, but that'll be pointless since Thea was the one who was the aggressor. If anything, the school could go after her."

The horse bumped its nose against Leana's shoulder. "It's not the school's fault." She looked down, kicking at some loose hay on the ground. "I didn't mean to hurt her that bad. It just kind of happened. I watched her break Myanna's ankle. I just reacted."

"I get that. I understand where you're coming from, but I saw what happened. You slapped her across the face and broke her jaw. I've been boxing since I was six, and I know what it takes to break someone's jaw. What I don't understand is *how* you did it."

"I don't know," Leana said with her hand on the stall. "All I thought about was protecting Myanna. Everything else just happened. I can't explain it."

"Try," encouraged Annette.

"It was a rage. I still feel the tightness in my gut when I think about it."

"What do you mean?"

"I mean I knew what I was doing, but it was like I wasn't the one in control. I don't know. I've never hurt anyone before. It was like something inside me took over."

"Yeah, it was weird seeing you hulk out." Annette stepped forward only to quickly step back again at the snort of the horse. "Oh, come on," she complained at the animal.

"I don't know what it was, but it scared me." Leana picked up the handful of hay from the ground and held it out to the horse. Its lips clamped around her fingers, pulling at the hay. "It's probably good that I came here."

"Why?"

"If I went home I'd just want to curl in a ball and hide from the world. But here, I don't know, I feel different, like more *me*."

"Well, good. That's why Justin and I came out in the first place, to check on you. Besides, you don't have to feel bad for what happened. It wasn't you who started it."

"Thank you. It means a lot." Leana hugged Annette.

The moment of silence was broken from the clicking of a camera shutter. "What the—" Annette whipped her head to the side.

"Howdy." Justin grinned behind the camera.

"Seriously?" Annette rolled her eyes and sighed. "You're such a troph."

"Oh I am, huh? Do you agree, Ana?" He clicked a picture of her with the horse peering over her shoulder.

Leana laughed. "You're invading our lady time. Shoo!" She smiled and leaned her head against the horse stall.

"Yeah, you stalker." The black horse whinnied suddenly and stomped a hoof. Annette jumped and spun around with her hands to her chest.

Belting out a laugh, Justin snapped a final picture. "Yep, no worries. I didn't know you two were here. I'm decampin'."

"I don't even know what that means," said Annette.

"He's leaving," Leana said, rolling her eyes.

Leana and Annette watched Justin leave the barn. They followed and peeked out to see if he'd actually left. Leana's eyes followed him as he got closer to the big, red barn which her father said was off limits.

"He's not supposed to go in there, right?" Annette asked Leana.

"Yeah, but I don't think he will."

"He's a guy. He's gonna at least peak."

Leana watched nervously until Justin walked past the large, sliding door. Relieved, she started to turn away, but noticed Annette still watching. Leana looked back to see that Justin had stopped and cocked his head towards the barn as though he'd heard something. Her stomach knotted. "Don't, Justin."

"Come on, we need to go get him before he's caught," Annette said, grabbing Leana's elbow.

Leana hesitated, torn between reprimanding Justin and upsetting her father. "Yeah, you're right." The girls exited the barn and latched the door.

As they approached Justin, Leana called out to him. He apparently didn't hear and instead began muscling open the giant, sliding door. It moved just enough for him to peer inside. Leana picked up her pace. Justin froze, staring inside.

"Whoa." He reached for his camera and brought it to his face eager for the shot.

Out of nowhere, Otis appeared and slammed the barn door shut abruptly from the far end, making a loud, dramatic thud as it latched.

All three teens jumped.

"What exactly are you doing?" asked Otis, wiping his hands on the rag he had pulled from his pocket.

"I... the... um... uh," Justin stammered.

"I remember asking that you stay *out* of this barn. There's equipment, tools, and other things I don't want you getting close to." Otis was talking very pointedly, clearly trying very hard to keep his composure. He looked pissed.

"There was a sound," Justin said quickly.

"A sound?"

Justin's hand shook nervously as he pointed at the barn door. "In there. In the barn."

A wave of embarrassment swept over Leana. She didn't like seeing Justin so scared, but she also knew he had messed up. The last thing she wanted today was for him to get in trouble with her father. *What if this ruins what he thinks about us? I don't want him to blame me.*

She spoke up quickly, trying to defend Justin. "He didn't actually go in."

"I can understand that, Leana, but—"

"He didn't mean to do anything," she defended.

"Leana," Justin said softly. "It's okay."

"No, it's not." Looking at Justin, she didn't want this day ruined, but anger filled her stomach quickly when she realized her father was doing just that. That anger snowballed immediately as it connected with the years of disappointment she had felt towards him.

Otis held up a hand, forcibly calm. "Leana, give me a second to explain."

"There's nothing to explain. They don't have to go just because he looked in your *precious* barn. It... was... an... accident." Her voice rose.

"Honey, I didn't say they had to—"

"Don't call me 'honey'. You don't get to call me that."

Annette stepped forward, placing her hand on Leana's arm. "Leana, it's okay. I don't think he's asking us to leave."

"I don't care. I don't want to be here anymore anyways," Leana responded. She saw Otis purse his lips and scrunch his eyebrows, puzzled.

"Leana," said Justin. "Stop. It's okay."

"What's in the barn, *Dad?*" She spit his name. "What's so important that you don't want us going in there?" Leana crossed her arms. She waited for a response, but everyone stood silent. "Fine." Leana stepped over to the door and gripped the handle. She leaned her body to slide it open it, but it wouldn't budge. She looked to see Otis standing with his hand on the far end.

"Don't," Otis said gently, but firmly.

"Leana, just leave it alone," said Annette as she grabbed at her arm to guide her away from the barn.

Leana yanked herself free. "Stop. You leave *me* alone!"

Annette drew back looking hurt. "Okay. Sure." She grabbed onto Justin's sleeve and pulled him behind her as they headed towards the car.

Leana looked at her retreating friends, and then back at her father. His face only showed concern, which made Leana feel horrible. "You guys, wait." She jogged to catch up, getting in between them and the car. "Annette, I'm so sorry."

"No, Ana, it's okay," she replied, holding her hands up to keep space between her and Leana. "You've obviously got stuff going on between you and your dad, so I think it's best for us to head out."

Justin stepped forward. "Leana, I'm sorry. I should have listened. I feel terrible."

"It's not a big deal. My dad shouldn't have reacted that way. I'm sorry. I wanted this to be fun."

"Hey, it's fine. We got time to see you. That's all that matters." Annette hugged Leana. "Besides, we'll see you Monday morning at school anyway."

Justin opened the trunk and placed his camera inside.

"Yeah. Okay," Leana said unsure as she watched Annette lift the car door.

Justin slammed the trunk shut. He walked around to his door and tried opening it, but it was locked. The window rolled down.

"What do you think you're doing?" asked Annette as she peered from inside the car at Justin.

"Uh, I'm getting in?"

"Nope, sorry. You came out here for a reason," she teased. "This trip will be completely pointless if you aren't going to ask."

"Annette," he whispered.

"Just do it." She pointed over at Leana. "Now."

Justin looked at her with wide, panicked eyes.

Annette sighed.

Slowly pacing around the vehicle, Justin faced Leana. "Um... Hi."

"Hi?" Leana felt uncomfortable now. There was too much going on emotionally today and she was ready for things to calm down. As he stood in front of her, she remembered the kiss and felt the tightness in her stomach fade slightly.

Leana noticed Justin's forehead perspiring. "I want to know..."

She waited.

"Oh, come on, Justin," Annette hollered through the open window. "Be confident for crying out loud and just ask." She dropped her head back against the car seat.

"To the dance," he said, not making eye contact. "Would you go to the dance with me?"

Leana didn't hesitate. "Yes, of course." She smiled and reached out to hug him.

"Really? Great!" He squeezed back.

Annette tapped the windshield. "Okay, finally. Now let's go. Later, Ana."

Justin turned and got in the car quickly. "Take it easy on the gravel. I don't want dust getting all over my mom's car, Annette," said Justin while shutting his door.

Leana laughed. "Bye, guys." Leana watched her friends coast down the driveway slowly, lost in the thought of how nice it would be going to the dance with Justin. Leana turned toward the house. There was her dad, sitting on the porch, watching.

She was pretty sure she hated him.

CHAPTER 14

Leana stormed towards the house as Otis opened the front door to let El out. She didn't know what to say or how to say it, but she could feel every drop of blood in her body boiling. She hated him for acting like a father when he'd never been around to be the father she needed, and now he thought he could just step in and play that role. Otis sat down in his rocking chair, his hand on El's head.

"What was that? You didn't have to make them leave. You didn't have to be so rude to them." Her fists were clenched tight and she didn't break eye contact with Otis. El sat quietly watching. Leana wasn't scared of her father, but she *was* scared of this anger she was feeling.

"Look, Leana, I'm sorry for how that went, but I wasn't upset. I didn't mind if they stayed, but I did set pretty clear boundaries. I just didn't want them going in there. They are still strangers to me." He began calmly petting El's back.

"Strangers?! They're my friends. They wouldn't be 'strangers' if you'd been in my life longer than you have!"

She wanted her words to hurt. She wanted him to be angry, sad, and embarrassed just like her. At this point, she didn't care what she said. She wanted him to feel her pain.

"That's true and you're right. I'm sorry."

"Well that makes everything better, doesn't it?!" She felt even more unsatisfied that he didn't look upset. *He doesn't even care.*

"Leana, you need to understand, I wasn't trying to scare them or hurt you. I'm trying my best, but this isn't easy for either of us."

"Well you did. And maybe your best isn't good enough." She turned and walked away from the house toward the woods. "I'm done here."

Otis stood from his chair. "Where are you going?"

"Away from you," she yelled as she kept marching. She didn't want to look back at him. She needed to be away from him. She hated how he acted so calm. She turned to face her father and kept marching backwards, yelling, "Now I know why you're alone!" Spinning violently, she continued her angry pace toward the woods.

In seconds, El was by her side clearly intending to follow.

"Whatever. Fine," she relented with a scowl.

CHAPTER 15

Leana trudged through the dead leaves as she zigzagged between trees. She barely felt the breeze as the sun penetrated the combination of thick canopy and slightly cloudy sky. Even though El was trailing behind her, Leana felt alone. She reached into her pocket and pulled out her pocket watch. As she had time and time again, she listened to the rhythmic ticking, focusing on the mechanical heartbeat to calm her.

Leana replayed the situation in her mind, trying to make sense of her father's reasoning and reaction to Justin. She couldn't understand why he had pushed her friends away so quickly, and why he was so completely emotionless when she yelled at him. Most of all, she wanted to know what he was trying to hide from her.

She knew only one person to call.

Leana activated the phone on her wrist and the display lit up.

"Call Mom."

Leana paid no attention to her surroundings.

"Come on," she urged as the phone rang. She stopped walking and leaned back against a tree.

"Hey, baby girl." Danielle was in her scrubs when she popped on the screen. "What's going on?"

"Mom, I hate it here," exclaimed Leana.

"Oh, honey. What happened?"

"It's all his fault." The words tumbled out of Leana's mouth. "He embarrassed me in front of my friends for doing nothing wrong, and they ended up leaving, and then I yelled at him and he just didn't seem to care at all."

"What do you mean?"

"I'm so angry right now."

"Why did he make your friends leave?"

"Well, he didn't *actually* make them leave…" Leana paused, gathering her thoughts. "They left because I got upset."

"So he wasn't the one who made them leave?"

"Are you kidding me? You're defending him?" Leana yelled. "First, you make me come here and now you make excuses for him."

"Whoa, honey, it isn't like that. Look, I'll be on my break in about half an hour. I'll call you back and we can talk more. Okay?"

"Whatever." Leana gritted her teeth, stopping herself from saying anything else.

"Leana?"

"What, Mom?"

"I love you."

The hologram disappeared as Leana ended the call.

Her sigh turned into a growl as frustration ripped through her throat. She pushed off the tree to keep walking then realized she had no idea where she was. There was nothing but trees in every direction. For a moment a knot of fear began to grow in her stomach, but then El bumped her hand with a wet nose. Leana laid her hand on the wolf. At least she wasn't actually alone. She wanted to turn back, but didn't want to face her father just yet.

"You want to keep going?"

She hated to admit it, but these thick woods didn't allow much light in and were a little scary.

"I'm glad you're here, El."

She started walking again but nearly tripped over El, who had stopped and turned suddenly with her ears perked up as if listening to something. Before Leana could turn around as well she heard a blood-curdling scream. Goosebumps crawled up her skin and she held her breath as she slowly turned around.

Leana let out her breath. "Annette? What are you doing here?"

El leaned forward, exposing her teeth. She let out a deep growl.

"Oh my god. That's a…" Annette backed up against the closest tree, her eyes wide of terror.

"El, no. Come here." The wolf turned back to Leana. "Sit," she demanded, pointing at the ground. The wolf looked at Annette, then back at Leana who pointed at the ground again. The wolf sat. "Good, girl."

Annette looked at Leana, stunned and silent.

Leana looked at her while she rubbed El's ear. "What's up with you and animals? I've never seen you so scared for as long as I've known you."

"Leana… That's a wolf. Where did that come from?"

"It's my dad's pet. This is El. El," Leana pointed her finger at her friend, "this is Annette."

Annette just kept breathing heavy.

"Annette, it's okay. El is very sweet. You can relax."

Slowly, Annette took a couple steps away from the tree without taking her eyes off the wolf.

"So, what are you doing here? Why are you back?"

"Justin's mom called. She makes us pull over if we're talking on the phone in the car. She thinks Justin's the one driving. It's ridiculous. Anyway, while he was talking with her I saw you in the rearview mirror, running into the woods, so I wanted to see if you were okay. Plus, I didn't want to hear Justin's mom talk for hours."

Leana rolled her eyes. "And you didn't see the giant wolf with me?"

"No! You think I would have followed if I had?"

Leana laughed. "I guess not."

"Why are you even out here?"

"My dad. I yelled at him and couldn't stand being around him anymore, so I came out here to get away."

"You doing okay?"

"Not really. I just hung up on my mom a couple minutes ago."

"Man, you're angry at everyone today."

"Yeah," said Leana. "Anyway, I'll walk you to your car."

"Uhh, sure," hesitated Annette, keeping her distance from the wolf.

As they walked, Leana bent down and picked up a stick. "Fetch?" She lifted it above her head.

Leana heaved the stick as deep into the woods as she could. The girls watched the leaves spit from the ground as El sprinted towards it. Watching El was a good distraction from the overwhelming emotions filling Leana. The wolf navigated through the trees effortlessly. Without stopping she retrieved the stick mid-sprint then changed directions, bringing the stick back.

"Are you kidding me?" Annette whistled under her breath. "That's so sizzlin'. Almost makes me want a pet wolf."

"After that display a minute ago?" Leana laughed. "You're such a liar. You don't even like horses when they're locked in a stall."

"Just picture it: me walking up to the ring in my next bout with a wolf by my side. People would love that."

"Keep dreaming, Annette."

They both turned in time to see El skid to a sudden halt inches from their feet. Annette instinctively put her arms to her face.

Leana laughed.

"What?" asked Annette.

"That's how I reacted the first time too." The sound of the phone ringing drew the girls' attention. "Great. It's my mom. I gotta... talk to her."

"That's fine. The car isn't too far from here. I'll go see how Justin's doing."

Annette ran through the trees as Leana opened the screen on her phone.

"Mom, hey."

"You sound better. How you doing, honey?"

Leana took a deep breath and looked around. "I'm doing okay. Annette found me in the woods. She calmed me down a bit."

"Okay, good. How about you tell me what happened?"

Leana sighed. "Okay, so I, uh, think I was the reason my friends left. Otis—Dad didn't kick my friends out. He wasn't even mad. I kind of freaked out and made them feel like they should leave because of how I reacted to Dad, and then when they did I got even more upset and, um... yelled at him. So I left."

"Left? Where'd you go?"

Leana slid the hologram screen over her right wrist, and used her hand to flip the screen, showing her mother where she was.

"Well, I'm not *gone*, but I'm in the woods. I don't know how far out I am."

As Leana kept panning her arm around, El appeared with a large stick in her mouth.

"Well, at least you're not alone. Be careful out there."

Leana twisted the screen back at herself.

"So, I assume you plan on going back soon?" Danielle was making it clear what she preferred.

"I don't know. Yeah. I guess. I don't want to, though."

"I understand. He's not an easy man to be around sometimes. He's very stubborn. Kind of like a girl I know..."

Leana snorted. "No kidding."

Leana looked up as El dropped the stick. The wolf padded forward slowly, growling quietly.

"Hold on, Mom. I think El smells something."

"What is it?"

"I don't know. It's probably just Annette coming back."

"Or an animal. Listen, you need to be patient with him."

El growled again, this time slightly louder. Leana tried to distract the wolf, so she wouldn't scare Annette again. She walked over and threw the stick.

"Go get it, El."

El didn't move, continuing to growl at the dark underbrush. Starting to feel a little creeped out, Leana stood behind the wolf. She felt like something was watching her. Officially nervous, she crossed her arms to hide her discomfort.

"Everything okay?" Danielle asked anxiously from the hologram display, now tilted slightly away from Leana's face due to her crossed arms.

"Yeah, fine," she said distractedly. She continued talking without taking her eyes off the void El appeared to be fixated on. "Hey, Mom?"

"Yeah?"

"Look, I'm sorry. I came here because you said it was for the best. I still trust you, but I don't think he cares. He's so closed off. I think this is a waste of time. What should I do?"

"Just be patient, baby girl. I'm so proud of you. You're so grown up now. I know you'll be able to make it work with him. He's a good man. He needs to remember how to be around people."

Leana glanced at the wolf. "Apparently he's good around wolves, right El?"

El didn't move. Her back was straight and fur raised, her head and ears lowered giving her an intimidating presence. Getting more nervous by the minute, Leana's eyes scanned the woods ahead of them, still unable to see anything. She took a step closer, afraid to blink.

"Leana?" Danielle said, getting her attention.

"Yeah?"

"I have to go. Anything else you need before I do?"

For a second there, Leana didn't have anything else to say. Then she remembered the kiss. She was excited to share it with her mom.

"Actually—"

El burst into a louder growl. Louder than she'd ever heard from a dog. Whatever was out there, El didn't like it and Leana couldn't hear or see it. A knot was suddenly stuck in her throat and her mouth went dry. Her heart raced as she struggled to keep a steady breath.

"What's out there, El? What do you hear?"

"Leana, what's going on?" Danielle asked.

"Hold on. El is freaking out."

El didn't move. Her front feet were planted far apart and her tail down. The dark pattern in the fur on her back continued to stand on end. Her ears twitched; Leana knew she heard something. A branch snapped and Leana whipped around, stifling a scream.

"Oh my god, Annette, seriously!"

"What? I told Justin where we are."

Leana turned back to El, expecting the wolf to have relaxed, but she was still facing away, unmoving. Just then, Leana thought she heard something.

"What's with you," Annette asked loudly.

Leana shushed her. "Quiet. Listen."

Annette raised an eyebrow. "I don't hear anything."

El crouched a bit lower.

"I hear it now, girl." Leana said softly.

At first, a sound reached the girls' ears like a distant vacuum cleaner, but it rapidly grew closer and louder. Before they knew it, the noise was overwhelming and the ground around them started to vibrate.

"Leana! Leana!" yelled Danielle.

"What the heck?" Annette looked around panicked.

The sound turned into a roar, forcing Leana and Annette to clap their hands over their ears. El stood still, her teeth visible and muscles tense.

"Mom!" Leana yelled, struggling to keep her footing.

"What? I can't he-- you. --'re –uttin-- --t."

The screen began flickering. "Mom? Mom!" The screen cut out.

El was now staring up at the location of the sound. Leana stared up too as her body continued to shake with the ground's rumblings. Through the thick greenery overhead, Leana struggled to get a clear view of what El was looking at, but she knew it was close because the sound was getting louder. A squirrel ran past her as the trees shook.

"Oh my god, Leana!" screamed Annette.

Leana saw a metallic object streak across the sky through the thick trees. *What the...*

She only got a glimpse, but it appeared to be about the size of a bus, and had a tail of blue flames. It was so close to the tree line she could feel the heat as it passed over. The metallic, flaming roar pierced her ears through her hands as the projectile came violently into contact with the earth. The ground shook so much it knocked Leana over and she curled up in the fetal position, squeezing her eyes shut. El straddled Leana like a shield, growling ferociously.

Whatever it was crashed a couple hundred yards from Leana, sending a shock wave through the woods and spattering leaves and dirt in every direction. The impact caused Leana to bounce off the ground and come back down hard, almost getting the wind knocked out of her.

Animals darted past as acorns and twigs fell from the surrounding trees. Leana cautiously opened her eyes, seeing the belly of El still hovering above her. Leana quickly scanned the area for Annette, struggling to see through all the dust and leaves.

"Annette!" she called out.

Catching her breath and shakily getting to her feet, Leana noticed El was standing between herself and what appeared to be a crashed airship. El's eyes were fixed on it, ready to strike at any moment.

"El, where is she?"

The wolf ignored Leana.

She yelled out for her friend again, this time getting a faint response.

"Over here."

Leana spun around, seeing Annette holding herself up against a tree. Besides being coated in dirt and a little shaken up, she appeared to be fine.

"Are you okay?"

"Yeah. Got the wind knocked outta me, but I'm good. You okay?"

"Yeah," Leana responded, hugging her friend tightly.

"What was that, Ana?"

Leana turned around, facing El's direction. "I don't know. Maybe we should go."

"We need to see if anyone was hurt. We don't know if someone was in… that thing."

"Annette, we don't even know what that *thing* is. What if it blows up or something?"

"We have to check it out."

Leana stepped forward, putting her hand on El's back. El only looked up momentarily.

After watching the smoke spew up into the sky, Leana turned to Annette. "Alright, let's go, but we have to be careful."

With every step Leana took, she felt her nerves tensing up her body, as well as adrenaline shooting through her veins. She wondered if Justin or her father had seen the crash. She didn't know what to do. She looked down at her phone, but it was still dead.

"Is your phone working?" she asked Annette.

"No, it's acting messed up," Annette responded, fiddling with her bracelets.

"Mine too."

"Well, maybe Justin will be able to call for help."

"I doubt—"

"Guys!" yelled a sudden voice.

Both girls startled.

"Justin!" said Annette with her hand on her chest.

"What?"

Annette punched him in the arm.

Leana looked down at El who was still looking forward. "Thanks for the warning, El."

"Holy… Leana, look out!" yelled Justin who stepped back.

"What? What?" Annette looked around.

Justin pointed. "There's a wolf behind you!"

Leana sighed forcefully. "It's fine. That's El, my dad's pet."

"Yeah, Justin. Relax," Annette said, hitting him in the arm again.

"Well, how was I supposed to know?" he asked, rubbing his arm. "And stop hitting me." He looked up at the smoke. "Did you see what came from the sky?"

Leana and Annette looked at him. He looked over their dusty, dirty clothes and wide-eyed expressions. "I'll take that as a yes."

"Please, tell me you called for emergency help before you came out here," said Leana.

"I tried, but my phone went dead."

"So did ours," Leana said frustrated. The girls sighed. Just then, El dashed towards the ship.

"El, no!" Leana yelled, chasing after the wolf.

She sprinted, trying pointlessly to catch up to the wolf. She didn't want El to leave her sight, but there was no way she could keep up. The other two tried to keep pace, but Leana was faster.

"Leana. Wait," they called after her.

By the time Leana caught up to El, she was standing meters away from the ship. Leana could feel heat radiating from the hull. El lowered her head and growled under her breath, her paws digging into the dirt as the hair on her back stood on end. Leana suddenly felt like she was going to be sick. She wanted to be away from all of this. Far away. But she knew if it was a ship, then there had to have been someone flying it. She took a step forward.

"Leana. Hold up," yelled Justin. He gasped for air, bending over once he had caught up. Annette followed closely behind also gasping, with her hands on her hips.

"Wow," Annette said, looking at the steaming metal. "This is unreal."

"I know," Leana said, keeping her eyes on the craft.

"One thing's for sure," Justin said, catching his breath. "This is *not* from the United Countries of the World. It doesn't even look man-made."

"What?" asked Annette.

"I mean look at that under the wing," he said, pointing as he bent over. "That does *not* look human." He paused.

The girls both looked underneath and saw strange symbols etched into the metal. Leana saw something click in Justin's mind.

"Oh man. It's just like Professor Vincent's theory. Maybe this is the kind of ship he was talking about," he added, holding his arms out towards the craft, indicating its size. "Someone's gonna come looking for this," he continued. "No way this went unnoticed, guys."

"Then we need to see if anyone is inside," Annette said, stepping forward.

Justin reached for her arm, but she shrugged it off. Leana stepped in behind her.

They were close enough to see the details along the ship's hull. It looked damaged, as if it had taken fire of some sort – but they didn't look like normal bullet holes. There was a large, scorched symbol toward the front of the craft that looked like a flower, almost like a rose. The colored markings that still showed through the damage appeared crimson red and gold. It seemed impossible that anyone would have survived the crash.

"El, come on," Leana whispered.

She took a deep breath, accidentally filling her lungs with the burning smell of the smoke. She coughed several times, trying to cover her mouth. That's when she heard it; a clanking, then a grunt. Something was moving inside the ship. Someone was still alive. She felt paralyzed. The sounds moved to the back of the ship, right where Leana was standing.

"Annette," she whispered forcefully.

"I'm here."

The tense muscles in her legs made it hard to walk. Slowly, Leana stepped back, one foot after the other, quietly and cautiously.

Leana tried yanking on El to get her to follow. The wolf brushed Leana off with a jerk of her head, making it clear that she wasn't moving.

"El, let's go. Now," she hissed.

A pounding erupted from the side of the ship, directly in front of Leana. She jumped back and gasped, trying not to scream.

Annette stepped forward, her arm grabbing onto Leana's elbow. They exchanged a scared look.

El growled deeply.

"What is it?" Annette said unsteadily.

Leana didn't know what to think or say. There was nothing in this moment she could control, not even her own nerves it seemed. "I have no clue."

The loud pounding continued to echo through the ship. They both jumped as the hull started to hiss violently.

Slowly a door on the side of the ship was forced open by a pair of hands. Swinging up from the bottom, the door shrieked as metal ground against metal. A body stumbled out from the ship, collapsing to the ground just short of El, who strangely didn't move.

For a moment, Leana stood frozen. This was beyond anything she was expecting to find in the woods – or ever, for that matter – and she didn't know how to handle it. She was terrified, but she knew something had to be done.

"Uh," Leana tried speaking.

"Is that... a person?" Annette asked, taking a tentative step forward.

"No, don't," Justin warned.

"They might be hurt." Annette approached the visitor cautiously. She knelt down slowly.

"I don't think you should touch them, Annette," he warned again.

She laid her hand on the visitor's back. "Well, they're still breathing. Leana, help me roll them over." She looked up at Leana, but Leana was staring at the ship. "Leana."

"Yeah. Yeah," she said weakly. She and Justin knelt across Annette, rolling the stranger over onto their back. Leana couldn't make out the person's face, but could see they had a muscular frame. A leather-like, dark blue hooded cape covered their entire head, but when Annette slowly pulled the hood off there was a helmet underneath. Lights and images flashed across a cracked visor, but they faded out before Leana could get a good look at them. The visor covered portions of the visitor's face, but she was still able to make out features that appeared distinctively masculine.

Without warning, the man's eyes shot open and caught Leana's gaze; he struggled to breathe, looking desperate.

He tried to speak, but they couldn't understand what he was saying. He wasn't speaking English. Leana flinched as the man suddenly grabbed her arm, pulling himself up slightly and reached up with his left hand. Touching two of his fingers to the back of her ear, he moved them over her skin down to her throat.

"Run." he said hoarsely, then passed out.

As he slumped back to the ground, his hooded cape fell away completely and revealed that he was wearing light armor over a finely woven garment. She noticed immediately that the armor matched the crimson and silver hull of the ship. There was a dark purple liquid smeared across his armor and cape, and it had gotten on her hands. The texture was thick between her fingers. She looked closer, removing the visor, noticing his sweat soaked face and more of the same purple liquid.

Looking down at his hands, she noticed an open wound, seeping purple. Her heart raced. "Oh my god," she said, looking at her own stained hand. "It's blood."

"And he's losing a lot," Annette added, stepping in and putting pressure on the wound. "We need a tourniquet."

Annette checked his pulse.

"Is he okay?" Justin asked.

"I'm not sure. I think he's just unconscious."

Leana sat back and sighed. "Thank god."

El sat quietly next to them. Leana looked at her friends. "What do we do now?"

A distant *vroom* came from behind Leana. They looked behind them. In the distance, headlights approached from behind the trees along the road. Leana realized how close the road was when the pair of headlights suddenly turned into the woods.

Justin said. "People are coming."

"What do we do, guys?" asked Leana.

As the lights came closer, Leana could make out a white vehicle. It skidded to a stop and a figure hopped out.

"Leana!"

It was her father.

"Here!" She was actually relieved it was him.

"Over here, Mr. Rayne," yelled Annette.

Otis raced towards them and knelt next to his daughter. "Oh my god.

Leana!"

Leana didn't respond, she just looked down at the body she was still touching.

Her father put his arms on her shoulders. "Are you guys okay?"

"He needs help," Leana said.

"He's lost a lot of blood, Mr. Rayne," added Annette.

Otis rubbed his head, nodding. He looked at Justin. "Help me get him in the truck."

"Yes, sir," Justin hurried over to the unconscious man's feet, grabbing them at the ankles.

Otis lifted the man's shoulders. Together they carried him to the truck. After they got him in the back, Otis walked back toward the ship.

Annette looked at Otis. "What about the ship?"

"Should we call someone or something?" Leana asked.

"No, we can't call *anyone*," said Otis. "Come on, girls."

"But, Mr. Rayne, what about his ship?" Annette asked again.

"Esu will take care of it. We need to get back. I need to patch him up. Come on."

Annette turned to Leana. "Esu?"

Leana stayed, staring at the ship. The hull appeared cooler now. Leana stepped closer.

Otis was beside her. "You okay, Leana?"

"I, uh... I don't know." She reached for the hull, but quickly pulled back as heat still radiated from the metal.

"Leana," he said, turning to face her. "We need to get him back to the house. Come on, honey."

"Okay. Okay." She forced the words around an unexpected lump in her throat. It was really weird hearing him call her that after everything that had happened today, but that should have been the least of her concerns right now.

Wrapping his arm around her shoulder, Otis guided her back to the truck. El jumped in after her and Otis slammed the door shut. Annette and Justin sat in the bed of the truck with the stranger.

"Hold on, you two," he said to them before opening his door.

Leana stared at the ship through the dusty window. Otis hopped in and turned to his daughter.

"It's going to be okay, rose petal. I'm here."

CHAPTER 16

The sun had nearly set as the truck stopped short of the porch, spitting dust and dirt into the headlights. Otis moved quickly to the bed of the truck.

"Justin, get his shoulders."

They pulled the man out, hurrying towards the house. His arms flopped as the two carried him up the porch stairs. Esu was at the top, holding open the front door.

"The office is prepared for him, sir."

Annette sprang to the ground from the truck and looked at Leana through the open window. "Leana, you coming?"

Leana continued to sit in the passenger seat, staring out the window. The ship, the stranger's armor, the colors, it all reminded her of something, but she couldn't remember what. It was just like trying to recall her dreams. She could never remember the details, only the residue of the emotions she felt after waking up from each of them. This experience had left her feeling the fear and terror that filled her body every night she woke up screaming. All Leana could do was sit in the truck and try not to scream now.

A short moment later, Otis ran back outside, leaping down the porch stairs in one jump. He pushed past Annette and swung open the door, breathing heavy.

"Something's wrong," said Annette as she stepped to the side so Otis could get closer.

"Leana? It's me," Otis spoke gently.

Leana stared blankly out the front window completely lost to the world.

"Hey, hey. Come back to me. Come back," whispered Otis.

Slowly, Leana turned her head with tears streaming down her checks. She was startled to find that the touch of her dad's fingers as he dried her face felt safe and familiar.

"Dad… What's happening? What—who is he?"

"Leana, I need you to help me. Can you come help me?" Slowly, one hand on each of hers, Otis guided Leana from the truck.

"What?"

"I need you to bring El in the house and watch her. Can you do that for me?"

"Yeah. Yeah." She nodded weakly.

"Okay. Come on, then. I'll help you in the house."

"My phone is broken," she responded still in a daze.

"I'll fix it for you later. Promise. Come on," he encouraged. It was obvious that she was in shock.

Slowly, Otis helped Leana up the stairs and inside the house with a concerned Annette close behind. El was already at the door.

Esu held it open for them. Otis stopped and let go of Leana's arm. "Esu, I need you to go take care of the rest."

"Are you sure, sir?"

"Yes. I'll take care of the kids. You need to go now."

"Leaving now, sir," said Esu, closing the door behind him.

The sound of the truck peeling away from the house could be heard inside. Leana turned the corner past the stairwell towards the office.

"Leana, where are you going?" asked Annette.

"I have to see if he's okay."

As soon as Leana entered the office, she saw Otis' old collectibles: a gigantic globe in the corner next to a book shelf, hundreds of dusty books, pictures on the walls, and even more books that took up the entire back wall. Next to the closest book shelf was an old leather wingback chair. Companion to the chair was an old desk covered with papers, books, and pictures. Leana was oblivious to the mess, instead focusing on Justin standing at the side of a lounger sofa.

She came up next to Justin as he gently wiped away the blood from the stranger's face who lay there unmoving. Leana circled around and sat in the big windowsill on the other side of the sofa. El walked in, her claws clicking on the hardwood floor.

"Is he going to be okay?" Leana asked.

"Your father said he'll be fine." He kept wiping away the blood, his white rag now colored purple. Leana noticed the water in the bowl matched the rag.

"Is that really his blood?"

Before Justin could answer, Otis walked into the room with a glass of water.

"Leana, can you take El to the kitchen and get her some food, please?"

"Yeah. Sure." She wobbled as she stood.

Otis stepped forward as if to catch her. "You okay?"

"I'm okay, I'm okay." She put out her hand. "Come on, El."

She trudged out of the room into the hallway where Annette was waiting. The office door closed behind her.

"Leana, are you okay?" asked Annette, seeing Leana lean against the door. For a moment, Leana had to focus all her energy on standing as still as possible. She still felt dizzy from the panic attack she experienced earlier.

She nodded then shushed Annette when she heard Otis' muffled voice.

"Justin, hand me that glass of water." A moment passed, then she heard the coughing and groaning of the stranger. She pressed her ear against the door, listening.

"Do you think he's dangerous?"

"I don't think so."

"How can you be sure?"

"I just am. I don't know why he came here and I don't care, but I want you to know that if he tries anything it won't go well for him. Okay?"

"Okay."

Leana pulled away from the door. Her father's tone of voice was chilling. She decided it was best to walk away and feed El like her father asked her to do. She and Annette walked into the dining room to see there was food in El's bowl already. Leana grabbed the food dish and empty water bowl and walked into the kitchen.

"Leana, you doing okay?"

"I really hope so," she said, turning on the faucet and filling the bowl. Leana stared at her fuzzy reflection in the sink's metal. It was difficult to process everything that had happened. *He's an alien, isn't he?* Leana tried to find her composure again. She put the water on the floor next to the dog food, then put her hands back under the spout and splashed her face with cold water. It felt good. The sudden temperature drop made her momentarily focus on something other than the stranger, her father, and how she and her friends had just seen an alien ship crash-land.

Still dripping with sink water, Leana reached with a wet hand into her jeans' pocket and pulled out the pocket watch wrapped in a cloth. It felt heavier than normal, but she assumed that was because she was weak after an exhausting day. Pressing it against her ear, without unwrapping it, Leana was able to collect herself as she focused on the ticking. With each tick, her muscles relaxed. She suddenly thought about her friend. She turned to Annette, "Are *you* okay?"

"Me? I'm fine. Saw an alien ship crash-land, saw an alien bleed purple blood... Oh, *and* I saw a pet wolf. You know, I'm great," she said sarcastically.

Leana hugged her, knowing Annette was probably just as much a mess as she was. "It's okay. My dad will take care of everything... I think."

"I feel like I'm losing my freakin' mind, Ana."

"Ha, yeah me too," responded Leana as she squeezed Annette tightly, and then released her.

They stepped out of the kitchen to be followed immediately by El who had long-finished her dinner.

"That was fast," said Annette.

They headed back to the office, sliding the door open. "Is he awake?" Leana asked quietly.

Otis was sitting at the man's side, handing Justin an empty glass. "No." He stood up and walked around the lounge chair.

Leana took her father's place, checking to see if the visitor was awake for herself. She noted his wet hair and face.

Otis slid his hands into his pockets and watched her examine him. "He's still resting."

"How's he doing?" asked Leana. She timidly put her hand on his forehead.

Otis smiled. "That's just like how your mother does it."

"What?" asked Leana.

"Nothing. He'll be better by tonight. Most of his wounds are from the crash, but he didn't break anything. He did get a nice knock on the head though." He turned to leave the office.

"Where are you going?"

"Back outside. Gotta take care of a few things tonight."

"Want me to stay and watch him?"

"That's fine, but you three stay together and keep El close. I don't want you alone with him. Understand?"

Annette walked up to Justin who wrapped his arm around her shoulder. Leana nodded without looking at her father.

He stepped into the hall then turned back around.

"Leana?"

"Yeah?"

"I'm sorry about earlier."

"I know. Me too." She smiled faintly.

The apology was comforting to Leana. Maybe this was the side her mother was talking about.

"Okay, then." Otis tapped the wall with his hand and left the room.

"Justin, do you really think he'll be okay?"

"Well, your dad said he has a concussion along with all his cuts and bruises. I think the dude is lucky to be alive, Ana."

Leana still couldn't believe it. It was a miracle that this man had gotten out alive – well, mostly alive. "This is *crazy*."

"Uh, yeah. We know, Leana. We were there," said Annette as she stepped closer to the stranger. "I wonder what his name is."

"Bob. His name is Bob," said Justin.

"Way?"

"Yep. That's what he told me earlier, Annette."

Annette glared at Justin. "You're dumb."

Justin grinned. "Almost had you goin' though."

"You're such a troph."

He chuckled as El walked into the room. "How about you, girl? You think I'm funny right?" he said to the wolf as he leaned in to pet her.

El growled and bared her teeth. Justin jerked back quickly, bumping into the stranger. "Jeez!"

"El, leave him alone," said Leana. She looked at Justin. "My dad says it takes her time to get used to new people."

"Ha! See even the wolf thinks you're a troph."

"Shut up, Annette. I don't know why it tolerates you so much already, you've only been here as long as I have."

"I don't know," Leana said absentmindedly. She hardly registered the comment – there were much more interesting things happening right now.

She looked back at the stranger, her hand running along El's head. "He should have been killed in that crash. Right?"

"Most humans would've been," replied Justin.

Whatever he was and wherever he was from, he was quite a survivor to be able to make it through something so horrible.

"Well, might as well get comfortable," Leana said, walking around the stranger.

She went back to the windowsill, sitting opposite her friends and watching the sun that was finally setting. Strangely, at this moment, when hardly anything made sense, Leana now felt calm, like everything would be alright. She remembered how her father had apologized, and maybe that's what brought her comfort. She sat there, fighting to keep her eyes open. She didn't want to miss anything if the stranger woke up.

Her eyes became extremely heavy, her body weak, and her breaths deeper. Keeping her eyes open became difficult to manage. Just before drifting off, a thought popped into her mind. Her father has been so calm throughout this whole situation. He hadn't flinched at the sight of a crashed alien ship, or the blood, or anything. He had simply handled everything quickly, without question. *Strange.*

Next thing she knew, she was being woken up by her father softly nudging her shoulder. His flannel shirt and jeans were covered in sweat and dirt. He looked exhausted and she noticed a cigar sticking out of his front pocket. She wrinkled her nose, then peered past him and saw Annette passed out in the chair in the back of the room with Justin sleeping at her feet.

Leana took a deep breath, sat up and stretched. She rubbed her eyes.

"How long was I out?"

"Little over two hours. How you feeling?"

When Leana looked out the window again, it was dark and lightning bugs were flickering in the distance over the field.

"Are you hungry?"

She looked at the stranger resting next to her. He was sound asleep.

"He doing okay?"

"Yeah, he's good."

Leana noticed that the stranger's armor had been removed and he lay quietly under a blanket. She also couldn't help but notice how attractive he was without the dirt and blood smeared all over. He had dark hair and a chiseled jaw line and looked to be in his early twenties.

She felt embarrassed for ogling.

"Yeah. Looks like it," she muttered.

"Well," chimed Esu as he entered the room, "I'll whip up a quick snack for you. I haven't had time to prepare supper yet, but I can fix something up in a jiffy."

"Esu, don't say jiffy... And thank you," Otis replied with a smile.

"Yes, right. You are welcome."

Esu exited loud enough that Justin and Annette slowly woke up.

"Food?" asked Justin groggily.

Leana looked at Otis. "Did you finish whatever you needed to get done?"

"I did. Didn't take as long as I thought it would. I need to go shower. Sorry for the smell."

"It's okay. Your cigar smells worse."

"Yeah, but they taste *good*."

"I doubt that," she snorted.

"Leana... I'm glad you're feeling better," Otis said with a fatherly look that was both comforting and foreign to Leana. "You had me worried there for a while."

"Yeah." She looked back at the unconscious man. "Me too."

The stranger lay there, unaware she was inches away from him. She wondered if being this close was dangerous, but with her father around she felt safe. So much had happened in the last few hours and she didn't know how to process any of it. She was still somewhat unconvinced he was even a real alien. He hardly looked it. Aside from the purple blood, he seemed very human.

She thought about how she couldn't understand his words until he touched her, and then all he'd said was '*run*'.

"Hey." Otis spoke, drawing her attention away. "Mind if I ask you about it?"

"Umm... Yeah, sure."

"Was he awake long? Did he say anything to you before he passed out?"

"Well, he was barely conscious. I *thought* I heard him say '*run*.'"

"He definitely spoke something, but it was gibberish," Justin chimed in. "I know it wasn't English."

Otis looked back at Leana. "Are you sure?" He looked at the other two. "I want to be sure."

"Yeah, we're certain. It sounded kind of like radio static," replied Justin. Otis looked at Annette.

"Don't look at me. I don't know what it was, Mr. Rayne," said Annette.

"Interesting," he said.

"You know, we kind of saved his life," Annette said proudly.

"Yes you did, and he'll have you three to thank when he wakes up." Otis looked back out the window, repeating softly, "He'll have you three to thank."

Leana looked at her father. "Can I ask you something?"

"Hmm?"

"I'm sitting next to an 'alien.' Should I be freaked out?"

"Why would you be?"

She shrugged.

"You have your mom's strength and courage. You know that, right?"

"What does that have to do with anything?"

"I just wanted to remind you since he's staring at you right now."

Leana gasped and jumped away out of her chair only to discover the stranger still sleeping and Otis laughing quietly behind his hand.

"That wasn't funny," she exclaimed, sitting back down.

Otis' laughter rumbled deep in his chest. "It was kind of funny."

Justin and Annette chuckled behind him.

His cigar fell to the ground and he picked it up and twisted the long, pungent cylinder between his fingers.

She glared at him and her friends. She could still smell the rank stench of his cigar.

"Okay, okay. I'm sorry."

Leana sat as she pouted a moment, then let out a small giggle. Catching herself she forced her face to look stern and upset.

"See? Funny." Otis said smiling.

"You done?" she asked faking annoyance. "On a serious note, don't you think we should call the ambulance, or police, or something?"

Otis sighed. "No."

"Why not?"

"Because it would make things worse."

"How?" Leana thought she saw the stranger's hand twitch. She looked quickly, but he was still unconscious.

"He's obviously not from here, and we have no idea what people might

118

do if they did get their hands on him. One thing I've learned over time is that this world isn't all sunshine and rainbows, Leana."

She sensed a bitterness in his words as if he was speaking from experience. She hadn't thought that far. What *would* happen to the stranger if he were put in the wrong hands? He was lucky he had crashed on the farm. Otis was willing to care for him here where no one else knew about him.

"What about his ship?" Leana continued.

"It's been taken care of. He should be safe for now."

Leana watched him cross his arms over his chest. "You don't seem like you believe that." She could tell her father wasn't being completely forthcoming with his opinion on the situation.

"No, I don't. With him here, none of us are actually safe." He sighed. "That's why he needs to go as soon as possible."

"What? Why?"

"He can't stay here, Leana."

"Well he can't go either. Obviously. Look at him. We saved him, he's our responsibility."

"Okay, let's say he stays," Otis responded calmly. "What happens if he wakes up and threatens our lives?"

"We call someone. They can deal with him."

"Then *they* will know we helped him. That would put us in a different kind of danger. Do you want that?"

"No!" She was getting more upset with each new question. "Look, we can't just make him leave."

"We might have to."

She looked at the stranger, thinking of how she could protect him. She tried playing to her dad's emotions. "Well... What if he isn't dangerous? What if he's a fellow soldier? Would you just leave him behind?"

She could see her words startle Otis as his eyes stayed on hers and the wheels in his head turned. His jaw clenched as he turned his head away. She had obviously struck a nerve with that comment. Annette and Justin looked at each other.

"I'm sorry," said Leana.

"For what?"

"If I offended you."

"No. You didn't offend me." He sighed and looked at the guest. "Look, I don't trust him, but you seem to. I made the mistake once going against your judgment about pushing people away," he said, nodding toward her two friends.

"What are you saying? Are you saying he can stay?"

"For just one night."

Leana was already on her feet, wrapping one arm around his midsection in an impromptu side-hug. "Thank you."

"You're welcome. I hope you're right about him."

Leana realized this was the first hug she had given her father since she was a little girl. She hadn't really planned on hugging him, it had just kind of happened. She broke the hug awkwardly before he could return it and turned to look back at the stranger.

"Me too," she agreed. "And thank you." *Maybe he didn't like the hug?*

"Listen, though," Otis said, placing his hands on her shoulders, drawing her attention back. "We need to be careful." He looked at the other two. "All of us. Don't be alone with him. You three need to stay together if I'm not with you. Got it?"

Leana nodded. "Just give him a chance."

"Fine. And El stays with you."

"Got it—"

"At all times," he interrupted.

"Okay, okay. I understand."

"Alright, then. I'll be back. I need to check one last thing outside."

"Okay," she said, feeling his hand squeeze her softly before he left the room.

The minute he was gone, Leana turned and gave her friends a huge thumbs-up. "I think we made the right choice."

Judging by the looks on their faces, they didn't agree. She started to ask them what was wrong when without warning she felt the bruising grip of the man's hand on her wrist. Fear shot through her as she turned to find him staring at her from the couch.

CHAPTER 17

Leana wrenched her hand from his grasp and stepped back behind El. She rubbed her wrist, wincing at the pain as the stranger groaned and slowly turned his body towards her.

"Leana," said Justin protectively, already at her side.

"Where…" the stranger trailed off weakly.

Leana stepped backward, cautious to stay out of his grasp. "Don't move."

"…Where is he?" He continued to look around the room. He grimaced in pain.

"Who?" asked Leana.

"What'd he say?" asked Annette, not coming any closer.

The man inhaled sharply, eyes wide. It looked as though his breathing was painful.

Leana yelled towards the hall. "Oti--. Dad… Dad. Esu!" she called out. "He's awake!"

El stayed between Leana and the stranger, growling.

Leana spoke again. "I can't believe you're awake. It's a miracle you even survived that crash."

The man shifted positions again, but El stepped closer. "Get back, El. It's okay. He's not going to hurt us." She looked back at the stranger. "Are you?"

His brown eyes appeared warm and unthreatening in the dim light, but Leana could see they were also wrought with pain. His weak smile didn't appear threatening. "No. Of course I won't." She noticed he spoke with an odd accent. His deep voice was strangely calming. He gazed at the wolf. "That is a curious creature."

Leana ran her hands through the black fur along the wolf's back, trying to keep her calm. "This is El," she said slowly. "She's my father's wolf."

The stranger lowered his head and made eye contact with the wolf, greeting her. "El."

The stranger looked back at Leana. "Rychur," he introduced, touching his chest with his bandaged hand.

She put her hand on her chest. "Leana." She pointed at her friends. "Justin. Annette."

"Wait, wait, wait. Leana, do you understand him?" asked Justin.

"Yeah, he just introduced himself."

"Leana, he's not speaking English," said Annette shocked.

"What? You didn't hear him say his name? He said 'Rychur'."

"Well, we heard him say something, but it wasn't our language," responded Justin.

Rychur swung his legs to the side slowly as if to sit up. He groaned at the pain as he held his side.

El growled and stepped forward.

"Easy, girl," Leana said quietly.

Keeping his eyes on the wolf, Rychur slowly reached out his hand. El exposed her teeth, which frightened Leana but didn't seem to faze the stranger. She watched him lean his hand a bit closer, slowly.

"What're you doing?" Leana asked nervously.

"Giving her a chance to decide if I'm friend or foe," he said.

Leana looked at her friends questioningly to see if they understood. They shook their heads. She didn't know how, but she definitely understood him. *How's that possible?*

"Smell," he said. "Easy, girl."

"Leana, what's he saying?" asked Annette.

"I don't know," she lied. "I was surprised I even caught his name."

"So, you *don't* know what's he saying?"

"No, I—I was just guessing," she lied again.

Cautiously, El leaned in, sniffing Rychur's hand while keeping her eyes on him. Leana held her breath. She could feel her heartbeat in her chest.

El stepped back, closing her mouth then lay down comfortably relaxed by Leana's feet.

"She chose friend," stated Rychur. "What an amazing creature."

Leana exhaled.

Rychur continued, "She didn't want me to be scared, she just wanted to keep you safe. I showed her respect, giving her the time to decide what I was. As you saw, I'm no threat." He braced his elbows on his knees, sitting up as he tried to breathe.

Leana wanted to respond, but she didn't want her friends to know she understood an alien language. She stepped forward and grabbed his arm with her hands as he tried to get up. "Whoa. Where you going?"

"I'm looking for someone."

"You need to stop moving," Leana demanded. "You are not okay."

Leana was surprised her father hadn't shown up yet. "Can one of you guys go find Esu or my dad?" Her friends stared at her. "Please." She heard shuffling down the hall, which hopefully meant one of them was returning. "Never mind."

Esu walked into the office, carrying a tray of food and water. Leana saw a curious look on Rychur's face.

"Hello there, sir. I am Esu. How are you feeling?"

"You are an incredible contraption."

Leana watched Rychur study the mechanical structure of Esu, taking in the details and functions. Esu stood still, staring forward with a blank look.

"What's he doing?" asked Annette.

"I don't know," answered Leana. "Esu?"

A sound like a fan starting came from inside Esu's chest. Lights in his head began blinking, growing steadily faster.

Rychur stood up weakly, reaching out his hand. "I am Rychur. Who is your maker?"

Esu blinked like he was clearing his head. He reached out as if to shake hands, but Rychur instead moved his hands up Esu's forearms and toward his shoulders and head, exploring Esu with wonder. Leana watched as Esu stood confused, uncomprehending the stranger's poor boundaries.

"Leana? Is he an android?" asked Justin stunned.

Annette, who stood next to him, was just as surprised. "There is a talking, walking, human-like robot in this room with us. I've never seen one this advanced."

"Oh... Oh, yeah. This is Esu, guys. My father's... house... keeper?"

"Housekeeper?" Justin responded, bewildered. "Then how come he's able to interact with us?"

Annette agreed, chiming in, "He's like a person made of metal, Leana! I mean, come on! This isn't your ordinary household android."

"Otis Rayne. A marvelous and brilliant man," stated Esu to the alien, in answer to his question. He gestured with his hands, accidently bumping Rychur's arm and nearly spilling everything from the tray. Leana picked up an apple that fell to the floor.

"Esu, you understand him?" Leana asked.

"Otis?" Rychur repeated. He looked at Leana. "Is that...?"

Leana stood there unsure if she should answer. She didn't want her friends to know she understood him.

"Otis is her father and this is his home."

Rychur nodded, quickly falling back on the couch.

"Whoa, easy," urged Leana as she grabbed a water glass from Esu's tray. "Here. Drink this." She held it out to him.

He took the glass from her and swirled the water around then smelled it. Slowly lifting it to his lips, he tipped some water into his mouth. Leana noticed a slight improvement in his skin color as his face relaxed and his posture straightened. He no longer struggled to sit upright. He paused, looking at the water curiously, then emptied the rest of the glass. "This fluid, what does it contain?"

Esu quickly answered, "Two hydrogen atoms and one oxygen atom."

"Those are your elements?"

"Yes. That's the molecular make-up of *water*," responded Esu.

"Leana," said Annette faintly. "Your dad's robot is talking to the alien in an alien language."

"I know. It's amazing isn't it?" Leana caught herself. "I just wish I understood them."

"It's WA-TER!" said Justin slowly.

"He already knows that," Esu said, condescendingly. He looked back to Rychur. "Water: A colorless, transparent, odorless, tasteless liquid that forms the seas, lakes, rivers, and rain and is the basis of the fluids of living organisms. Earth's surface is covered by about seventy percent of water. The human body is more than sixty percent water. Blood is ninety-two percent water, the brain and muscles are seventy-five percent water, and bones are about twenty-two percent water."

"Earth is what you call your world?" asked Rychur, attempting to stand up.

"It is," replied Esu.

"We call your world Coreal."

"What's he saying, robot?" asked Annette.

"My name is E.S.U., emotional stabilizing unit. Feel free to call me Esu for short," he responded in English.

"Sorry, Esu." Annette apologized. "What is he saying?"

"Coreal is what his people call Earth."

"His people?" asked Leana.

Rychur twisted around at the sound of footsteps coming down the hall. Otis entered the room, but stopped at the entrance, staring at Rychur who was now standing.

Otis reached his hands into his pockets and pulled out five small, circular devices. "Kids, put these in your ears." He held one out to Rychur who put up his hand.

"That is not necessary. I am able to understand your language already."

"What are they?" Leana asked.

"They're Translation Aids. They're the same as the one in Esu."

"Are these another one of your inventions?" asked Justin.

"No, Esu actually developed these. He's very handy." He then reached in his other pocket and threw Justin and Annette their bracelets. "I did, however, fix your phones. Before you call your family though we'll need to discuss some things first. Okay?"

"Of course, Mr. Rayne," replied Justin.

Leana put the translator in her ear, as did Justin and Annette.

Otis looked at Rychur. "You appear to be feeling better."

"I am, and quicker than expected. I have you to thank it seems," he replied.

"Oh, wow. These are amazing, Mr. Rayne. I can understand what the alien is saying," said Justin loudly.

"Good, Justin," Otis replied. "He can also understand you. No need to speak loudly."

"Oh, sorry."

"These are so sizzlin'," Annette added excitedly. "Thanks."

"You're welcome," Otis said to Annette and Justin. He looked back at Rychur.

"Thank you for allowing me to stay at—"

Otis interrupted. "Listen, my name is Otis. You are a stranger in my home. We are happy you are better, but I'm very unclear of your intentions here, so let *me* be clear. If it weren't for my daughter you'd be gone already. Please, understand your position in my home, and we won't have any problems."

"I understand, Otis," said Rychur with a small smile, bowing his head slightly. "I am Rychur."

"That was subtle," said Leana.

Otis looked sternly at his daughter. She scowled back. She knew he wasn't happy, but Leana had no reason not to like Rychur and what Otis had just said reminded her of how her father had treated her friends earlier. There was a moment of silence. No one spoke as the nighttime bugs chirped outside.

"I'll get dinner started," pronounced Esu, turning to exit the room.

"Good, thank you, Esu," stated Otis, his face still grim.

"Your human-contrivance is very well done, Otis," praised Rychur. "An incredible craft."

"Thank you."

"How long did it take to build?"

"One year and twenty-seven days," said Otis bluntly.

"Esu... It took care of me." Rychur gestured to Leana. "Your daughter, she took care of me also. You raised her well—"

"Oh no, he didn't raise me." It burst out of Leana before she had time to think about why she would tell this to a total stranger. "In fact, he was never around. Isn't that right, *dad*?" Leana's resentment was palpable.

Otis interrupted, "Leana, would you give us a moment?"

Leana became quickly irritated. "Why?"

"Because I said—"

"What? *You* say so *I* do? No. I'm not going anywhere."

"Please, give me a minute to talk to him."

Annette and Justin looked at each other in the background. Annette stepped forward. "Leana, just listen to him."

Rychur chimed in as if speaking to a counsel on peacekeeping. "I apologize for whatever conflict I have created between you two, so I think it best if I leave."

"No," exclaimed Leana. "You can stay until you are better. My 'father' doesn't treat guests very well, but he said you can stay for one day."

"Leana," said Rychur gently, "that is not necessary."

She could see pain in Rychur's eyes that didn't seem to be from his crash wounds. She looked at her father. Otis was studying the hardwood floor with his hands in his pockets. Whatever was going on here, Leana suddenly felt embarrassed for being such a brat.

"Leana, please. Let's go," Justin pleaded.

She could tell by his voice that she had once again made a troph of herself. By her father's distant gaze, she could tell he was trying to stay calm.

"Okay," she sighed. Leana trudged out. "I'm sorry about that," she said to her friends.

Slowly, El stood up and exited the room with the teens. After sliding the doors shut, they all sat on the floor in the hallway opposite the office. Leana could hear the two men talking back and forth, but the voices were muffled behind the doors.

"I guess they don't want kids around while adults talk, huh?" she asked her friends.

"What was that all about? You were kind of a jerk in there," stated Annette.

"I don't know. I felt like Otis was *attacking* Rychur and I got protective. I feel like a total idiot."

"Well you should, Leana. You acted like one. Just because you don't have a good relationship with your father yet doesn't mean you need to disrespect him or fly off the handle every time he annoys you. He's trying to keep us safe and follow your wishes to keep Rychur here at the same time. You need to fix this."

Leana looked at Justin who shrugged, but nodded in agreement.

"You're right. I guess I still have a lot of resentment towards him."

"You've gotta stop being so angry with him. I think he's trying to make this work, so let him. Okay?" encouraged Annette. "You're lucky he wants to try."

"Yeah," Leana said softly, looking down.

Leana dragged her fingers through El's thick fur, thinking about

Rychur's peace-making and the look he'd had when he wanted the fighting to stop. She felt embarrassed by the way she had handled herself in front of him, especially towards her father. She didn't understand exactly what had happened in there, but she realized she had allowed herself to lose control of her anger.

Leana dug into her jacket and pulled out the pocket watch, unwrapping it from the cloth. Pressing the top button, she popped open the cover. Instead of looking at the time, she took in the details of her father's craftsmanship. She studied the watch like Rychur had studied Esu earlier. He was right about her father; he was very talented. She could see all the turning and moving gears inside. There was something behind the gears she had never noticed before. She lifted up the watch into the light for a better view.

"Huh, what *is* that?" she asked to no one in particular.

"What's 'what'?" responded Justin.

Leana squinted, trying to make out a glowing object in the back, behind all the moving parts. It was round almost like a watch battery, that much she could see, but there wasn't enough space in the tiny gap to make more details. She tried shaking the watch, but the object didn't budge.

"It almost looks like a…"

She was distracted by raised voices coming from the office. The men's conversation was still impossible to make out from where they were sitting, but Leana could tell the two were starting to argue. She moved to her knees, inching closer to the doors. Pressing her ear against the cold wood, she slid the watch back into her pocket. El whined.

Leana looked behind her. "El, quiet," she whispered.

She put her ear back on the door, but the voices had gone quiet.

The moment of silence seemed to stretch interminably when suddenly a portion of wall next to her exploded outward, spraying drywall and dust everywhere. Leana's heart stopped for a second as she gasped and fell back onto Justin and Annette. They stared at the large globe that now stuck halfway through the wall where, moments before, Leana had been sitting. El growled and Leana jumped up.

"What the heck?!" asked Justin.

"Leana, wait," said Annette.

Without hesitating, Leana burst into the room to find Rychur breathing heavy, his hands up in front of him in surrender. Otis stood across from him, his fists tight by his side. Both men stood silently, their eyes locked on each other's.

"What's going on?!" She looked at the globe sticking through the wall next to her. Justin and Annette stood in the hallway. "What happened?"

"I'm sorry," stuttered Rychur.

"No more apologies," said Otis sharply. He sighed, dropping his gaze.

"I need to clear my head."

Leana flinched as Otis turned in her direction. She knew things had gotten out of hand. She wanted to say something, she wanted answers, but seeing the look on Otis' face and the defeat in Rychur's made her simply stand aside and let Otis pass. She felt oddly responsible for whatever had just happened.

Otis stopped and turned halfway, gesturing to the wall. "I'll take care of my mess in the morning."

She saw a flash of guilt in his eyes as he tried squeezing out a weak smile as if to tell her everything was okay. It was pointless. She knew things weren't going the way they expected. Leana watched him leave, choking back her emotions as a knot swelled in her throat. Annette and Justin quickly moved out of his way.

Leana turned to see Rychur running his hands through his hair. Suddenly emotions raged back into her mind. "What happened in here, Rychur? What did you do?"

"I'm not sure."

"What do you mean? You've been here for only a couple of hours, and now there's a hole in the wall."

He ignored Leana's comment. "I made a mistake. I shouldn't have come here," he whispered to himself. Rychur sat down on the couch.

Leana took a deep breath and sat next to him. Nervously, she placed her folded hands between her legs and leaned forward. "Well, you're here now, so you need to start pulling yourself together."

He chuckled.

"What is it?"

"You," he said, humorously. "You remind me of someone very close to me. She used to tell me something very similar."

Leana felt butterflies in her stomach. "Like a loved one?"

He nodded.

"You have family?"

"I did… A long time ago."

"Why did you leave them?"

"I came here with a task, a purpose."

Justin and Annette made their way into the office. Annette walked over to the globe and Justin sat in the wing-back chair, watching Leana and Rychur talk.

Leana just stared at Rychur, waiting for an answer. "Yeah?"

"I'm searching for something."

"Here?"

"We believe so."

"You say 'we.' How many of you are there?"

"There are so many."

"Well, that didn't really answer my question," Leana said trying her best not to sound rude.

Rychur's head dropped. "Close to a million."

Her eyes grew wide. "Whoa, that's a lot."

"Our numbers were once nine hundred times greater than Coreal, so, no it is not," he said, looking sad.

"Oh, yeah... I see what you're saying," Leana responded hesitantly. "Do you think I can help you find whatever you're looking for?"

He looked her in the eyes, his brow low. "I don't think so. The item I seek is a weapon we hid from the evil of our world long ago."

"So why are you looking for it now?"

"The war has started again, and we will not survive without it."

"Is that what you and my father were arguing about?" She gestured to the globe in the wall.

Rychur briefly looked back at the floor. "Actually, yes. He did not care about our troubles, and when I asked about you he became angry."

"I can help you. He's not my boss, you know."

"Whatever you might see him as, he isn't. I can feel your resentment towards him."

"He's pretty much garbage for a father, a troph, and a jerk. He doesn't care about anyone but himself," exclaimed Leana. "So, yeah. I resent him."

Rychur spoke calmly, "That anger and hate you have for him will continue to eat away at you if you do not let it go. He's conflicted. You see him as one thing when he's something different entirely. You just have to *find* it through the rough exterior he puts up."

Leana leaned back on her hands. She wondered what gave Rychur the right to talk about her father as if he'd known him for years, but decided her other feelings mattered more right now. "You don't even know him. There is nothing to *find*. I'm already sick of him after one day."

"Leana!" Annette chided. "We literally just talked about this. Quit!"

"Your father is a complicated and confused man, but he's a very good man, a strong man. He defended you the moment I brought you up. To me, that is not a bad man, Leana."

"I never said he was a bad man. What I said is he's a really terrible *father*." She couldn't sit down any longer, her emotions wanted to pop out of her skin. She stood up and paced, rubbing her forehead with her hand.

"Do you have any respect for him?" asked Rychur.

"Of course she doesn't," Annette answered quickly.

Leana didn't hesitate. "No, I don't. Why would I?"

"Then why are you visiting him?"

"How do you know I don't already live here?"

"Because you just said you'd only been here a day."

"Well, I didn't have a choice. I was pretty much dragged here."

Rychur sighed. "No, I don't believe that's the reason. I believe you are here with him to fix what isn't broken. You talk like your bond is forever broken."

Leana stared out the window, turning over his every word, confused.

Rychur continued, "If I could go back to fix things on my home world I would, but I can't. Now there is only regret. You don't need to experience that."

There was a moment of silence as Leana saw the lightning bugs flicker in the distance.

"Who is your father to you?" Rychur asked solemnly.

Leana thought about it but didn't know how to answer. "I don't know."

"Then why do you treat him like you do?"

"You're not a parent, are you?" Leana asked turning back toward Rychur.

"No, I'm not."

"Then what do you know about being a father?" Leana quickly rebutted.

"Leana," added Annette. "What do *you* know about it?"

Leana glared at Annette. She saw Justin's disappointed look out of the corner of her eye. With the resentment of talking about her father, she didn't want to care how they felt right now.

Rychur appeared unaffected by her passive aggressive comment.

Leana looked away from Rychur again. She was angry and torn, which felt even worse. She didn't know what she wanted for herself. She had allowed her anger to guide her through life for so long that it had gotten to a point where she had trouble controlling it.

Leana sat back down next to him. "I didn't mean it like it sounded."

"You didn't, Leana. Anger is like a mask. It changes how we appear."

Rychur reached up, calmly holding his hand in front of her face. Leana flinched away. "It's okay. Just relax, Leana. I want to show you something."

Slowly, Leana relaxed, letting herself focus on his face. From his mouth, she heard the faintest of whispers. Her eyes turned heavy. All her thoughts of doubt began fading, leaving her mind empty and void. She struggled to speak clearly. "What are you..."

"What are you doing to her?" She heard Justin's muted voice behind her.

"Sleep now," whispered Rychur.

Leana felt the muscles in her body relax as her limbs went numb. She wanted to fight the overwhelming exhaustion, but she also wanted so badly to sleep. She welcomed the back of the couch as her body slumped. She thought she heard Justin's feet approach.

"Leana," his voice faded.

She welcomed the black behind her eyelids, without fear of her oncoming dreams.

CHAPTER 18

Feeling as though she had just fallen asleep, Leana awoke to find Esu shaking her shoulder. Looking around the office, she took a deep breath.

"How long was I out?" she groaned, stretching out her arms.

"About an hour." Esu replied cheerfully. His head lifted as Leana sprung to her feet. "You seem to be feeling good, yes?"

"I feel great, actually. I must have slept pretty hard." She scanned the room again. Where is... Oh, there you are." She was relieved to see Rychur seated in a chair in the corner of the room. "Have you been sitting there the whole time?"

"Yes, I've been talking with your friends."

"I'm sure that was entertaining..."

"Yes, I learned quite a bit about them."

"Good."

"I would have liked to talk more with your father, but he hasn't come back in yet."

"Did Annette or Justin talk about anything interesting?"

"They both did. They demonstrate amazing feats at such a young age. A fighter and an artist and gymnast."

"Sounds about right," Leana said chuckling. "So you guys just sat there waiting on me?"

"Yes. It was something you needed. You're a very peaceful sleeper," Rychur added genuinely.

"Well, that's awkward." Leana threw her legs off the side of the couch and faced her friends. "He tell you much?" she asked nodding toward Rychur. She watched Esu fold the blanket that someone had laid on her while she slept.

"Oh yeah," started Annette, but Justin interjected. "He talked about his galaxy and planet!"

"Really?" Leana was intrigued. "What did you tell them, Rychur?"

"Just some memories," he answered quietly.

"Like what—"

"Dinner is nearly prepared," Esu interrupted, "Please, be in the dining room in four minutes."

"Heck, yeah. Finally," Justin said, standing up and slapping his stomach. "I'm starving!"

"I'm with ya, Justin," said Annette, joining him.

"Of course, Esu. I could kill for some steak right now," exclaimed Leana. "What are we having?"

Leana missed Esu's answer as she realized Rychur remained seated. "You're welcome to join us. I assume you're hungry."

"If that's appropriate," Rychur said.

"It is," replied Esu. "Otis made sure I prepared enough food for everyone, including you. You are most certainly welcome."

Rychur straightened his back, looking humble. "Thank you, my friend."

Esu didn't say anything, he turned and glanced at Leana, smiling, then walked past her towards the hallway.

"What are you smiling at?" Leana whispered to Esu as he walked by.

"He called me 'friend,'" Esu whispered back.

Rychur stood up calling after Esu, "Your generosity is truly appreciated."

"You are welcome... friend," replied Esu as he headed down the hall, out of Leana's sight.

She looked back at Rychur. "You just made his day."

"I'm not used to such kindness. Not anymore."

"Used to? Why not anymore?"

Justin groaned, "Come on, Ana! We can talk in the dining room."

Annette laughed. "Agreed. Lead the way, troph."

Justin gave Annette a playful punch on the arm as they both headed down the hallway, leaving Leana and Rychur alone.

"Sorry," Leana apologized for her friends. "You were saying?"

"That's not the people we are anymore. Our world isn't how it used to be."

"What's it like now?"

"It's a dark place. Full of terror and violence."

"Umm... That's terrible."

"That's just how we live now. Day by day, waiting for the suns to rise and the moons to set."

"Suns. Moons. *More* than one?"

"Yes."

"That's pretty nitro." said Leana excitedly. She added, "I dreamt one time about a sky with more than one moon and sun. I'll bet it's beautiful at night."

"It is. Every night." Rychur stepped towards her.

She noticed Rychur seemed stronger and his posture was upright. "You look like you're feeling better."

"I am. I don't know how, but I can feel all my strength coming back. I haven't felt like this since…" he hesitated, looking at his hands, "…well I don't think I've ever felt this strong."

"Well, that's great. Isn't it?"

"Yes, it is, but I don't know how it's possible. It doesn't make sense."

"Let's go to dinner. You can ask my father." She grabbed his arm and pulled him towards the hallway. "Come on."

"By the way," said Rychur. Leana stopped and looked back at him. "I'm sorry if I frightened you when you found me."

"That wouldn't have been the word I'd use. More like terrified. Traumatized, perhaps," she said in a halfway playful tone.

"Yet, you didn't leave me alone."

"Why would I have?" she asked shocked.

"When I crashed, I didn't expect anyone to be around."

"What did you expect?"

"I expected to die."

"Well, from the looks of things, you should have."

"You could have just left."

"I almost did, but Annette wanted to check for survivors. I knew she was right, especially when we found you. After that, I wasn't about to leave you alone."

Rychur looked at her silently and smiled.

Feeling herself blushing, Leana rushed through the awkward moment, "Okay, good. Now can we go eat?"

Rychur held out his arm, encouraging Leana to lead him to the dining room.

When they entered, Otis was already seated at the head of the table, waiting patiently. Leana sat down across from him. Rychur sat at the table between Otis and Leana, across from Annette and Justin. He stared at the assortment of meat and vegetables and potatoes. Leana could see how unsettled Rychur's presence made her father as he shifted in his seat unnecessarily. *This should be interesting.*

"Hey," she said, looking at Otis.

"Hello," responded Otis blankly.

"Finally," said Justin. "You move at a snail's speed. *So slow.*"

She ignored Justin, noticing now that Otis was covered in dirt except for his hands. "I see you washed up before dinner."

Otis smiled faintly, but said nothing.

"Did you get all your work done?" asked Leana, hoping to strike up any conversation to avoid the awkward silence.

"For the night, yeah." Otis offered quickly.

Leana felt Otis' distance. She was slightly relieved when El padded up next to her and put her head on Leana's lap. It was comforting to have El there, even though she was using Leana for table scraps.

Leana turned to Rychur. "What do you think of all this? You look confused."

Rychur chuckled uncomfortably. "New world, new food. I'm afraid I don't know your customs."

"Well, I can make it easy for you," Justin replied. He picked up the silverware. "We eat with these."

He pointed at a platter. "Cow meat." Then pointed at another. "Corn." He kept on pointing to each dish until he was done explaining. "Mashed potatoes and the gravy that goes on top. Steak sauce. Watermelon. Rice. And beans."

"It's a wealth of foods," said Rychur, impressed.

"Yeah, well I'd like to see how much I can eat," said Annette.

Leana laughed. "I said the same thing with last night's meal – so much food – but don't worry. My dad takes the leftovers to veterans who don't have food. Pretty cool, huh?"

"Very honorable," said Rychur, nodding at Otis.

Otis kept his eyes on the table. Leana could see the compliment made him uncomfortable. "Yes, very honorable," she reiterated looking at her father who finally looked up. Leana mouthed "You okay?" to him. His smile brought her some relief.

"Let's eat," encouraged Otis.

Leana waved her hand over the table. "Dig in, guys."

Ignoring Annette and Justin diving into the food, Otis watched Rychur who was studying Leana's process of filling her plate. "So how are you feeling?" he asked the visitor.

"Much better. Thank you," Rychur responded, a spoonful of potatoes hovering over his plate.

Otis took a deep breath. "Listen," he hesitated. "I want to apologize to everyone for the way I reacted." He looked at his daughter.

"It's okay." Leana rubbed El's head, "Mom told me I need to be patient with you."

"She said the same about you," he replied.

"Oh no… Mom!" Leana slapped her forehead. A moment of panic overwhelmed her. Danielle was probably on her way here at this very moment, worried sick that something had happened to her when the phone cut out.

"What?"

"My phone. It malfunctioned in the middle of the, uh… crash," she hesitated, looking at Rychur. "It cut off midway through my conversation with her. She's probably freaking out right now," exclaimed Leana.

"She's not freaking out," comforted Otis.

"How do you know?"

"Because she called me," he replied, grabbing a steak.

"Yeah, Leana," added Annette. "Justin and I already talked to our folks too. We told them we were staying with friends for the weekend."

"What? Why?"

"Your dad doesn't want us leaving right now just in case. He doesn't want us accidently saying anything right now," said Annette, then she smiled. "So, it's easier if we just stay the rest of the weekend."

"Your dad was okay with that?"

"Well, yeah, why wouldn't he be?" Annette sighed. "A weekend of no training. It's gonna be *so* nice."

Leana didn't know how to feel about her friends staying with her the rest of the weekend. It was unexpected. "What about you, Justin?" asked Leana. "You have your mom's car. She's going to let you keep it all weekend?"

"My mom is out of state right now. I told her I was staying with Frankie the rest of the weekend." He stuffed a huge bite of mashed potatoes into his mouth. His eyes rolled back in his head at the delicious flavor.

She watched Otis lather his steak with dark, red sauce. "What'd you tell Mom?"

"Nothing. I told her I'd fix your phone tonight and that you had a scare earlier today. She seemed fine."

"Seriously? That's all you said?"

"Honestly? I had no clue how to tell your mother what happened. I wasn't really sure myself," he said, gesturing to Rychur, who was smelling a cob of corn. "I told her I'd call her back tonight."

"Well you're screwed."

"Why?"

"She's gonna freak. That was *not* enough info for her."

"Probably," agreed Otis with a slight smile.

Leana sighed and looked over at Rychur who was starting to stick the corn into his mouth like a hot dog. El whined and licked her hand.

"Rychur," Leana warned.

He looked up questioningly.

She chuckled then demonstrated. "You eat the corn off of the cob. You don't eat the cob part."

"There's two parts of this food? 'Corn' and 'cob'?" Rychur's confusion was blatant. He watched Otis noisily chomp at his corn. "I see." He took a bite then grimaced. He leaned towards Leana. "Are you sure this was intended as food?"

Justin stared at him with a piece of meat sticking out of his mouth. Leana laughed at his expression. "Yes but it's okay if you don't like it. It's not my favorite either."

Rychur gently set the cob on the plate next to the potatoes. He leaned to the side, seeing El licking Leana's hand, which held a piece of steak. "She seems so loyal to you."

"Well she wasn't when I first met her."

"She grew to like you?"

"Yep, and actually, I've grown to like her too. She was literally the scariest thing I'd seen in my life when I met her." Leana leaned down and spoke in a baby voice, "but now you're not."

"Yeah, that wolf is nitro, Mr. Rayne," said Annette.

"You know I know you're feeding her steak, right?" Otis said matter-of-factly.

Leana's eyes widened. "Sorry." She dropped the meat, letting El eat the rest of the floor as she lay down next to Leana.

Otis laughed. "It's fine. Just don't let Esu see you."

"Okay," she said relieved.

El chewed happily as meat juice dripped on the wooden floor.

"Just like your Esu, she's so unique. How did you come to acquire her?" asked Rychur gesturing toward El. Leana forked a steak onto her plate, and then one on Rychur's plate, who replied with a "Thank you."

Otis wiped his face with his napkin. "I just did. She was injured and I fixed her up. When she healed, she chose to stay." He went back to eating his meal in silence, his eyes focused on his plate.

"Come on. Tell him the whole story." Leana watched Otis continue to eat then turned her body towards Rychur. "She was wounded, right? My dad found her, in the woods, alone and bleeding. He carried her miles back to the house, healed her, fed her, and now she's like his best friend."

"Best friend?"

"She's been very good to me," said Otis. "She keeps me company. Her and Esu." Otis took a big bite of his mashed potatoes and spoke through it, "Yeah... I'm glad she wanted to stay. No one else like her on the entire planet. She's most likely the last of her species."

Leana looked at Rychur.

"What?" asked Rychur.

"She's just like you. Alone on this world."

Leana felt bad as she saw her comment make him wilt over his food. "Oh, no. I'm sorry. I didn't mean it like..." She leaned her head into her hand, bracing her elbow on the table.

"It's okay, Leana," said Rychur. "I guess I hadn't really thought about that yet, but it sounds like El and I do have a lot in common."

Otis looked at Rychur, pointedly. "Don't get any ideas."

As they went back to eating, Leana's mind wandered through the sounds of plates clinking and mouths chewing. She worried her father was mad at her for taking an interest in the extraterrestrial, but Rychur didn't seem alien at all. She could see how uncomfortable her father was sitting next to this stranger. She could also see Rychur's discomfort, which he was trying to hide as he kept eating. She marveled at how weird it was to be in the same house as her estranged father, an alien, a pet wolf, a robot servant, two of her best friends, and yet it was difficult to find the right thing to talk about. She knew talking about her father's past would be inappropriate at the moment, and she didn't want to say anything else stupid to Rychur. She sat in silence, eating her food.

"Isn't it strange," she said aloud suddenly, "that we are all sitting here at this table together?" She listened to the clanking silverware on the plates. "And we're all eating dinner."

"Is it strange?" asked Rychur.

"Well it's gotta be for you, Spaceman," teased Annette.

"Come on, guys," Leana said. "Crazy, right?" she looked at her father.

Otis stared at her. "I'm trying not to think about it," he responded before going back to eating.

A moment of embarrassment filled her stomach, until both her friends looked at her and rolled their eyes. Breaking their eye contact, Leana dug into her mashed potatoes.

Leana continued. "Okay, I know it's freaky, but look." She said to Otis, gesturing to Rychur on her right. "He's an alien..." she turned her gaze to Rychur, "No offense." Then looked at Justin and pointed down at his feet. "And that's a wolf, one of the last of her kind."

Justin pointed at the kitchen door. "And don't forget the android. Right, Annette?"

Annette finally chimed in happily. "I know, and it's cooking! Sparklin'!" she yelled as she took another bite of her steak and swayed side-to-side.

"Right?! Thank you, guys," Leana said, nodding at her friends.

"Yeah," said Otis flatly. "Crazy."

Leana stared at Rychur who was still eating and refilling his plate. He seemed to enjoy the potatoes and watermelon more than anything else. The tension between her father and Rychur was beginning to stress her out.

"You don't see it?" she asked Rychur. She received a blank stare. "Seriously?! You're from *outer space* and you're sitting there scarfing down *earth* food. We're not scared of you and you aren't scared of this, or us..." she wanted a real response from Rychur or Otis. "Oh come on!" she exclaimed.

She grabbed her fork and held it up. "Fine," she said, focusing on her food since that's what the men were doing. Abruptly, a rare moment of clarity clunked into place in her mind. She felt focused, full of curiosity and adventure. She suddenly didn't want to just sit on a farm all weekend. She wanted more. She thought about all the nights she had looked up at the stars, longing to escape from normal life. Now, in this impossible situation she had an alien from the stars with a spaceship who crash-landed practically in her lap. Maybe fate was finally on her side.

Leana watched as Esu emerged from the kitchen and processed the tension at the table. "Having difficulties getting along?"

"Please," groaned Leana. "The adults are boring and grumpy."

"We're fine, Esu," replied Otis with a stern voice.

"Oh you are?" the android asked, obviously not believing a word. Leana could tell Otis' comment had just upset Esu.

"If you were *fine* then you wouldn't be tarnishing my meal with your tainted rudeness and taciturn social skills. And in front of guests! Smile and converse or—or no dessert!" He whirled back into the kitchen. Leana could hear him muttering to himself as the door closed. "Biologicals... so emotional!"

Justin and Annette looked at each other puzzled, and then at everyone else at the table.

"What was that?" asked Annette, gesturing at the kitchen door.

"Esu calculates, recognizes and processes emotions," stated Otis, "so he's responding emotionally in a manner in which he feels appropriate. To be more 'human' around humans."

The teenagers continued to look at him with wide eyes.

He smiled. "Okay, yes, I can see how that was unexpected."

"No kidding." stated Leana. "Does he usually respond like that?"

"Umm... Depending on the situation, yes?" Otis said uncertain. "Why?"

"Esu is an emotional stabilizer unit. If there are negative emotions occurring in his general location, then it is his job to confront the issue in a manner that resolves the conflict. He's supposed to constructively respond to conflicting emotions in order to put out the fire. He doesn't always get it right."

"Wow... I don't like it," stated Leana. "It's like having another parent around."

"Yeah," agreed Justin.

Annette nodded.

"I did," spoke up Rychur.

Leana and her friends stared silently at Rychur.

"Well, his programming is useful," Rychur continued cautiously, "I mean, look, we're talking again."

"Good point," said Justin.

"So, um ... Rychur," stammered Leana, anxious to keep the

138

conversation from dying again. "Do you have any family like a brother, sister, parents?"

He sat back with a heavy smile on his face. Leana knew right away this was a painful question. "No," he said softly then added, "not anymore."

Leana stared at him, hoping that she hadn't said the wrong thing... again.

"They're dead." Rychur added solemnly.

Leana was instantly filled with guilt. "Oh, no. I'm so sorry. I didn't mean..." She clenched her jaw as tight as she could to stop herself from saying anything else stupid. She felt like she couldn't stop triggering something the alien didn't want to talk about. She cursed her big mouth.

"It's alright. It was a long time ago and I grieved their passing as a son and brother should have. It's not your fault. Death is inevitable."

Leana allowed a cautious smile.

"They were very good," Rychur continued.

"Who were?" asked Annette.

"My mother, my father," he said looking at Otis, "and my sister," he added, looking over at Leana and the other two.

"What were they like?" Leana asked curious.

"Leana," Otis interjected.

"It's okay, Otis. I don't mind." Rychur said looking down and smiling to himself.

Rychur set down his silverware and laid his napkin next to his plate. He laid his wrists on the table and relaxed his shoulders. "I haven't spoken about my family for many years. And to think, here I am talking to people from a different world about them." Rychur readjusted in his seat, sitting up slightly with a sudden boost of energy. "You know, the first time I let myself think about my sister in years was when I saw you at my ship," he said, looking at Leana. "In the confusion of the crash, I actually thought you were her."

"So she was a dirty, scrawny, scared chick?" Annette joked.

"She was incredibly faultless, just like the two I came from."

"His parents," added Otis.

"Yeah, I know," replied Leana, shushing him right away.

"My father was a warrior, as was my mother. They were both honorable and merciful. My sister, Na'ala, was very innocent. She loved to play and she smiled at everyone, and was never allowed anywhere close to a battlefield."

"Na'ala. That's a pretty name," Annette said, her head leaning to the side and smiling at Rychur.

"Named after one of the first of our bloodline," he said proudly.

Leana noticed Otis fidgeting in his seat as he kept eating, staring down at his food. She wondered if war being brought up triggered things inside of him. "You okay?" she asked gently.

"Yeah. Just hungry." he said without looking at her.

She knew he was lying because he'd only been picking at his food for the past several minutes. Leana looked back at Rychur. "Can I ask what happened to them?"

"They were killed in a genocide in our quadrant. I tried to save my sister, but failed. She died much too young. I should have died along with her, but somehow I didn't." Rychur's face revealed no emotion. "When you appeared by my side, the look on your face, the innocence, it reminded me of her. I had to touch your neck to be sure I wasn't dead."

"Why her neck?" Justin asked.

"Because she had a scar," he gestured his finger from his ear to clavicle, "she got in an accident when she was very little."

Leana's heart felt like breaking. *How does he keep himself together?*

CHAPTER 19

As everyone finished up their dinner, Leana thought about how the alien sitting next to her was some kind of warrior from his world. She wanted to ask him so many questions, but she figured she'd have more time for that later tonight. She could see how uneasy her father was with all the questions.

She stared at the final bite on her plate and patted her stomach. "I don't think I can finish this." She took the last cut of meat off her plate and held it out. "Justin? Annette, want it?"

Justin shook his head as he leaned back in his chair patting his own stomach while Annette groaned and held up her hands, declining. Leana lowered her hand to give it to El. The wolf wasn't there.

"El? Come here, girl." Leana looked under the table. "Where'd she go?"

"I thought she was right next to you," Otis mumbled from within his mug.

"So did I."

Crashing metal rang in the kitchen, drawing everyone's attention to the door.

"El, no! Give that back!" yelled Esu.

Bursting through the door, El darted behind Otis with a large, roasted chicken in her mouth. Closely behind her sprang Esu, covered with soup and flour.

"You always do this to me, El. Now it's ruined!" pronounced Esu as he threw up his hands in defeat.

For Esu's sake, Leana tried holding in her laughter as she watched El lie down next to Otis and gnaw at the freshly cooked chicken. She growled in obvious pleasure at the juicy, flavored meat. Leana couldn't help grinning at the wolf's cheeky behavior.

"It's going to be okay, Esu. Just cook the other one, and I'll take it to the veterans in the morning," said Otis as he rubbed the wolf's head.

Esu stood upright and smiled. "Of course. I forgot the other chicken! Thank you. I'll get right to it." With a spring in his step, Esu went back to the kitchen, but not before shooting a final glare at the happy canine.

Otis looked around the table at his guests. "This is why I always buy more than one," he chuckled. "She loves Esu, but she loves messing with him even more. Don't you, girl?"

El continued chomping away at the chicken, her tail thumping the ground. Chicken juice coated her front paws.

Rychur began chuckling and Leana couldn't hold it in anymore. She let out a hearty laugh. "Oh my god, are they *always* like this?" Her laugh spread to her friends whose faces were already beet red from holding in their laughter.

"Pretty much. Those two squabble like siblings, but it's all in fun… I think," Otis responded.

Rychur leaned towards Leana, still smiling, his elbow on the table. "The closest thing we have back home to a creature like El is called a Croalack, but those aren't as, um, pleasant to be around as El is."

Leana noted Rychur giving a quick shudder. Her curiosity got the better of her. "Why's that?" she asked.

"Well, they excrete fluids all over their bodies when they're happy. Damp fur, soaked nostrils, and they stink. It's disgusting, but they are very cute and very gentle. They wouldn't hurt a fly."

"Aw, that's sweet… but gross. No, thank you," Annette chimed in.

"Agreed. I'll stick with the chicken-stealing wolf," said Justin.

Leana stared at her father as he looked down petting El. She was beginning to understand just how lonely he would've been without El or Esu. "You have good companions, Dad."

Seeing him smile at her words lifted a heavy weight within Leana. She was beginning to think that a relationship with him might be possible. She wanted to let go of the last thirteen years; she wanted to forgive him. Leana realized that she related to his struggles of feeling alone. She felt suddenly selfish to have thought she was alone when she'd always had her mother and he had nobody. Even though El and Esu were great, they weren't exactly a wife and daughter. These feelings surprised her.

For a moment, she felt she could have a father again, or even more importantly, a Dad. She looked at Annette who was giving her a supportive smile and thumbs up.

Rychur politely set down his spoon next to his empty plate. "Leana, what is your talent?"

The question caught Leana off guard. "Umm… What? What do you mean?"

"Well, I know what your father is good at and I know what your friends are good at, but I still know very little about you."

"Oh, well… I, uh, I'm good at soccer."

"Soccer. What is—"

Otis grunted, gaining Leana's attention. "That reminds me. I never got around to asking. How did your game go?"

"Um… Well," she hesitated, "we lost." This was the last place she wanted this conversation to go right now.

"Too bad! How did *you* play?" he asked.

She slouched deep into her chair. "I… don't necessarily want to talk about it."

"Why not?"

Leana sighed and looked pleadingly at her friends, hoping they'd help her out, but they were now avoiding eye contact. *Thanks, guys.* She took a deep breath. "I played pretty well, actually." She hoped answering at least part of his question would suffice.

"Good. Did the game start early or something?" her father continued to ask.

"No, why?"

"Because you got here nearly an hour earlier than we expected."

"Oh…" she didn't want to say anything more. She looked over at Rychur, hoping to change subjects. "How was your—"

"Leana," interrupted Otis, his face now obviously concerned. "What happened?"

"I don't want to talk about it."

"Why not?"

"Because I don't know how you'll feel about it. You might freak."

"Okay." Otis nodded. "But if you want to start trusting me then you have to start somewhere," he said assuringly. "Try me. And what's with you thinking I'm going to *freak* out?"

Justin snorted and Otis shot him a hard look.

"Fine," she said, sitting upright and resting her elbows on the table as if to brace herself for a negative response. "I slapped a girl unconscious because she broke my friend's ankle. I didn't start it, she did." She paused only to receive more silence. "I don't know what came over me, but I just hit her." She sighed hard, feeling her cheeks flush with nerves. She could tell her friends were tense as they waited to see Leana's father react.

Otis paused for a moment. "Okay."

Leana was taken aback. "That's it?"

"Well, I thought something *bad* happened," Otis said nonchalantly.

"It *did*, Dad. I hurt someone." She didn't know why she needed to explain this to her father.

Otis looked at her plainly. "But you didn't intend to."

"It didn't stop me from doing it, though."

"Sometimes, you can only be pushed so far, Leana, before you lose control."

"What do you mean?"

Otis looked at Rychur without answering.

"What?" Leana asked.

"The globe…" Rychur said.

"Oh," she said, dragging out the word. "Yeah, okay. So, you understand."

"I do," Otis said smiling.

His smile calmed the tension she was feeling. "I do understand. I have lost control like that… at least once."

Leana could see out of her peripheral vision Rychur's head dropping, but she didn't pay much attention. "Thanks for not being angry with me."

"What matters most is how you felt afterwards."

"Ashamed?"

He chuckled. "There is no shame in protecting a teammate and friend."

"Then how should I feel?" she continued to ask. Her two surprised friends kept looking back-and-forth between her and Otis.

"Regret would work," Otis said with a dip in his voice.

"Why? How is that different?"

"Because having that compunction for your wrongfulness reflects character."

Leana sighed. "I don't get what that means."

"You don't?"

"Not really," she said, lifting her eyebrows in embarrassment and shrugging.

"You reacted out of leadership. Do I agree you should always use violence? No. Perhaps, it could have been dealt with in another way, but I *do* understand the position you were put in. Sometimes certain people only respond to pain. It's not an easy choice to make."

She was starting to see what her mother might have seen in Otis. This was a side she didn't know existed… an empathetic side. "So…" she hesitated, "you're not mad then?"

"No, of course not. I get it."

She looked down at the table, confused and relieved. "Wow, okay."

"But do you understand what I said to you?"

"About acting like a leader? I think so, yeah," she replied.

Rychur slid his hand towards Leana. "No, you didn't *act* like a leader. You *became* a leader."

Strangely, Rychur's words struck her deep.

"He's right, Leana. Anyone can become a team captain or mascot or boss or chief, but *you*," Otis said with pride, "proved what it took to be a leader. You stood up for someone who was hurt badly by a tyrant."

"Thank you," she said shyly. She looked down, feeling the warmth on her cheeks. Justin's comforting look gave her relief that he was in agreement with the other two.

"What's soccer?" Rychur asked in the silence.

Leana chuckled, as did the others.

"A sport, Rychur." Leana took in his blank stare. "You know what a sport is, right?"

He shook his head.

"Well, I guess that makes sense. He didn't know about gymnastics or boxing either," Justin added.

"Rychur," said Otis. "A sport is a game of competition."

"Ah, a game! I understand now. Balachur also has games."

Leana saw Otis' eyes turn strangely cold. "They do? Like what?" she asked.

"We call them the 'Blood Games.'"

"Whoa..." she hesitated, "meaning what?"

"Games of combat. Four armies, each led by their king, battle each other in a designated battlefield. The last army left with their king standing, rules Balachur for a cycle."

"You mean like virtual combat?"

"I don't know that term, but combat, yes."

"Wait, wait, wait," interjected Annette. "No one *actually* dies in these games do they? Like it's not actual blood, right?"

He gave her a puzzled look. "Hundreds upon thousands die."

Leana stared, her jaw open. "Nuh-uh. That's probably the most ridiculous thing I've ever heard. You're making that up." Otis glared at her. "What? Oh come on, Dad, you don't actually believe this do you?"

Before he could respond, Rychur interrupted, "Why?"

"Well, because... I just think..." She was convinced he was joking. "You aren't serious, Rychur." She looked at her friends. "You don't believe this do you?"

"Leana, why wouldn't I be?"

"Because it's brutal," her voice trailed off weakly.

"Yes, but it's a sport... like yours; interesting, competitive, meant to defeat others through skill, strength, cunning and will-power."

"No, Rychur!" she exclaimed. "We don't *kill* people. Everyone is left standing at the end of our games, we stay alive, we don't kill—"

"Rychur," interrupted Otis. "Here, it isn't those types of games. Here, sports focus on teamwork through... aggressive, but non-violent skills and strategies to challenge and overcome the opponent. The sports and games here aren't as bloody and *pointless* as they are where you come from."

Leana flinched at the emphasis on "pointless." It was one of the harshest tones she'd heard her dad use yet.

Leana could tell the conversation was more or less over as Rychur responded with a succinct, "Okay, thank you. I understand now."

"Good," Otis responded. He leaned back and looked toward the kitchen door. "Esu!" he yelled a little louder than necessary.

Out popped Esu. "Yes? Everything splendid?"

"Yes, Esu. We just wanted to say thank you. The meal was wonderful."

Esu smiled ear-to-ear, "Wonderful? Well, thank you." He gave a quick bow then quickly and happily cleared the rest of the table.

"He smiled," said Justin, still obviously taken aback by the robot's abilities.

"Of course he did," responded Otis.

"It's creepy," Annette added.

"He wanted it," replied Otis. "He said it made him look more personable."

Leana waited for Esu to head back behind the kitchen door, and then slowly addressed Otis, "He's very overly, outwardly, emotional… in a good way. Are you sure this isn't just how you programmed him?"

"Not at all. As I said before, he has developed emotionally, very like a human would. If you treat Esu well, then he'll treat you even better."

"Like a friend," Rychur said warmly.

Otis nodded. Standing up from his chair, he threw the napkin from his lap onto the table, his demeanor instantly serious. He looked at the teens. "It's been a long day and I want you getting some rest." He then looked at Rychur. "We all need some rest."

"But, Dad—"

"Nope, no arguments. If you want to stay up the rest of the night that's fine, but you'll be staying in your room."

Otis looked at Rychur. "Your ship is in the back section of the red barn. There's a rear door that's unlocked. I've prepared a tent, food and water in case you need something late tonight. That's where you'll be staying."

"Dad!" Leana exclaimed, surprised by his curt tone.

"If you need anything I will be in my office. Esu will also be available all night."

"Dad?!"

Otis ignored her. "You have five minutes to get to your bed." He looked at Rychur. "That includes you."

"Dad!"

Otis darted his eyes at his daughter. "What?!"

"What about my friends," she asked, gesturing at Justin and Annette.

"Oh, sorry. Annette can stay with you," he answered, nodding his head.

"I assumed," Leana replied.

"Where do you want me, Mr. Rayne?" asked Justin.

Otis pointed behind Justin. "You can sleep on the couch right there. Esu will bring you blankets. And don't think I can't hear every move you make."

"Oh… okay," Justin stuttered.

Otis turned to leave the dining room.

Leana stood up, completely irritated. "Wait… can't I see the ship?"

"No!" Otis yelled from the living room.

"Tomorrow?"

There was a short pause. "Maybe. Tomorrow."

Justin and Annette smiled excitedly.

She listened to the feet stomp down the hall. "Thank you!" she yelled back gleefully.

Rychur leaned forward. "Why do you want to see the ship again? It looks the same as the last time. Wrecked and ruined."

"Yeah, but even though we saw it crash, I was too freaked to take a really good look."

"I see. Tomorrow it is then."

Leana grinned. "This is going to be totally nitro."

Rychur stuck out his arm, "You've used that word numerous times, and with much enthusiasm. How would you measure the meaning of that word?"

"Measure?" Justin looked confused.

"Um, I don't know," Leana responded as she sat back in her chair. "Fantastic, awesome, great, cool, I guess?"

Rychur stared blankly at her.

"Okay. Well, what's the greatest thing *you* could ever think of?"

"From my world?" he asked.

"From your world."

Leana watched Rychur pause and look past her while lost in thought for a moment. "When the Balachurian suns and moons align perfectly once every cycle the sky becomes filled with unimaginable colors, capturing an infinite, dark mystery which can be clearly seen from nearly everywhere on Balachur."

Leana paused, staring at him wide-eyed. "Umm, yeah. It's like that… Sort of. When I say 'nitro,' that's the feeling I get when I say it, except we don't have anything that cool sun-and-moon-wise. It's just something great that happens which makes me feel even better. Understand?"

"I believe I do."

Leana pushed her chair away and started to leave the table before stopping to turn around. "Oh, one other thing. What's a cycle?"

"It compares to one hundred of your earth years," he said with ease in his voice. "I've only witnessed the change of the cycle once. It'll be quite some time before I see the next one."

147

"Wait, what? How old are you *exactly*?" Annette asked.

"In earth years... approximately forty years old."

"What?!" exclaimed the two girls.

Leana's jaw dropped.

"You look good for an old guy," commented Annette.

Leana laughed in agreement. "Yeah, you definitely don't look forty."

Justin clenched his jaw and rolled his eyes at the comment.

"Okay... so tomorrow. See you then." Leana stood up, dragging Annette from her chair. "Come on, El!" she called. She looked at Justin and winked as she left the dining room. "Goodnight, Justin."

Justin waved slightly. "Goodnight—"

El burst out from under the dining table with the final chicken leg hanging from her mouth, almost knocking Justin off his chair. Rychur followed Leana, stopping at the front door at the base of the stairs. Leana caught Rychur's eye as he opened the door to step outside. She was happy he was here. She didn't know if it was because she had saved him, helped heal him, or because she reminded him of his sister. Leana only knew that tomorrow was going to be another exciting day. She was going to be one of the first people on earth to touch a space ship.

Esu returned to the dining room and threw his hands up. "You must be kidding me. El!"

Leana peered around the banister and saw a pile of bones and chicken skin. Esu shook his head. "Justin, you'll have to wait to sleep until I clean up this mess."

Leana saw Rychur laugh and they exchanged a smile as he paused on the threshold. "He's lost his circuits again," she said laughing as she turned to head back up the stairs behind Annette.

She heard Rychur mutter "What a funny world" before shutting the front door behind him.

Goodnight, my new friend from Balachur.

CHAPTER 20

Up the stairs and down the quiet hall the old wooden floorboards creaked as Leana and Annette made their way to her bedroom. This time Leana left the door open as an invitation for El to sleep in the room with them that night. They were both in desperate need of a shower since they had spent nearly the entire day in outfits coated with dirt, dry blood, and sweat.

Today probably shouldn't have been her idea of a good time, but Leana was surprised to realize it was possibly the greatest day of her life. After assuring Annette it was safe to be left alone with El, Leana threw a towel over her shoulder and carried her pajamas to the bathroom. In the peace and quiet of the small, tiled room, Leana's mind raced, thinking of the unbelievable events that had occurred in the last twenty-four hours.

The setting of the sun had been evidence enough that the hours of the day had really passed, that this wasn't all a dream, yet it still seemed surreal to her. She wondered if any of the day's events had been possible.

The water from the shower ran through her dark, curly hair, washing her body clean of dirt and blood. She relaxed as the warmth eased her stressed muscles. She was grateful for the help as she wasn't very good at relaxing on her own.

Standing still under the running shower with her eyes closed, her mind filled with more questions. She began processing through the events one-by-one. Her first kiss with Justin, the fight with her dad, the crash, an alien eating dinner with them; it was all so unreal. This was the sort of thing she saw in books, movies, or those fake newspapers. She couldn't help but wonder what tomorrow would bring; sleep was the last thing on her mind. She thought about the kiss; her first kiss. She never imagined it happening on a farm of all places. Especially not her dad's farm. She knew Emily would think it was a fairy tale moment and would totally flip, but Leana still wasn't sure how she felt about it herself. She had expected to feel something deeper, but instead it had felt kind of strange, like an experiment. She wasn't sure if the kiss had made her feel closer to Justin, or further away.

El hadn't moved from her spot at the door as Leana made her way back into her room. She draped her wet towel over a chair then looked at her arm, which felt naked without her phone on it.

"Your turn, Annette," Leana said, rubbing her wrists. "Did you find some clothes in my bag?"

"Yeah, thanks," Annette replied, carrying a towel and clothes with her to the bathroom. She gave El a wide berth as the wolf lifted her head to watch her pass. "Easy, girl," she muttered nervously.

"Oh my god, just go!" Leana demanded, laughing softly.

Leana felt the cold wood on the palm of her hand as she braced herself on the dresser, bending down and smelling the day old rose in its vase. The scent was still sweet but faded, and she was met with an unfamiliar disappointment when she realized she would miss this when she left the farm.

Leana plopped down at the end of her bed, her legs swinging just an inch above the ground. She looked around the room, noticing how homey it all looked with the moonlight coming through the window. Sighing deeply, Leana fell back and listened to the soothing sound of running water coming from the bathroom. She was anxious for Annette to hurry up so they could discuss the day. Finally, some excitement was happening in her life, and here she was stuck in her bedroom. She felt like she was grounded.

"I'm *so* bored now," she groaned. She turned her head to the door. "El, come here," she encouraged, holding out her hand.

Leana laughed as El cautiously took a step into the doorway, but stepped back, sitting on her haunches. "Come on, El. What are you doing?"

El whimpered uncomfortably and wagged her tail on the floor.

"Fine. Well, at least you can sleep in the doorway tonight where I can see you." She smiled as El lay down.

She got up, feeling the carpet press between her toes as she made her way to the doorway. She bent down and patted the beast who already had her head lying on her paws.

"Goodnight, wolfie," she whispered. She flipped the light switch then walked back to the bed and sprawled out. Bright light illuminated the bedroom.

Annette emerged from the bathroom; her shirt wet in spots, especially where her wet dreads hung.

"That was fast." Leana observed, looking up.

"Well, I didn't bring a razor and it's not like I do my hair every day," she said, throwing her towel on the ground and crawling in bed on the opposite side from El. "Move over," she demanded.

"Annette, you are ridiculous. El's not going to hurt you, or she would have by now."

"I know, I'm just not ready to get close. That's all," Annette said comfortably.

"Whatever."

Leana crawled under the covers and rolled over to face Annette, grabbing her hand. They smiled at each other. "I'm really glad you stayed," Leana said.

"Me too, Ana. This was a crazy sparklin' day!"

Leana sighed, looking past Annette.

"You're thinking about him, aren't you?"

Leana gave a wry smile. "Thinking about who?"

Annette stared. "Yeah," she said quietly, rolling onto her back and letting go of Leana's hand.

Leana didn't want to admit that Rychur was the guy she'd been thinking about, but she knew her friend was referring to Justin. "Annette, don't be like that."

"Like what?" she snipped.

"Like *that*. Please, don't shut down."

Annette laid still, looking out the window at the moon.

"Please, talk to me." Leana waited patiently, knowing her best friend was hurt. "Please?" she begged softly.

"It's this thing between you and Justin..." Annette hesitated.

"What about it?" Leana was a bit relieved her friend didn't mention Rychur.

It's just that... I don't want to lose you," Annette said softly.

"You won't."

"I'm sorry, Ana. I really am happy for you." Annette's voice cracked.

Leana pursed her lips. "There's nothing you have to be 'happy' about. We're not a thing, Annette. Nothing's changed."

Annette's eyebrows raised and she snorted. "I'll bet Justin doesn't see it that way."

"He's my friend. I'm sure he understands."

"Yeah, maybe I'm just being dramatic," Annette said, looking again. "I'm sorry."

Leana crawled closely and hugged her friend tight. "You don't have to be sorry. I love you, Annette. You are my best friend."

"I love you too, Ana."

"Everything is going to be okay. I promise," Leana said comfortingly.

Reassured that her friend was feeling better, she rolled back, reaching to grab the cold, metal watch off the side table. The moonlight radiating through her window shone on the intricate designs as she rubbed the watch between her fingers. She thought about her father. *Maybe I held onto this for so long because I hoped it wasn't over between us. Maybe there's still a chance.*

On impulse, she kissed the watch then set it back on the side table. She lay still for a while, looking at it in the silver light. Her thoughts finally wandered beyond today and into the coming night. Her smile left her face.

Even with her friend by her side, Leana was afraid to fall asleep.

CHAPTER 21

I felt petrified of the dark. From the sound of my own whimpering, I knew I was a very young child, hiding in the pitch-blackness. I couldn't tell where I was, but I knew there were others yelling above me. I felt as though I was trapped underground. I was tense and frightened, but there was an older boy and girl with me, trying to keep me calm and quiet. The fear and sadness coursing through my body overwhelmed me. The boy put his hand on my chest while the girl stroked my head. Their touch was so loving. I felt safe. Somehow I knew they were my brother and sister. He was visibly much older than her, but I wasn't sure of their ages or mine.

Why was I so terrified?

My chest was sore as my breathing became heavier and heavier. The pounding noises over our heads were getting more violent and causing dust to fall from the barrier above. They were trying to keep me calm, but it wasn't helping. I wanted to scream and cry. I opened my mouth but my brother's big hand covered it to stop me. He whispered something, but I couldn't hear what he was saying because my attention was focused up above me.

THUD -- THUD

I looked up only to catch dust in my eyes. I cried into my brother's hand and rubbed them hard which only made it worse. I couldn't see anything.

Then I heard my sister shushing me lovingly. She stood up slightly over me as I laid there helpless. Through my tears I could see her face was full of love, but also terror and determination as well. As she whispered something I couldn't understand, a familiar glow faintly appeared from her hands and her eyes.

I could see her face more clearly now. She was so pretty. Her hair was long and flat. She was wearing a gold crown that came to a point in the middle of her forehead. I could see a small scar on the right side of her cheek. Still, the scar didn't take away from how pretty she was. She wore it with pride.

I watched her claw her fingers into the ground, picking up a handful of dirt. She opened her fingers as the dirt rested in her palm. The underground room lit up more as the boy's hands and eyes also began glowing the same color. He had short dark hair, and I couldn't help but notice his ears stuck out a little too much. Just seeing their faces brought comfort to the child's body I was in.

He raised his hand above the dirt in our sister's hand, closing his eyes. For a moment, it was quiet and nothing happened. Then slowly, the glowing haze descended down on the dirt, swirling around the girl's palm. The dirt began to shake and quiver. She smiled at me as I watched the dirt turn into different shapes. He made it twirl like a tornado, and then it melted flat and sprang up like a mountain. Then somehow the dirt was dancing in the shape of a beautiful woman.

Happiness filled me. I laughed. Suddenly their eyes grew wide and the pink from their hands disappeared. Darkness took over again. I felt a hand cover my mouth tightly. I could barely breathe. The yelling had stopped above us. Had they heard me? What was happening?

A woman screamed and there was more scuffling. I felt nauseas and weak. After a moment, everything was quiet again. I thought maybe they had finally left.

The metal door directly above us swung open violently and fear jolted through my body. Two black figures stood above us. One reached down and squeezed my arm. It hurt. The pain was almost too much to bear as I was yanked upward. I screamed in utter terror.

Leana shook violently as the fear from the dream coursed through her. Her chest rose and fell as she tried to breathe. She sat up quickly sucking desperately at the air around her. Like nearly every other nightmare she had woken from, her skin was heavy with sweat and her sheets soaked.

A hand grabbed onto Leana's arm, causing her to pull away in panic, almost falling off the other end of the bed.

"Hey, hey. It's me."

"Mom?!" Leana exclaimed.

"It's okay. I'm here, honey." Danielle sat at Leana's bedside. She leaned in and hugged the perplexed teen. For a moment, Leana still wasn't sure if this was another dream or if it was real.

Leana threw her arms around her mother's neck, crying softly. "Mom," she whimpered.

"You're okay, baby girl. You're safe." Danielle returned the tight squeeze.

Leana stayed in her mother's arms. Apparently, last night had been a fluke. The nightmares weren't going away as she'd hoped. She could see, feel, and touch everything in the dreams like they were actually happening. It terrified her.

"What are—what are you doing here?" Leana asked confused.

"When our call cut out yesterday, I got worried. I had to be sure you were okay." She placed her hand on Leana's knee. "I felt that you needed me here."

"Oh, yeah." Leana had completely forgotten about the dropped call. "I'm glad you're here."

While trying to find comfort in the safety of her mother's arms all Leana could think about was the overwhelming fear the child in her dream had felt. She couldn't understand why that fear was lingering even after waking up. *What's happening to me?*

"They're not getting better, Mom." Leana was tired; tired of rarely sleeping a full night, tired of always being scared to even attempt to go to sleep. She didn't know what she would've done if her mother hadn't been here to help her right now. As her breath slowed, the dream and the emotions began fading. She breathed deep. "Thank you."

"For what?" Danielle rubbed Leana's back.

"For coming here." She sniffled hard and caught the scent of a new rose on her dresser. She looked over surprised. "When did that get here?"

"The rose? Your father brought it. He left you a rose every morning up until..." Danielle rubbed Leana's back a little more.

"Wait... Morning? I slept till the morning?" She finally took note of the early morning light and Annette's empty spot in the bed. "I can't remember the last time I've slept this long."

"That's good, honey. You feeling better?"

Leana sniffled again and cleared her throat. "Yeah. I think so. I just needed to cry a little bit I guess." She and her mother shared a wry smile.

"Do you remember anything?"

Leana sat there looking at her mother. "No, not now."

"Well, it's nice to be able to actually *be* here for you..."

"Yeah..." Leana's eyes were closed as she soaked up her mom's soothing presence. Realizing the silence meant her mother was waiting for more of a reply, Leana looked up at her. "Oh, yeah. Sorry." Danielle laughed as Leana hugged her again.

"I'm just glad you didn't have the door locked."

"So... What did Dad say about you coming?"

"He was fine with it. He's downstairs helping Ryder—"

"Rychur," interrupted Leana. It felt strange that her mother had already met him. She had so much to fill her in about the crash landing of an alien who was apparently somewhere in the house. Not to mention getting her first kiss from Justin. This was by far the strangest weekend of her life.

"Sorry... Helping *Rychur* with something."

"He's kind of cool, huh?" Leana grinned.

"He's definitely fascinating, and definitely cute." Danielle chuckled, a twinkle in her eye.

"Mom!" exclaimed Leana.

A whining noise came from El in the hallway as she waited patiently outside Leana's door. For a brief second, Leana had wondered how Annette had managed to sneak past the wolf.

Leana grunted. "I love El. She's just awesome." She peered over her mother's shoulder to peer into the hallway. "I love you, El."

Danielle shook her head with a smile on her face. "I know. You don't see wolves like her anymore except in lessons at school and in museums. It's so sad that they're all gone."

"They aren't *all* gone, Mom. She's still here."

"True, but she's the last of her species as far as we know. Strange how life changes so fast."

"You're telling me."

"Yeah." Danielle slapped her legs and stood up. "So, you get up and get ready. I'm only here for a few hours, so get moving. I'll see you downstairs in a few minutes."

"What's the rush?"

"Breakfast. Everyone is down there waiting." Danielle left the room, patting the wolf as she passed. "Good morning, El." She headed towards the stairs down the hall, calling over her shoulder. "And hurry up, Ana. I'm hungry."

Leana's furry friend responded with a whine. The wolf had barely left Leana's side since she arrived. She didn't mind, although Leana didn't understand why El wasn't downstairs watching Rychur, a stranger to the house, instead of being so interested in her.

Leana walked over to the rose in the vase, inhaling the sweet scent. This was at least one thing she liked about her father. There was a gentle side to him that she had gotten to experience two mornings in a row now. *At least he's got one redeeming quality.*

Grabbing her towel, she stepped into the bathroom, closing the door as El whimpered for attention. She turned on the shower and waited for the water to warm up. The steam rose from behind the curtain as she stared at herself in the mirror. She could feel the warmth in the air. Looking at herself, she realized something in her reflection had shifted. Flashes of last night's dream flickered across the mirror surface. The person Leana was looking at seemed different than before. Something had changed in her, and Leana could see it in her haunted eyes. Was it real or another twisted part of her imagination? And why did it seem to be getting worse?

She turned away in frustration, stepping into the shower. She wanted a normal life like all the other kids in her school seemed to have. She wanted to play soccer, go to college, hang with friends, and everything else a girl her age should be doing. She thought of the way Justin's kiss and Annette's reaction. She wondered if it was going to change things. They'd all been friends for so long. She thought of the stranger who had crash-landed in the forest and how she had been one of the people to pull him from the wreckage. Thinking about Rychur confused her even more than thinking about Justin. She thought about the gray wolf that had hardly left her side. And she thought about her father who had invited her to his home to help her, but was still keeping his distance. Why was all this happening to her?

CHAPTER 22

After a quick shower, Leana made her way back to her room wrapped in her towel. She was greeted by a playful yelp as she made her way to her travel bag; El hadn't moved from the doorway.

She could feel the fresh morning air sneak in through the window, chilling the skin not covered by her towel. El's head turned quickly to look down the hallway, and then back at her. Not thinking anything of it Leana began to remove her towel just as Esu stepped into her room. "Leana, are you—"

"Esu!" yelled Leana. She quickly rewrapped the towel around herself. "Get out! Now!"

"I'm sorry." Esu backed up slowly into the hall, but continued to face her. El yipped in pain as she tried pulling her tail out from underneath Esu's foot.

"Oh, apologies, El," he said, lifting his leg.

"Close your eyes! Don't look at me! Shut the door!"

Esu stood there unfazed by the situation. "Even if I 'close my eyes'," Esu made air quotes, "my sensors will still know you are 12 feet in front of me. What is the purpose of obstructing my view of you at this time?"

Not bothering to explain, Leana marched towards the door. "Knock next time."

"How do I knock—" Leana interrupted him by slamming the door in his face.

She sighed and shook her head. "Unbelievable." Walking back to the bed, there was a knock. "Seriously?!"

She opened the door a crack. "What, Esu?"

"Breakfast is ready. Your mother told me to tell you…" His voice tone changed to a recording of Danielle speaking but Esu's lips were still moving. "*She needs to hurry up. The food's getting cold and I'm hungry.*"

Leana was taken aback. "What… Did you just… Okay, fine. Just go somewhere else."

"Certainly." He turned to head back downstairs.

"And Esu?"

He turned around at the top stair.

"Don't ever do that imitation voice thing again, please. It's really creepy."

"Of course."

Leana watched Esu proceed down the stairs. She noticed El staring up at her. "So awkward." She closed the door.

CHAPTER 23

Leana bounded down the stairs with El closely behind. In the living room, Rychur was sitting on the couch, still wearing the same clothing as yesterday. On the table in front of him was a blue, holographic image of a spaceship. It hovered inches above his white coffee cup. She walked over to him, curious to see what he was doing.

He spun the holo with his finger, zooming in and out, as though looking for something specific. There were flashing red highlights on different parts of the ship. Whenever Rychur touched the spots, texts popped up, but Leana was unable to read the foreign letters.

El darted past her into the kitchen.

There was a coffee pot, nearly empty, sitting on the table next to Rychur's cup. She noticed his hand shake as he reached up to move the hologram.

"What are you doing?" Leana asked, peering over his shoulder. On the image of the ship she could see that the hull looked damaged. There was a lot of red flashing on that section.

"This is my ship. I'm examining the parts that were most damaged." He kept his eyes on the hologram. He continued spinning the image, expanding parts of the ship and touching red spots. He zoomed in and out quickly as he worked with practiced ease. At times, he held his breath or sighed, seemingly becoming more and more dejected as nearly each blue spot he touched flashed to red.

"Looks like a lot of damage." Leana's eyes had trouble keeping up with Rychur's movements. She wanted to ask him more about the ship and where he'd come from, but he didn't seem to be paying her much attention.

"Indeed," he said distractedly.

"Can you fix it?" By this time, about half of the ship was highlighted.

Rychur rubbed his forehead. "Not all of it. But I'm hoping I can fix the most important parts to at least get her back into flying shape."

"Her?"

"Yes, my ship. Na'ala. I named her after my sister."

Leana felt a flash of guilt for bringing up his sister again, knowing it had to be a sensitive topic for him. "Good name."

"I thought so too. You better go eat. Maybe later I can show you more."

"And you'll tell me more about where you come from?" she asked. Leana was curious to learn as much as she could before he had to leave.

Rychur nodded then looked towards the dining room.

Leana turned around to see her parents and friends talking and laughing at the dining room table. This was a side of her parents she'd never seen and it felt so foreign. At the same time, it was good to see them laughing.

"Finally," gasped Justin, spotting her. "I'm hungry."

"Took you long enough," added Annette.

"Thank god you all survived," Leana joked. She looked back at Rychur. "You coming?"

He kept his eye on the ship and lifted his coffee cup at Leana, his hand still shaky. "No need," he said quickly. "This drink will suffice."

Smiling, Leana walked to the dining room. *This could be weird.*

"Good morning." Leana sat down across from Otis and between Justin and Danielle.

"Morning," greeted Otis.

"Hey, baby girl," Danielle said cheerfully. "Hope you're hungry."

"Always." Leana chugged down her orange juice, and then layered her plate with Esu's perfectly scrambled eggs, toast, and sliced fruit. She paused and looked up, her hand still holding a spoonful of hash browns. "You guys not eating?"

Otis sipped his coffee. "Already did."

"We waited, Ana," interjected Annette.

"Leana," Danielle said, "it's 10 o'clock. Your friends have been waiting for almost an hour for you to get ready."

"Oh." Leana didn't realize she'd taken so long. "Sorry, guys."

"Once you get done, I thought we three could spend some time together while I'm here? Go into town—" Danielle started, but Leana interrupted.

"Oh, uh, I kind of have plans." She had better things to do like helping an alien work on a spaceship. She didn't want to leave her friends with all the fun stuff to go hang with her parents.

"Ana, I only have a few hours to be here before I have to leave and I wanted to spend that time with you and your dad."

Otis just sat, sipping his coffee and watching their conflict. Justin and Annette exchanged looks.

"I don't want to go into town, Mom."

"Then what do you plan to do today?"

"I don't know. Help Rychur probably. Hang with my friends." She looked over at Rychur who was still sipping his coffee and analyzing his ship, oblivious to the conversation. Leana wondered what affects the coffee might be having on him.

"I'm *not* leaving you here with a stranger," Danielle stated.

"A stranger, Mom? Hardly more than *he* is." She gestured at Otis. "Besides, I practically saved Rychur's life."

Danielle looked over at Otis. "Help here?"

He coughed down his sip of coffee. "Uh… She did save his life, Danielle."

"Not helping, Otis."

Esu entered from the kitchen. He rounded the table, clearing plates, bowls and silverware from the table, and leaving only Leana's and her friend's plates.

"So you're agreeing with our teenage daughter?" Danielle raised her eyebrows and looked at Leana, who was surprised Otis had her back. "Ana, I'm not comfortable letting you stay here with him."

Esu interjected, his back pressed against the kitchen door. "If I may, you need not be worried. I've been programed in thirty-seven different forms of fighting styles and self-defense as well as being an absolutely perfect shot with any form of rifle." Esu gestured to a rifle in a nearby stand. "There is no need for concern for your daughter's safety. Statistically, I have a better probability of protecting her than you do."

El whined from behind the kitchen door. "El would also be a help, I suppose," Esu said begrudgingly.

"Yeah, Mrs. Rayne, we'll be here too, so…" Justin added.

Leana smiled triumphantly at the end of the table, while taking bites of her breakfast. Otis couldn't help but chuckle as Danielle's mouth hung open. She cleared her throat as Esu backed into the kitchen, unaware of the pointed stare he was receiving. "Okay, then. I can't fight all of you," Danielle said sighing. "*And* he's lucky he's an android, Otis."

"I know he is." Otis laughed and leaned back in his chair, catching the napkin Danielle threw at his face.

"You're ridiculous," Danielle exclaimed.

"Gross you guys. Just stop." The flirting made Leana feel weird. "How about you two go into town and flirt where I can't see you. You're making me want to puke. I'll stay back with my friends and metallic protector."

Danielle sighed in disappointment. "I don't know, honey."

"Danielle, she's right. She'll be no fun if we make her go, and she's perfectly safe here. El has barely left her side since she arrived here. She's in good hands."

"Paws." Danielle responded.

"What?" he said confused. "Oh, right." Otis laughed.

"Bad joke, Mom." Leana groaned, finishing up her eggs. She picked up a half-eaten piece of toast and tossed it off the table.

"Leana, don't..."

Danielle was quickly interrupted as El bolted from behind the kitchen door and caught it in her mouth before the bread could even hit the floor. She swallowed the food in one gulp.

"Sorry, Mom."

Danielle shook her head, rolling her eyes.

"*Both* of you are ridiculous." Danielle pointed her finger at Leana and Otis with a smirk.

"So you still up for a trip to town?" asked Otis.

"Well I guess so. I mean, if you're okay with her staying."

"Yes, I'm okay with it." Otis stood up. "Esu," he pronounced.

They could hear clattering behind the closed door then Esu emerged, holding three boxes wrapped with tinfoil. "Here you are, sir. Breakfast for the veterans. Also, I loaded some of the strawberries and onions from the greenhouse into your truck, as well as a few empty crates just in case. You are set and ready."

"Thanks, Esu. I couldn't manage without you."

Leana was surprised to see Esu look as if he was going to cry at the compliment. She shot a confused look at Otis as Esu sprang back into the kitchen.

"I love that android. So polite," Danielle said as she stood up.

"It's so odd that he does that," said Leana. "I'm still getting used to it."

"Does what, Leana?" Otis tucked in his chair with one hand while holding the boxes Esu had passed to him.

"Acts all emotional like that. I mean, *really*. Does he actually feel... feelings?" She stacked the plates and bowls to help Esu clear the table faster after they had left.

"He isn't acting," stated Otis confidently as he walked to the front door.

Leana stopped what she was doing and turned to him. "I was thinking about that yesterday. I don't see how that's possible. How can Esu have feelings if his emotions are programmed?" She knew her estranged father could do a lot with his skills, like build an extremely intelligent, emotionally-conscious android, so it didn't make sense that he chose to abandon her and do emotional damage just to be a farmer.

"Honestly?" He asked as Leana nodded her head. "It's complicated," he teased, smiling as he opened the door with one hand.

Leana growled, frustrated at not getting an answer. She wanted to understand how programmed emotions made Esu seem so human despite his transparent skin and interior mechanics, while her own father seemed to be in need of human emotions in general. She still struggled to believe he made Esu.

Danielle grabbed her purse and headed to the door. "You want help carrying the food?"

"I got it. Come on." Otis gestured with his head.

"Are you sure it's safe to leave her here?"

"Yes, Danielle. Come on," he encouraged.

"Okay. Bye honey. See you guys in a couple hours. Esu, please take care of them." She stepped onto the porch. "Oh, it's a bit chilly this morning."

Otis looked at Leana and she saw a smile on the side of his mouth. "See ya."

Before Otis could step out, Leana spoke up.

"Dad?"

He stopped. "Yeah?" he said with his hand still on the door.

"Thanks for the roses," she said nervously with her hands in her pockets.

"You're welcome." He stepped out on the porch, closing the door behind him.

Leana sighed, and then looked at her friends. She hoped this was going to be another interesting day. She glanced over at Rychur, who still hadn't moved from his spot on the couch. She flinched as Esu sprang from the kitchen to clean the dining table quickly.

Leana walked over to Rychur. "So what do you want to do?" she asked hesitantly.

"I must work on my ship if I ever want to make it off-world. Were you all still wanting to assist?" Rychur took a deep breath and leaned back into the couch, looking questioningly at the three teens.

They all nodded back. "You don't mind?" Leana asked Rychur, watching the hologram of his ship spin slowly.

"I don't mind. Can you manage laboring work?" asked Rychur. He leaned and hit a button on the display of his equipment. The image of the ship blinked off.

"Of course! Besides, we've got nothing better to do."

"For a land as flourishing as this one, I'm surprised to hear you have nothing else to keep you occupied."

"Well, nothing fun," responded Annette.

"What's 'fun' for you?" Rychur asked, looking at the three teenagers.

Annette hesitated and looked at her friends. "You know… Doing stuff…"

"For instance?" He blinked and continued staring at her.

"Well, we enjoy… boxing, training…" said Annette.

"Not everything is 'fun'. Must you only do things that are?"

Leana shrugged. "Well, no…"

"We go to school, but that's lame," interjected Justin.

Rychur asked quickly, "What about playing with El? That appears 'fun'."

"Yeah, that's—"

"Or you could stare into that reflector and organize your," he paused, motioning to Leana's head apparently unsure of the correct word for "braid."

Leana laughed. "It's called a *mirror*, and *hair*, and mine's fine the way it is. Thank you."

"Then you *do* have other things you can do here, right?"

"Okay, yes you're right, but we don't want to do any of those things. We want to help you. Is that okay?"

"Then that is fine with me, but do not make excuses when you have none."

"If you're going to talk like an adult then we aren't going to help," Leana responded as she heard Annette snicker behind her.

"I merely brought attention to your—"

"You know what? It doesn't matter. When do we get started?"

Rychur stood up and stretched, prompting El to appear at Leana's side. "We can begin now if you'd like." Leana suspected from his swinging hands and fast exhales that the coffee had hit Rychur with full force. Leana wondered if it was a good idea to let an alien drink it.

"Are you feeling okay?" Leana asked, laying her hand on his arm.

"I feel very well and quite strong."

"No I mean are you *okay*?"

Rychur stared at her, blinking rapidly. "I'm not sure I understand."

"You know... With everything that's happened? The crash?"

"Thank you, Leana. The breath in my lungs is all I need now." He patted his chest with vigor. "Come," he gestured to the front door with his hand.

"Your hand is a bit shaky," Annette noted.

"Yes, I noticed that. I believe it's from the coughing."

Leana and Annette looked at each other puzzled. "Huh?"

"Do you mean 'coffee'?" Justin laughed.

"Oh, yes. Coffee." Rychur dragged out the last syllable. They all laughed.

"I'll grab my coat and meet you guys outside," Leana said then sprinted upstairs as Rychur and the other two headed out the door. El sprang up after her.

"Come on, El. Let's go see this thing!"

CHAPTER 24

Sprinting into her room, Leana grabbed her coat off the chair sitting under the window and threw it on. On the side table was her phone. She slipped on the bracelets and sprinted back downstairs.

Reaching the door, she twisted the knob hard and threw it open, hurdling all the porch steps with El right behind her. Filled with excitement at the chance to possibly see Rychur's ship in action, Leana sprinted to the barn, swerving around a tractor sitting lifelessly between an old oak tree and the barn.

Leana was glad for her coat. A steady breeze kept the temperature cool, and a cloudy sky wasn't helping either. On the plus side, the wind carried the smell of pasture grass to Leana who was learning to love farm-fresh air.

Turning the corner around the rear of the barn, Leana nearly ran into Rychur and the others who'd been waiting on the back side. Her enthusiasm brought a smile to Rychur's face. She moved quickly to the door, lifted the lock, and pushed hard to slide it open. It wouldn't budge.

She changed her position, digging her feet deep into the ground to pull with all her strength, but it barely moved. She ignored Justin's encouraging cheers and Annette's laughter.

"A little help would be great," she proclaimed, gesturing at Rychur to help open the door.

He grasped the edge of the door and motioned for her to step back. "Are you ready to see her?"

Leana moved next to Justin with her hands folded together in glee. She nodded excitedly, waiting for the unveiling. Rychur barely strained as he slid open the heavy, wooden door. The sunlight snuck in inch-by-inch, revealing the charred metal of the spacecraft and reflected off the unbroken windshield.

"Wow." She couldn't find any other words to express what she was looking at. Excitement, adventure, wonder, and exhilaration filled every inch of her body.

"Holy…" Justin started.

"Sizzlin'," Annette finished, her eyes wide.

Now that the ship was no longer half buried in a crater, it was twice as big and even more incredible. It gave Leana goosebumps.

"Don't you mean *nitro?*" Rychur said smiling, bracing his body against the doorframe. Dust particles floated in the air as beams of light penetrated the old barn. Hay was stacked on the upper loft behind the ship. Rychur entered the barn with his arms behind his back.

Justin shook his head. "No. No way. This is so much better than that. This is absolutely sizzlin', Rychur."

"Do you people ever take time to listen to how you talk?"

"Umm…" Justin wasn't sure how to answer the question. "What?"

Rychur shook his head. He approached his damaged ship, rubbing the fractured and splintered metal exterior. "She took quite a beating entering the atmosphere."

"I still can hardly believe you came from space," Justin said, his face expressing complete shock. He still hadn't stepped into the barn.

Leana spoke up, "When we found you after you crashed I didn't notice all the damage at all. It was so hot, and I was kinda distracted by you being nearly dead. All this was caused by entering the atmosphere?"

"Some of it, yes." He continued running his hand under the wing of his ship, scanning every inch of his craft. Leana watched him stroke the ship like it was something precious. She could see the hope in his eyes. She didn't understand how such an incredible spacecraft could have gotten so damaged by entering the atmosphere.

In the warmth of the barn, Leana removed her jacket and threw it on a hay bale. "What do you mean some of it? Is the rest from your perfect landing?" She smiled teasingly, but Rychur didn't seem to notice. He was very deep in thought. There was a long pause.

"The crash didn't do all of this either," Rychur said.

"What do you mean?" Justin asked, finally entering the barn and stepping towards the ship.

Rychur led the girls closer. Just the fact that it existed made Leana realize how small she was in a giant universe she knew nothing about.

Rychur grabbed her wrist gently, guiding her hand along the hull of the ship. El growled but Leana shushed her quickly. Justin stepped forward as if to say something, his eyes on Rychur's hand. He kept silent.

The metal was cold and rough at the same time. Leana felt the divots and chunks that had been ripped from the exterior. She noticed even the smell was alien – definitely metallic, but it seemed to have a very earthy smell to it as well, almost like flowers.

"Go on, you two," Rychur said to Annette and Justin. "You can touch it."

Walking alongside the ship, with Annette peering underneath, Rychur flicked the metal while he examined and checked the lower wing. "Phase blasts," he said, pointing at the damaged parts. "Atmospheric-distortion pull, and... claws."

"What?" She looked at where Rychur was pointing, touching the impaired section. "Did you say claws?"

Rychur explained to Leana, "Remember the blood on my armor?"

She nodded.

"I do!" Annette added.

"Well, it wasn't all mine. I had to fight my way off-world in order to escape. Fortunately, I made it to my ship, but that means it took on most of this damage while leaving my planet. If I find what I'm looking for, it'll be worth it."

Leana didn't know what to say. She couldn't imagine what that battle must have been like. "Do you know for sure that whatever you're looking for is still here?"

"What do you mean?"

"Well, are you positive it's on Earth?"

"Wait... what are you looking for?" asked Annette.

Rychur paused at a large gash on his ship, but didn't seem to be looking at it. He avoided Annette's question. "I know it's here."

"Suppose you do find it," Leana interjected, pursing her lips and shaking her head slightly at Annette. "Then what?"

"Everything will be taken care of in time, Leana."

"You can't know that."

Rychur smiled wanly. "You're right, but I believe."

While Leana and her friends explored the underneath of the ship, she noticed Rychur move to the front of the vessel, stopping right behind the frame of what she assumed was the windshield. Suddenly his feet lifted out of sight impossibly fast, and she could hear Rychur moving around on top of the craft. Before Leana could wonder how he'd gotten up there, Rychur started stomping his feet, making a rhythmical beat that filled the previously quiet barn.

Leana ran out from under the ship's wing just in time to see a latch pop open in front of Rychur. He knelt down to slide open a small, heavy door. With one arm, Rychur covered his face. Reaching in with his other hand, he yanked hard. A loud clank echoed inside of the ship and a small door swung open to his left, shooting pressurized air into his face.

"You okay?" Leana called up to him.

"Yes." Rychur peered inside the hull, and then slammed his hand down in frustration.

"What's wrong?" Justin asked.

"This door didn't open right."

"What do you mean? How is it supposed to open?" asked Leana.

"The pressure valve released where it shouldn't have." He pointed to the other opening next to him. "It should have come from here. The main pressure valve is completely dysfunctional."

Leana could read the disappointment on Rychur's face.

Rychur slammed both doors shut. He ran to the end of the ship, jumping down to the ground. Reaching into his pocket, he pulled out a small flat remote. He ran his thumb over the top, causing a blue light to swipe across the device and scan his finger.

Suddenly, the hydraulics on the side of the ship hissed loudly, releasing pressure. The sound was almost deafening. Leana shielded her face as the barn's dust shot in every direction. She backed away from the hatch, ears ringing as a ramp slowly lowered to the ground, revealing the interior of the ship. Without the flames and Rychur's falling body in the way, she was finally able to see inside.

Rychur leapt onto the ramp before it even made it to the ground and sprinted into the ship. He turned a corner and was out of Leana's sight.

"Alright," Justin said excitedly. "Let's check it—"

"No!" Rychur yelled from inside, loud enough to make Justin and Leana flinch.

"Okay then," Justin said quietly.

"Oh, no," she whispered to herself. She had heard the anguish in Rychur's voice and knew the condition of the ship was worse than he'd hoped.

Rychur trudged back out, staring blankly at the ramp.

"It won't make it home. The *only* piece that I needed to still function is beyond repair."

Leana felt sadness overwhelm her as she thought of all his friends and family who were surely waiting back home for him, lost forever. She didn't know how to help him, but for some reason she felt like she needed to.

She approached him and placed her hand on his back. "I'm so sorry, Ry. We're here for you. Whatever you need help with, we'll do our best."

"Thank you," he replied weakly, bracing himself against the hull of the ship.

Leana watched emotions play across Rychur's face. *Guess we're not that different*, she thought.

She could see the defeat in his eyes and posture. She felt so helpless in this situation. She had no way to help an alien get home.

Rychur turned and began banging around on the hull, pulling her attention away from her wandering thoughts. Under the ship, a previously hidden storage compartment lowered, holding large, metallic crates stacked on top of each other. She watched him unload a couple of the heavy crates from the storage unit after peering inside each one, as if looking for something. He threw out random devices from each of the boxes, some metal, some different shapes, some lit up, and others made of unknown materials. It took her a moment to realize they were tools.

She could see the desperation in his eyes as he piled the tools on the ground by his feet. He was deep in thought, as if trying to find an answer he'd forgotten.

Leana looked at her friends, who were still studying the ship, but they were not going to be of any help. Leana felt so frustrated as she took a quick step outside the barn, hoping to clear her head. Seeing Rychur's inability to deal with his problems made her think about her own.

Her mind started to churn as she thought about her mother and father being together, alone today. Thinking of them like that made her feel upset and jealous. It wasn't supposed to be like this. She didn't like being part of a broken home where both of her parents pretended they were still a married couple. They couldn't just ignore the last thirteen years. She suddenly wanted to be back in her home with her mother and her friends. She wanted to laugh with Annette and Emily about the awkwardness with Justin. She wanted to be somewhere where she knew what to do and what to expect.

Leana could only think about the problems she was going to face back home on Monday. She kept asking herself how she was going to deal with the school board and her coach, and what Thea Williams' family were going to do when they came face-to-face with her. Would she get suspended? Would Chandler be penalized somehow? Leana didn't want these problems, and she most certainly didn't want to think about any of them right now.

She wanted to know why she had been dealt a hand she never asked for. She wanted simple problems, teenage problems, like boys, grades, curfew, anything else that didn't involve estranged fathers and aliens. The excitement she'd felt waking up this morning had somehow evolved into an overwhelming swirl of negative emotions.

All the weight she'd been carrying finally took over. She leaned her arm against the nearby tractor tire while pushing at the knot inside her stomach. Everything around her was happening too fast and she wasn't processing it at all. *Why is this happening to me?*

Leana thought about blaming her mother for bringing Otis back in her life. She liked it better when it was just the two of them. Her friends never would've met the strict, secluded man she called 'Dad' and she'd be at home planning a prom dress right now with Emily and Annette.

Leana needed to sit down, and she stumbled to the ground, leaning against the big tire. El approached slowly, lying next to Leana and licking her hand. Leana pulled her knees to her chest and tried to hold back her tears. She didn't want to be here.

"Hey," yelled Rychur from inside the barn. "Are you unwell?"

"No, I'm fine," she lied, tucking her head into her knees.

Leana heard Rychur's feet approaching. She wanted to cover her face to keep him from seeing her cry, but she just didn't care anymore. She kept her head down so she didn't have to look at him, filled with guilt for feeling like this when he had much bigger problems. She hated being a girl and the mood swings it came with.

A heavy rush of wind swirled around Leana and she shielded her face from the dust until it died down again.

"Leana!" yelled one of her friends from the barn.

Peeking between her fingers, Leana looked up and realized Rychur was floating just a few feet off the ground in front of her. He appeared completely relaxed as he began lowering himself very slowly to the ground. Beneath him the grass moved in different directions below a small pocket of air.

"Are you... flying?" Leana couldn't blink.

CHAPTER 25

Annette's hand was on Justin's wrist tight as they both stood frozen, staring at Rychur. The moment his feet touched the ground, the wind stopped swirling around him. He wore a smile on his face like everything was perfectly normal. Leana's mind emptied of the troubles she'd been focusing on just moments earlier.

"How did you do that?" she asked, struggling to speak.

He knelt down next to her. "I just can," he said softly, reaching out his hand. "Here."

"What?"

"Take my hands."

Leana hesitated, then held out her own.

Helping Leana to her feet, Rychur walked back a couple steps, not letting go of her. "Now… Step on my feet."

"What?"

"Do it," Annette called.

Rychur, still smiling, winked at Leana. "I want to help you. I see how you struggle to be here with your father and with me. You have many questions and concerns. I know this is not that easy for you, and I know you think you're not okay, but you will be."

Feeling shy at the closeness, Leana stepped onto his feet. Suddenly weightless, she gasped and tightened her grip on Rychur's hands. She felt shivers crawl up her spine as she realized she was floating a few feet off the ground. She looked down and saw the wind was swirling on the ground again. Her friends stepped back, covering their eyes from the blowing dust. She began to panic.

"Keep your eyes on me, Leana," Rychur said. She was instantly drawn to his command and locked her eyes on his. "Trust me."

Leana didn't know why, but she felt like she *could* trust him. She allowed her body to relax.

After spinning them around slowly, Rychur gently brought them back down to the ground. Leana let go of his hands and stepped back quickly, her breathing heavy. She looked at her feet and at her friends, her eyes wide with shock and amazement. Annette's face mirrored her own, but Justin appeared less than thrilled.

Rychur put his hand on her shoulder. His touch was no longer strange or uncomfortable, but safe like a friend. Leana was glad her father had said Rychur could be trusted.

Leana didn't know why, but she felt an unexplainable urge to hug him. Without thinking, she wrapped her arms around him. She was just about let go when she felt the surprising embrace of his returned hug. He released her and smiled.

"Do you feel better?" he asked.

"Yes, thank you." She wiped a small bit of dirt from her face.

"Did I do okay?" asked Rychur.

"What do you mean?"

"I used to watch my father make my sister's sadness go away. I wasn't sure if I did it correctly."

She smiled and nodded. "Yes, you made my sadness go away."

"Good." He reached out his hand again.

"Where are we going?" Leana asked. She brushed off some of the dirt from her clothes; dust sprayed into the air around her each time she swiped at her pants.

"Follow me," Rychur said and headed back to the house.

"Cute," Justin muttered to no one in particular.

"Shut up, Justin," Annette replied, backhanding his shoulder. "You're trophin' the moment."

"That's not how you use the word, Annette."

"It is now… *Troph*."

"Whatever," he said, turning to follow Leana and Rychur.

Between the barn and the house was an open lot of grass where Otis usually parked his truck. Leana peered down the driveway, hoping her parents weren't on their way back just yet. She smiled in satisfaction at the empty lane.

Rychur walked beside her, observing her actions. Leana could feel his eyes on her.

"What are you doing?" She felt like a new recruit being judged by a drill sergeant.

"Do you believe?" he asked, testing her.

"In what?" Not a question she'd ever been asked.

"Anything."

"Like what? I don't understand."

"Your *Earth* is full of distractions. Things that pull you away from seeing your world. Your mind is drowned in emotions and thoughts. How can one be great if their gifts are blanketed by mental interferences?"

Leana stood there completely confused. "I'm sorry I don't—"

"Potential, Leana. Potential." As he continued walking he raised his arms to his side. His body spun as he floated off the grass. "No potential can be met without failure. And if you wish to become something more than yourself you must get rid of distractions and mental barriers."

Leana watched Rychur rising and moving around her just feet off the ground. He landed softly and continued forward, like it was nothing. She realized she needed to shut her gaping mouth again.

He continued, "My world may seem incredible to you, but I see my world for what it is. A Dystopia."

"Dystopia?" she asked, surprised by the direction of the conversation.

"A world that was once beautiful and filled with life, potential, and good. Now, it's a world consumed with war, death, and hate. Our world's potential is nearly gone." She saw the anger in his eyes as he spoke about it.

Leana's eyes caught at a pink glow beginning to beam from Rychur's hands as a colorful haze began steaming from his eyes. Her breath caught in her throat as she instantly flashed back to her vision of the man in the hood. His hands had done the same thing. She watched in stunned silence as he took a deep breath. He thrust out his right hand. The moment his eyes shut the wind around swirled like a vacuum towards the center of Rychur's palm.

She didn't understand what she was seeing, but it appeared that the air around them had condensed into a giant, transparent bubble in front of Rychur's outstretched arm. The glow from his hand illuminated the sphere.

An eerie stillness surrounded the two, but just twenty feet away, where her friends stood, she could see the wind was still blowing in the trees and grass.

He opened his glowing eyes. "Potential is everywhere. You choose not to see it."

Rychur threw up his hand to the sky, causing the condensed air to blast out around them. The breeze boomed like an explosion, shooting the air pressure out and blowing through the trees and grass around her once again. Her air whipped across her face.

"That's not possible. How is that possible?" she stuttered.

Rychur smiled peacefully at Leana.

"As with most things, the answer lies within."

"That doesn't really answer my question," Leana replied.

"Listen more carefully and perhaps it will."

"Okay?" Leana looked away frustrated and a little embarrassed at her lack of understanding. Her friends were staring at Rychur, shocked.

"My bloodline," Rychur continued warmly, "the bloodline of my people, is able to manipulate the air and elements of the environment around them, gathering energy into our bodies and releasing it. It's like an arm pulling and throwing the atmosphere."

"Your bloodline... As in, your family?" asked Annette.

"Yes, my family is separated from three other family clans. I am from the clan Malachur."

"What does that mean?"

"It's not a meaning. It's a title. We're a people who love the air. We can manipulate and control the very atmosphere around us."

Despite the impossibility of what she was hearing, Leana was overwhelmed with questions. "Who are the other three clans?"

"The Elchur are manipulators of the elements within the land around us. The rocks, dirt, trees, and metal ore of our land."

"So like things of the ground. The earth."

"Precisely. They absorb and control the element within the *earth* to create deadly weapons. They, unlike Malachurians, must physically touch whatever they want to manipulate. They are researchers. Constantly studying the elements within everything around them. Even themselves. They're obsessed with Balachurian biology. They're incredibly powerful, but sadly their story is..."

Leana watched Rychur trail off in his thoughts. Justin and Annette hurried over to them as anxious as Leana to hear more. Just as Leana was opening her mouth to ask what the Elchur story was, he continued. "Then there are the Onites. A warrior people of soldiers with unmatched tactical minds and agilities. *They* are many who make up an army of *one*. Beyond that they are able to create with their hands the most powerful weaponry, armor, and mechanics. They are also manipulators of the metal ores of Balachur, but don't have to touch them to do so. They are extremely talented and detailed in their work, and the results are remarkably beautiful. Some even call it artistic. It's quite amazing. Onites can build or fix just about anything."

Leana wondered what kind of weapons they crafted. The weapons on Earth, before the crash, were very primitive, but military improvements had climbed to new heights within the last couple decades. She remembers how her teachers had taught that the weaponry of the Earth was considered necessary. She realized Rychur had stopped.

Leana saw his posture had changed. He hesitated. Something made him not want to continue. "Go on. Who are the others?"

He sighed. "Then there are the Baramats. 'Beasts of Balachur' we call them. They were once enslaved people, controlled by the Balachurian Seven. But when they were freed, they acted out irrationally, fueled by anger and hatred. They never learned to control their strength and skills, so instead they've created a people simply fueled by negative power. Like the other clans, they also have special abilities, but as you would expect from such a brute group, theirs are unrefined."

"What do you mean?" Leana's head was spinning from all the information. She could not believe she was learning about the history of another planet.

"When activating the essence within them, they are able to build up their bodies to great stature, becoming strong, wild-minded, and extremely violent. Over the cycles of time, they have become the dominant force of our world, led by a king made up of pure hatred. They kill any who defy them."

Rychur paused again. He looked full of sorrow and pain. A bird chirped and she saw him blink at the sound. He shook his head and took a deep breath, turning to Leana with a smile.

"*We* are a people of Balachur."

Leana returned the smile, but her curiosity was still controlling her. "What do you mean 'a people'?"

"That is what we are. Just as your science says atoms make up you and me and everyone anywhere, Balachurians are 'atoms' of Balachur. And like you and your world, we make up the world of Balachur. Even though we don't work as one, we live as one. Without us, Balachur doesn't exist. Without Balachur, we don't exist."

"Umm, no, not 'just like us.' Our people and nations are more like cliques. We do not work together or see eye-to-eye. We don't get along. We've been waging war with one another from the moment we were born on this planet. We never agree on anything. We fight over things not even worth fighting over."

"Then do you see the missing potential? A world does great things when working together. Weakness in unity leads to chaos. Balachur is broken, and I wish to fix that. That's why I am here."

"And that is what you believe, isn't it? You believe you can fix what's broken."

"No, I can't fix it, but I desire to heal what's scarred. I believe in good, peace, honor. Through time, war is how we came to achieve that healing."

Justin finally spoke up, "Wait, you just said war is your people's answer? That's not 'peace' or 'good'; fighting and killing and war are evil. You kill, so how is that honor? How is that peace?"

Rychur looked over at him. "When evil exists, peace will not. Just as it is in any world."

"Why not? There can be peace." Annette sounded frustrated. "If there is potential in one person then there can be potential in most, right?"

"You are right, but as long as evil is allowed to survive, peace will dim and fade. It's like the two-headed Yargnuff. It doesn't die off easily. Even if you chop off one head, as long as the other head remains it continues to flourish. Do you think that evil should be allowed to grow, or should it be destroyed completely?" he asked Annette.

"Well... No, evil shouldn't be allowed to grow."

"Why not?"

"I don't know, but war is ugly. Innocent people die. Isn't that evil?"

"Innocent people can die at any time. While death, pain, and cruelty do come of war, without it there can never truly be a victor. War, to Balachur, means cleansing immorality for the sake of the innocent. I aim to cleanse."

"That's contradictory, Rychur," Justin said. "You can't protect the innocent by allowing the innocent to die."

"Yeah, it isn't right. War isn't the answer," Annette added.

"Then what is?"

"I don't know."

Rychur returned his gaze to Leana questioningly.

She shrugged, looking down.

Rychur nodded. "I don't know either. I do not wish for war on any world, only peace. That is what I believe. If you have an answer to stop my world from destroying itself, then I will listen."

CHAPTER 26

Leana looked at the time display on her bracelet and realized over two hours had slipped by, and her parents still weren't back. She wondered if she should be worried. Danielle never missed work, and she was definitely never late. She had been so distracted by Rychur's stories she hadn't even *thought* about her parents. *If they aren't home soon I'll call them.*

The stories of Rychur's world were like the movies and books she'd read growing up. It was so incredible, Leana just wanted to hear more. She was still in a place of partial disbelief. How so much had gone on throughout his world's history was unimaginable, and far more interesting than Earth's history.

Rychur went on to describe how one of the smallest plants on his homeworld was called the Junsur. It was also one of the most beautiful and could survive any terrain. Its nectar produced a poison that was deadly if eaten at the wrong time of day, and its thorns were used to numb wounds. The stem of the flower cured infections, and it never died unless it was removed from the ground.

He told them of the Agrioc, a four-legged creature that had colors of Earth's sky during sunrise with layers of teeth that shredded its prey in one single bite. It grew fur overnight for warmth, but would shed the thick coat by mid-morning. He said their fur was immensely valuable and was used to ward off other creatures.

Then Rychur began to describe the night skies he was used to back home, and how the nights were so clear anyone could see the stars and orbiting planets with ease. He spoke of how there was a once-in-a-cycle eclipse where the two moons and three closest planets all aligned, causing the light from their sun to reflect concurrently and brighten the black sky, revealing clear images of the orbiting spheres in half of the atmosphere.

Leana knew she'd never experienced moments like these, but somehow it all sounded vaguely familiar. It reminded her of the beautiful sky and lush planets she'd written about in her journal; the documentations from her nightmares. She realized, with everything going on, she hadn't thought about her dreams for a while – which was an incredible feeling – and she didn't want to go down that rabbit hole now. She was having too good of a day. She wanted Rychur to keep talking.

"How long have your people been on Balachur?"

Rychur smiled. Justin and Annette sat down in the grass. Leana joined them. The three looked up at Rychur as he sat on the porch stairs.

The visitor's voice was proud as he looked out at the farm. "Balachur started peacefully for many cycles. We were a happy people, building a utopia and flourishing. We went off-world to other galaxies, explored the deep space, and established lasting relationships with peoples of different planets." Rychur paused for a moment.

Leana saw his eyes drop slightly.

"That was until the Galactic Space War began," he continued. "Fierce races from neighboring galaxies came out of the Deep. There were millions of them to our thousands and they invaded our galaxy quickly. We had only known peace before that time, and were not ready for what the enemy brought with them. The battle lasted for nearly an entire cycle, we barely held our own. Our allies throughout the galaxy aided us as much as possible, but it wasn't enough. They suffered too much loss and eventually left us to fend for ourselves. That's when we fell, but not before the Seven took their stand."

"I'm sorry, Seven what?"

"The Seven. Seven pureblood Balachurians who are part of our planet's original families. The oldest, wisest, and most powerful Balachurians to ever live."

"So these are good guys, right?" Justin asked with hope in his voice. "Like superheroes?"

Rychur didn't answer at first, but after a moment he continued. "I'm not sure your meaning, but before you understand the Seven and their power, I want to explain the source of Balachur's abilities. Just like the air and the water that makes up your planet's biology, the Sa'rael makes up ours. It's in everything on our world: the people, the land, the creatures. It surrounds everything, and binds us together. We cannot live without it.

"The Seven were able to manipulate and utilize the Sa'rael in a way we had never seen before. They tapped into the elements and created energy fields and weapons from the planet's resources around them. Their power was unmatched. Within months, they were able to wipe out our enemies with unimaginable strength. Though the war eventually left Balachur, it remained throughout the rest of the surrounding galaxies. We chose not to care. We thought we, at least, were safe.

"Then the Seven turned their newfound power and took control of the planet. They knew we were weak from the battles. Going into the war as pacifists, and being forced to learn how to fight, took its toll on my people. The Seven used this to their advantage, swiftly establishing control and enslaving us. For the next two cycles, they ruled over the four families. Two of the Seven stayed in each of the Malachurian, Onites, and Elchur lands. Only one ruled over the Baramats and he was the most vicious. He was the source of the Baramats' rage. All four of the clans suffered, but the Baramats were mistreated far more than any of the others.

"It all happened so quickly. In the end, the Baramats were turned into slaves, forced to do the will and beckoning of the Seven. We don't know why they were singled out, but they were. It's possible that's why they are the way they are today."

"What happened to the Baramats?" Of all the questions roaming through Leana's mind right now, this seemed to be the right one to ask.

Rychur paused, as though collecting his thoughts. Finally, he continued, without answering her question. "That was when one of the Seven opened his eyes and saw what the war had turned him and the others into. Perhaps his guilt grew to be too much to handle. Regardless, he turned his power to help us fight back and regain our peace.

"We lost many, but we did finally win back our freedom. We just wanted to gain back the existence our people once knew. The problem was that now the clans were so filled with anger and bitterness from our enslavement that no one knew how to keep Balachur in peace. Our ancestors who had helped rule in the idyllic times had become mere memories to us. So we turned to what we now know... fighting. This time as a sport."

"You're talking about the Blood Games!" Justin exclaimed.

Leana thought of the barbaric Roman gladiators from Earth's ancient history. She wouldn't wish that on anyone.

"Exactly. Once every cycle, there are the Blood Games. The king of each family – Baramat, Onite, Malachur, and Elchur – and their chosen army fight against the others. The clan of the last king standing rules the planet for the next cycle."

"That's insane!" exclaimed Annette.

"Is it?" Rychur raised an eyebrow. Leana didn't know how to respond. "Peace reigned again throughout Balachur and we were becoming the people we once were. The peaceful people we remembered. That is..." he hesitated.

Leana suddenly saw shame and anguish sweep over his face. He looked at her and spoke weakly, "until Renisis came to power."

"Renisis?"

Rychur suddenly seemed very detached from what he was saying, forcing the words out of his own mouth, his voice flat. "Yes. Renisis, King of the Baramats. King of Balachur. He is still the king. No one knows where he came from, but from the beginning he seemed to only know rage and greed. *Obsessed* with power. His army was victorious during the Fourth Blood Games. What he did next was—"

The horn from Otis' truck cut off Rychur's story.

The three teens startled at the sound.

Leana checked her wrist again and realized another hour had passed. Otis and her mother had been gone for over three hours. She felt instant disappointment that the story couldn't continue. She wanted to keep asking questions and learn more. She had been imagining what the war and the people were like. She wanted to see it. She wanted to know more about this Renisis and what had happened after the Fourth Blood Games.

The engine's truck turned off and both doors creaked open.

"Hey gang, you been out here all day?" Danielle called as she got out of the truck.

"Yeah mostly. Where have you guys been?" Leana asked.

Otis turned off the truck, slammed his door shut, and grabbed the stack of crates in the back of the truck. "Work!"

"Work where?" Leana could tell something was up. Something about her father was different. He was happier, and her mother was full of smiles. Leana looked at her. "And *you* were supposed to be back in time to go to work."

"I actually had a friend fill in for me. She owed me a favor. It's all taken care of, honey."

Leana looked at Rychur. He sighed deeply but smiled, and stood up to head back to the barn. She turned back to her parents.

"So, are we hanging out now, Mom?" She already knew the answer was 'yes,' but she still couldn't stop thinking about her new friend's story. Even if she couldn't fathom it, it was fascinating to listen to. She decided to keep Rychur's story to herself for now. She didn't know how her parents would take it.

"Of course, honey. I'm sorry we took so long. I helped out at the market, we visited with the veterans, and we spent some much needed time together, but I'm all yours now." Danielle wrapped her arm around Leana as they walked into the house. El stood on the porch, wagging her tail at Otis.

Right as Leana was about to enter the house, she stopped. "Hold on, Mom. I forgot my jacket in the barn."

"Oh okay. We'll go inside and see if Esu needs any help getting ready for dinner. Run quick."

"Be right back." Leana turned around and ran towards the barn just in time to see her father enter ahead of her. She slowed her pace, not wanting him to see her, and curious to what he was up to.

Just before entering the barn she stopped and stood outside the door, straining to overhear what might be going on inside. She jumped when she heard pounding on one of the metal crates Rychur had stacked near the front of the ship. She slowly peeked around the corner to see Otis holding one of Rychur's larger tools. He hit it against the crate again.

"You hungry?" yelled Otis as he looked into the cockpit of the ship. She couldn't make out Rychur's muffled response.

"You doing alright in there?" Otis yelled again.

Again, Leana couldn't hear his response.

"I can't hear you. Mind if I come up?"

Rychur must have agreed, as Otis walked around the cockpit and into the ship. Slowly and quietly, Leana crept to the ramp, following Otis unseen. She was nervous and excited at the same time. She hadn't seen the inside of the spacecraft yet and she definitely hadn't seen Otis interact with Rychur like this. It was as if they were now friends. Silently making her way up the ramp, Leana could see a short corridor on her right that led to the cockpit. Otis' back was to her, blocking her view of the cockpit where Rychur was.

She watched as her father shifted his weight to lean against the entrance frame and his head turned to Rychur, who leaned forward, bracing himself on his knees. Rychur looked down at the floor.

"You don't look so good," Otis said. "Thought I'd check in on you. You feeling alright?"

Leana had a difficult time making out Rychur's response, but she was able to hear a little. She held her breath, listening.

"I am the best I can be. Thank you," Rychur responded then sighed. "I need your help."

"You know I won't. I'm sorry," Otis said, sounding irritated.

"Why?"

Her father sighed before replying, "I see it was a mistake I came up here." Otis turned to leave. Leana panicked, thinking she was caught, but just then Rychur stood up, punching the roof. Sparks shot out from the ceiling and nearby console. "I need your help! Why don't you see that?" Leana was taken aback by the desperation in his voice.

Otis stepped forward. "You are in my home now. *My* home. I have family here. *My* family. A life. *My* life. I will let you stay, and do what you have to, but *I* will not help you."

Leana felt her stomach tighten at her father's voice. She decided now would not be a good time for either of the men to see her. She backed away slowly then exited the ship, grabbing her coat off the hay bale. She shook the dust from it and turned to leave, only to run smack into her father's chest. He stood there, looking at her, clearly upset.

"Forget something?"

"Yeah," she said nervously, holding up the jacket. "Found it." She could see various emotions flickering across his face. She thought she saw frustration and maybe disappointment, but she wasn't sure. Whatever it was, his behavior towards Rychur wasn't sitting well with her.

"Alright then. Better hurry, food is going to be ready soon," Otis said, turning away quickly.

"Wait, Dad. Why did you yell at him?" Leana slapped her hand over her mouth, surprised at the words that had just come out. She was so confused by the way he spoke to Rychur.

Otis turned and sighed. He took off his hat, slapped it gently in his other hand and looked up as if collecting his thoughts. "I don't know why. I shouldn't have though. Are you upset?"

Leana only nodded.

"Then I'm sorry. It probably wasn't right." Otis turned his head to look at Rychur who was now standing in the entryway of the ship. "I'm sorry, Rychur. You didn't deserve that... and, uh... It won't happen again." Otis raised an eyebrow towards Rychur as if saying, *"okay then?"*

Rychur nodded back and Otis turned around to walk out of the barn. He passed Leana, pursing his lips into a weak smile and rounded the corner out of sight.

Leana dropped her head, worried that she may have just upset her father again.

"Thank you for that. You didn't need to say anything." Rychur came over to Leana.

"I know," she said, putting her coat back on. "I didn't really mean to." She smiled. "Do you want to go for a walk? I'm not really ready to go inside yet."

"Of course." Rychur smiled back.

Together they walked out of the barn. She waited with her hands in her coat pockets as Rychur slammed the barn door shut with ease. The chilly air brought goosebumps to Leana's skin.

"Your world is so beautiful," he said, looking out into the acreage and up into the clear sky. "The creatures of the air and ground roam free without concern, just like you do. I haven't known peace like this in so long. This is what I want for Balachur."

Leana watched some birds fly to the willow tree a few yards down the driveway. She and Rychur strolled down the gravel lane outlined by the white, wooden fence on each side. The ground crunched beneath their feet.

Halfway down the long driveway, they stopped and perched on the fence near the huge tree by the pond. A lovely landmark on her father's property, the willow's branches drooped to the ground, dancing as the wind blew past. In the tree, birds sang as two squirrels chased each other around the trunk and through the grass.

Leana saw the happiness on his face as he watched the animals. "They live such simple lives here. Do you see how they appreciate their home and their freedom? They are completely content with life, singing and dancing and playing in that tree. I would give anything for a life like theirs right now." He sighed deeply and breathed in the fresh air.

Leana stepped down to the lower rail of the fence next to him and swung around to face him, holding on with both hands. "Are you alright? I hope my dad didn't say anything too bad." She recognized the flicker of loneliness in his eyes. She saw that same look in the mirror almost every day.

"Leana, will you do something for me?"

"Uh... Okay?"

He looked over at her, examining her face. "You need to believe in yourself, Leana. Always. Make the most of your life because this is the only one you get. You seem so tired of your life and the challenges you face. You still don't *grasp* your family and friends."

"I *grasp* them, Rychur," Leana said, copying his tone defensively.

"No, Leana, you don't. If I could choose anything it'd be to have my sister back. Even for a breath, it would be the happiest breath I ever took, to hug her and look into her eyes once more. It would be a moment that I would grasp onto forever. I see you with them and they don't seem to matter to you; at least not enough. You have all of them here, together, for you. Make your life matter with the people who are in it."

Leana nodded slowly, slightly taken aback by his sudden reprimand. He stared at the tree as it continued swaying with the wind. A fish rippled the water in the pond next to it. He now looked sad.

"You don't look like you're doing too well, Ry."

He smiled wanly. "You're right. I'm not. But for the first time, I feel a bit at peace with the world. This world, at least."

Leana didn't know why, but she felt so drawn to him. Despite his age, he didn't really seem that much older than her. Being out here on the farm with him made her feel somehow less alone than when she was with her parents. She felt a connection with him. She understood his loneliness and sorrow. "How can I help you?"

"What do you do when you feel entirely lost?"

Leana thought for a while, realizing she'd been unable to answer this question since the nightmares began. "I don't know. I usually fall apart." She crossed her arms in front of her on the fence, resting her chin on them. "What do *you* do when you feel lost?"

"I just keep wandering and waiting until I find my path again." Rychur looked at her. "That's what I'm doing now. I'm waiting. I know why I came here, but I'm not sure what is actually here for me anymore."

"What do you mean?"

"I'm not quite sure what that means myself, but I know I am here for a purpose."

She was comforted by his words somehow. She felt glad but selfish, thinking how nice it would be to have him around a little longer. His presence gave her unexplainable reassurance that things were going to be okay. Listening to his life and how he lived in a different world made it easier for her to cope with what she was going through here.

She felt guilty though. Her struggles awaiting her back home in Core City were nothing compared to what Rychur faced every day. The man next to her only knew a life of chaos, war, pain and loneliness, and yet he was kindhearted and wise. He stayed fixated on the potential of what his world could be: peaceful. He seemed willing to do whatever it took to make that happen.

For now, he was here with her and he was safe. She didn't know what to do to help him, so she decided she would stay by his side and wait with him.

"Let's go get some food," she said.

CHAPTER 27

The rest of the night went by slowly and uneventfully. After dinner, Rychur went back outside and Danielle and Otis spent most of their time in the living room with the teens, talking amongst themselves about things going on in their lives. Annette sat in an old fold-out chair next to Leana with El lying between them on the ground. Justin sat on the floor on the opposite side of the room.

Most of the conversation was boring after the more interesting conversations of the day. To Leana, this felt forced and unnecessary. She hated listening to her parents talk about lives right in front of her. She stared out the living room window at the silhouette of Rychur looking at the horizon. He was alone out there and she was stuck in here. Neither were where they wanted to be.

Just then, Leana's phone blinked. Annette had messaged her from across the room. The message included Justin and Emily in a random, pointless but delightfully distracting group convo. She started by sending a funny picture of Axel Stormweather, the lead singer of Brailtrot, completely wiping out on stage. Emily's response was classic – she'd had a crush on him for the last four years. Before long, Emily was asking for updates on the other three's activities. She was still out of the loop on what her friends were up to at the farm.

Leana felt good being on her phone again. Emily was finally getting over being ditched, and she was excited to plan a Girl's Night when Leana came back home.

At times, Leana caught Justin glancing over at her during the chat, and she knew they still needed to talk about what had happened between them. She had no idea what to say and wasn't looking forward to having the conversation. She kept her eyes on her phone as much as possible.

Her mind was stuck between two places, the farm and home. Back home, she had the life she'd been living for so long, but that also came with the nightmares she'd suffered each night. Here, she was able to make a new friend, Rychur. She knew that once she left, her father would send Rychur packing. She felt responsible for Rychur now. She was literally his only friend on Earth.

They shared a bond now, a connection that went beyond being human or alien. They both felt alone. He trusted her and she wouldn't do anything to break it. She couldn't stop trying to think of ways to get him home, but she knew she couldn't really. Otis was probably Rychur's best chance, but she knew her father wasn't going to lift a finger to help. He'd made that very clear, although she didn't know why.

She felt the familiar knot in her gut, but each time she acknowledged it, El would lick her hand or her phone would buzz, bringing Leana back to reality.

Leana felt slightly ashamed that she finally had both her parents together and was spending quality time with them, but right now she didn't *want* to be with them. She wanted to be with the alien whose life seemed more interesting and exciting.

"Leana," Otis said with a tender voice, trying to get her attention. He sat directly across from her in front of the window she kept looking out of.

Leana looked at him and realized both her parents were looking at her. Leana's right hand dangled off the side of her chair, rubbing El's fur mindlessly as the wolf lay quietly on the ground. "Yeah?"

Danielle slid down the couch, closer to her. She reached over and placed her hand on Leana's. "You haven't said much for the last couple hours. What's going on?"

"Nothing."

"I know you better than that, baby girl. It's never 'nothing'."

Leana looked out the window again, deciding if she wanted to open up or not. She sighed. "Why am I here?"

Danielle looked confused. "You know why."

"Okay, then why are *you* here?"

"Leana, I came to see you."

Leana pulled her hand away, gripping her pocket watch through her jeans. "No you didn't. You came to see him."

"Leana!" exclaimed Danielle.

This was going to be yet another moment Leana didn't want to remember. She had been angry with her mother for sending her away and yet now that Danielle was here, Leana wanted her gone. Her life was torn into so many pieces, and her heart wasn't able to put them together. She needed to be away from her parents, it was too hard to be around them. Her chest began to ache and her head throbbed.

"Why didn't *you* just come here instead of me? Then I could have been the one who stayed home." Her frustration made her heart beat faster.

Otis watched quietly, his hands on his armrests.

"Is that what this is about, honey?" Danielle asked gently. "Is that how you truly feel?"

Leana didn't say anything. She stared down at the table as her eyes began to tear up. She felt Annette's hand on her shoulder.

"I can leave if that's what you want." Danielle waited. "Leana?" she asked, lowering her voice. "What do you want?"

"I don't know. I don't want to be alone anymore."

"Alone? You're not alone. We're both here… for you. And so are your friends." Danielle gestured around the room.

"I know that. You don't understand. Both of you being here makes me feel even more alone. I just want to go home."

Danielle looked at Otis as they shared a disappointed look. "But you were supposed to be here to get help. That's why we're here."

Leana raised her head, looking at Otis, not hiding the tears filling her eyes. "I want to go home."

"That's fine," Otis said, the words sounding forced.

Leana stood up abruptly and walked outside to the porch, slamming the front door. El darted out the door just before she shut it, her constant shadow. She could hear her parents begin arguing inside the house. She knew they were arguing about her and about Otis giving in to Leana's request without a fight. She felt like her life was falling apart all over again, and all the pieces were getting buried deeper and deeper. Before long, they were going to be impossible to find. Her father's abandonment made each minute here with him more difficult to bear, and it only got worse with her mother coming around. All of the feelings Rychur's arrival had distracted her from were rushing back full force.

She leaned against the railing and looked out, watching the sunset. This day was closing on a bad note. She knew she was pushing Otis *and* her mother away. She didn't belong here and it didn't feel right having them here together. She had hoped that being away from her city life would have done her some good like getting away from her nightmares. It did, somewhat, but everything wasn't as good as she'd hoped, and it's not like the nightmares were gone. She hadn't even had Otis help with them at all. She didn't know what was worse: the dreams or the reality. She wanted to scream, yell, cry, or run away; anything but be here. She looked up into the sky, wishing she was somewhere else. Anywhere else.

The arguing grew louder as she stepped down from the porch. Just then, the door opened again. The tension in her muscles relaxed slightly as Justin and Annette stepped through the door.

"Uh… Thanks for leaving us in there, Ana," commented Justin.

"Stop," Annette said, hitting Justin to shut him up.

"I'm sorry, guys," Leana said, pursing her lips. Seeing her friends come after her made her want to give into her built up emotions. She was torn, but she knew they were here for her.

Annette embraced her quickly without saying a word, and as she did, it broke down her defenses entirely. Her shoulders began to shake as her face pressed against Annette's shoulder. She began crying softly. Her family, life, and mind were all so messed up and now her friends were beginning to see it all too clearly. She knew there was no way she could share all of her secrets with them. She cried for several minutes. Justin patted her back comfortingly.

Finally pulling away, the three sat down on the steps of the porch, Justin directly behind Leana and Annette next to her.

"What do you want us to do, Ana? How can we help?" asked Annette.

She gestured vaguely. "Well, I don't think you can. You heard my mom, right? I came here to get help and so far you've seen how that's gone."

Justin reached down and wrapped his arms gently around her shoulders. His touch was comforting. She instantly felt safe. He said softly, his mouth next to her ear, "There have been more incredible things that have happened here in one day than in my entire life. That's gotta count for something, right?"

Leana sniffled, thinking about what he said. She knew he was right and that her parents arguing shouldn't ruin everything she'd experienced in such a short time. "No, you're right," she said, sniffling again.

"Yeah, see?" Annette added. "It's going to be okay. We're here for you."

"It *is* going to be okay, Ana," whispered Justin. "Promise."

She wanted to believe him. She held onto Justin's arms. She let out a small chuckle as she remembered Rychur's words from earlier. She wanted to grasp this moment with her friends and remember it.

"By the way," Annette asked, "does your mom not realize Rychur crash landed here? That he's an alien?"

Leana laughed again quietly. "Oh my god, I didn't even think about that. I'll bet she doesn't." Leana grabbed Annette's wrist. "Do you think my dad lied to her about him?"

"Well, he's one smart man if he did," responded Annette. "Knowing your mom, she would *freak* if she knew what was really going on."

"Good point," said Leana. "It's kinda funny that she doesn't know."

"Speaking of," Justin said, pointing out to the barn. "Rychur's just standing over there."

"Yeah, I know," Leana responded. "He's been watching the sky for a while now."

They all sat quietly for a moment, staring at their new friend. "Have I told you yet that he's really good looking?" asked Annette.

"Seriously?! My dad *and* him? You really need to get yourself a man," Leana said teasingly.

"Uh-huh… Right," replied Annette, looking at Leana and shaking her head. "Look, I'm gonna call my dad quick."

"Okay, I'm gonna go check on Rychur for a bit. See if he needs anything," said Leana.

"Oh. Want me to go with you?" asked Justin.

"No, it's okay."

For a moment, Leana saw a disappointed look on his face. She patted his arm. "I'll be right back."

He looked at her and smiled. "Okay. I'll be right here."

Annette rolled her eyes.

"Go call your dad," said Justin, "or I'm going to elbow *you* for once."

Leana got up and walked towards the barn before turning back around to her friends, smiling. "Thank you, guys. You mean the world to me."

As she approached Rychur, she rubbed her chilly hands together, and then shoved them deep in her pockets.

Rychur was watching the sun set while leaning on the tire of Otis' rusted tractor that sat outside the barn. He turned as he heard her approach. "The sunsets here are beautiful."

"Yeah, mind if I join you?"

"Not at all," he said with a smile.

Leana leaned on the side of the tire, staring out into the red and orange horizon. They watched quietly as the sun continued setting, changing the colors of the sky as it descended below the horizon. The first few stars of the evening blinked into view, greeting the two onlookers.

"Thank you, Leana." Rychur studied the constellations as the sky continued to darken.

"For what?"

"For saving me. For giving me this," he said, reaching his arms out into the sky. "If you and the others weren't there, I wouldn't be here."

"You're welcome, Rychur," she said.

Behind her, she heard the front door close and feet approaching.

"Be kind-hearted to her, Leana. She is your mother," Rychur encouraged quietly.

"Leana," Danielle called as she walked towards them.

They both turned to see Danielle with her purse over her shoulder. "What happened, Mom?" Leana already knew.

"He yelled. I yelled. It doesn't matter. Things are fine now. I informed him you're staying." Danielle exchanged looks with Rychur and received a gentle nod of encouragement.

"I'm sorry for what I said. You don't have to go, Mom." Leana felt protective, knowing Otis had yelled at her mother.

"I know, but you were right. I should have let you two have your time. Coming here was a mistake."

"It wasn't," she said, grasping her mother's hands. "You two needed to have some time together, it looked like."

Danielle inhaled hard. "Your hands are freezing." She started rubbing warmth into her daughter's hands.

"You know I didn't mean what I said, right?" asked Leana.

"I know, baby girl. I was sixteen once." She wrapped her arms around Leana. Times like these made her regret feeling so distant. She missed the closeness of the only person who knew everything about her.

The door closed again as Otis made his way out. He looked much calmer than when Leana had left.

"Honey. I need you to listen to me really quick, okay?" Danielle said quietly.

"Okay?"

Danielle's words came out in a rush. "When you came into our lives, your father wept. You have always been his whole world. You are a part of him just as much as he is a part of you. I know things are hard for you, but you need to be here with him. You need to trust him. Make the most of tonight because you never know what tomorrow will bring. Okay? Can you do that for me?"

"Yeah, okay, Mom."

Stepping up to them with his hands in his pockets, Otis looked at Danielle and Leana. "I, uh... I'm sorry for earlier."

Leana had a difficult time looking at him, and didn't know what to say. There seemed to be too much apologizing lately, and she didn't know how to deal with it.

"It's alright, Otis," Danielle responded. "I was just saying my goodbyes."

"Yeah," Otis said, his voice disappointed. "I'll walk you to your car."

"Me too, Mom," said Leana. She looked at Otis. "If that's okay."

"Of course it is," Otis said.

Danielle started to head to her car then stopped.

"It was nice meeting you, Rychur," Danielle said softly.

"I will remember you, Danielle."

"Really? Why's that?" She tilted her head.

"Kindness is never forgotten," Rychur said firmly.

Danielle looked at her daughter. "I like your friend."

Rychur watched them as they walked away.

Danielle linked arms with Leana. "I can see the way he looks at Otis, and the way *you* are around him. He's been *so* grateful and friendly. I was wrong about him." She turned and looked at Otis. "He's put up with *your* rudeness long enough. Time to change that."

Otis opened his mouth, but nothing came out.

She grabbed Otis' hand and brought him in close to her. "*This* isn't the man I know, or the man I fell in love with long ago. Just because you live alone doesn't mean you get to treat people the way you have been. I don't care where he's from or how long you two have been around each other…" Danielle stepped toward Otis and took his face in her hands. "Be kind. You'll only regret it later if you don't."

She kissed him on the lips and wrapped her arms around his neck. "I'm going to miss you, honey."

"I'll miss you, bee."

Leana cleared her throat uncomfortably.

"Ana," Danielle said, wrapping her arms around her daughter. "I love you, and I know what's best for you. Right now, this is what's best. Okay?"

"Yeah, okay, Mom. I love you too."

"Okay. I want a minute more with your father before I go. I'll see you soon?"

"Yeah. Bye, Mom."

Leana turned towards the house. She didn't like seeing her mother have to go, knowing she was the reason Danielle was leaving. She wanted to take back what she had said and how she'd reacted. She wanted the emotional rollercoaster to stop. She walked back to the porch, passing Justin who was sitting on the steps, and sat at the rocking chair. It was no surprise when El joined her.

"You okay?" asked Justin.

"Yeah, I'm okay," she replied. "Mom's leaving."

"Yeah, I got that. You sure you're doing okay?" He leaned back on his elbows, studying her.

"I just feel so alone when she's not around, ya know?" she said, looking at her mother from the distance.

"Well… you aren't."

Annette came up the steps, finished with her phone call. She slapped the back of Justin's head. "What'd I miss? Where's your mom going?"

"Home," Leana answered.

Justin rubbed the back of his head. "What was that for?"

"Just cause," Annette said, laughing.

Leana watched Rychur's faint figure at the tractor, still facing the sun that had already set. He appeared to be staring up to the sky, studying the stars and constellations. She knew this was a new sky to him. She could only imagine the wonder going through his mind.

Leana heard Danielle's car door shutting. She couldn't help the sudden wash of guilt as her mother drove away. She felt so stupid for how she had acted, and now she was alone again with her father. Watching Otis approach didn't make her feel much better either. She could see by the way he was walking, that he was hesitant to come over and speak to her. She sat there looking out, hoping to avoid eye contact and the inevitable awkward interaction.

He stood at the bottom of the steps to the porch and knocked on the railing." Mind if I join you?" he asked calmly.

"If you want to." Leana shifted in her seat.

He looked at her friends who sat quietly, staring up at him, and then he looked back at his daughter. "Look, I'm sorry."

That wasn't what she expected. *Another apology?* She had expected a lecture for making Danielle leave and for throwing a fit in the living room. "Okay."

"I'm not the type of person who likes to apologize, yet already this weekend I've apologized too many times."

Leana agreed. "Yeah, so why are you apologizing this time?"

"For everything, Leana. From all the way back when you were three-years-old. I wasn't able to be around, but I did miss you. Every minute of my life here on this farm I thought of nothing but you and your mother."

Leana stared at him. She tried opening her mouth, but couldn't speak. The lump in her throat was too much. She felt tears fill her eyes. She didn't want to cry again, especially not in front of her father.

"You don't have to say anything, but I want to show you something. Let me steal you from your friends for an hour or so. Uh…" he suddenly sounded nervous. "Consider it like a date."

Leana felt a shock zing through her body. "A what?"

"A date. A first date. Father-daughter, you know? I want to show you something. It's a hobby of mine, but I want to share it with you. I should have done this sooner."

Leana didn't know how to react, but her mother's words kept ringing through her head. She looked at Justin and Annette who stared back with encouraging smiles. Annette nodded and mouthed 'yes'. Justin winked at her.

"Yeah… Sure. I guess."

Otis smiled and nodded before going back in the house. "Good."

CHAPTER 28

Leana sat on the porch impatiently waiting for her father to come back out. She didn't know why she agreed to a *date,* but it was obviously something he wanted and she knew her mother would want it too.

"Leana, you know how sizzlin' this is, right?" asked Annette.

"Yeah, I agree," said Justin. "This is what you two have needed since you got here. Some time together."

"You're probably right... I think," said Leana, as she hugged her cold body.

"It's good to see your father smile," said Rychur's voice, unexpectedly.

Leana looked around, but couldn't see him. She stepped to the edge of the porch, leaning over the railing.

"Up here," he called.

Looking up, she saw Rychur's legs dangling from the edge of the roof of the house. He chuckled, and then looked up at the stars that decorated the night. Leana turned and sprinted through the front door.

"What are you doing?" Annette called after her.

"Be right back," Leana replied, slamming the door behind her.

She sprinted up the stairs, down the hall, and into the attic. El, who had gleefully chased her the entire way, yelped as Leana climbed up into the dark room above where El couldn't follow.

Leana looked down. "Sorry, girl."

She hit the light and hurried to the far window. It took some effort, but she was able to lift open the sash. "Mind if I join you?" she asked.

"I don't."

She turned and grabbed a blanket that had been stacked next to her father's antique sword, and then slowly and cautiously made her way out onto the roof. In her excitement she hadn't thought ahead to the fact that she had never been on the roof before or any roof for that matter. As her feet hit the steeply sloped shingles, this suddenly seemed like a terrible idea. Her heart began beating through her chest as she held her breath.

"Are you crazy?" yelled Annette below her.

"Annette, seriously… You are scared of *everything* here," Leana yelled back, shakily. "Spine up."

She heard Justin laugh below, followed by a grunt. "Stop hitting me… dang."

With great caution, Leana sat down next to Rychur, wrapping herself in the blanket. "That was… harder than I thought."

Down below, she heard the front door shut and saw Otis walking across the yard, carrying a large telescope. "What is he doing?" asked Rychur.

"He's setting up our… *date*, I guess," hesitated Leana.

"He looks happy."

Leana gazed over at her father spread out a blanket and set out some chairs. "Yeah, I guess he does."

Rychur sighed and looked up into the black sky, watching a shooting star stream across space.

"You feel pretty far from home right now, don't you?" Leana asked, watching him for a moment.

"I feel like I'm without a home. When I was a child I would watch shooting stars from the Great Cliffs. The night sky is the only thing that feels like home. This sky is different from ours. The stars are in the wrong places. It's strange."

"Yeah… So, what are you doing up here?"

"Enjoying the quiet."

Leana jerked her head to the side. "I can leave if you want. I'm sorry if—"

"That's not what I meant."

"Oh, okay." She relaxed.

"This life *here* is what I've longed for for many years. Is this what your world is like everywhere?"

"Some of it, yeah, but there are lots of other places that aren't as nice as this."

"Then you are appreciative of it."

"Well, I guess so. Honestly, before you, I didn't really take time to appreciate much in my life."

"Then I am jealous," joked Rychur. "You have so much to enjoy and you forget to take the time to fill yourself with that goodness."

"Well, it's not always like this. I have my own problems going on—"

Rychur interrupted, "Why do you push your family away, Leana? What obscures you from fixing those problems with your family, your life?"

"Oh, please. Not again. I don't need another lecture."

"What you have here is incredible. Whether you care for your father or not, you've become so distracted by the tiniest things—"

"I don't want to talk about this anymore," she said quietly, but firmly.

For a moment, they sat silent. Leana understood where Rychur was coming from. There was no excuse for the way she treated her mother and the way she was around her father. She knew Rychur didn't have much family left back home, a home that had few moments of peace or time to heal. She felt guilty and convicted when she ignored his problems and focused on her own.

She watched him think. Looking from his point-of-view, Leana could understand his feelings about the little things she was dealing with. But to her, everything in her own life was too much to bear. She didn't know how to let it go.

"I'm sorry," she whispered. "I just don't know who I am here... or *anywhere* for that matter."

"Your friends and family seem to want the best for you, but you... You don't see the best in yourself to know who you really are. So the question needs to be asked."

"Yeah? What's that, Rychur?" she asked sarcastically.

"Who do you *want* to be, Leana?"

I, uh... I—I... don't know," she stuttered.

"Only you can know who you are. You are so blind with everything around you. It's what's inside that makes the individual. Your worries and troubles distract you, change you, twist and distort you."

"So... What? Are you saying to find new friends? Make up with my dad?"

Rychur sighed in frustration. He opened his mouth to continue, but Leana interrupted him.

"I'm sorry, but you don't get it. Women don't just turn it off like men. We can't think about our feelings and thoughts one at a time. They come at us in a tangled mess, and our brains don't stop until it's all resolved.

"Almost every night, I wake up screaming from these horrific nightmares. The only thing that calms me is this stupid pocket watch which makes me think about my father," she said pulling it out of her coat. The rose on its cover glistened in the moonlight. "I've hated him every day that I saw my mother alone. I've become jealous when I see how normal my friends' lives are. I just want a normal life - I want a family. I don't want to hate my father anymore. And I don't want my mom to be alone. And I don't want the nightmares."

Tears followed this outpour of emotion and Rychur pulled Leana close with his arm around her shoulder. For a moment she wept. She hugged her arms around his waist, feeling embarrassed that she had poured out all her problems to a complete stranger. But it was too late; she couldn't hold it in anymore, and he didn't feel like a stranger anymore. She could feel all the weight of the last thirteen years come crashing down on her, tearing her up inside, making her feel worthless and alone. She wanted so bad to be normal, to know who she was.

Rychur gently stroked her hair, keeping her close.

Leana knew she needed to let it all out. She needed to break in order to put herself back together. She needed someone to pick out her flaws and bring them to light. She'd spent nearly a decade holding in her pain and built-up emotions from the people who would care, hoping she could make it just one more day as the person she wanted people to see. She couldn't hide any longer. Not tonight. She didn't want to.

"Can you do something for me?" she whispered as she sniffled.

"Of course, anything," he responded quietly.

"Talk about something else. Please?" She looked out into the open sky.

"Like what? What would you want me to talk about?"

"I want to know more about what happened to your world. About Renisis, was that his name?" She felt his muscles tense at her words.

"I'd prefer to talk about my people and how we came to be."

"That's fine." She felt bad for mentioning the name.

"The Malachurians, my family, are a beautiful people. We are also known as the 'Nightseers' because we see very well at night. This is also the reason I appreciate the skies so much."

"What are your nights like?"

"Unlike anything you've experienced. At a certain time of the night, in the Dark Lands of Balachur, there is 'The Fall'. They are very special nights," he said passionately. "The element—"

"The Sa'rael," added Leana.

"Yes." Rychur smiled. "We also call it 'The Sa'. It is able to change its density, making it visible to the Malachurians. The ground is covered from The Fall, and when the suns rise, it settles in the ground, giving life to everything it touches. The Malachurians believe Balachur, as in the planet itself, chooses where The Fall occurs."

"So... Balachur is alive?"

"Of course it is. If we are alive it is because Balachur is. No life can be sustained on a dead planet."

"What about your family?"

"My family, my bloodline is heir to the Malachurian Rule."

Leana sat up breathless. "What? Are you like a prince or something?!"

"Yes."

"Shut up!"

"What?" he asked confused.

"No, I mean... That's *nitro.*"

"I see... Yes, I am a part of a bloodline that runs to the first

Malachurian King. Being king isn't what you might think it is, though."

"What are you talking about? You get a castle, money, servants, and you don't do anything unless you want to."

"Is that the life of your kings?"

"When kings were actually around… Yeah, I guess."

"Your world's kings seem to far outrank the privileges of the kings of Balachur."

"How so?"

"Remember what I told you of the Blood Games?"

"Yeah, four kings enter. One king leaves."

"That's right. Why would one desire kingship when its sole purpose is to make a last stand in battle?"

She gave him a blank look.

"The kings are replaced by another heir of the bloodline when their previous king falls. There is no honor going into a battle to be protected. And while honor comes to those who choose to serve and protect, three out of four will die."

"So who is your king?"

"Currently, my father's brother. He was chosen after my father fell during the previous Blood Games."

"I'm so sorry, Rychur. Who won those games?"

"The Beasts of Balachur."

"I thought you said they were wild-minded creatures. How did they manage to win the last Blood Games?"

"The last *two* Blood Games."

King Renisis, she remembered. "I'm sorry. We don't have to talk about this anymore." Leana shifted away from Rychur.

"It's okay." He sighed, and looked at her. "Do you really want to hear the story?"

She nodded. "But only if you're okay talking about it."

"As I said earlier, Renisis climbed to the rank of King out of nowhere. He earned the respect of the Baramats after he'd won the Games. But he was a *vicious* ruler.

"When they were victors of the fourth Blood Games he became power hungry. He wanted to create the perfect warriors for his army. He immediately assigned his brother, Nach, to be his right hand."

Leana saw Rychur tense as he spoke.

"Renisis was able to manipulate the fourth family, the Elchur, to side with him. They were desperate and feared him greatly."

"Why the Elchur?"

"They never became victorious in any of the Games. The Elchur are… were the intelligent ones, the scholars of Balachur. They had a wisdom and thirst for discovery. They would use their own bodies and the planet's elements to manipulate the Sa. A very loyal family, they would often risk their own lives to save others, Elchurian or not. This was why they never ruled. They were considered weak.

"Renisis somehow tricked the Elchur King, his own Royal Bloodline *and* the Elchur Elders. Renisis turned on them all, killing the entire Royal bloodline while they were trapped in the Baramat kingdom. The Elchur and Baramat peoples witnessed the slaughter, and were too petrified in fear to fight back. Renisis took the Elchur queen as his queen, hoping to start a new race, a zenith race comprised of all the Balachur families' blood. He wanted them to be perfect, all-powerful beings."

"Why didn't the Elchur fight back?"

"Once the bloodline was wiped out the only royalty left went to the Elchur Queen. The Elchur were forced to be slaves to the Baramats. And slaves they are still to this day – forced and controlled by the Baramat hands."

"You mentioned the Elchurian Elders. Why were they important to the Baramats if they already had the queen?"

"Renisis had other plans for them. Obsessed with developing the perfect race on Balachur, he forced the Elders to experiment on Renisis' own people. Their first goal was to create the greatest soldier. This cycle was known as the 'Time of Blood' because tens of thousands of Baramats lost their lives during these experiments."

"Why didn't anyone stop him?!"

"We tried. Each of the clansmen and their kings worked together to find ways to kill this king. Each attempt failed, usually costing lives. Renisis was stronger than any of the Baramats; he was faster, smarter, more cunning, and merciless. They never stood a chance."

"Did he succeed with what he wanted from the Elders of Elchur?"

"He did, and we paid dearly for it. We failed to stop what he managed to create."

"What did he create?"

"The Porters."

"What are—" Leana started, but Rychur continued.

"They were the catalyst to creating absolute chaos on Balachur. The Elders of Elchur were able to utilize their abilities of manipulating the Sa, and discovered a way to implant it into the Baramat bloodstream. They created a fusion race of Balachurians."

"I don't understand. How is that even possible?"

"The Porters would be unable to survive if they didn't wear masks to cover their mouths. Their skin looks as if they are as old as The Seven. They walk like animals, and their bodies are covered in tubing around and throughout their limbs. They can liquify the Sa and it flows through their bodies via those tubes."

"What does that mean?"

"Instead of exploding into immense strength and hulking size, these Porters *implode* using the Sa which allows them to move through space."

"You mean they can teleport?" she exclaimed.

"Yes. During the fifth Blood Games, the Baramats walked onto the battlefield with their king in front and three Porters behind him."

"That's all? How many did you have?"

"Thousands."

"What happened?"

"The three Porters disappeared, and within seconds reappeared next to each of the kings of the other clans. Each one laid a hand on one of the kings, then disappeared again, dismembering the kings. The fight was over within seconds. They won."

"What do you mean 'dismembering'?"

"When the Porters move through space, they use the Sa'rael as their means to teleport. Doing so, they use an unimaginable amount of this element to travel, so when they teleported with their hands on a king, the Sa was sucked from the kings' bodies, leaving only the shell. It pulled their souls from their flesh, leaving only a corpse. It has now become the worst way to die."

"That's horrible. What happened to the Elders of Elchur?"

"They were killed by the Porters."

This was a story of nightmares, and she didn't want to believe it. The mention of Baramat beasts reminded her somewhat of the figure who had towered over her in her vision on the soccer field. Leana also remembered reading something in her dream journal that sounded similar. Even though she couldn't remember for sure, it felt familiar. She wondered if she should tell Rychur. Leana didn't understand how it was possible, since they weren't from the same world, let alone the same galaxy, but she felt the stories and dreams were somehow connected.

"What does that weapon you're looking for have to do with all this?"

"I don't think you want to hear any more of this. I've told you enough, Leana."

"No, I need to know. Why would it be all the way out here?"

Rychur sat quietly with his head down.

"Where is it, Rychur?"

Rychur gritted his teeth. "I don't know, Leana," he said defensively.

"So who does?"

"An old friend."

Leana twisted her head at him, "You mean someone else like you?"

Rychur simply nodded.

"Here?"

He nodded again. Suddenly, she remembered 'The Crash' they spoke so much about in their History classes. It all began clicking into place. Her eyes widened.

"Okay, so where is this friend?"

"Self-exiled a long time ago. Far from Balachur."

"Why? What did they do?"

"A burden was carried. Something no soldier should ever carry."

"What burden?"

"Killing Renisis' baby which he shared with the Elchur queen."

"What?! Your *friend* killed a baby?"

"When word got out that Renisis was planning to create a clan of zeniths, the other families panicked. My friend was forced into murdering this child while the fifth Blood Games waged. When the Porters took their first steps on the battlefield, he snuck into the Baramat kingdom and killed the infant."

"How do you know all this?"

"Because I was there. I helped him escape off-world."

"You? You helped kill a baby?"

"In our world, orders are orders, no matter how dishonorable they may seem. If you refused to follow, you and your bloodline were given to the enemy. Weakness was worse than evil. So, we followed orders."

"It sounds like your culture is evil... not weak."

Rychur pursed his lips and dropped his head. He hesitated for a moment before looking back at Leana. "Those were the same words my friend spoke before leaving."

"I think your friend was a coward."

"My friend would have agreed with you.'"

Leana could feel anger fill her stomach. She wanted to rage at the injustice, but that would have been pointless and she knew it. "So, anyway. The exile. Why'd he leave? Why did he come here?"

"Could you live with yourself if you had done the unthinkable, the unforgiveable?"

Leana could see the shame Rychur felt for his actions. He couldn't hide it.

"Leana, he was filled with complete guilt and shame for what was done—"

"Stop saying 'he.' What was his name?"

Rychur sighed. "His name is Galavon, and he never forgave the king for forcing his hand. He struggled with so much anger and dishonor; he even considered killing some of his own people, those who had put this dishonor on him.

"When I helped him escape off-world, Renisis returned to find out that over a dozen of his soldiers were dead, along with his son. After that, he sunk into an unquenchable thirst for revenge, killing any who resisted or whom he felt would betray him. He was completely blinded by rage and paranoia.

"To this day, Balachur continues to bleed over the death that fell upon that Baramat child."

"So that's why you came. To find your lost friend and whatever thing he has that can help you. How long have you searched for it?"

"Long enough. You know, it was a strange luck that brought me to your farm. Had I crashed anywhere else I wouldn't have survived. Maybe this is where I'm supposed to be when I die, exiled just like Galavon."

"Well, it's not so bad here." Leana was trying to be positive.

"No, you are right. I would have liked to see him one last time. Of all the galaxies and worlds filled with life, Coreal was the best choice."

"I really like what you call our planet. It's beautiful."

The sound of footsteps approaching interrupted them, but Leana wasn't done listening and wasn't exactly in the mood for a father-daughter date right that minute. She felt confused by the story of Rychur's friend and the life he must have kept living. Maybe it was a good idea to step away from this dark story for a bit.

Otis approached the house, standing below Rychur and Leana. "Hanging out, huh?"

"Oh, hey," said Leana, forcing herself to sound happy to see him.

"I have everything set up except for our drinks. Meet you over there?" He pointed behind him.

She nodded and received a smile. Otis walked back into the house. "You guys need anything?" he asked Justin and Annette as he passed.

Leana turned her ear to listen.

"Nah, we're good, Mr. Rayne," Justin replied.

"Mr. Rayne, could—"

"Otis. Just Otis from now on."

"Okay, cool. Is it okay if we join Rychur," Annette asked hesitantly, pointing up to the roof, "up there?"

"Sure. Just grab a ladder and be careful, you two," he said, heading back into the house.

"Sizzlin'," Annette exclaimed. "You cool with that, Rychur?"

"Of course," he replied, looking at Leana. "It is time for you to go. I will see you at sunrise," he said smiling.

"Umm… not *that* early. I will see you tomorrow though." Leana realized the stories she had just heard probably wouldn't help her in the sleep or dream department. Perhaps she should be looking forward to spending some alone time together with her dad. It might be a good distraction. Besides, her mom would want her to, and she knew Annette wanted her too as well. This was kind of a big deal. She could feel a bit of nervousness run up her arms.

Leana stood up slowly and grabbed her blanket. "Okay, I'm going."

He looked at Leana. "Don't forget, grasp this moment."

"Goodnight, Ry." Leana crept back into the window, slower than when she came out.

Leana wanted to make Rychur happy, so tonight she was going to be a bit kinder to her father. Listening to Rychur's story made her want to fix things with Otis, knowing he had been on this farm alone for all those years. He deserved a decent date even if it was their only one.

"Leana." Otis stood at the bottom of the stairwell with two steaming white mugs in his hands. "Are you ready?"

Making her way to the porch, Leana heard the ladder slam against the eaves of the roof. Justin and Annette rushed each other up to the roof, causing Leana to smile. She hoped they'd enjoy their time with Rychur.

After exiting the house together, Otis handed Leana the mugs. "I'm right behind you," he said softly.

Leana walked ahead while Otis lingered behind for another moment. He rubbed his hands together and looked up to the roof. "You okay?"

Rychur sighed. "I am. Thank you."

CHAPTER 29

Otis clapped his hands on his thighs, then took a deep breath and caught up with Leana. "Some sky, huh?" he asked.

"Yeah, it's the clearest it's been since I got here."

Leana loved what she was seeing - the darkest dark with startlingly bright stars arranged everywhere in the velvety black. She remembered feeling almost the same way back when she was staring at the stars outside the soccer stadium. Now that she was able to really see the beauty of the night sky without the city lights competing, she felt so much more peaceful. To her, it seemed like no matter where she was the stars never changed. They were the one thing in her life she could count on. Looking up into the blackness, she felt like she had momentarily escaped her normal life.

Otis interrupted her reverie. "This is what I wanted to share with you, Leana." He gestured at two folding chairs and a mini-table set up on a large blanket. In the center of the blanket was a long, red telescope. It looked brand-new.

"Do you recognize the blanket?" asked Otis.

"No... Should I?"

"I guess not. It was one of the many blankets your grandma made you. I took this one with me the night I left."

"Oh..." Leana always felt a sting when he would say things like "*the night I left.*" She kept her eyes on the blanket. "Why did you take it?"

"I wanted to have a piece of you with me. Every night I've stargazed I used this blanket. I look up into the night sky and I think of you, hoping you're looking at the same sky." His eyes met hers before looking back up at the stars.

Leana wondered if he somehow knew how often she'd looked up in the sky, wondering about him. It weirded her out that they had that in

204

common.

Otis gave a slight awkward laugh, and then reached for a steaming cup of hot chocolate.

Leana smiled as she inhaled the sweet aroma of her favorite drink. She held out her cup. "Cheers."

Otis smiled. "Cheers." They tapped cups.

Leana sat down in a new-looking green lawn chair.

Otis chuckled. "I only had one, so I bought one this afternoon... Just in case. You like it?"

Leana didn't know what to say. She was starting to see the sweet side of her father Danielle had talked about. She sat back, stretching her legs. "Yeah, sure." She looked up again. "The sky... I've never seen it so clear." She ignored her cold hands, instead staring up above her into the infinite mystery, getting lost in the incredible canvas of space and stars.

"That's one of the reasons I chose to live outside the city. The farther out from Core City I got, the less the light pollution, the clearer the sky."

"Well, it's beautiful." Her eyes tried to catch each and every star. "You don't get to see it this clear at home, that's for sure."

"No you don't, but the stars have always been beautiful, no matter where you are." Otis took a sip of his hot chocolate.

"Do you come out here every night?" Leana realized she was curious to ask her father questions right now. The starlight and hot chocolate had relaxed her, and she was enjoying the moment with him.

"Every night I can, yes. It's the only time I can embrace the silence of my life." Leana's eyes had adjusted to the dark, and she could see he was smiling.

"What do you do when you're out here?" She swallowed, feeling the hot drink warm her stomach.

"I think about how small I am. How small we are." He leaned in and looked through his telescope. "Every night since I came out here to the farm, I would look out into the stars, wondering about my life, wondering about you." He looked directly at Leana; she could hear the sadness in his voice. "And of the choices I made in my life."

"It's funny," Leana sipped again. "Whenever I look at the stars I feel this—this overwhelming sense of peace. And for a moment, just a short moment, my mind is completely clear."

"You lose yourself entirely. You just appreciate it."

"Yeah." She pulled up her legs and cuddled up to her hot cup, wrapping both hands around it. It was unexpected to have someone understand her like this. For the first time, he didn't feel like a stranger.

"Think about it," Otis continued. "With a sky so big, so distant, so open... looking up establishes the reality of how tiny we are, whether we realize it or not. It's a moment of clarity to the lives we live and the things we do. But also, it makes you wonder what else could live out in the deep black. Who else. When you recognize these things, you can appreciate it more. For example, you've befriended someone from a different world. It answers that question of 'Are we alone in the galaxy?'"

"Yeah, I never really expected to get that answer." Leana laughed. "Have you always been a philosopher?"

"There's a lot you don't know about me. And there's a lot I know about you."

"Oh, really?" Leana felt irritated at the comment. "I doubt that."

"You'd be surprised how much I know." Otis leaned back in his old raggedy chair, sipping from his cup, and stared up.

Leana sighed and turned towards him. "Okay, fine. When was the first time I scored a goal in a game?"

"You were four. First game. Landings Park, winning goal. That was when you knew you'd love soccer the rest of your life."

"How'd you know that?"

"How do you think?"

"Fine. Mom probably told you, so that doesn't count. Too easy. Next question. When was my first broken bone?" she asked, sterner.

"Trick question. You've never broken a bone."

She hesitated. "Okay, well then... favorite drink?"

"Besides your sugar-loaded coffee?" Otis lifted his cup and smirked. "Hot chocolate." Leana was annoyed he was right. *How does he know all of this?*

Otis laughed and twisted the telescope. "Enough questions for now. Want to take a look?"

Leana peered into the eyepiece, soaking up the beauty in the sky, but continued thinking of more questions. Still looking through the scope, she asked, "Favorite celebrity?"

"Oh, tough one. It's either James Dean or Marilyn Monroe."

"How the heck did you know that?" Leana was baffled.

He laughed again. "Educated guess. Your mother *loves* them, and seeing how close you two are I knew there was a good chance you had the same taste."

"Impressive... and you're right. I grew to like them both."

"I figured you for an oldies kind of gal."

"Okay, here's another toughie. What is my favorite color?"

"That's easy, it's red, and you hate pink."

"Ah ha! Wrong." She pointed her finger.

Otis threw his arms playfully out to the side to argue. "What do you mean 'wrong'? I'm not wrong."

Leana laughed. "You're wrong. You are."

"Okay, then." Otis leaned in, "Tell me, what is your favorite color?"

She leaned in too, feeling completely present. "Jungle green. Red *used* to be my favorite."

He paused, and then smirked. "Okay, fine. But you still hate pink, right?"

"Yes, Dad. I still hate pink." She leaned back to peer in the telescope, scanning it across the night sky.

Otis paused, staring at Leana.

Leana looked back up at him. "What?"

"Thank you."

"Umm…" She went back to the stars. "For what?"

"For calling me 'Dad.' I was starting to think I'd never hear that again."

"Well… You *are* my dad." She didn't want the conversation to get awkward again. "It's no big deal."

"Leana?"

"Yeah?" she asked.

"I'm proud of you."

She was surprised. "Why?"

"You've been through a lot, and yet you've become an incredible, young woman. You're mother raised you well."

"Thanks," she whispered, holding back a rogue tear as she pushed her eye against the telescope again. "So, how did you know all this?"

"Your mother tells me," he said.

"How much—"

Otis interrupted. "Do we talk?"

"Yeah."

"Every week since the day I left."

"What'd you guys talk about?" Leana never knew how much her parents cared for each other. She had always pictured her father as a worthless guy who wanted nothing to do with his family, but she was apparently very wrong.

"You… and her… but mostly just you."

"Why me? And why did you guys talk so much?"

"Why do you think?"

"Please," she said with hope in her voice. "Just tell me."

"Leana, your mother and I…" he hesitated, "ever since I left… Leana, we've never stopped loving each other. Or you," he added gently.

That was the words she'd waited over a decade to hear, and they brought absolute joy to her heart. After thirteen years, she finally had the answer she'd been looking for: her father did love her, did miss her, and had always loved her mother deeply. Otis moved from his chair to kneel in front of her. He hugged her. Something inside of Leana crumbled, and she finally let go of all that hurt, pain, anger, and loneliness she'd been holding onto throughout her entire life. The hate began melting away as she allowed love to wash her heart. For a long moment, she quietly wept in his arms.

"I never knew. I hated you for so long," she said into his soggy shoulder.

"I told her never to tell you."

"But why?" She gripped the back of his flannel coat, still angry at the lost time.

"I would rather you hated me than be scared of me."

"Why would I be scared of you?"

"I knew my presence would eventually hurt you, in some way, because of where I came from. My background, my history, broke me apart inside. You mother held me together for so long, but I knew things would have eventually fallen apart if I stayed any longer."

His words resonated inside her mind. She remembered what her psychiatrist told her about how fear can lead to unexplainable choices and actions. Leana remembered how her doctor addressed the fact that perhaps her father leaving wasn't an act of neglect or hate, but of fear and mistrust within himself as a parent. The hardest thing her doctor had told her was to let go of all the built up anger that she'd accrued over the years. All those years of wanting to hate him were finally being flattened as she heard the brokenness and love in his words. "You hurt me anyway."

Otis leaned her back in her chair, but continued kneeling in front of her. "Listen, Leana." He gently lifted her chin with his fingers. "Listen to me. There are things you don't know about me, about my past."

"Yeah, I know." She sniffed hard, wiping her damp face. "Mom told me. You were a soldier, and she said you had a hard time coping." It was difficult to breathe and speak.

"She was right, but there's so much more than you could possibly imagine." He rubbed her knee. "And that was why I had to leave. Not because I wanted to, but because I needed to."

"Was Mom angry with you?" Her throat was sore from crying.

"At first she was, but she understood better than anyone else. She knows everything about me, so she forgave me even before I left. The problem was that I never really forgave myself. I couldn't until you did."

Filled with overwhelming emotions, Leana wrapped her arms around her father once again while he just held her. He rubbed her back, squeezing her tightly. It made up for every hug she had missed out on the last thirteen years. She didn't want to let go. Finally, Leana pulled away, taking in a deep breath.

"So, what now?" She asked, drying her face. "What's going to happen to me and you after tomorrow?"

Otis sat back down in his chair. "I don't know, but for right now, let's enjoy this moment." He gestured to the telescope again, pointing out constellations. Leana paid attention to his every word, finally learning from her father for the first time in her memory. He knew so much about the stars.

"Why do you know all of this?"

"I've studied these stars ever since I met your mother. They were something that was a constant in my life. Besides Danielle, of course." He finished his cup of now cold chocolate. "Your mother and I did this almost every night while we were dating."

"What was that like, meeting her for the first time?" asked Leana.

"Hmm," he thought. "Did you know we almost never met in the first place?"

"Seriously?"

"I actually was planning on leaving town after the crash because of how people were acting, but I had a bad accident so I stayed. After the accident, I had nowhere else to go, so I went out. That was actually the night I met her."

"Leaving sounds like a common theme for you, huh?"

Her father didn't respond right away. She wondered if she had ruined the moment, but instead of sounding hurt, he just smiled and continued. "You could say that, but fate had other plans apparently." He rotated his body in his chair. "If I hadn't had my accident where I did, I may never have met your mother. And maybe, making the choice to leave later wasn't the worst decision."

"How can you say that?"

"Well, it led to you being here, with me now, instead of you pushing me away like you might have if I'd stayed."

"I wouldn't have done that," Leana responded defensively.

"Oh, yes, you would have."

"Well I'm not right now."

"I see that. I think it's fate that fixed us into this position."

"Fate, huh? What do you think my fate is?" she asked. "To become a professional soccer player, a wife, a mother? Or is it the bad dreams that forced my mother to send me here?"

"We *are* going to talk about those dreams of yours, we need to get those under control, but before we do, would that be enough for you? To be a soccer player or mom?"

"Yes? I don't know," she hesitated. "No, actually. I want more than that."

"Then what do you want?"

"I want people to see me the way I see the stars," she said shyly. "Heck, to be out among the stars if that was possible. Like Rychur." Leana was getting excited, realizing she now knew someone who could maybe make that dream come true. *I should ask Rychur about that later.*

"No," said Otis.

"'No?' What do you mean?" she asked, tension in her voice.

"I know what you're thinking. That's not happening."

"I wasn't..." She could feel her father's glare. "Okay, maybe I was."

Otis sighed, shaking his head. "We're a lot alike, you and me."

"Well, I wasn't *actually* going to." She felt disappointed.

Otis smiled, and then looked back into his telescope. He adjusted his body, gripping the focus tube tightly. "What the—" Otis peeled his eyes away and looked up. "What is that?" Slowly he stood.

"What? What is what?" asked Leana, his tone of voice making her skin suddenly tingle with nerves. The only thing Leana could see was another shooting star crossing the sky.

Otis turned around suddenly, staring over Leana and back toward the house. Out of earshot, Rychur was still on the roof but now he was standing. Leana caught the look on her father's face.

"Dad... What's wrong?"

"It's time for bed. Now."

CHAPTER 30

Leana woke to another morning filled with the smell of a fresh rose on her dresser and Annette fast asleep next to her. Joy filled her when she saw the rose and realized she hadn't had a nightmare the previous night. For the second time in months, Leana had been able to sleep completely through the night.

She immediately thought about the incredible time she'd had with her father. She'd finally been able to drop her guard and open up to him. She'd given him a chance to fix things and he had done so, or at least told her everything she'd needed to hear at that moment. She had forgiven him and was ready to start moving forward with their relationship. The anger and bitterness had been exhausting and she felt lighter this morning, knowing she had let them go. There was too much pain in the past, and she just wanted things to be better.

It had been nearly impossible to fall asleep the night before, thinking about how the night had gone, and especially how it had ended. She knew something had gone wrong when her father's mood had changed and could tell Rychur was somehow involved. For the sake of keeping the peace, she hadn't argued with her father then, but she was dying to get some answers this morning.

She put her phone on to check for alerts from last night. With everything else that had happened, she'd forgotten to check her phone before bed. The blue light was blinking. *Missed message from Justin.* She hadn't focused on her friends much this weekend yet, especially him, so she decided today she was going to make it a point to do so. She took a quick shot of herself, laughing at the picture he'd sent of Annette passed out cold on the porch, and sent it back.

She then listened to Emily's three messages asking how she was and if everything was okay. In each of her voice recordings, her hair and appearance were immaculate, as always. Leana felt a little sad that her other friend wasn't here. She knew it would have been great watching Emily witness a ship crash, a wolf, an android, and an alien. Maybe it was for the best though. Out of all of her friends, Emily was the most unpredictable one. There's no telling how she would have reacted.

She had one last message from Danielle. It just read: "I LOVE YOU". Three words that made Leana smile, and reassured her that her mom wasn't angry with her. The screen faded and Leana slid down her bracelet.

After a quick shower and getting dressed, Leana took one long sniff of the rose, turned to the bed, and tip-toed around it. Raising her hand high in the air, she smacked it down hard on Annette's butt, yelling, "Sun's up! Butts up!"

Annette jolted awake, swinging her fists, but Leana already sprinted from the room so fast that she forgot about El lying in front of the door. The thud of Leana hitting the ground and rolling into the wall quickly turned Annette's scowl to howls of laughter. "That's what you get. Karma!" She rolled out of bed still laughing.

El stood, staring at Leana who lay looking at the wolf upside-down. "Good morning, El. Sorry."

El turned her head to the side, and then hopped over Leana, and headed downstairs. Leana jumped to her feet, heading downstairs as well. "Come on, Annette!" she called.

"I'm coming…" Annette replied groggily, rubbing her eyes and stretching. "Give me five minutes."

As Leana made her way to the dining room, she expected her father to be in as good of a mood as she was, and she was hoping to get to learn more about Rychur before he left. At the bottom of the stairs she could smell the aroma of hot breakfast being prepared by Esu, who had easily become her number one favorite chef of all time.

"I see you, girl." Leana giggled to El who now lay quietly in the living room, watching her. She glanced at the couch, but Justin wasn't there. Hearing voices in the kitchen, Leana assumed Justin was helping with breakfast. She looked around the main floor for her father and Rychur, hoping to avoid any of Esu's long, overly wordy morning conversations. Rychur wasn't in the living room either and her father wasn't at the dining room table with his morning coffee.

"Where is everyone, El?" El whined sadly. "What's wrong, girl?" Leana asked as she bent down to rub the wolf's head.

El closed her eyes enjoying Leana's hands running through her fur. "It's okay." Two intense, muffled voices could suddenly be heard talking out on the porch. Leana stood quickly and peered around the windowsill to see who was out there. It was Rychur and her father.

Leana quickly moved to the front door and swung it open quickly to see Rychur gesturing with his hands animatedly. His voice was raised. "I don't understand why you—" Rychur stopped abruptly as he saw Leana and appeared to be trying to regain his composure. "Good morning, Leana."

"Morning," she said puzzled. Otis was silent. "Morning, Dad."

"Morning." His voice held no emotion.

Leana hoped he wasn't back in a bad mood again. It certainly looked like he was. She tried to stay positive and upbeat. "You guys been up for a while?"

"We didn't go to bed. Your father and I have been up all night... talking," said Rychur.

"Oh? What about?" She stepped out onto the porch curiously with El close behind.

"Nothing. We were just talking. You don't need to worry about it." Otis said distantly. He definitely seemed to have shut down again.

"Dad... Are you okay?"

"Fine, Leana. Just tired."

She could understand what that felt like, being up all night. "Okay..." she hesitated. "I had a great time last night." She smiled hopefully at her father.

"That's good."

The awkward silence kept weighing Leana down, second by second. "Thanks for the rose," she added.

"You're welcome."

Leana's heart hurt a little. This entire time her father never once looked at her, or smiled. She didn't know what was going on, but it was worrying her. After such a great night last night she didn't want to go back to him being so standoffish. She didn't want to feel unwanted and unloved like before. It was confusing.

"Obviously something is going on, but sorry for bugging you." She could feel tears gathering behind her eyes.

"Leana," said Otis, raising his voice. "Just leave it."

Leana couldn't help but feel emotional.

"Leana, it's okay," Rychur tried to interrupt with a positive tone.

Otis quickly jumped in. "I called your mother. I asked her to come get you sooner today. You should pack up your stuff after breakfast. And let your friends know."

Overwhelmed and confused, the ache in her chest filled her with complete disappointment. She was heartbroken. "Did I do something wrong?" Leana stepped closer to her father, still holding back her tears, trying to be strong. "I thought—"

Otis stood up quickly. "Leana. Stop. You can't be here anymore. I'm sorry, but you have to go."

Those were the words Leana was afraid to hear, and he'd said them without hesitation. She saw no remorse, no guilt, and no regret in her father. He just stared into Leana's eyes. To avoid showing weakness, Leana stormed off the porch and walked quickly away from her father before he saw her cry.

"Where are you going?" yelled Otis.

"Away from you!" she screamed back.

"Not this time. El!" Otis made a clicking noise with his tongue.

El sprang from the porch and blocked Leana's path. At first, Leana was irritated at the wolf. She tried to order El to move, but the wolf remained where she was. Taking a deep breath, Leana twisted around. "Why can't I go? It's what you want."

Otis stared at her.

"Well?" she exclaimed, throwing her hands in the air.

Otis said nothing. He turned and walked back into the house.

Leana felt the pain from her father's silence. "Dad?"

She couldn't fight the tears any longer. She had never expected to be crushed by her father like this, especially after last night. This is what she got for trusting him. Seeing him push her away made her think of how her mother must have felt the night he left all those years ago. And now Danielle had to take pills every night to sleep. Her mother's face filled her thoughts. Leana realized if she walked away now she was just like him. She felt hate for her father refill her stomach just like before. There was no way Leana was going to cry another tear for him if he was going to run away again. *No, not this time. I'm done.*

Leana headed back to the house, screaming her father's name. "Otis!"

Rychur stood with a hand out, trying to stop Leana, but she shouldered past him and stormed into the house. Otis was sitting on the couch in the living room watching the news on the HoloVision. He sat hunched forward, scowling and avoiding eye contact with his daughter.

Leana walked angrily around the couch and stood directly in his line of sight. "Are you running away from me again?" She clenched her jaw when he refused to look at her. "Look at me!"

She realized she was yelling when Justin sprang from behind the kitchen door, eyes wide. She heard Annette's footsteps sprinting down the stairs behind her. Leana didn't care anymore that her friends were watching. She was sick of hiding her anger. She no longer felt shame or pity in her heart for this man.

Otis finally looked at her and, for a moment, they stared at each other in complete silence. The only noise in the room was the news anchor. Leana caught a short part of what the man was reporting. "*Twenty years after the anniversary of the first visitor, another spaceship seems to have crashed—*"

Leana slammed the remote down, turning off the HV. "You can't keep running away, Dad. This has to stop… Now! You have to decide who you're going to be."

"I'm not running," he responded quietly.

Leana threw her hands up confused. "Then what? What is it?!"

"You wouldn't understand." Otis put his head into his hands.

"How can I understand?" Leana raised her voice. "You won't talk to me!"

Otis rose to his feet quickly, looking into Leana's eyes. "I'm protecting you."

Protecting me, right!

She scoffed, "From what? You? Because *you're* the one doing all the damage."

"It doesn't matter. You'll be leaving soon." Otis turned to walk away.

Leana grabbed his arm. "I'm not leaving until you tell me. I'm tired of all your secrets. Tell me."

"I have nothing to tell you," whispered Otis, looking defeated.

Leana was done. *I give up.* He completely had distanced himself from her all over again, and he was going to keep his secrets from her. She shoved his arm back towards him and turned away. She walked down the hall, passing the stairs and office. Just before turning the corner, Leana looked back one last time, still somehow hoping Otis would stop her and change his mind, but instead, he sat back down, his back towards her. The only thing she could feel now was emptiness and anger. She dug deep in her pocket and pulled out the pocket watch she'd carried around with her since she was a tiny child. She looked at it for a short moment. It was a gift from her father and it disgusted her.

She squeezed the watch tightly in her hand, tensing every muscle in her body, and heaved it across the hallway. As it crashed into the HV, Leana turned and ran into the back room, squeezing out the window. She had only made it about a hundred feet before she could hear her name being yelled from the house. She didn't stop or turn around, she just kept running. She needed to get away. She wanted to be alone.

She never wanted to see him again.

CHAPTER 31

Leana ran until her breath was ragged. She knew how to power through pain from her training in soccer, but she welcomed the physical discomfort now as she struggled to ignore the aching in her heart. She couldn't bear thinking of her father and the false hope he had pandered since her arrival. The fire in her chest burned as she ran hard, but she ignored it.

She was now deeper into the woods than she'd been previously, and this time she was by herself. She had passed the crater where Rychur's ship crashed a little while back, but she still didn't feel far enough away. The dark, cloudy morning didn't make for good visibility, but she actually found comfort in the dim, cool somberness of the woods. Anything was better than being around her father.

She ran until her legs felt like they couldn't go any farther. She stopped and put her hands on her hips, trying to breathe as her legs shook violently. The dead sprint had taken its toll on her body. Leana turned to look around and was relieved to see there was no house in sight, only the dark expanse of the woods. She didn't know what to do from here; she just wanted to be away from everything. After having such an incredible night where she had felt closer to her father than she'd ever dreamed she could, she couldn't fathom what had happened. The familiar pain of abandonment filled her again. It made her feel overwhelmingly betrayed and deceived. *Why doesn't he want me? Why doesn't he love me?*

She thought they had settled some things last night, had begun healing those deep wounds, but it appeared the man was exactly what she had thought all this time: a coward. She wanted to hate him more than ever, just thinking about it made her feel sick. She leaned over, still breathing heavy, trying to quell the nausea.

Leana needed to hear her mother's voice, her guide through anger, but she knew her mother would tell her '*to stop hating him because it isn't what he deserves*'. She desperately wanted to stop caring about him altogether, to stop having a father again. Not knowing what else to do, Leana kept walking, trying to make sense of why her father didn't understand her or even care to try. With each passing thought, Leana had to constantly wipe at the cold tears falling from her eyes while she held her hoodie tight across her chest to stay warm.

"Child," growled a deep voice.

Leana jumped backwards in surprise. She looked up to see a tall, pale figure standing a few yards in front of her. It felt like she had been electrocuted. The air was suddenly charged with tension.

"Who are you?" She couldn't think of anything else to say.

The thin, bald man stood staring at her with a disturbing smile across his face. His clothing was a strange, rough material, black from head to toe. He wore a tattered cloth, similar to a cape that started at his waist and hung to the back of his knees. His clothing was so tight she could see every lean, wiry muscle.

"Hello," the man murmured, tilting his head to the side. "What is your name?"

The empty eyes of this new stranger sent a cold shiver up Leana's spine. She wanted to turn and run back to the house, but her feet seemed unable to move. Fear crept up her scalp and crawled through the hair on the back of her neck. She felt frozen, afraid to take her eyes off the man.

"Um…" she struggled, staring wide-eyed at the deep scars across his face, head and neck.

"I asked for your name," repeated the towering man, more loudly. He took a step forward.

Instantly, Leana took a step back.

He grinned coldly. "I won't hurt you, child."

"Who are—" Leana tried to force the words out again.

"*Where* is the better question. Where am I?" He looked around him and back at her. "Where?!"

"Uh… Prescott, Iowa?" Her legs were heavy and breaths rapid. She wanted her father, El, Rychur, Esu… Anyone.

"We have always called this Coreal. But I have never been here before."

Leana stared silently as cold fear shot through her veins. Rychur had also called Earth "Coreal." This stranger was from Balachur.

"From up there," he said, pointing slowly at the sky, "it seems quite busy down here."

Leana felt like he was toying with her, but she didn't have time to wonder why. She was more concerned with how to get away.

He tilted his head down. "Yes?"

Leana didn't speak. She flinched when his brow fell and his eyes glared.

"Speak!" he yelled.

Every muscle in Leana's body started to shake; she closed her eyes hoping he'd be gone, but quickly reopened them as she heard him take a heavy step forward.

"Yes," she whispered. "Yes."

He began pacing around Leana, leaning in to study her. He was so close she could now smell him – he smelled of burnt ash. The way his gaze raked her as he paced was unnerving. "What name were you given?"

"L—Leana," she muttered, clenching her fists to try to stop the rapid shaking. Her jaw felt locked tight, making speech difficult. She'd never been this scared in her entire life.

He kept pacing. "Are you afraid?"

This time he only waited a second before yelling again. "Speak!"

"Yes," she whispered. Tears began streaming down her face. She lowered her head, but lifted it quickly, afraid to take her eyes off him. "Why are you here?" she stuttered.

"I'm tracking a deserter from my world. He crashed somewhere near this coordinate, and I'm here to take him home."

Rychur. She knew he was watching her every move, looking for tell-tale hints or twitches.

He waited patiently this time, and then lowered his voice. The deep resonance of his whispered voice made him even more terrifying. "Did anyone come through here that didn't appear *normal* to you?"

Besides you? She didn't want to say anything, but she didn't want to make this man angrier either. "No."

"Liar!!"

The man in black was suddenly behind Leana, wrapping his long, gray fingers around her neck. He whispered into her ear, "You are brave, Leana."

Knowing he was looking for Rychur gave her courage. She knew she had to protect her friend. She straightened her posture with his hand still on her neck, noticing the stench of his breath under his cold touch.

He squeezed a bit harder, but Leana wasn't going to give him the pleasure of screaming. She knew her lack of response made him angry when he pulled her head back, forcing her to bend backwards, looking up at him. "You're *very* brave."

Leana tried ignoring the pain shooting through her neck. He was so strong, she feared he was going to break her. With a sudden jerk she yanked free and whipped around to glare at the man. She could see the rage fill his eyes as he reached for her again, his arm extended forward towards her throat. She closed her eyes anticipating whatever pain she was about to endure. Her only thought was protecting her friend.

A sudden grunt flung her eyes open. She gasped in shock. "El."

CHAPTER 32

Leana could only scream the wolf's name. "El!"

El was on top of the alien, growling, his forearm in her mouth. Leana saw the purple blood running from between El's teeth. Leana didn't know what to do. She couldn't leave El and she was no use in this fight. She watched as the wolf dug her claws into the chest of the man as he lay pinned on his back.

"Get off, beast!" he yelled, swinging his fist. El yelped as she flew across the air and smashed against a tree, going limp on impact. Her body lay motionless on the ground.

"No!" Leana screamed. The fear was gone, instantly replaced with rage. She glared at the stranger as he stood up. "You!"

Thinking only of her wounded friend, Leana stepped toward the man. Her vision went black.

CHAPTER 33

The screams were too much this time. I was trapped and I didn't know where. The night was hiding everything around me. I was terrified. Looking up I saw the suns streaming across the sky, lighting everything around me and burning away the agonizing voices. For a moment I felt comfort, but the suns didn't stop in the sky. The beating heat on my face was too much; the feeling of my blood boiling consumed my mind. I felt an overwhelming weight on my back, bringing me to my knees. Lifting my head, I witnessed the lushest and most beautiful forest of trees and plants springing from the ground, different than anything I had ever seen before. They were reaching for the sun as if trying to be pulled from the ground, almost like hands reaching out to be rescued. The screams started again. I plugged my ears, but the horrifying sounds didn't dull. The cries grew louder and louder and I screamed out myself for the pain to stop, but it didn't. In my mind I was trapped with this enemy, this shadow of haunting souls. Finally, the suns dropped behind the horizon, but I was still trapped in this nightmare of black. The forest died and melted into the black ground.

Again, the suns rose, faster this time, as did the trees and the forest around me. The screams rose and flooded the air again, filling my head with the pain and agony suffered by the shrieks and cries. Again, the tree branches and bushes stretched out to the sky where the suns threw down the unbearable heat, refusing again to stretch out to help the plants and trees below. The screams built and built, then quickly disappeared as fast as the suns setting behind the horizon.

Again and again, the suns rose, each time shooting faster across the sky. The screams ripped out into the air, disappearing faster as the suns hid behind the horizon.

The voices yelled out in pain again, they grew and faded over and over. I couldn't stop the pain, the agony. I cried out to them, begging for them to stop. The suns rose and set, rose and set. The forest grew and reached out, and then melted again and again into the ground.

My head spun as the sky brightened and blackened faster and faster. I didn't know what to do. The pain in my head became too much to bear.

I opened my eyes. It was quiet. I was in the black again. I didn't want to cry out because I didn't want the voices answering back. I took a step forward; there was no texture to the ground under my feet. It was smooth. I took another step, hesitant of a cliff or edge I might fall from. I took a few more steps, one after another.

There was a sudden yank on my pant leg, stopping me from going forward. Fear jumped up my spine and I drove my feet forward, trying to get away. Hands sprung from the ground all around me. I heard the ground open up, but I still couldn't see it. I heard the sound of moaning. I stepped onto rocks, but they weren't stable on the ground. I stepped on two more, softer than the others. The hands continued to reach for me. I could feel the fingertips reaching out to pull me down with them.

I stepped onto a pile of boulders, finally getting away from the grasping hands. The moans grew loud, closing in on me. I had nowhere left to go. I didn't know why, but I knew they were coming for me. They came closer and closer.

Suddenly, the suns rose again. I was so relieved to see them.

The light exposed the vast land around me, but now I could see it was a wasteland of corpses clear to the horizon. They were everywhere. Children, women, soldiers; both old and young lay lifeless all around me. I looked down to see I had climbed up on a pile of corpses. They were staring through me and I stared back. I could see the lifelessness of their glare.

I jerked away as another hand grasped onto my arm. It wouldn't let go as I tried to pull away. I twisted around, and saw standing there was an old man in white. I'd seen him in my dreams before. His eyes were first pink, and then they faded to a sky blue. Those eyes… They stared straight at me.

"Leana, find me!"

A gasp of oxygen raced into Leana's lungs as she shot up from bed with her eyes wide open, feeling as if she had been suffocating just a moment earlier. Disorientated, Leana noticed the sun was already down. The night sky instantly reminded her of the evil man in black she had encountered. *He must've been a dream,* she thought. *A dream within a dream.* Leana wasn't sure how to make sense of this. She felt so weak and her body hurt so much everywhere that she didn't want to move, let alone try to figure it all out. Gathering enough strength to turn her body so her legs hung off the bed, Leana looked out the window to see the cloudy, night sky. She felt something touch her hand and she jerked it to her body quickly, then realized it was El.

"Hey," a voice whispered from across the room.

Leana jumped again which wasn't easy since her muscles were incredibly sore. Rychur was sitting in a chair near the bedroom door. El was in the room by the bed.

"How are you feeling?"

CHAPTER 34

Leana tried to scoot to the edge of the bed, but her muscles shot pain through her body, and she ended up lying back down.

"Everything hurts," moaned Leana. She scanned the rest of the room.

"Oh my god, Ana!" exclaimed Annette, running into the bedroom with Justin right behind her. She jumped on the bed, embracing her friend, ignoring Leana's grunts of pain. "We were so worried."

Justin slowly sat down next to her, gripping Leana's hand with both of his and staring deep into her eyes. "Are you okay?" he asked.

Leana could see his genuine concern. "I'm okay," she said softly, squeezing his hand.

Leana looked around the room for a second before Justin let go. "Where's Otis?"

"I don't know," Justin responded. "As soon as we brought you back he left again."

"Brought me back?"

"Ana," said Annette, "we found you… unconscious in the woods. El chased after you when you left, and we followed her. When we got to you, you were on the ground."

So it wasn't all a dream.

"El, as you see, is doing fine," Rychur said, comfortingly.

Knowing El was there, alive and by her side, brought her instant relief. "What happened?" She sniffed hard and brushed her fingers through her hair. She winced at the pain shooting up her arm.

"What do you remember?" Rychur stood up as Leana slowly swung her legs to the side of the bed again.

"A man in black," she said, gazing at the floor.

"Did he give a name?" he asked.

She shook her head in response. "No, but I think he was looking for you." She looked up.

Rychur held his breath for a moment. "What did he look like?"

Leana tried to stand, but couldn't hold herself up. Annette and Justin quickly braced her from falling backwards as she sat. She leaned forward onto her shaky knees, cupping her face in her hands.

"Just relax. You gotta stop moving," said Justin worriedly. He wrapped his arm around her back, and Annette laid her arm across his, holding Leana together.

Rychur approached and knelt down in front of her. "Leana," he whispered, "it's okay now. You're safe."

Leana began crying into her hands, trying to take deep breaths, remembering the terror that filled her when encountering the stranger. "He was just so... awful."

"Do you know who she is talking about?" asked Justin defensively.

Rychur ignored him. "Leana, what did he look like?"

She tried to keep her mind from flashing the images of the stranger from space. She wanted to forget everything. She wanted it to be a dream.

Rychur looked impatient with her hesitation. "Leana, you need to tell me, so I can help you."

Sniffling, Leana took a deep breath. "Okay. Okay." She looked at her friends, then Rychur. "Uh, he was tall. He had gray skin and was bald. And there were scars covering his face and head."

"You mean, like a..." Rychur gestured his finger above his left eye, dragging diagonally across his face. Leana responded with a nod.

"Ry, who is she talking about?" asked Annette. "There was nobody else out there."

Rychur stood fast, rubbing the back of his neck.

"Whoa, whoa, Rychur. What's wrong?" asked Justin.

"This is not good. We're in trouble. All of us."

"What do you mean? Who is he?" Leana watched him walk to the window and stare out.

"His name is Nach. The fact that you survived an encounter with him--"

"Wait. What do you mean *survived?*" she asked.

"That is what I do not understand. Leana, you never should have survived." He breathed out and looked back at her. "He's the general of the Baramat army... and he's the brother of King Renisis."

"What?!" exclaimed the three together.

"The evil villain from your story? That's his brother?" Leana still couldn't believe what she was hearing. Leana wondered why she couldn't remember anything after El had collided with the tree, or where Nach had gone.

"What do we do now, Ry?" asked Annette.

"First off, we need to hope he doesn't find this place," Rychur said.

"Why did he come here?" Leana asked.

"Me. He came for me."

"Why?"

"Yeah. What'd you do?" asked Justin.

"He's here to stop me from bringing back the weapon that was supposed to stop the war."

Leana watched Rychur look at the ground. She recognized the look of defeat.

"What's wrong?" Leana didn't like his silence and wanted an answer. "Rychur?"

"You are, Leana. *You* are what's wrong." He pointed at Leana.

She was startled by his response. "What?"

"You do not understand. Until tonight, he didn't know someone like you existed. You are a threat to him."

"Why? Because I'm from Earth? I don't understand. There's millions of us."

"You are special, Leana." Rychur received a blank stare. "You have no idea how special."

Before Leana could find out more answers, Esu strolled into the room carrying a tray. "Oh good, you're awake. How do you feel, Leana?"

"Fine, Esu." She didn't want to be interrupted.

"Well that's good. Here, drink this," he encouraged, handing Leana a glass of water. "Are you hungry? Of course you are. Here is a sandwich, apple, and carrots for energy. Eat, eat."

Leana was juggling the food Esu handed her, grimacing at his fast movements. Justin and Annette picked up the veggies falling on the bed in Esu's haste.

"Esu, Esu." She reached up and took the tray gently. "Thank you," she whispered, as she put the food back on the tray.

He smiled and bowed. "You are so very welcome, Leana." Esu exited the room. Even in all this craziness, Leana couldn't help but smile at the silly android.

The apple was placed back on Leana's tray with a bite taken out of it. Looking up she saw Justin grinning. She couldn't help but laugh. "Hey!"

El continued nudging her nose against Leana, wanting to be petted. Leana wiped her hand on her shirt from El's wet nose. "Thank you, El," she said, rubbing the wolf's head. "Wow. You healed fast didn't you, girl? Glad you're feeling okay. That was quite a hit you took, and thank you, sweet wolf, for saving me." She looked back at Rychur.

"Rychur, where did my father go? I know you know."

Rychur hesitated, and then sighed. "I don't know where your father went. He just… left."

"No, Ry! Where did he go?"

Rychur's head dropped and his voice quieted, "I honestly know nothing."

"Leana," said Annette, "he's being serious. We haven't seen him."

Leana looked at Justin who nodded in agreement.

Just then, something crashed into the side of the house, shaking the walls violently and shooting a shock through Leana. Her friends gasped and Rychur twisted his body around. Leana's body became numb as she stood up from the bed.

"Rychur, what was that?"

"Not what... Who." he said ominously.

El stepped in front of Leana, between her and the hallway. Leana thought she heard Esu's voice downstairs, but it was overwhelmed by more smashing sounds. Whatever it was, it was inside.

"Is it him?" Leana stepped closer to Rychur.

She gripped Rychur's arm tightly as a terrifyingly deep voice rang through the house. "RYCHUR!"

Leana felt Rychur's body tense up.

"Nach," he said faintly.

An explosion erupted through the floor. Wood flooring shot upward like a geyser directly in front of the bedroom door. Two large hands reached up and grasped onto the doorframe. Slowly rising through the gaping hole was Nach, this time twice as large as before. His body was enormous and he towered over Rychur and the teens. His skin was pulled tight, popping veins out all over his muscled body.

"Rychur." His voice was deep and hollow. It resonated around the room.

"Nach," Rychur responded, clenching his fists.

Leana looked down at Rychur's hands. They were glowing. She looked up to see the same glow in his eyes. "Rychur?"

He lowered his head, but kept his gaze on the monster. "Everyone get back."

Thrusting his hands out at Nach, Rychur roared as a bright collection of energy slowly condensed around his hands. He released it in an explosive blast, forcing Nach backwards through three walls and out of the house. Leana's eyes and ears rang violently, throwing off her equilibrium.

"We need to go." Rychur grabbed Leana's arm, looking up at the other scared teens. "All of us."

"Go where? What's happening?!" asked Annette, eyes completely petrified.

"Ry, what do we do?" exclaimed Justin.

"Nach is going to kill us. We must go. Now!"

Leana had a sudden flashback of Otis' globe being sent through the office wall. She now realized Rychur had done that.

"Is he dead?"

"No, barely scratched," Rychur said. "Come on!"

The thought of anyone or anything surviving that blast scared her. It scared all of them. "What? How is that possible?" Leana asked, still frozen.

"Leana! We have to go." He threw his arm towards the window, shattering it into a million pieces without touching it. "El, go!"

El sprang out of the window onto the porch roof without hesitation then landed gently on the grass below. Justin followed quickly after her, showing just how skilled of a gymnast he was. Leana stepped out with Rychur and Annette. She looked down, seeing El smelling around for Nach. The wolf lifted her head and howled.

"Jump, Leana, jump!" Rychur shoved her towards the edge of the roof. "I will hold him off," he said, stepping back into the bedroom.

After watching Annette jump down slightly less gracefully than Justin had, Leana looked back in fear, pulling Rychur towards her. "I can't leave. I can help."

"No. Just go!" he yelled.

"Leana, come on!" Justin yelled up to her.

As Leana turned to jump, a crash from downstairs told her Nach had plowed his way back into the house. She could only imagine the destruction happening on the floor below.

Rychur turned around towards the door with a fierce grunt, reigniting the glowing haze in his hands and eyes. He stood in a ready position, his shoulders rising and falling from his heavy breathing.

"Come on out, beast. Face me!" bellowed Rychur.

A loud bang erupted from the floor beneath Rychur. Leana looked down at his feet, seeing hands spring through the floor and grab Rychur's ankles, yanking him down violently.

"Rychur!" Leana screamed, reaching her body back through the window, scrambling to get inside.

She heard El growl as the wolf sprang back into the house through the window on the floor below her. Leana peered down through the gaping hole to see Rychur get thrown across the room as the pink energy blasted from his hands point-blank at Nach. She heard Rychur grunt as his body smashed into something hard. El erupted in a ferocious growl as Rychur made his way back at Nach, shooting the energy discharges from his hands.

Through the loud explosions and destruction, Leana could hear her name being screamed by her friends outside, but she knew if she turned away now she couldn't help Rychur and El. She wanted to fight, but she was frozen. *What can I do?*

A deep-voiced grunt echoed below from Nach as she heard another outburst from El, followed by a shrieking yelp.

"El!" Leana tried to see what happened, but the wolf was out of eyesight.

"Justin, Annette, no!" screamed Rychur. "Get out of here you two!"

Justin? Leana edged further into the hole and saw Justin running after Annette into the living room.

Nach slammed his fist against the wall, causing a part of the ceiling to collapse on top of Annette, and knocking Justin back. Annette's legs weren't moving.

"Annette!" screamed Justin as he picked himself back up. He charged Nach, who had turned again to face Rychur, and jumped on the beast's back. He wrapped his arms around Nach's neck and looked up at Leana, bellowing, "Leana, run! GO!"

Jerking Justin's body to the side effortlessly, Nach swung the human off his back, slamming him against the ground hard. Justin staggered to his feet and swung a weak right-hook to the side of Nach's face. His punch did nothing. Nach returned the punch with a back hand that shot Justin across the room and out of Leana's view.

"Justi–" Rychur started to yell, shooting another blast of energy toward Nach. The beast charged through the energy beam and landed a vicious uppercut on Rychur, shooting him up through the floor behind Leana.

"No!" Leana screamed desperately.

Rychur's body went through the bed and landed in the pile of debris he had just created. Leana was able to roll out the way just in time, almost falling into the first hole Rychur created.

She rushed to his side. "Rychur." She shook him. "RYCHUR!"

Leana didn't have time to help Rychur regain consciousness. A thud followed by heavy breathing drew her attention. Nach stood behind her; a subtle glow came from the gashes where El had dug her claws and teeth into him. She watched horrified as the wounds closed. He took a step towards Leana.

Fear swept over her body as he approached.

He reached out to her, grinning and cackling maniacally.

Leana's scream was quickly muffled as everything went black.

CHAPTER 35

Leana opened her eyes slowly to the sound of heavy marching. Her stomach ached from the boney shoulder she was slung over. She could see Rychur was slung over Nach's other shoulder, still unconscious. Looking around, she realized they were back in the forest, but she had no idea where. It all looked the same. Cautiously, Leana reached over to her unconscious friend and tried to shake him. She was afraid to speak.

"Awake, are you?" spoke Nach in his deep voice.

The tone of his voice sent chills up her spine. She tried pushing away, groaning. "Where is El? Where are my friends?"

"Dead. Alive. It does not matter to me." His strides were powerful, jostling her stomach hard.

"You better not have killed them… monster!"

"Or what?!" he yelled, grabbing the back of her shirt and lifting her high above him. His strength didn't scare her now, but the sneer on his face made her angry. For the first time, she felt the courage she needed and smashed the heel of her foot into his face. It was like hitting concrete, but she was satisfied when he grunted, turning his head to the side.

"That was foolish," Nach responded, throwing her back over his shoulder. "It does not matter though."

"Where are you taking us?" She tried to press her stomach away from his shoulder just enough to breathe.

He stopped again and threw her to the ground. She crawled back a bit as Nach bent down to look piercingly into her eyes. "I'm taking you home, Leana."

The sound of her name coming from his mouth made her feel sick. Nach grabbed Leana by her wrist and yanked her to her feet. "Go," he growled, shoving her onward into the woods. He continued to prod her anytime she slowed.

"What do you want with me?" Leana reached deep into her pocket for the pocket watch, wanting to hold it tight. She felt a moment of panic when she couldn't find it, then she remembered she'd thrown it at her father right before she left. Her heart sank. She thought about her friends and El who had tried to help save her, and wondered what had happened to them.

"You are unique, child. I am surprised I did not recognize it sooner." She listened to the crunching of sticks and leaves under his footsteps.

She stopped and turned to look at him, noticing the glow of some freshly healing wounds on his chest and stomach. She knew they were from Rychur's blasts, but she couldn't believe how insignificant the damage appeared to be, considering how fierce she thought his attack was. She looked up and glared. "What do you mean?"

He smirked. "Don't you know? You do not belong here, Leana." Nach shoved her hard. "Go."

Leana stumbled on through the underbrush. "What did you do to my father?" She kept her eyes forward, realizing she wasn't scared anymore. His chuckle forced her to look back at him.

"Nothing," the horrid voice echoed in the dark. "Yet."

The only thing that made Leana feel somewhat safe right now was the unconscious, yet still living, Rychur. "What are you going to do with him?" She nodded at the limp body on Nach's shoulder.

"I will take him back with us. My brother will want to meet with him."

Leana remembered Rychur's stories. "You mean your psycho brother Renisis?"

"Silence!" he yelled, slapping her across the face. Leana fell to the ground, struggling to stand up. Nach grabbed her by her hair and pulled her to her feet.

Leana struggled to get herself free from his grasp. "Why did you come here?" Pain seared through her scalp and the bruise on her face. She wished her father were here.

"Enough questions. Walk or I will carry you again."

It felt like they'd been walking forever, though it was most likely just the exhaustion of her body from all the adrenaline and fighting. She wanted this nightmare to end and everything to go back to normal. Unfortunately, she didn't know what normal was anymore. She desperately wanted Rychur to wake up, and could only pray that El was okay. She also feared her missing-in-action father had left them all to die.

"We're here," grunted Nach. Up ahead, Leana could see a ship. It reminded her of Rychur's ship, but it was bigger. It had the same structural build and design, but the exterior emblem and color were different. It had a large gold emblem that resembled claw marks. The rest of the ship was gray and black. Without any battle damage, the smooth design was more noticeable than with Rychur's ship. "Sit here," ordered Nach as they arrived at the craft.

Leana felt the heavy weight of Nach's hand as he forced her to the ground. She flinched as Rychur's body was slammed down next to her. The impact woke him up. He groaned and moved his head to the side, eyes still closed.

"Rychur." She shook him gently, and his eyes flew open, focusing on her. "Oh, thank god," she said, resting her head on his chest. "You're okay."

"Where are we?" He tried sitting up.

"We're at Nach's ship." Leana looked over at the man in black who stood about twenty feet away, staring into the forest. She leaned against the ship and hugged her legs to her chest. She stared at the monster quietly. She watched as he went up the ramp of his ship, and then returned quickly, peering at the prisoners to be sure they hadn't moved. Leana knew they could never move fast enough to get away from him in the shape they were in.

"Why are we still here?" She tried to speak quietly so as not to get Nach's attention.

"I think he's waiting for someone," Rychur stated, staring into the pitch-black forest.

"You think there's more?" Leana asked surprised, trying not to feel afraid again.

"I don't know, Leana," whispered Rychur. He'd been able to pull himself up next to her, resting against the ship.

"Are you okay?"

"Yeah, he just got a lucky shot in. I hesitated when Justin jumped on him, and I shouldn't have. Won't happen again, I assure you," he said confidently.

Suddenly, holding back tears, Leana thought of Annette's lifeless legs under the debris. "I hope they're okay, Ry. I don't want them to die."

"Your friends are very strong. I'm sure they are going to be okay, Leana."

Leana wasn't so sure.

Nach turned quickly and stormed towards Leana. He bent down, shoving his hand into her chest. Leana felt pain shoot through her spine and head as she slammed against the hull of the ship.

"Silence!" He wrapped his hand around her throat and began to squeeze.

Without hesitating, Rychur shot an energy blast into Nach's wrist. "Stop!"

Nach fell back a few steps.

"Do not touch her, Nach."

Nach regained his balance and charged back at them. He raised his fist as Rychur stretched out his hands and calmly closed his eyes.

Leana sat up straight, bracing her body for impact. At the last second, she shut her eyes, flinching. A loud echo rang around her. Reopening her eyes, she saw a force field of light trapping her and Rychur inside like a bubble.

Nach began pounding on the protective layer of energy, but he wasn't making a dent. Ripples of light vibrated around the bubble, radiating from where his hands slammed into the barrier. Even though Leana felt like Nach couldn't get to them, his anger still terrified her. He was filled with such hatred; she could see it in his eyes.

When the pounding didn't work, he began clawing at the bubble like a wild beast, to no avail. He stopped, staring into Leana's eyes with his hands relaxed at his sides. He placed his right hand on the energy field and tapped it, giving her a mocking grin. He then turned around and walked back to the front of the ship, to once again peer into the dark woods.

Leana looked over at Rychur. His eyes were closed with his hands stretched out, glowing the same familiar color as before. His head was tilted down and he looked to be entirely at peace. She felt instantly safe, seeing him focused and calm. She sighed and leaned back against the ship.

Nitro, Rychur.

CHAPTER 36

Leana continued to stare at Nach through the transparent, colorful wall. *Who is he waiting for?* She had the sudden fear that if there were others they probably had her father. It would explain his untimely absence. *Or maybe he's still just running away.* She didn't want to worry about him too. Her mind ran wild not knowing what had happened to her friends, El, Esu, and her father. She wondered if she was going to die.

Leana could see Rychur was still focused on maintaining the force field, keeping her safe the only way he could at the moment. Leana was grateful for his company. He sat silent and focused. In the quiet, she realized the force field gave off a peaceful, droning hum. She sat back and listened, waiting.

The tension continued to build in her mind. She thought about El's final yelp in the battle with Nach back in the house. She thought about the sounds of Esu probably being ripped to pieces in the dining room. Even the thought of her father abandoning her again came into her mind. She was too worked up to think of the good things. It appeared there was no help coming, no savior. She knew she was going to get taken away and no one was ever going to know where she went or what happened here. She knew once this energy field went down she was most likely dead. She so badly wanted to just go home to her mother.

"He's here," whispered Rychur, lifting his head. Leana saw his eyes were wide and hopeful. He was smiling.

"Who is it?" Leana looked out into the woods.

"Him." He nodded at the dark trees.

Leana squinted into the forest only to see El stalking out of the dark woods. She was ecstatic to see the wolf looked uninjured. Leana could see Nach's chest puff up and his fists clench tightly. She leaned to the side,

233

trying to see past him, but Nach's huge frame blocked her view.

It wasn't until Nach shifted to the side that Leana could see who was with El. It was a man in a sleeveless, brown, leather cloak over armor that looked unlike anything she had ever seen before. A hood covered his face. He stood confidently, and Leana's first thought was that he was one of Nach's soldiers. Then she realized El would never have been next to an enemy. She only sided with people she trusted, and she didn't trust many.

As the stranger approached Nach, Leana could better make out the armor underneath the exterior hood attached to the long cloak. The smooth, shining armor was crimson outlined in gold and silver. The armor was fitted and made the muscular shape of the stranger's body obvious. His forearms and legs were tightly layered with plates of armor as well, close against his skin. There was a symbol on the center of his chest plate, but she couldn't make it out clearly. It resembled a flower of some sort.

"Rychur, who is that?"

"*That's* the weapon, Leana," Rychur said confidently.

"What? But—Who *is* he?" She leaned in closer to try and make out his face.

"Galavon, the greatest general of the Onites." Leana heard the pride in his words.

Just then, Galavon pulled back the hood, exposing his face. Leana's stomach flipped in shock as she recognized him.

"Dad!"

Galavon looked at his daughter for the briefest of seconds, sending her a nod then focused on the villain.

"Hello, Nach," Galavon said firmly.

Leana couldn't believe how much more tense Nach became. He was arched forward as though he had a hunchback.

"Galavon. I knew you'd come. It has been a long time." Nach began to pace slowly in a circle, staring at him with Galavon following suit. "A very long time, *old* warrior."

"I'm not a warrior anymore. At least, I wasn't until you came here and threatened my family. You never should have come."

"And miss my opportunity to seek my revenge? Why would I do that, *murderer?*"

Murderer? Leana looked at Rychur, but he avoided her gaze, watching instead the two men.

Galavon continued circling Nach, keeping his eyes on his opponent. "You were a fool to come here, Nach, and then you capture a child like the cowardly insect you are instead of facing me honorably. Or did you leave your honor back on Balachur?"

"No, Galavon. My honor is what kept them alive while I waited for you. You are the one who lost your honor long ago...'Murderer of the Innocent' is what they call you back home now."

"A name I have earned and suffered with for many years. You cannot shame me any more than I have already shamed myself. Now, let them go, Nach."

"You want me to release the bloodline of the Malachur and your *special* daughter? No, murderer. That will never happen. After they watch you fall tonight, I'll be taking them to the king."

"You will not, beast."

"My brother always gets what he wants." Slowly, Nach's claws grew longer and sharper from his fingertips. "I will remove your spine, Galavon, and avenge my baby brother."

"That may be justice." Galavon grasped the hand of his weapon still sheathed in his belt. "But you will not find it to be a simple task. You will not walk away from this fight." Galavon unsheathed his sword.

Instantly, Leana recognized the weapon. It was the ancient sword she had found in the attic on her first day. She'd never considered that the foreign weapon might be alien. She remembered what had happened when she held it. It seemed so small and insubstantial at the moment.

"Last chance, Nach," Galavon snarled.

"Fight me!" Nach bellowed. He crouched down and screamed again. His eyes began to glow bright, and his body bulged in size even more. Leana could hear the stretching skin and cracking bones as the Baramat soldier grew in size. The man in black now towered over her father, but Leana was shocked to see her father stand his ground. He wouldn't be running from this fight.

She suddenly noticed El. The strange black markings that ran along the wolf's spine stood up on end. As if light filled every fiber of the black fur, her back started to glow and change color. Pink illuminated within her markings, and as she growled her eyes also began glowing fiercely. Leana was shocked to see somehow El was drawing upon the same power the aliens used.

Nach took one massive step forward. Fear filled every inch of Leana's body; fear for her father and for El. She wanted to help fight, but she knew she couldn't. She remembered how violent Nach had been last time and wondered what her father could do against such strength. Instantly it hit her *why* she was special: she had her father's blood.

As Galavon placed both hands on the handle of his meager sword Leana realized she had misjudged him for a coward.

He lowered his stance with his legs wide and strong, and the sword held out straight in front of him. He closed his eyes and took a deep breath. Leana could almost hear the tightening of his hands around the hilt. For a brief moment he seemed to forget he was in front of Nach. He looked completely at peace, as if he were meditating. His eyes opened suddenly, glowing bright. Energy ignited out of his body like an intense fog.

Galavon looked down and the energy slowly ran through the creases of his armor. As he did it flowed through his hands into the handle and up the blade like blood flowing through a body. The fog engulfed the blade and it started growing, stretching out towards Nach. It looked almost like a claymore sword, but as it continued lengthening the blade became thinner more like a katana. As a silvery gleam reflected off the edge, it became clear that the sword was also becoming sharper as it grew. Leana heard the screeching sound of metal stretching. She cringed.

By the time it stopped, the blade had stretched to be nearly four feet long. Leana watched her father look over at a tree next to him. He swiped his blade through it with little effort, cutting through the wood as though it was paper. It toppled noisily, forcing Nach to step to the side to avoid being slammed by the trunk.

Leana was stunned by her father's strength and ability – never once had she expected anything like this from him – but she couldn't help but notice that Nach's breathing had become louder.

Leana's attention shifted as she realized Rychur had dropped the energy field and was slowly standing up, his hands and eyes still glowing.

A monstrous scream immediately drew her attention back to her father and his opponent. Nach roared, charging the smaller warrior. He swung his claws with lightning speed, but Galavon ducked easily. The momentum sent Nach stumbling past Galavon. He stopped himself from falling over, digging his claws into the ground, then turned to face Galavon, who stood ready for his next attack.

Nach blew the dirt from his fingers.

As Galavon stared Nach down, Rychur appeared next to him in a stance that clearly indicated that he was there to fight as well. He bent down into a stance with one fist up by his face and the other stretched out towards Nach. "It is good to see you, Galavon."

"Same to you." Galavon kept his eyes on Nach.

Nach puffed out his chest again and clenched his fists. "Welcome to the fight. This is going to be fun."

In that short moment in time, Leana remembered all of the moments she had watched her father and Rychur together, acting like complete strangers. Her father had brushed him off so rudely. She realized now they had both been acting. *But why? Why didn't they just tell me all of this?*

She understood now what her mother had meant when she'd said her father was a soldier who had seen war. She'd never imagined he was a soldier from another planet.

And, now, here he was fighting to protect her from the evils of his homeworld.

Leana felt a surge of confidence as Rychur and her father stood side-by-side, against this brute, to protect her. In the momentary silence, all she could hear was her own breathing. The energetic glow from each of the warriors illuminated the darkness of the night as they just stared at each other. She felt the coldness creep up her skin.

Nach moved first. His feet shot huge chunks of dirt behind him as he charged. He slashed his claws at the other two, but they both jumped back and evaded. Rychur shot out both his hands, forming the same pink bubble around Nach that he'd used before for protection. His hands came together, interlocking his fingers. The bubble started closing tightly around the monster. Nach screamed as his body began being crushed.

Leana hoped this was the end, but Nach gave a snarl and flexed his body. With a loud howl he thrust his chest and arms outward, freeing himself instantly. The pink haze disintegrated as pieces of the bubble fell to the ground and disappeared. The recoil of energy blew Rychur back into the undergrowth.

Before Nach could reposition, Galavon slid in and drove his elbow into the beast's ribs. Bones cracked and Nach roared in pain. Getting behind him, Galavon then drove his elbow hard into the center of the monster's back, shooting Nach forward. He collided with a thick tree trunk near the rear of his ship. He fell to the ground hard, but dragged himself up immediately using the tree for leverage. He was breathing hard, staring at Galavon whose elbow remained outstretched.

Rychur began floating inches from the ground. Leana had seen it before, but was still amazed. She felt the cold breeze blow from around him.

Nach swiveled his head desperately, then sprang at Leana.

She turned quickly, ducking.

Nach reached out towards her face and grasped at air, missing his target by inches. Leana was close enough to see the dirt on Nach's palm. Looking over, she saw Rychur's hands stretched out toward Nach. He moved his hands across his body fluidly then shot them in Nach's direction. Like a puppet on a string, Nach's body was yanked away.

Leana gasped for air as she realized Rychur had just saved her life without even touching Nach. Even though he kept getting beaten back, Leana could see there was still a lot of fight left in his eyes. He had taken a pounding, but seemed unstoppable purely by his unrelenting willpower. Each time he was hit he'd attack harder than before. Leana cringed at the thought of how pulverized Nach's body was becoming, but that sliver of empathy was quickly replaced by the fear she had for her father and Rychur's lives.

Nach's next attack was aerial. With claws splayed and a massive roar, he targeted Rychur. The rage in his eyes was unlike anything Leana had ever seen. The size and speed of the mountainous demon wasn't enough to break Rychur's defenses. Rychur threw his hands up and with a blast of energy tossed Nach like a ragdoll, throwing the giant backwards towards the trees. Nach exploded through a tree, then smashed hard against the ground. Leana heard him grunt as his body slid a few feet before stopping. Without missing a beat Nach rose to one knee and inhaled hard, seeming to calculate his next move.

As he stood up, Nach grasped two tree trunks at their bases. With a furious yell he yanked them from the ground, ripping the soil open. Leaves fell like raindrops as Nach shook his new weapons. They appeared almost weightless as he held them out towards Leana's father. She couldn't believe his monstrous strength. If King Renisis and his clan were anything like Nach, Leana could see why Rychur was convinced everyone was in danger.

She watched helplessly as Nach slowly approached the other two, brandishing his enormous, wooden clubs.

SHIIIING. Galavon unsheathed his sword. With weapon outstretched toward Nach, he glanced beside him where Rychur stood, his hands and eyes glowing with energy.

Using the trees as sledgehammers, Nach smashed his weapons hard into the ground, where Galavon had stood just moments before. Branches snapped violently as Nach continued swinging the trees, attempting to flatten his opponent. The trunks splintered more each time they struck the ground or surrounding trees. Nach's attempts were futile as he missed his target with each swing.

Nach continued his desperate rampage, but eventually Galavon stopped dodging and started using his weapon. With each swipe of his sword, chunks of the assailing trees flew off.

Attempting to avoid the other combatants, Rychur leapt into the air and hovered, but Nach noticed and quickly turned. He locked eyes with Rychur then crouched deep and leapt after him.

Rychur smirked and held out his hands, palms facing the beast.

He screamed powerfully as energy burst from his hands like a tornado. Leana watched as it blasted down on Nach, who fruitlessly tried to use what was left of the huge trees as a shield. The leaves and branches erupted into flames as their wielder crashed back to the ground. Unfazed, Nach hurdled back into the air, swinging his flaming weapons. Each blow was useless as they pounded against a shield Rychur had quickly created.

Galavon took advantage of the distraction. He charged, leapt, and kicked Nach forcefully between the shoulder blades. Nach jolted forward, smashing his face against the earth once again. He rolled to his back and sat up, never letting go of the tree clubs.

Relentless, Nach rose to his feet and ran at Galavon again. At the last second before contact he juked to the side, narrowly missing Galavon's deadly blade. Using the momentum of his massive charge, Nach spun and smashed the trees together against Galavon's head, spraying embers and flaming leaves.

Momentarily stunned and blinded, Galavon dropped.

Leana gasped, cupping her mouth at her father's pained grunt.

Nach had raised both massive stumps high above his head, ready to deliver a final blow to his long-time nemesis, when a weak energy blast hit his back. He quickly turned his attention to Rychur who had floated into the air about to attack again. Rychur drew his hand back for another blast. Nach leapt forward and swung at Rychur, who hastily created a force field at the last second.

With awesome strength, Nach swung both trees, batting the energy sphere with Rychur inside to the ground. The force field disintegrated on impact, ejecting Rychur into the forest floor. He bounced once before coming to a stop.

Leana's horrified scream drew Nach's attention. The only thing worse than the sight of the wrath in his eyes was the sound of the wood splintering as Nach squeezed his grip tightly around the trunks.

"Coward!" yelled Galavon, standing behind the beast.

Nach turned his body slowly towards Galavon, his taunting eyes on Leana until he stood face-to-face with her father.

"Stay away from her, beast!" Galavon bellowed, pointing his sword. "Your fight is here." He gestured, hitting his chest. "Come on!"

Nach howled and charged with his weapons held high. He swung one of the trees down towards Galavon who blocked with his sword, cutting through the tree like paper just as the other trunk slammed against his rib cage. Leana gasped as her father flew chest-first into a distant tree. He dropped to the ground. Nach smiled smugly, obviously believing he had won until Galavon started to slowly get up, grasping his chest as he looked up for Nach.

"Look out!" Leana screamed.

SNAP

Galavon turned his head quickly to look behind him. Nach leapt through the air, logs above his head. Galavon ducked as Leana screamed again.

The trees smashed down violently on the energy sphere suddenly surrounding Galavon.

"What?!" yelled Nach.

"Not that easy, Nach," called Rychur as he approached the men, hands up supporting the energy shield he had just created. Keeping one arm up, Rychur dropped his other hand and with as much energy as he could muster he shot Nach backwards twenty feet.

"Thank you," Galavon said hoarsely, rising fully to his feet.

Rychur smiled. "You're getting slow."

"Shut up," Galavon said before chuckling with a returned smile.

Standing to his feet, Nach was taken aback for a moment as he stared at the two stunted tree trunks still left in his grasps. He threw them angrily at Rychur and Galavon like a stubborn child. Leana could see Nach's expression become more determined that ever. He sprang to his feet, anger filling his eyes. He charged Galavon, claws out. As Nach approached, Galavon countered with his foot to the beast's gut. Nach grunted as he smashed against the dirt and skidded back. He started to get up, slower this time and holding his stomach. Rychur and Galavon were hurting him. Rising to one knee, Nach raised his head and wiped the blood running from his mouth. He wasn't wild; he was hesitating.

"Don't try touching her again or I will end you," Galavon demanded, pointing the sword out.

"It's not possible. I have bested you once. I know I'm stronger than you. Where did you get your strength?" Nach grunted, trying to push himself up from the ground completely.

Galavon laid his sword on his shoulder. "It doesn't matter, Nach. Get up."

Nach's head hung low. He was enraged, but Leana could see him wincing in pain. He wrapped his arm across his ribcage. Leana assumed his ribs were broken. He grimaced at the pain, trying to hide it, but his eyes showed the amount of agony he was experiencing. He spat blood on the ground.

He leaned forward to charge again, but was instantly yanked back to the ground. El dug her teeth into his back, growling heavily and yanking her head to the side. Nach screamed, trying to reach for the wolf. She released him, only to dig her fangs into the side of his neck, lashing her jaw backward and pulling. He howled again in pain and rolled over, pressing the wolf against the ground. Before he could pull back and swing, Galavon was in the air delivering a swift kick hard to Nach's face. It threw Nach off balance, toppling him to the ground once again. He looked up to see Galavon lay his hand gently on the wolf. Blood dripped from her mouth; Nach's blood.

Nach tried futilely to push up, but he was weak. He couldn't find the strength to rise. He grunted and moaned, falling back to the dirt.

Leana saw Rychur was keeping Nach pressed down with another energy field. Unexpectedly, Rychur threw his hands up, yanking Nach high into the air. Rychur threw his hands down again, smashing Nach against the ground like a hammer. He repeated the motions. Each time, Nach grunted in pain.

Leana didn't know how to feel. Nach's purpose was to destroy, but watching him get pulverized was disturbing.

As the slamming stopped, Rychur raised Nach limply to his feet. Galavon took a step forward, close enough that Nach weakly swung his claws, striking only the ground again. Leana saw shock in the monster's eyes as her father began floating high above him.

"Now," Galavon ordered.

Rychur let go of his control of Galavon who dropped swiftly from the air, slamming both his fists down onto Nach's head. The impact was intense. Leana averted her eyes before the collision, but could still hear cracking bone and a thud as her father landed next to Nach, creating a small crater in the ground.

Nach howled as Galavon backed away. She looked back up to see the monster stand slowly. The energetic light began shining from his many wounds, but not as bright as before. Leana couldn't believe it; he was still willing to fight. Seeing the blood covering his body, Leana began to feel something like pity for him. Something was driving Nach to keep standing. He wasn't going to give up. Despite herself, Leana respected his will-power.

"You will have to kill me, Onite." Nach could barely speak through his battered face.

"Attacking my home and my daughter... You won't ever stop, will you?" Galavon stated calmly. "You will not harm anyone ever again."

Leana didn't want this. She didn't want to see her father kill anyone. "Dad, don't—" she called out.

"Leana, if he lives, he will bring war to this world. I'm sorry." Galavon's voice was loud and firm. He pointed his sword. "Nach, to quote your people: 'One last fight.' Are you ready?"

"Are you?" Nach sneered. He breathed deep, drawing upon whatever energy he had left and grew his hulk just a bit more. As Leana watched Nach's relentlessness she understood just how powerful Baramats actually were. Rychur's stories had been incredible, but seeing it in person was even more so. Nach continued to grow stronger even after the wounds he'd received. It didn't seem possible.

Galavon leapt forward, swinging his sword.

Nach sidestepped, punching Galavon and knocking him to the side. Rolling with the momentum, Galavon leg-swept the beast, knocking him off balance. Before Nach could regain his footing and strike back, Galavon circled around behind Nach, slashing his sword violently across his back. Nach screamed, trying to grab at the fresh laceration. He stepped away from Galavon, shaking. For the first time, there was fear in his eyes.

"How did that pierce me?" Nach roared. "Where did your power come from?"

Not bothering to answer, Galavon sprang in front of Nach. Gaining momentum, he swung his sword, slashing its target. The blade sliced across the beast's chest above the abdomen.

Leana watched purple blood drain from Nach's chest. He placed his hand in the center of the long wound as blood flowed heavily between his fingers.

"Finish it, Galavon." Nach breathed harshly, clenching his jaw.

Galavon paused, waiting with his sword held up above his enemy.

"Do it!" Nach screamed.

Leana watched as Galavon stood there, motionless. She felt frozen with him. For a brief moment, she felt if she didn't move her father wouldn't kill him. *Dad... Don't.*

"Galavon, you must," said Rychur. He stood behind Nach; his hands and eyes still glowing. "He will go back to his king. Renisis will come if you don't kill him!"

Galavon squeezed the handle tighter as the blade shook above Nach. He looked from his daughter to the kneeling enemy.

"Please, Dad," she whispered. "You don't have to do this."

"You are a killer," taunted Nach. "Infant-slayer. Coward!"

Leana saw a flash of something unreadable in her father's eyes. Galavon opened his mouth and screamed, thrusting down his sword.

"No!" she screamed, closing her eyes and throwing up her hands.

CHAPTER 37

Leana felt a blast of energy surge from her hands. Opening her eyes, Leana saw that the blade of her father's sword had sunk into the ground, inches from Nach's neck. *He missed?*

All three men stared at her. She couldn't understand why. Galavon looked at his sword in shock, and then back at his daughter.

"What was that?" asked Rychur. The tone of his voice was indecipherable as he slowly let his guard down. The glow in his hands and eyes disappeared.

"Leana?" her father said calmly.

She stuttered. "What just happened?"

"You did," he replied, his voice proud.

Nach smirked. Taking advantage of the moment, he smashed his fist hard into Galavon's chest, and then drilled his foot into Galavon's stomach, slamming him backward into Rychur. Galavon gasped violently.

Nach sprinted at Leana. Fear swept over her like a hurricane, and she couldn't move; she could only scream. She knew she was going to die. Just then, a fierce growl roared from above. El leapt from the top of the ship, hurdling down on top of the charging beast. Nach swiped the wolf to the side. El bounced off the ground, landing on her feet and charged again, exposing her teeth as she tried to catch him.

The closer Nach got, the more Leana's heart raced. She saw him and everything around her as though in slow motion. She could hear Nach's breath and the pounding of his feet on the twigs and leaves, the ground quaking at his charge. She heard the whisper of the wind blow by her ears and through her hair. She could hear her own heartbeat and the ways she was about to die ran through her mind.

Leana turned away, throwing her hands over her head protectively. Her knees buckled, dropping her to the ground. Nach reached out with both hands and snarled.

Leana screamed as something warm and wet sprayed her.

She heard a massive crash. Turning back, she found herself looking into the crazed eyes of Nach. He was on his knees before her, staring at her in shock and pain.

Her eyes moved down to the blade sticking out of Nach's chest. Slowly, Galavon removed the sword. Nach slumped over, grabbing at his new wound, his eyes rolling in agony. She assumed he was done for, but impossibly he put his giant hand on the ground and began to slowly push himself up. Staggering to his feet, the beast turned to face his enemy. He was so mountainous he blocked her view of her father.

Without warning, her father's blade pierced Nach again; this time staying.

Falling to his knees, Nach coughed, purple blood soiling the ground in front of him. He turned towards Leana, meeting her eyes. For the first time she saw wretchedness in them.

"She probably would've been like you."

Leana was confused. She saw her father look at her behind sad eyes. Her father seemed to know who Nach was referring to.

She watched Nach close his eyes and slumped further. *Is it over?* She felt a moment of relief, but backed away from him anyway just to be safe.

She looked up and saw Rychur approaching the scene clutching his side. Leana met Rychur's eyes, welcoming one of the warmest smiles she's seen in a long time. She could see that he was proud of her, though she didn't know why. Rychur was clearly in pain, and her body ached all over, but somehow she smiled back.

It was finally over. They could relax.

As they held each other's gaze, a small rock hovered into their line of sight. They had only a moment to exchange confused looks, and in the next instant Rychur's expression changed to horror. Leana watched his gaze shift to Nach's body a couple meters to Leana's left.

"LEANA LOO—"

Before she could react, Nach let out a deafening roar that shook the very ground. A burst of energy exploded from the beast, knocking Leana back several feet. She watched in disbelief as Nach's eyes, now completely pale with rage, burned fiercely in her direction.

Nach reached his arm back and swiftly grabbed the hilt of the sword still stuck through his body. He pulled it out, raining purple blood from his body and poised his arm to throw the dripping blade.

Leana ducked, trying to make herself a smaller target. This was not how she expected to die, with Nach's insane yell as the last thing she heard. Out of the corner of her eye, she saw Rychur reach toward her and a burst of energy flew at her and started to pull her to him, out of the beast's reach.

The only thing she knew to do was close her eyes. And then it all stopped with a jolt. There was no pain.

She looked up to see Nach's white eyes staring at her.

"Leana... you have to run..."

Leana looked over in the direction of Rychur's weak voice, and her stomach dropped in horror. He was lying on the ground, propped up by her father's sword which was sticking so far into the front of his chest that the handle had cracked his armor. "NO!"

"Rychur!" Galavon bellowed.

Nach started to get up, laughing manically and reaching for Leana. She hunched frozen, filled with overwhelming emotion and fear.

Galavon sprinted toward the monster. Before Nach could stand, Galavon jumped in the air in a roundhouse kick to Nach's temple. The power was explosive. Its force sent Nach into the ground face-first, unconscious.

Leana looked up to see her father staring at the motionless body. He looked at her and held out his hand, "Get up."

Leana reached up and took her father's callused hand. He pulled her to her feet. She was suddenly weak as she fell into his chest.

"You're okay." Her father's voice broke.

"Rychur!" she gasped. She pushed past her father and ran to her friend's side, kneeling down. "No, no, no."

If Rychur was breathing, she couldn't tell. His body was limp, his arms dangling at his sides.

"Rychur, please. Please wake up." She put her hand on his shoulder trying to pull him up. The sword had dug into the ground at least six inches, and she was afraid if she pulled it out she would hurt him more. Her mom would know what to do.

It was too much. Tears flowed silently down Leana's cheeks as she lowered her head, her hand still on Rychur's chest.

"...Leh...Leana..."

She jerked her head up. Rychur was awake, but barely. His eyes were slits.

"Don't talk. We're going to fix you up, just like before."

"Leana... Your father..."

"Please Rychur..." she said through tears.

"Forgive... Trust... him..."

Leana looked back at her father standing behind her. He was staring silently, watching. He looked at his daughter. Her eyes pleaded with him to do something. She looked back at Rychur as he coughed.

She shushed him. "Okay. I will. We'll talk more later."

Rychur's mouth moved slightly as he tried to smile. He looked up to her father. Leana watched them exchange silent looks for a moment.

Galavon broke the brief moment. "Chur…"

"Umi ba'la," Rychur said weakly. He turned his gaze back to Leana.

Rychur reached up his hand and placed it on Leana's cheek. "Don't…" He coughed up blood. "Don't be afraid."

"Of what?" she pleaded.

"Your… destiny…"

As the breath left Rychur, his hand fell from Leana's cheek, leaving a small streak of purple blood behind.

She picked up his hand and held it close to her chest. "Rychur! Ry! I won't be afraid! Please don't go! I won't be afraid! Rychur!"

Leana felt her father's hands on her shoulders. "Leana," he whispered. "Leana, he's gone."

This can't be happening. He can't be dead. "Wake up, please," she begged.

But Rychur wasn't going to wake up. Nothing had ever hurt like this before.

The Balachurian was gone.

CHAPTER 38

Leana stood up and buried herself in her father's chest, sobbing uncontrollably.

"I'm sorry, Leana," her father said with a thick voice. "I'm so sorry."

Seemingly forever, Leana stood in her father's embrace. Only the sound of her crying could be heard in the silence of the forest around them. Slowly, her father let her go and she stood there staring at the ground.

Right behind her lay her friend's body. He had been someone who believed in her and cared for her. He had felt like the mentor she had needed for so long. He had even saved her life more than once. And now, she had been unable to return the favor.

She turned to face his body. "I'm sorry, Rychur," she said, dropping to her knees next to him. She sniffed hard, wiping her face, then leaned over to kiss his forehead. "Good bye."

She looked up and watched her father bending over to grab the hilt of his sword. Carefully, and with considerable strength, he removed it from Rychur's body and turned to Nach's motionless figure behind them. Walking over then looking down, Galavon calmly but with great precision, pierced Nach through the heart. He pulled out the sword and wiped it clean on the grass.

He returned to Leana's side, a single tear falling down his battered, dirty cheek. As he dropped the sword on the ground beside them, it shrank back to its original size and shape.

Leana stood up in her father's direction. He quickly reached out his hands and pulled her into his arms again. She felt his heart racing underneath his armor. "I've got you, rose petal," he whispered, kissing her head.

"Dad..." she replied, squeezing her arms tightly around him.

"It's over… It's over."

In that moment, in her father's arms, Leana felt like *she* was there for *him* now. She melted in his arms. She felt loved. She trusted him. She loved him. The confusion of this morning meant nothing now. Leana finally understood everything.

All she felt she could do was cry.

"I'm sorry," he said again. "For everything."

Leana squeezed her father. "I forgive you," she stuttered, struggling to speak as she cried. "For everything." She felt his body relax at her words, but he hugged her more tightly.

After a moment they broke their embrace and started walking back over to Nach's ship. Leana looked down at Nach's body. A burst of anger and confusion filled her at the sight of him. She wanted to somehow hurt him more, but knew it was pointless. His eyes, just like Rychur's, were lifeless.

She remembered what he had said earlier: "she probably would've been a lot like you." *Who was the "she" he was talking about?*

From out of the brush, El emerged and nudged herself gently against Leana's leg. Welcoming the living warmth in this moment, she rubbed the wolf hard and lovingly. She hugged El, remembering what her furry friend had done for her earlier. "Thank you, El. You saved me again." Leana laid her head on El's forehead.

Her father put his hand on Leana's back. "Leana?"

She looked up at his resolute face.

"I have to leave."

"What do you mean? Where are you going?"

He paused then answered. "Home… To Balachur."

CHAPTER 39

Leana's head swam against the tidal wave of emotions. The way Nach stared lifelessly into the night sky unnerved her. She thought of her terrifying experiences with him earlier that day. She was exhausted from all the fear, adrenaline and physical exertion, and now her father was saying he was leaving – again. She didn't want him to go. She didn't want him to abandon her and her mother, not again, especially not now when she had just learned her heritage. There were too many questions that needed answering.

"I don't understand," she said thoughtfully, staring at the dead enemy.

"What don't you understand?" asked her father. "I have to go."

"No, that's not what I meant. How did *I* make it home? When you found me."

"You really don't remember anything?" He paused, waiting for her answer, but Leana shook her head. He continued, "You overpowered him. You protected yourself."

"How could I have, Dad? He knocked me out, and then I woke up in my bed."

"That's because it worked."

"What worked?"

"Your pocket watch."

Leana reached in her pockets then remembered she didn't have it. "Where is it?"

"It's fine. Esu has it. I gave it to him after you threw it at me."

"What does the watch have to do with me?"

"When your mother and I found out we were pregnant, we weren't sure what the future would bring for you here on Earth. So we needed to do something to protect you."

"What do you mean?"

"Leana, you are the first mixed-blood between human and Balachurian. I had no idea how Earth would affect you, so I started exploring ways to help you transition. If you were anything like me, I knew we needed to figure something out, so I made you the pocket watch. It suppresses your powers so your Balachurian abilities were never revealed."

"Powers? Me? That's ridiculous."

"Leana, without your pocket watch you reacted and naturally defended yourself when confronted by Nach. Something happened between you two that triggered your powers. What I don't understand is *what* you did."

"Oh... great." She didn't know how to feel.

"Where we found you unconscious, the whole area had been wiped out, almost like an explosion. Nach was nowhere to be seen. It doesn't make sense. You seemed to have shown Malachurian abilities, but you are of the Onite race. It's nearly unheard of to have the abilities of another clan."

"Nach wasn't a Malachurian, right? He was Baramat."

"Exactly. Rychur was Malachurian."

A painful sting shot through Leana's stomach at her friend's name. She looked away from her father for a moment. She didn't want to think about Rychur right now. The pain was too much.

It didn't help that Leana couldn't fully comprehend what he was saying. There was so much running through her mind.

She suddenly remembered her father being absent when she'd woken up in her room earlier that day. She didn't know why it mattered, but for some reason she had to know. "Wait, Dad, where were you this morning?"

"I left El with you and the others, and I went out to find Nach. By the time I made it to the woods, he was gone. I deactivated his ship to be sure he couldn't escape."

Leana nodded. *Of course, the 'shooting star!'*

He continued, "I had to make sure he didn't tell anyone about you. I searched the entire woods for him, but when I came back to the house you two were already gone, and your friends were badly injured."

Justin. Annette. Leana gasped. In the chaos she had forgotten all about them. "Oh my god. Are they okay?"

"Leana, they're fine. It's okay. They're safe and Esu is taking care of them."

"Oh, thank god." A wave of relief filled her. Thinking of her friends brought to the surface Rychur's fate again. She glanced over at where he lay, but couldn't bear to look too long as the grief was overwhelming.

Leana couldn't believe it. Any of it. She'd had a secret her entire life and no one had told her. It was brand-new to her, and now her friends definitely knew too, but instead of running away they had protected her, and paid a high cost. She wondered if her mother knew everything already.

Did she see this coming? Why didn't she warn me?

As the reality of all this came crashing down on her, something that felt like a wall in her mind suddenly opened up. She started seeing forgotten images from the nightmares and dreams she'd been having. Flashes of warriors, battles, gorgeous alien landscapes, and mystical, powerful beings. Her eyes opened wide in shock.

"I'm remembering," she said aloud to herself.

"Remembering what?" her father asked confused.

She plowed ahead, needing to know more. "What about the dreams? How are those all related?"

"Those were memories, Leana," he responded calmly, "but not yours exactly. They are pieces of your bloodline's history passed down through generations. They appear in your mind as memories, moments from history long past that we can call upon at any time. It's a Balachurian method of preserving history and tradition, but it seems to have manifested itself in you through your dreams which isn't... typical."

"Hold on, what? What do you mean *memories*?"

"Leana," her father interjected, "it's the stories of my people, of *your* people. Your *other* family."

"So I was dreaming the memories of Balachurians?"

"Yes, from their point-of-views," he said, nodding his head. "That's why I made the inhibitor. It was to hinder your power and those memories. But I guess it couldn't block it all. You're stronger than I calculated you would be."

Leana didn't know what to think or feel. "So you created this, this inhibitor and then just *left*? Why?"

"I left because if I had stayed it would have increased the chances of you realizing you weren't human. It could have triggered your abilities or had some other unknown result. I exiled myself to protect you and give you a normal life. You would have never had the life you did if I were around."

"But this life you gave me, you weren't even a part of it! I wanted you there. And because of that I wanted to hate you so much. I *wanted to* hate you for a long time."

"I know. I made a choice, and it wasn't the best one."

"You think?!" she exploded, and immediately turned away from her father. The silent moment in the woods was deafening, but there wasn't time for this. She didn't want to have this conversation influenced by her anger. Not after all the loss she'd suffered today. Leana took a deep breath and turned back around. "I'm sorry. It is in the past, and I want to move on from all that now."

"Thank you," he said smiling.

"Mom did everything she could to save me, and she succeeded."

"I know. My actions also hurt her more than I could have imagined. I sometimes wished her love for me wasn't so strong. It would have been easier for her and you."

"No, her love for you kept me from truly hating you. She was proud of me for how I lived my life. She told me love carries a burden."

In that moment Leana was aware her entire life had been a mask, hiding her from who she actually was. She'd lived this life for sixteen years and still didn't feel like she really belonged. Now she knew why. She wanted to know her father, her people, and the other world they came from. Even though her dreams scared her most nights, she wanted to see where they originated, and meet the people who shared the same blood as her. Her curiosity was overriding her anger. She was thankful Rychur had already taught her so much. She wanted him to tell her more, but that wasn't going to happen now. Leana had to bury that pain for the time being. She didn't want to cry anymore, she just wanted to get away from this place.

She looked at him and paused. "Dad, can I ask you something?"

"Of course."

"Can I go with you? I want to go."

He stared at her, shocked. "What do you mean, Leana?"

"Balachur. I want to see it and—"

"No!" Galavon interrupted. "You can't go. It's not safe."

"I stayed with you for one weekend, here on a *farm*, and all this happened," she exclaimed, waving her hands. "And you're telling me I was safe? If you leave now, Dad, I know I won't be safe after you leave. None of us will. We'll be alone. What if they come back or come for Mom and me? What if I develop my powers more and have no idea how to control them? What then?"

Galavon looked at her with a raised eyebrow. "Yeah… You're definitely my daughter." There was a hint of pride in his voice. "But I don't know, Ana."

"Dad, Rychur believed in me. He seemed to believe there was something great in me. I want to believe that too, but I don't know if I can right now. There's almost nothing left for my life here. Not anymore." Leana stared at him, ignoring the flash of Justin's face crossing her mind. She knew this was right, and she knew that her father knew it too. She wouldn't be safe on Earth by herself if he went away.

"I—"

"Please," she pleaded, her voice breaking. "Rychur said I need to believe in something like he did. I don't even know what this is," she said, motioning to her entire body. "And it scares me. If you leave me here, I'll be more alone than ever. I need to start by believing in myself, but I need you to help me get there."

He put his hand to his cheek absentmindedly rubbing his scruff as he thought. "Leana." His voice was serious. "It will be extremely dangerous for you if you come."

"But I'll have you with me. And we can bring El and Esu. We're family, and we need to stick together. Right?"

"What about your mother?"

Leana hadn't thought about that. She would be leaving her mother behind and didn't know when the next time she'd see her would be. Leana wasn't sure she could bear the thought of being away from her. They'd become more like best friends over the years. She then thought of her girlfriends and Justin. She didn't know how to explain to any of them that she didn't belong here. She didn't know how to face them without thinking of herself as different anymore.

"Leana, you still have a choice," Galavon continued sternly. "I won't lie. If you come with me it will not be easy."

Leana felt disheartened. Staying wouldn't be much better. Not anymore. She didn't fit in already. She wasn't really challenged by anything at school, and now knowing she was literally part alien would make her feel even more isolated. She wanted to become something more. She wanted her eyes opened to a new world outside of her own. She wanted answers so she didn't have to feel so lost anymore. She wanted to feel whole. She needed it.

Her father added, "If you come, you will see destruction and you will likely see more death."

Leana quickly erased the thoughts. "But I will also see unbelievable and amazing things."

"Yes, you will." He was being very straightforward.

"That's what I want, Dad. I need this. I feel like I need to do this."

"What about your friends?"

Leana couldn't think about what her friends wanted. She knew how much it would hurt them if she left. She knew she would always cherish the great times they'd had together, but she also knew being around her friends while keeping a secret this big wouldn't be fair to them, or her. Staying here would keep her from ever truly discovering what was hiding deep within her, and she'd come back to them some day. She knew in her heart the decision was made.

"They would never understand me if I stayed. If you left and I stayed behind I would regret it the rest of my life. I don't know if my friends would ever be comfortable with me being different." Leana cleared her throat. "I don't know if I'd ever truly feel normal here."

Her father held out his hand, holding her phone. "Then tell them."

"You mean—?"

"You're right. I can't teach you anything, or keep you safe, if you're here alone. Nach's people will come back for him when they realize he never returned. We need to make sure that doesn't happen."

She took the bracelets and put them on. "Dad, is this what you want?"

"Yes, it really is, but we have to do what's best for you right now. What do you think?"

Leana hugged her father. Her emotions felt like a blender of complete relief, excitement, and fear. "Thank you, Dad," she said, smiling up at him. While she knew this was not going to be a vacation, it *was* going to be the trip of her dreams - literally. Turning to see Rychur lying on the grass, her heart hurt that he wasn't going to be with them. Leana had never thought she'd be the one leaving him behind.

Her father knelt down and Leana could tell his sadness mirrored her own. "You've got to call your friends and your mother. I'm going to tend to my friend."

Leana turned around and walked away into the forest. It was still dark, but she ignored the cold. She didn't want to experience any more painful emotions. If she wanted her life to change from this point on she needed to get through these next few moments. Calling her friends seemed impossible. She didn't know what to say.

Doubt slammed into her gut. Her mind was telling her to stay, but her heart was saying different. She had felt a hole inside of her for such a long time now, something she'd been missing, something important. If she made the decision to go with her father, to trust her gut instincts and chase this wild dream, she was going to have to leave her entire life behind; not forever, she hoped.

She loved the idea of being with her father, but the thought of leaving her mother behind made her sick to her stomach. Despite it all, she knew it was the right thing to do. This needed to happen. Her mother was the only person who had always been there for Leana, and now she knew she hoped her mother would understand this unforeseen situation.

Leana stopped walking when her father was out of earshot. She looked up and saw a gap in the tree line above. Staring up into the stars, through the trees, she tried to calm her thoughts. She closed her eyes and listened to the world around her. She surrendered herself to the blackness, freeing up her mind. She knew if she was going to do this she needed to make a decision that might appear selfish. *I don't want to be afraid anymore. I don't want to question who I am for the rest of my life. I have to do this.*

Leana had decided. She was leaving Earth and everything she knew behind.

CHAPTER 40

Leana braced herself to call Annette. She briefly hoped her friend would talk her out of going, but Leana knew that wasn't what she truly wanted. She had to accept the fact that she was going to be leaving her best friend behind. She had no idea how to tell her, but Annette always had the right words to say that helped Leana think through situations, and that's what Leana needed to hear right now.

The holographic screen popped up, illuminating the dark forest around her with its blue light. She gave her eyes a moment to adjust. Ignoring the devastating feeling in her stomach, she commanded the phone to call Annette.

While the phone rang, Leana waited, staring at the picture of her and Annette as freshmen in high school. Annette's face finally popped on screen.

"Leana! I was just about to call you. Emily called Justin, but he's passed out so I answered and she went off on how her dad is looking for you and... what's wrong?" she stopped suddenly. "You okay?"

Leana didn't register anything Annette had just said. All she could focus on was how exhausted her best friend looked, and the canyon of guilt that had formed where her stomach used to be.

"Yes, I'm fine. How are you feeling? How's Justin?" Leana choked at the lump in her throat. She struggled to hide it.

Annette didn't answer. She could see the tears running down her friend's face. "Ana, what's wrong?"

"How's Justin?" Leana insisted.

"He's resting. A bit rough around the edges, but he'll be okay." Annette sighed as she answered. "Now are you going to tell me what's wrong?"

Leana swallowed hard, suddenly finding it hard to form words. She pushed through.

"I'm... I'm going away." Leana felt the welling pressure behind her eyes. "What? Where?"

Leana leaned forward, trying to be closer to her friend. "I'm leaving with my father and I don't know when I'll be coming back." That felt like a lie. She was scared that she was never going to see her best friend again. Leana felt awful breaking the news over the phone. She wanted to hug Annette in person and tell her goodbye, but just speaking over the phone was hard enough.

"Did something happen?" Leana could hear Annette struggling with the words.

"Annette..." she paused. "Rychur is dead. Nach killed him. I can't explain more right now... but I'm okay," she hesitated. "I have to go – I want to go – but we don't have much time."

"Can't we come say goodbye?"

"No," Leana said, her heart pounding. "If you do then I won't be able to do this. It's hard enough as it is, but I just know I have to do it."

Leana waited for Annette to say something. She knew Annette would default to trying to act strong in this moment. She watched her friend's tear-stained eyes dart back and forth as she thought of what to say next. Finally she stuttered out, "Wh... When are you leaving?"

"Tonight." Leana watched Annette covering her quivering mouth with her hand, holding back tears. "As soon as possible. We have to go right away."

"Can't you just come back here and—"

"Annette, please. I can't. It'll be too hard."

Annette paused, sniffling hard. After clearing her throat, she asked, "Where are you going?"

"I can't believe I'm saying this, but I'm going to Balachur. I don't know why, but I have to. It's hard to explain" She wiped the tears that dripped from her chin. "I'm so sorry. I didn't mean for it to be this way."

"When are you coming back? You won't be gone for long, right?" Annette was starting to sound desperate.

"I don't know. I really don't. I don't even know how long it takes to get there." Leana felt so guilty, hurting her friend like this. After a couple of deep breaths, she looked directly in the screen, "We *will* see each other again."

"No, don't say it like that. I know you're somewhere out in the woods, I'm coming to find you right now," Annette demanded.

Leana watched as Annette tried to stand, but the video feed jerked harshly as she fell back to the ground, groaning in pain. "Damn it!" She sighed deeply. "Leana, please... don't go."

For a moment, the girls just stared at each other, wiping away their own tears. Leana wanted to hug her friend one last time. Annette stubbornly tried to get up again.

"Annette, stop. You'll only hurt yourself worse. It's not worth it."

"You can't leave me," said Annette, raising her voice.

"I know. I'm sorry," Leana responded, crying. "I need you to do something for me. Can you... Can you tell Emily and Justin for me? I can't do it, not right now. I still have to call my mom and talk to her." Leana knew she couldn't handle watching Justin's reaction to the news. It was already too painful.

"No!" Annette sniffed hard. "I will *not* do that for you. You can tell them yourself!"

"Please, Annette. Please," Leana begged. "I need you for this."

Annette glared at Leana. She sighed hard, her cheeks damp and lips pursed. Shaking her head, she finally spoke in a whisper, "Fine! Okay." She sniffed again. "I will see you again. We're friends forever. Nothing can keep us apart. We'll just... Talk a lot while you're away, get together as soon as you're back."

Leana continued crying as she listened to her friend try to make both of them feel better with unfounded optimism. She couldn't speak anymore, and resorted to nodding her head.

"Say it again, Leana," Annette said firmly. "Say 'we'll see each other again'."

"We'll see each other again," Leana said. "I promise. And thank you." She could feel the pressure continue to push up against her eyes. "I love you... so much." *I hope she can forgive me,* she thought to herself.

Annette continued crying. "I love you too."

Leana took a deep breath. "Okay. I have to go."

"No, Leana!"

"I'm sorry."

Leana ended the call quickly, unable to take anymore. She was overcome with emotion and collapsed to her knees in the middle of the forest. The weight of this decision was crashing down on her. She held herself, her arms wrapped around her stomach, and sobbed quietly.

She flinched at the sudden feel of arms wrapping around her. She looked over her shoulder to see her father kneeling behind her, holding her close. "I'm sorry, sweetheart."

Together they knelt in the forest, rocking gently, not saying a word. Eventually Leana's breathing slowed down and her body relaxed.

She sniffed. "Okay."

"Okay what?" her father leaned away.

She turned and looked at him. "I have to call Mom now."

He sighed and nodded. "That one we'll do together."

Leana looked at her phone. "Mom," she commanded.

The screen showed a picture of Leana as a baby, being held by her mom and dad, the same picture that was face down on her bedside table back home. Leana had updated it after the date with her father. It felt right seeing that picture again. She saw her father smile wistfully at the sight of the picture.

"I remember when that was taken." he said, his voice thick.

"Yeah?"

"You spit-up all over your fancy outfit, so I changed you into those red overalls for our family pictures. Your mother wasn't happy that you ruined the clothes, but it's still a great picture." He gently rested his chin on Leana's head. "Call," he whispered.

The phone began to ring while they both stared at the screen, waiting to see Danielle's face. Galavon wrapped his arm around Leana. Danielle answered, "Hey, sweetie." Her eyes widened when she saw her husband right next to Leana. "Hey," she said wistfully.

"Hey, Mom." Leana quickly became overwhelmed, but she felt stronger with her father's hands on her shoulders.

"What's going on?" Danielle said, taking in their bruised, tear-stained faces. "Why are you in your armor? And what happened to your face?"

Leana was about to speak, but her father did first.

"Danielle, it happened."

Leana looked at him in surprise, then back at her mother.

"Does she know everything?" asked Danielle.

"Not everything, but she will soon enough."

Danielle sighed deeply, shaking her head. "You just keep getting farther and farther away from me, don't you Ana?"

Leana suddenly realized her parents had been preparing for this moment all along. Somewhere, throughout the past sixteen years, her mother had accepted the fact that Leana would leave her. Leana couldn't imagine what the weight of holding that secret for so long would have done to her mother.

"I love you, Danielle," Galavon said.

"And I..." Danielle's eyes began to water as she cupped her mouth, much like Annette had. She pulled her hand away and replied, "I love you too, Otis. From this world—"

"To the next," he finished.

Danielle sniffled as she watched Galavon rest his head on their crying daughter. "Leana, you will be okay. Your father will protect you. I've taught you what I can. It's his turn now."

"I know," Leana whispered, squeezing out the words as she exhaled.

"Hey," exclaimed Danielle. "Be brave, baby girl. You are destined for something great." She was forcing a positive attitude. "From what your father has told me, you're going to see some amazing things. Be sure to have him tell you about their moon."

Danielle forced a smile and for a moment the two women stared at each other not knowing what to say next.

Leana's head dropped. She couldn't stand the reality that she was going to leave her mother alone.

Danielle continued, "I wish I could be there with you to watch you grow, but I will be right there in spirit, and I will pray for you *every* day."

Leana couldn't shake the guilt she was feeling and doubt took over. "Am I doing the right thing? I was convinced it was until I talked to you and Annette. Now I'm so unsure."

"Big steps are always scary. Letting what's behind you stand in the way of reaching your full potential is the fastest way to never go anywhere. All you have to decide is to make the most out of the time you have."

Leaves bustled around them as a soft breeze swept through the forest around them.

"I love you, Mom." Leana curled up her shoulders against the cold breeze, dragging in a ragged breath. She was so tired, so weak, so emotionally drained.

"I love you too, Ana," her mother responded. "Good bye. Be brave. Be strong."

"I'll try."

"And listen to your father," she joked.

Everyone smiled through their tears.

Galavon spoke over Leana's shoulder, "I've already planned on Esu arriving at your place to keep you company. No arguing, Danielle."

She smiled again. "Okay. It'll be nice having a friendly face around. What about the kids?"

"Esu is taking care of them now, but I need you to help them transition back to normal life. It's going to be hard for them. They've seen a lot. Try not to let them talk to anyone about this weekend."

"You know I will," Danielle replied compassionately. "I haven't been a mom for sixteen years for nothing." She tilted her head to the side, looking deep into Galavon's eyes. "Goodbye, honey."

He smiled and responded. "Goodbye, bee."

Danielle ended the call before Leana could say anything else.

"Mom? Mom?!"

She leaned her head into her father's shoulder and let the moment linger. Despite everything, in this quiet moment in the woods with her father, she felt peace and safety she hadn't felt in a very, very long time. It was encouraging, empowering even. The time had come. She took a deep breath, sighed, and looked up at her father. "Okay. I'm ready."

They walked back to where Rychur was laying. She looked at him one more time. "I already miss him, Dad. So much."

"I know, rose petal, but you will see him again." He pursed his lips. "He left you something." He handed her an object.

She recognized the device and rubbed her hand over it. "Why did he give this to me—"

The device activated, projecting a hologram. It showed a transparent sphere that looked like a planet.

"Is that Balachur?" she asked her father.

"It is."

She startled when a woman's voice began speaking. *"Please hurry, Rychur. Renisis has sent out his men to search for the rebels who helped you escape. It's only a matter of time before they're found."*

"Who was that?" asked Leana.

The woman continued before he could answer. *"If you find Galavon, please let him hear this message."* The voice was filled with desperation.

"Push that, right there." He pointed at a small, blue button on the side of the device.

Leana obeyed. A new message began.

"Galavon, please. We beg of you... I beg of you. Please, we need your help. You know we must be desperate to reach out to you. Our people are on the brink of annihilation and we won't make it much longer without you. We need you back. Pleas—" The screen turned off.

"Wait. What happened?"

"It looks like the recording cuts off there. Maybe that's all Rychur had been able to get transmitted to him as he escaped."

Leana swallowed hard. She felt fear flush over her from the distressed voice. *Am I making the right choice?*

Galavon hit another button, sliding it across the device. Rychur's face popped up. He looked happy. *"Leana, hello. If you and your father are watching this, then I am sorry. Something happened and I can't be there with you. I told your father to play this if you chose to leave with him, and I am very glad you have chosen to do so. Now you must listen. On Balachur, you will face many trials and hardships, but you must understand when I say I believe in you. You must face the beast head-on and conquer your fears."* He smiled again. *"I want you to know that because of you... I am happy again. For too long I have carried a guilt and burden with me, but in the short time I knew you I learned that I no longer had to let my past define me. There were people still in my life I could care about and help. I know you have many questions, but your father will answer them when it's the right time. Thank you for being you,"* he said, pointing at her through the screen. *"I am sorry I couldn't continue this part of your journey with you. I hope I will see you again in another time. Goodbye, my friend."*

Leana's eyes teared up as the screen cut out and the lights on the device dimmed out. "Goodbye, Rychur." She looked at her father, smiling shakily. "I want to be done crying now," she chuckled softly.

"I know," Galavon said. He pointed up. "We're almost done."

Leana's attention was suddenly drawn upward where she saw several beams of light shining down on them. Leaves, dirt and heavy wind began blowing everywhere around them. Leana shielded her eyes from the light to see a ship descending. It was neither Nach's nor Rychur's ship, but was smaller. Understanding quickly, Leana knew it must be her father's ship.

"Who's flying it?" she asked, raising her voice over the gust of wind.

"Esu's controlling it from the house. I couldn't risk him leaving your friends."

"Where did you keep it?" She had to yell now to be heard over the loud rumble of the ship's engine. Slowly, the vessel lowered and landed next to them, throttling down.

"In the barn. Your friend, Justin, almost took a picture of it."

"Of course! So that's why you got upset with him."

Her father simply nodded as he looked over his ship.

The ramp lowered from the bottom of the ship, stretching down to the ground. From the sound of the smooth hydraulics, Leana could tell Galavon had taken excellent care of his ship over the years. It was in much better condition than the other ships she had experienced so far. She squinted her eyes against the bright lights inside the hull.

Galavon looked at Leana and yelled, "Are you ready?"

"Yes," she responded without thinking. She swallowed again, and then looked down at the wolf panting beside her. "What about her?"

Galavon just whistled and El sprinted into the ship.

Leana felt relieved. She was glad she would have another familiar face on this adventure.

Thunder began rumbling in the sky above. Just then, her projector popped up, showing Esu on the screen. "Dad, look. Hey, Esu."

"Leana, I'm very glad you are alive. I apologize for hacking your phone, but I need to speak to your father. Goodness! What a racket."

"Yeah, of course."

Galavon stepped up next to her while he unstrapped the armor on his chest. "Esu, I need you to get the tractor. As soon as we're gone, I need you to clear everything out quickly. Once you have deactivated the energy field around the property, it will only be a matter of time before people start searching you out. They'll be coming for the ships. Destroy everything, including the two ships, and Nach's body. Take care of Rychur, please. He... won't be making the journey back with us."

"Oh dear. I'm so sorry to hear that. I will take care of everything promptly."

"I know. Thank you, Esu. When you're done, please take care of the rest of the farm and the kids. Just like we discussed, activate all automation and security protocols. After that, I want you to go to Danielle's and stay with her."

"Right away, sir. Goodbye, sir. Good luck."

Galavon smiled. "Goodbye, old friend. Thank you for your services and company."

Esu smiled back. "You are welcome O—"

Her father interrupted, "You can call me Galavon. I'm no longer Otis."

"—Galavon," Esu finished.

Leana wanted to hug him just once, and was sad she couldn't.

"Goodbye, Esu," she said.

"Goodbye, sweet Leana," he said, winking and smiling. The screen cut out.

Galavon looked at his daughter. "We need to be gone before he gets here. Time to move." He saw that Leana's bracelets were lighting up. It was a call coming in from Justin. "I'm guessing you'll need to take care of that. I'll be on the ship waiting. Okay?"

"Okay. I'll be quick," she said as he stroked her head sympathetically.

Leana watched her father disappear into the ship, then looked at the screen. She knew if she answered Justin would try to convince her to stay. She couldn't handle any more disappointment. Leana choked back her tears, declining the call. Instead, she sent him a message; only three words.

"I... AM... SORRY!"

She turned off her phone, unbuckled the bracelets, and put them in her pocket. Leana knew that was the last message she'd be sending for a long time. She stepped forward, inches from the metal ramp and looked up into the hull's bright lights. Once she stepped inside she couldn't turn back.

It was starting to rain. Leana took in a deep breath of rain-soaked Earth air then walked up the ramp. Slowly, she reached the top, just outside of the hull, and looked back out into the forest.

"Goodbye, Earth."

She stepped into the ship as the door closed behind her.

• • • • • •

The ship's engine boomed to life, smoothly lifting it from the ground, higher and higher. The nose pointed towards the sky as the rear engines fired, shooting the ship through heavy clouds and into space, leaving nothing but floating leaves behind.

Lightning flashed and thunder boomed through the sky as it lit up with flashes, exposing the rain-soaked forest and everything in it. The hollow sound of pouring rain soaked the grass and dirt, which was quickly turning into mud. The clatter of drops hitting Nach's ship echoed throughout the woods. His drenched body lay lifeless in the woods.

As the rain began pouring harder and harder, blood and water mixed together, pooling on the ground around him. The exposed lacerations and open wounds started glowing with a pulse like a faint heartbeat. As the rain continued falling, the glow became brighter.

Nach's hand twitched and his eyes opened wide as he sucked air into his lungs violently. He sat up, his eyes on Galavon's ship shooting up towards the stars.

He grinned and tightened his fist. "I will see you soon, Galavon."

LEANA WILL RETURN IN BOOK TWO
See you on Balachur

ACKNOWLEDGEMENTS

This two-year journey has been an incredible adventure, and it has only just begun. Along the way, we have come across some incredible people who helped us.

To Myanna, Isabelle, Keenan, John, Matt, Andrew, and Rachel, thank you for the time and energy you spent reading early drafts of the book, and the invaluable feedback and insight you provided.

To Zach, Craig, and Thomas, thank you for your editing. Your time, words of encouragement, and constructive criticism helped us become better storytellers, and you fed us enthusiasm and encouragement through your passion and support.

To Aubree (from Will): This book wouldn't have happened without you. Words can't express my gratitude. Thank you so very much.

To Aubree (from Jordan): To my beautiful and wonderful wife, Aubree. You have been there for me since the beginning. You always supported me through this project. You pushed me to get on my computer after an exhausting week at work. You constantly questioned my ideas, forcing me to think deeper and deeper into the characters of the story. You kept me dreaming and keeping my eyes on the prize. I thank you for sitting with me as we read through the book, twice over, editing it sentence by sentence. You birthed our child in the middle of the book's editing phase, and still helped me when you were more exhausted than I was. You are my Balachurian warrior and Earthy wife. I love you from the bottom of my heart, and I thank you for everything you've done for Will and me. You played such a gigantic role to make this book and myself better. LYMYWKY!

This book wouldn't be what it is without you all.

NOTE FROM THE AUTHORS:

Thanks so much for taking the time to read our work. Please consider leaving a review wherever you bought the book, and telling your friends about Destined, to help us spread the word. Thank you so much for your support!

JOIN THE ADVENTURE

Join hundreds of fans who get sneak

peeks, latest news, and early copies of all

things Destined, at DESTINEDBOOK.COM

Connect with us too!

@DESTINEDBOOK

FACEBOOK.COM/DESTINEDBOOK

Made in the USA
Charleston, SC
06 May 2016